Queen of Lies

To Amalia-Eleni and Nicholas,
To the Erasmias of my life,
To David, my very own Parakoimomenos ...

... whenever they might read this

Queen of Lies

Achilleas Mavrellis

EFU ◊ *London* 2012

First published in Great Britain in 2012 by
Empire Forever Unlimited (EFU), London
Contact: www.empireforever.co.uk

A catalog record for this book
is available from the British Library

ISBN 978-0-9575046-0-8

Typeset in Literaturnaya

Main cover image adapted from a 9th century wall mosaic of the
Archangel Michael at the Hosias Loukas monastery, Greece
Embedded image of Claire-Monique Martin, Kaveh Beyk and Gioele
Silvestri as Ingerina, Vassilis and Michael from YouTube clip

Esdras is witness that the race of women,
together with truth, prevails over all

Kassia the Nun

Contents

To the Reader

This is an untold tale of love, loss and the quest for power that took place during a major turning point in world history, in what was once called New Rome, later Constantinople. Although much of what I describe here is unsettling, and the way of things quite alien, the story is based on recorded events and occurrences.

The historical sources of the period complement yet contradict each other, much like disparate tesserae of a mosaic that need re-working before they can be placed together to create a single, recognizable whole. Rather than being a window into another world, the stories and people of this time — like the religious Icons at the heart of events — project out relentlessly from that world into ours, demanding some kind of response. To inform that response I offer the following context, and have provided some explanatory notes at the end, along with lists of most of the characters mentioned. I also encourage you to visit my website: www.empireforever.co.uk for background information.

You may still come across people referring to the place and time of this story as "Byzantium". This rather unfortunate label is the product of an outdated, nineteenth century paradigm that tried to distance New Rome from its more "noble" predecessor. While Rome may have collapsed, the Roman Empire never died; in the fourth century the Emperor Constantine moved the capital of Empire east, to the ancient port city of Vyzantion, in what is now north-west Turkey. The inhabitants of New Rome spoke Latin for several centuries, before becoming completely Greek-speaking. They also drew on and evolved many ancient Roman traditions, often by placing them in a Hellenized Christian context. But they never stopped thinking of themselves as Romans.

That the New Roman Empire lasted for just over thirteen centuries is a testament to its robust self-identity and extraordinary level of political administration and largely due to a very old Roman sense of order in the face of adversity. While the Empire's goal — to preserve its classical heritage and Christian values until the Second Coming — was ostensibly not fulfilled, it is worth noting that Constantinople was one of the most successful cities of its time. "The City", as it became known, was a strong draw for outsiders from China to Scandinavia for almost a millennium, much as it is today in its modern form — Istanbul.

Today the Empire lives on in invisible ways, through the ancient literature it preserved and re-interpreted, through its evolution of Roman law and through the gifts of art and written language it bequeathed to the maturing cultures of Europe. Perhaps most significantly, it was the first medieval sovereign entity in which women not only had occasion to govern, but were recognized as rulers in their own right, an ancient world view which, apart from this largely forgotten period in late antiquity, took until well into the last millennium to re-emerge fully into global consciousness.

Achilleas Mavrellis, London, 2012
www.empireforever.co.uk

Major characters

Eudokia Ingerina — daughter of a Viking emissary to the Romans, lady in waiting to the Regent, then Empress herself. She writes in the winter of late 879 AD.

Vassilis — Macedonian teenage peasant, groom, bodyguard, later Companion to the Emperor, and then some!

Michael — the only surviving son of Theodora and the last Iconoclast Emperor Theophilos, he became the sixty-fifth Emperor of New Rome.

Photios — Chief Imperial Secretary, scholar, diplomat, commander, later patriarch; he is partly responsible for what later became known as the Great Schism of the Eastern and Western Churches.

Theoktistos the Eunuch — Michael's appointed guardian and the Logothete, the most senior civil servant.

Theodora the Regent — Empress Regent and Michael's mother, also known as the final restorer of Icon worship.

Vardas — older brother of Theodora, soldier, patron of the arts; after his return from exile he becomes Caesar.

Petronas — younger brother of Theodora and Vardas, and a seasoned soldier; later a General of Thrace.

Ignatios — Archbishop and later Patriarch of Constantinople, a devoted Iconodule.

Cyril and Methodios — Greek orphan brothers from Thessaloniki; they are largely to thank for spearheading the conversion of the Slavs to Christianity.

Symvatios — Vardas' ex-son-in-law and the second Logothete in this tale, with his heart set on becoming Caesar one day.

Part I

Iconoduly

842–850 AD

1. The end, and a beginning

When did this river of opportunity start, and how did it spring up and take us, especially me, by such welcome surprise?

Perhaps as a small trickle of happenstance, on a plain somewhere between the villages and hills of Macedonia. Nearly forty years ago for me now, perhaps just as the Eunuch had completed his campaign to free the Macedonians from the wild Bulgar.

I imagine my young Peasant and his older brother, Marianos, grinning in anticipation as they stalk a wild mare, its nostrils steaming in the icy wind. She stands transfixed, as we all did, by these village bumpkins.

Marianos nods to his younger brother. "Now! Take her!"

The boy hesitates. After all, he is still just a lad.

"She's yours, come on, boy, she's waiting!" chides Marianos.

The boy springs on eager heels, slides onto the mare's back, grapples, then nearly slips off as the mare bucks.

"That's it!"

The wild creature rears up, casting a hopeful eye on the open fields. Marianos is also on her now. He squeezes her to stillness with thick legs, a broad hand on his youngest brother's shoulder, arms surrounding him as he holds on to her mane. Marianos tries the old trick, to pull her over, to blind her with the glaring sun.

"She's a good one — show her who's in charge right now — and she'll be yours forever."

Young shoulders lean forward, eagerly embracing the mare. But she bucks and throws both of them off. The boys collapse into laughing limbs, oblivious now to the retreating snorts.

"Don't worry, there will be more," Marianos says.

My Peasant rolls onto his elbows and gazes into his brother's eyes. "Yes, but will I ever get one?" he asks.

Marianos gently takes him by the ears, taps forehead to forehead. "Every young prince deserves his own horse. For someone already twelve years out of his mother's womb, I expected more! Next time we will tie you on."

Then abruptly, mock roughly, "Now get going before I give you a good beating for doubting yourself. Next time I'll tell Father about it too."

Marianos leaps up, pretending to be a ferocious predator. Hands and feet everywhere as my little Peasant scatters toward a nearby clump of trees. He is fast — Marianos reaches him late but manages to grab him by the ankle. He scoops him down onto a waist-high branch and throws open a bag, revealing some bread. The bleating of goats in the distance echoes off gray mountains and snowy peaks. A lone eagle hangs in the air.

"Why do you say every young prince needs a horse? Am I a young prince?" His eyebrows rise quizzically.

"You are — and more besides!" Munching. "Father's father is from a land far away. Across the mountains. Across the Black Sea. The land of Hayk, or, as they say in Greek, Armenia. Great-grandfather was a king."

"Is the sea that place where there is so much water? Like a stream, but much more? How do people go over it?"

"They have boats — like big huts — that float on the water."

"Mother says there are people who live in nice places by the sea and are very happy. She is not happy because she wants to live there too."

Marianos snorts. "I think Mother says many things just to annoy Father. Wives often do that. She loves him so she always expects more of him." He casts an eye in the direction of hooves thundering nearby. He wants to try for another one.

"One day you will see such places. All you need is to be strong and brave, and have a good horse. Enough talk."

The boy yelps and drops his bread as Marianos plucks him from the tree and sets him on broad shoulders. He bucks and rides his older brother's chestnut curls before Marianos sets him down again on their own mare.

"Silence!" Marianos commands in a whisper.

They creep up to within twenty paces of the herd. Marianos slips some rope out of his sack. The herd ignores them, especially the largest, a dark stallion.

This will be the catch of the month, Marianos knows it. Many meals could be earned today if he could just get this handsome creature to the Adrianopolis market. He crosses himself, kissing the Virgin in his mind's eye, all the while hoping that Father won't want to hold on to the catch for too long.

† † †

Do you see, my darling Leo? You must not let Photios get away with telling this tale the way he has, now that I have found this myth he so cunningly thought to weave into my Peasant's past. Where did I find it, I hear you ask? Deep in the bare-stripped gloom of the Virgin of the Lighthouse chapel, but not deep enough to escape the probing of inquisitive fingers.

As Eudokia, the daughter of Inger, envoy of Thule to the Holy Realm of Vyzantion, I did not always understand how important it is to speak simply; but now, as Empress, I know it more than ever. For those who control the understanding of the people control the people themselves. Photios, with all his erudition, has never understood this.

So, my son, mark well the tears in the binding of this volume. I have removed Photios' tedious droning and inserted my pages in their place. I want you to know what happened from me, not from some old soldier turned troublemaker like Photios.

I know things he could never have known, or would be too afraid to speak about. Where was he when I held the hands and heads of both my Emperors, listened to their childlike yearnings, and kissed their eyes, when their bodies enclosed mine in a hot cocoon of love on many a lamp lit evening?

My earliest memory, perhaps when I was five or so, is that of a late autumn dawn in the Palace gardens, fresh after a night of rain. The morning service is over. Mother, Father and I walk home from the Ayia Eirene past the labyrinthine hedges, where I love to play whenever possible. The dew on the carnations sparkles in the morning light. Beads of water cling to rain-tattered spider webs like pearls poised on strands of silk. The sun rises and the hedges flash in the light. I have always found this remarkable.

Mother and Father are at each other's throats. Mother grabs me as I run between them and a hedge. Her fingers pinch me fiercely, as if I am about to vanish, and she hugs me to her. Father seems to be serious but I can see his eyes twinkling at me.

"All I ask is that you let her go for a few days. Is that so much to ask?" says Father. "She is already old enough to be with the other girls."

"She is still far too young. I will not have her become a slave," says Mother, "not even to the Emperor himself. And certainly not to a filthy Icon worshiper like the Augusta."

I slip out of her arms, and run to grab the head scarf that she had let drop to the ground, enjoying its silky feel around my shoulders as I climb onto the base of an eagle statue. The broad plinth cuts into my knees but I can just about balance on its edge when I grab hold of one of the eagle's claws.

Father slips me a sly wink. I try to wink in return, but I haven't mastered this skill yet, and shut both my eyes for trying, nearly slipping as well. Instead, I grin back.

"It's just for her to play and make friends. There is no guarantee she will enter the Augusta's retinue," says Father. "But it might help me at court if she were invited one day to the Gynaeconitis. The Emperor holds me in high regard but ... who knows what might happen in future."

I launch myself at him knowing that he will catch me, then perch snugly on a broad arm, tickling my forehead on his beard, letting his long hair, gleaming red in the morning sun, fall on my cheek. "Papa, when will we go to live in the snow castle again? I want to slide on the ice and roll in the snow." I have vague recollections of eating hot soup by a fiery hearth, and being wrapped in reindeer skins when put to sleep.

"You remember that!" Father's amazement pleases me. "You were just a *selurinn ungviði* then, how do you say in Greek ... a seal pup. No, not for a while, my sweet. I think mother has had her fill of the cold."

The Norse words fall like welcome snowflakes on my hot ears. But Mother glowers in silence.

"In a way, so have I," he continues. "Of this cold, that is. I will be going back soon. Alone."

Tears sting my eyes. I hate it when Father leaves us. And it breaks my heart to see Mother ignoring us now, in one of her usual fits, so I run over and throw my arms around her knees.

Then I am back in Father's arms, where I want to spend every second. He is the only one who dares throw me up and swirl me around him without any effort. I imagine I am a seagull, coasting behind him as he takes his boat away to the delicious cold and thrilling ice. Real birds must feel less dizzy though.

"Come on," he cries. "I'll race you to the pig statue, the one in the market."

He is already racing away as my feet land on the ground, and I tumble after him, my head spinning. That is what I remember. Along with the memories, later acquired, that we all share as the proud descendants of the first Constantine, the one who mounted old Rome and made it buck under him, more than six hundred years ago. So in these pages is my story, written by a mere woman who knows her letters as well as her stitches, no better, no worse. Know this, and you will know all you need to know.

How marvelous it was when Constantine left old Rome and took us Romans to this most womanly of towns, old Vyzantion. Here, washed in golden sunshine and adorned in marble and granite, Europa laid her bosom around a natural harbor into which the docile Aegean laps, stretching a lazy arm across the sparkling Bosporus, but never quite reaching our motherland, Anatolia.

Theodosius was among the earliest to adorn that bosom, by building the walls of our great City. Much later came Justinian – the sleepless one – whose Ayia Sofia gave us the means to worship her. That all of us survive and live well, even the oldest peasant still breaking his back at the olive tree in the early morning chill, we owe to these and other great Romans.

But where would these great men have been without us women to knock some sense into their heads, eh? Where would Constantine have been without Helen, his mother? Or Justinian without his whore-empress, Theodora? Need I remind you of Theodosius' sister, Pulcheria? Not to mention your own grandmother, another Theodora, who strode rough-shod through our lives long after her Theophilos died.

Like any beautiful woman, our City was desired. But desire brings both fortune and bad luck. Perhaps we didn't take enough care of her. Surrounded by enemies on all sides our men fought bravely and well, but lost often. In our despair, we gave in too easily to an empty idea born of vanity. Remember this always, little Leo. Ideas are far more dangerous than devils or demons. And men are obsessed with them.

They said that God had deserted the Romans, that he sided with our Abbasid foes who knelt to Allah and shunned all images. Our men struck at Icon-loving ways, claiming that these harmless images — which offered the poor a taste of heaven beyond the daily misery of life — corrupted the natural order. Women were especially to blame because they held the Icons closest to their hearts, by their bedsides, and over their hearths.

This is how ideas can turn the minds of men to the study of hate, and what lies in their hearts into the objects of that hate. Learn this well, my wise little Leo, as you embark on your own studies. We women set our City on a straight path when it stumbled along the wayside. We have been more than just mothers or wives or sisters. Some might even say that we have ruled with the wisdom of Emperors ourselves.

And they would be right!

2. The myth unfolds

LATE FALL, 842 AD

The myth still lingers in the murky past, at a time when my Peasant is still barely aware of his toes, let alone me, or even us. Let's give him his proper name — Vassilis. He sits on the back of their old mare as Marianos guides it around the herd, doing his best not to startle it. Marianos wants him to let the horses get accustomed to having men nearby before striking — perhaps a good lesson for the future!

A sudden lunge into the center of the herd sends the rope spiraling out, the noose mesmerizing a stallion into brief immobility. It heaves, tearing at the rocky ground as it tries to twist free. Marianos digs heels in and winds the rope around his arm. Seconds grind past.

Then he is on its back, calling out in victory, pulling its head down as it tries to rear. Vassilis circles around on their mare, desperate to be a part of the new catch.

A solitary peal of thunder rolls in from the distance toward them. The herd bolts. Marianos sees Vassilis racing away on their panicked mare, toward rising smoke on the horizon. He takes the stallion by the mane and forces it into a gallop.

Over the hilltop, the town comes into view, swarming with men on horseback, thick limbs waving firebrands, braids flying out from under iron helmets. The Bulgar colors of red, black, and white burn Marianos' heart. I'm sure the thug resorts to peasant curses at this point.

Marianos panics as hears Vassilis scream. He spots him vanishing on their mare into a forest. An age seems to pass as Marianos catches up to where he last saw him. He picks his way through the trees but Vassilis is nowhere to be seen. Like the peasant that he is, Marianos feels instinctively the need to return home, to return to look for the boy later. After all, he expects Vassilis to know the lie of the land well.

I imagine the town ablaze, perhaps a collapsed wall lying across a bridge strewn with people scrambling, screaming, some in burnt horror, dizzy with pain, clutter everywhere, hens underfoot. Where is Vassilis? Perhaps the mare has taken him home.

Marianos gallops down the main street, then into a maze of alleyways. The Bulgar are already at the marketplace — going straight for the livestock, of course!

He leaps to the ground and charges through the shambles to the hovel that he once called home. On his knees, he tears away at the rubble that covers tattered limbs. Blood drips from his father's face. Next to him their mother groans in agony, badly burnt.

Marianos roars with rage. His wife screams his name. The smoke is perhaps too much and he passes out for a moment, but then the ground thuds against his head. He fights to get up. Where is she? A flaming beam picks her out as it topples to the ground.

Now he is pushing and kicking, doing anything he can to get the burning wood off her. She frees herself but — a loud creaking overhead — he leaps aside in time to avoid a collapsing timber pinning him to the ground. The whole place is on fire. He pulls her away, thoughts racing. What to do first? Where is the little one? Where is their dim-witted mare?

The call of a horn echoes across the town. What now? Romans as well?

Back out on the street, a clear view of the hills opened up by the toppled wall shows Cataphracts pouring through the gates. Pennants fly the Iconoclast's black cross. This is as much the fault of the Romans as the Bulgar, Marianos rages. He prays for the arrows flying across the streets to find their target in the rears of the fleeing men.

Animals mill about. The smoke drifting across the town adds to the confusion. He hides behind a smoldering pile of rubble; waiting for a chance to . . . he knows not what.

Then he lunges out at a passing Cataphract, toppling him from his horse, pinning him easily to the ground, thanks to the Cataphract's heavy chain mail. A moment later he draws the Cataphract's sword across his neck.

"Tell me what is going on before you die," Marianos hisses.

"No need, we are just in time, you are safe," chokes the Cataphract. He tries to get up.

Marianos forces him down again and shoves a knee in his throat. "How can we be safe? Where do you come from?"

"The City …" the Cataphract chokes. "This area returns to Roman rule."

More invaders, under the mask of freedom. The myth that Photios has built on is that their father's father had been forced to settle in this land by the Romans and had died at the hands of the Bulgar, who dragged Vassilis' father to this town. Perhaps Vassilis hadn't even been born yet; let's say that Marianos, his senior by some seven years, had been very young when the barbarians threw their family down on the rocky ground, leaving them to struggle for survival.

Marianos brings the sword hilt down on the Cataphract's exposed cheek, leaving a bloody gash. A burning fence nearby starts to collapse and they both jump away just in time.

But Marianos is back on him again, pinning him down in a crushing hold.

"Which city … Constantinople? What do you want here? Why don't you bastards leave us alone?"

A horn sounds again.

"My commander calls," the Cataphract splutters as Marianos tightens his grip. "Kill me or let me leave."

Marianos lets go. The Cataphract scrambles for a horse.

Marianos watches him ride off, the sweat drying coldly on his back in the rising wind, the smell of death and chaos choking him as he struggles to decide what he should do next.

† † †

Theodora the Regent awakens in the Imperial quarters, the afternoon sleep dropping away from her eyes. But there is no peaceful calm to be had. In the long moments at waking, Theophilos' wordless pleas fade like tired stars into dusk. His agony has returned. Their embraces over the past months have become fewer, the nights of suffering longer and more painful for both of them. Now, encased in bedclothes, only foreheads and fingers touching, not even a kiss is exchanged. His incontinence and fever are a constant, relentless battle against himself, subjugating his once fierce pride.

I imagine Theodora cursing the miserable rascal as much as she feels his pain. She had once been so gullible, this pig-farmer's daughter from the provinces. In her youthful naivety she had lavished adoration on this most noble of living Romans, convinced that the light that poured from her young Emperor was that of the Savior himself! He had rewarded her by crowning her Augusta.

Then she had watched him throw himself away, mostly on campaigns, trying to set things right, driven by guilt, by his desire for justice. The vanity of men such as him is also their greatest asset. Having taken all the faults of his predecessors on his shoulders, he felt he had to sacrifice every vestige of strength to make the Empire stand firm again.

But why squander himself on her attendants? She forgave him because, as Emperor, he gave everything of himself, and so she felt he was allowed small indulgences. But how could she forget the affronts to her family, such as the time when Theophilos humiliated Petronas, her brother, for building a house that obstructed a widow's sea view? He had ordered Petronas' mansion torn down, awarding the property and the left over building materials to the widow, and had Petronas flogged in public. Dear Leo, that was your grandfather!

But it wasn't just the dallying with her maids that left a bitter taste in her mouth, like aubergines badly prepared for a stew. His raging against her Icons, so unbecoming to an Augusta, made her love for him dissolve into contempt at his single-mindedness.

The last few weeks pass before her eyes as Theophilos tosses and groans. She had been called away on several occasions, first to meet with officials, then to announce to the people that little Michael was to be crowned, and then to the Senate that Theoktistos, the Logothete, would assist her in watching over the little Emperor until he could be let out of his cage. What pleasure was there in it for her, I wonder, to watch all those grand counts and generals scraping the ground, the senators pledging allegiance to Theodora the farmer's daughter? She would be able to bring men up or push them down, issue decrees, even engage in war. But for her it is all duty, not power.

The court officials had been terrified of Theodora from early on. She would find them hiding behind their sheaves of documents, behind their bowing and bustling, all covering intricate plots to

implicate each other while really doing as little as possible to satisfy Imperial whim. Then their scorn and arrogance would wilt
under her gaze. Even before Theodora was appointed Regent,
legend has it that she challenged the Comptroller and his officials
openly when he couldn't explain payments that had gone astray.
She tallied up the figures in her head as Leo the Mathematician
had taught her; which troops were stationed at which outposts,
and the costs involved, and the results disagreed with what she
saw in the papers before her.

I laugh aloud when I imagine the waxen smiles of officials
melting as they back away from her presence, dripping excuses as
they flee. Theophilos had to acknowledge her quickness then, as
well as in her private business pursuits, pursuits that he despised
in an Augusta. But how he humiliated her over these later!

So what does Theodora feel when she places her hand on
Theophilos' swollen, feverish belly and slides it up to his chest?
Suspicion laced with pity rather than fondness? Perhaps there is
a touch of nostalgia for the once handsome cheeks, now gaunt
under a fragment of beard. Who can ever really know?

Someone pulls a curtain aside. Theodora nods in response.
The final Lenten vespers are upon them. The court will take it
amiss if they do not see the Emperor lead the procession, even if
he is at death's door. Theophilos knows as well as she does the
consequences of the slightest show of weakness.

† † †

So here is Theophilos' last Lent, in the darkness of the Virgin of
the Lighthouse chapel, bursting with plagal chant, and in the winter of his life. Like the senators gathered behind the Emperor, and
indeed like all our people, Theophilos was still trapped in the aus-
terity of spirit that the Iconoclasts — even my own mother — once
approved of.

Of course, later on Michael had the Chapel filled with every
imaginable form of ornamentation. So much so that it seemed to
glow with its own light when Photios officiated at Michael's union
with Vassilis. This chapel is where Photios hid this volume. We
ripped his own library apart at first, to find the records of the final
acts against the Pope. But who would have thought of looking for

a book beneath an altar, until one of my eunuchs stumbled upon it one day, and brought it to me.

A simple cross etched into the ceiling looms over the endless bows and turns of black, purple and white robes, as sandals and soft velvet boots slide over the cold stone. A cloud of smoke coils away from a censer swinging in Patriarch John's hands. Photios writes that John the Grammarian was an intelligent man whom he would have respected much, if only he had not devoted himself to defending the Iconoclasts as much as he did.

Theophilos' lean shadow hunches in prayer and crosses itself, his mumbled prayers barely audible over the Patriarch's chant. Theodora is at his elbow as he struggles to keep on his feet, while a wooden staff strains under the weight of his other hand.

John trips over the usual words as he rushes to finish the service. "We pray for our mother and father in Christ, the Augusta and the Emperor, may they live long and carry our burdens through adversity into prosperity."

With a final "God have mercy on us" and sweep of the censer, the Emperor turns and shuffles, three-legged, out of the chapel. Do the shouted commands of a cohort of the Palace Guard assembling outside — once a source of pride to Theophilos — now startle him? To Photios he seemed very nervous near the end.

Outside the chapel, the blinding sun burns down on the Mese, the road that connects the heart of our City for seven miles to the Gates and the great walls that protect us. The guard is changing, as is usual at the sixth hour, before entering the larger formation marching toward the Gates. I imagine the midday sun making long shadows of the guards' beards on the chain mail over their broad chests, while their sweat-soaked shoulders yearn for the whisper of a sea breeze. Some of them are my people, far from Thule, home of the Norsemen. They will endure anything to find a better life in the City.

A towering brass gate swings open at the walls to reveal a moat. I have seen the midday sun strike right onto the water and watched it glisten in the bright heat. If the guards were off duty, I am sure that a quick, naked plunge would definitely be in order, though it is strictly forbidden.

Let's imagine that calls and hooves echo across the walls to-day. Curtains of dust make way for the pummeling of horse's hooves, perhaps the very same Cataphracts who are returning from Adrianopolis, perhaps even from Vassilis' village. It is conceivable that one of these knights rubs his neck gingerly, still recalling his encounter with Marianos.

Now the lead Cataphract emerges from the dust and reins in his mount at the gate. He takes off his helmet, revealing a bald, long head and marble-chiseled chin, in sharp contrast to the thickset, bearded men who ride past.

"This is the Logothete," Theoktistos the Eunuch says. "Stand down. We are needed immediately at the Emperor's side." He shakes the dust from his cloak. I smile as I imagine the pompous tones, reeking with contrived precision that accompany this declaration. Such a show-off!

The guard at the gate probably greets the Eunuch with something like "Good news for the Emperor?"

Perhaps exhaustion makes the Eunuch even more annoyed at the over-familiar greeting. He ignores it and dismisses the commanders, before easing his mount into a trot, hooves crunching the broad path, lined with fruit trees, huts and vegetable beds receding into the distance.

Surely he must be satisfied, perhaps even proud, at what he has done. Compared to the grinding failures in recent months, in particular the campaign to rescue Crete from the Emir of Còrdoba — whose forces never cease trying to secure every island in the Mediterranean — this campaign has delivered a modicum of success. He knows we can never give up our struggle to preserve the City from the loss of more lands. At least his Augusta, Theodora, knows and appreciates how difficult it has been for them, and for what we now know was their hidden cause — the Icons.

The route that Theoktistos must have followed that day is a breathtaking one: along the hills of Thrace, the horses racing behind him, the great Aqueduct never far from sight to the north. How I would love to see this marvel, built nearly five hundred years ago by the Emperor Valens, its monstrous arches and pillars, like some gorgon of old, straddling forests and valleys for more than a hundred miles as its watery load races down to the bowels of our thirsty City.

Now, with the Aqueduct still on his left, close cobbles eat up the path as horse and rider sweat their way through the crowds, along the Mese, and up a gradual but long incline. The vegetable gardens have deferred to rows of orange brick homes under a sea of flat roofs.

At the top of the hill the Palace complex erupts into view below him. A familiar sight, but one that always makes my heart stand still, a frozen topple of white marble cascading through pockets of green, up and over the next hill, to a cerulean sea flecked with white. The Ayia Sofia, toward which all good Christians are compelled to genuflect, squats in porphyry on the left. The vast expanse of the Hippodrome lies straight ahead. He casts an eye to the chariot boxes at the far end, and perhaps a gleam of sunlight from the giant copper horses above fires the illusion that they are springing into action toward him? They certainly do that to me sometimes.

Exhaustion finally catches up with him. The chill of the late afternoon breeze stirs him into motion again, and he leads his perspiring mount down the slope to the stables. He must get a fresh cloak, report to the old tyrant, and then, God willing, get home quickly to a delicious bath and his sweet bed.

3. No way back

LATE FALL, 842 AD
Everyone knows that Photios' learning knows no bounds. But how many know how well he can fabricate? No doubt all his reading provides fertile ground for this tale. But what he writes about our story is only half the story. The rest is really my story.

So mark well the pages that I have torn from the binding of his codex, my fine boy. I will take up Photios' mythology here, and tell the plight of my Vassilis, those many years ago, the one that Photios calls the Usurper in his version of this tale. I hold the power now. I have done so for the past twelve years — since your father died. And the stories of the women in this tome will be mine as well. Somehow that is very fitting — one might even say that Vassilis has taken on the nobler role of a woman himself in some circumstances!

His faithful mare gallops for what seems like an age, leaving my young Peasant nodding off, as he grows tired. He awakens to find himself lying on the ground and that his horse has vanished. Does he weep and thrash around in fear and frustration?

Of course not! He enjoys the time alone at first, playing in the streams, eating berries and trying to catch fresh fish as his brothers had taught him. He climbs trees, looking for the occasional egg, leaving many a confused nest behind. After the first few days of doing this, he stops wondering about his family, at least in the beginning. For my Vassilis is very pragmatic about these things.

I have always marveled at his simple, quiet awareness of God. It often confuses me, even terrifies me. For me, God is — to be frank — somewhat irrelevant. Why does He care about what we do? Surely people should matter more.

But Vassilis can now wander where his heart most wants to be, freed from the clutter of village life, alone amid the forests, the plains and the peaks where only the rustling trees break the silence. For my Vassilis prays without words. Even now, when he holds me in his arms, I wrap myself in the peace that surrounds him like a comfortable blanket. He says that God has no need of babble or priests. I agree completely. So why would it have been any different back then?

Here then is my Peasant, learning to be old at twelve, lost in the dark forest yet content with his lot, in spite of the cold. Though being alone for too long must fill him with some sort of dread, especially when he remembers that soon it will be his name day. Maybe that day is even today? How his brown eyes sting! Where are his parents, not to mention his aunts and uncles? Who do they gather around, singing the songs of the arrival of Saint Vassilis from Caesarea, bearing parchment and quill to write blessings for the start of the New Year?

Now this little one's body shakes with sobs. He cries himself to sleep. With the lightness borne of release, an empty stomach and the cool dark air, he dreams all night of his family, singing together with them at church, and then calling out greetings in the early morning hours in front of each other's homes. Sad dreams, in which they do not hear him when he calls, do not even notice him as he runs to tug at their tunics. Their tunics seem to melt away in his hands, just out of grasp.

But now the bleating and sour smell of goats poking their hot noses at him have woken up my young Vassilis, as has the shouting of strange voices and the neighing of horses. He is a little afraid, so he pretends he is still asleep.

The previous night he had curled up under some dead branches at the edge of a clearing. Now he peers out to discover that brightly colored hangings on wooden poles fill the clearing. He can't understand the strange words being spoken around him, but the men speaking them seem not to have noticed him, too hard at work to care about anything else. He slips away when they start kicking around for more sticks.

But as much as he tries he cannot resist the smell of boiling milk that coaxes his hunger into a painful flame. He moves resolutely over to the fire and sits down beside it. My Peasant is the most cautious man I have ever known, but also the bravest.

The men can't help but notice him now. Vassilis looks them in the eye, at which they shake their heads and grin. They speak but he understands nothing, and says nothing. Comments fly — one laughs loudly, while another passes Vassilis a bowl. I am sure he takes it with a smile, that smile that still sends my heart beating. The sourness of the hot curds makes him grimace, but it goes down very well, burning comfortably in his stomach. He wanders over to the horses.

He wonders if these people might take him to Chariopolis, back to his family, or perhaps to Adrianopolis, from where he could try to find his cousins and ask them how to get home. How to explain all this in words the strangers will understand?

Now that Vassilis feels people near him I'm sure he yearns for his family even more. He fights back the tears and decides to wait and see. If he were to win their favor, maybe they'd let him tag along. There were several trees he had not climbed in the last few days, several nests recently unexplored. Perhaps the men might take him more seriously if he rounded up some fresh eggs for them?

† † †

A roaring fire darts shadows across a large oak table, across maps and charts scattered across it. To Photios' horror, the Emperor, gaunt cheeks resting in his hands, appears to be ... drooling!

Theodora bustles in, all busy concern for her husband. She is everywhere at once, yet somehow veiled.

"Husband, you are too tired," she whispers at him. "The service was long and the fast is not yet over."

Theophilos reaches out to her and beckons vaguely. "Where is the Logothete? He knows I want him here straight from the field!"

Panic — from the fear of life's consequences — lies low in the room. Theophilos has made many choices, too many for a man of his thirty years. He has seen too much pain, both from his choices and from the stupidity of others. There is no way back. We live in the wake of our choices, as life washes back out to the great sea of approaching death. Is there a life after life? I doubt it sometimes. There is only one hell, the hell of now.

Theoktistos glides in, although I can see that he is doing his best to hide his weariness. Theodora holds out her hands as if to greet him, but brings them to her mouth instead. Then she moves to stand behind her husband, the cowled marble of her glare ready for the worst.

"Worthiness, I'm here with good news ...."

"Welcome back, brave Logothete," groans the Emperor. "Although we mourn losing our worldly wars against the Abbasid, and our very cradle of Amorion, I hope we stand firm in securing the Kingdom of Heaven?"

The Eunuch and the Augusta are behaving quite strangely, stealing glances at each other constantly. Something is afoot.

"Let's get some rest, dear heart," Theodora says, perhaps a bit too loudly. "You still have not recovered from the fast!" The bustling concern seems contrived, even excessive.

An earthquake convulses in Theophilos' chest. "We stay until we are done!" he says.

Embarrassment mixed with concern alight on every forehead. Theophilos doubles up in pain, clutching his sides.

Is there perhaps divine retribution after all? Is He as capricious as the gods of old were?

I wasn't there to see any of this. But this is what Photios wrote of events. He wrote also of Lazarus. Not the New Testament saint, that is, but the old monk who lived on Terebinthos — one Lazarus Zographos, a man who nearly lost his hands to this cruel-hearted bastard of an Emperor because he, Lazarus, insisted on painting the saints that the people revered.

Theophilos himself ordered the monk's hands to be pressed into sheets of red hot steel. Only the stumps of his fingers remained. Far fewer know that Theodora was the one who stopped Theophilos from going any further. At any rate, the pain silenced both his lips and brush for more than a year. But it took longer for Theophilos to forgive her meddling. One wonders if he ever really forgave it?

The Emperor has regained enough strength to rant again. Sweat glistens on his forehead. "Oh God, where is my Amorion, why should it have fallen to the devious Abbasid, once our fellow worshipers of the one God but now our foes. Did so many thousands need to fall!" The fine meter and elevated language Theophilos reverted to, especially in times of anger or distress, was legendary.

The Augusta takes the Eunuch aside. She touches his arm, their eyes meet and their lips exchange a silent message. Then she whispers to him. "He has been like this since you left. He lives in the past, his mind clinging to recent losses. I try to remind him of his earlier work, the peace we brokered with the Abbasid, the hospitals and the Bucoleon Palace so recently built and where he now refuses to rest."

"Our coffers are in a better state than expected," says Photios to no one in particular. "We won't need to raise taxes in our newly acquired Themes, at least not for the time being."

But we all know that our prosperity has been due more to Theodora's careful husbandry than anything else. Now she holds Theophilos' face in her hands and pleads with him. "Husband, husband, hear out these good men. They speak only good of what you have done. Courage!"

She straightens and turns back to the Eunuch. "Logothete, tell us your news."

"We have covered the plains and valleys of Thrace. The last of the obstinate Bulgar have been expelled and the ... Icon worshipers put to the sword. I have reappointed the General in Adrianopolis to restore the Macedonian Theme."

The Eunuch's words seem to have a calming effect, and he knows it, if his smug expression is anything to go by. That a General feels confident enough to resume responsibility for this fractious but vital Theme is an impressive achievement indeed.

"I think we can safely say we have our bulwark against the Bulgar..." he begins.

"Not good enough!" the Emperor slams his fist down on the table, nearly launching himself, like a puppet with broken strings, into the air. The flames in the hearth sputter.

"I want death to the Icon worshipers, all of them. We should not stop until they all roast in hell!"

Suddenly he doubles over and sags to the floor. A guard helps lift him to the table. It is all hands as he comes to. Everyone freezes in horror. A pendant has slipped out the Eunuch's robes. The Emperor's eyes flicker open, glazed at first, then they focus on it. A powerful gust outside sends the fire into sudden brightness, the light reflecting off a miniature Icon of a Mary Theotokos that swings in the air before everyone.

The Emperor grabs the pendant and pulls the Eunuch toward him as if to kiss him, then tries to rip the pendant from his neck.

Groaning, he vomits and lists onto the table. Theoktistos leans over him again, listening for a heartbeat, while slipping the pendant back into his tunic. His silent frown says it all.

Theodora reaches across her husband, shuts his eyes, and rests her head on his chest. Yet her expression belies no real emotion.

Upright again, she pulls a small pendant of John the Baptist from her robe. She places the miniature Icon to his lips, then on his forehead. Then she is back on her feet — all business again.

"Let it be known that the Emperor of all the Romans passed into heaven this hour with the Mother of God on his lips," she announces. "Enough talk. We must move quickly. There is no time for a great mourning. A brief display will suffice. We crown the infant on the morrow. Bring me the Patriarch now."

† † †

Indeed, I can see how Photios' fiction has worked, how his myth that Vassilis is descended from kings, rather than just horse thieves, has smoothed his path back to the Patriarchate.

But I will not shirk from relating absolutely everything I imagine or know to be true. For I know my Peasant in ways no one else would dare relate, and I want you to know of them, my boys — may the Theotokos shield you from all harm!

I can see a clearing, and a squirrel darting off one end of a fallen tree. My young Peasant sits perched on the other end. The surrounding purple peaks peer down at him and themselves in the smooth waters of a wide river below.

The bread in his mouth tastes flat. He has decided that the men are Abbasid, from stories that Father had told the boys. Distant travelers, olive-skinned, friendly, though clearly weaklings. All is slowness, comfort to them. Though their horses are handsome beasts, much better even than what his brothers would normally bring home from the hills around Chariopolis.

He strolls to the nearest tent. The caravan has brought him all the way to this river, the river Marianos had told him about once — a river he had only dreamed of seeing. But he has no real idea where the men are headed.

They have stopped on a steep bank beyond which Vassilis imagines he can see the river mouth to the east, through grow-

ing mists. He wonders if the sea is beyond that and whether they
will take him there. Or are they going north, to the wilderness that
haunts every Macedonian child's dreams, bedeviled by wolves and
bears, and fierce tribes such as the Bulgar? He is not afraid. Let
the Theotokos show him the path.

A hand touches his shoulder. He throws it off, but regrets it
straight away when he sees the toothy grin and cheerful eyes facing him. These people look so different, Vassilis thinks. Just like
women, long and thin, with shapely hips and slender hands. Especially this fellow — perhaps seventeen or so, almost as old as Marianos. The young Abbasid hands him a bowl of soup and squats,
his strange, harsh sounds contradicting gentle gestures.

"Hello, stranger," Vassilis says pointing at the horses. "I like
my new friends. They are good and true, and want nothing from
anyone in return for work and hardship."

The Abbasid points at himself and says something ending in
"Wasim". That must be his name.

Vassilis takes in the strange smells from this one: horse leather,
sweat, and something like ... origanum. He marvels at the fellow's cinnamon skin and shining black curls.

"I don't understand. Can't you speak Greek?" Vassilis says.
"Doesn't matter." He gropes for something to break the tension,
sips from the bowl and puts it down on the log.

Wasim says something, points to a horse, and indicates a riding motion. Vassilis takes a moment to understand, then nods. A
chance for a ride with a new friend!

They fly away from the caravan, down the slope, to the river.
The saltiness of the sea blows in from nearby. The restful smell
of warm fir trees fills the air. He finds it hard not to feel a little bit
happy again. The sand whips up from the horses' hooves as they
race beside the river.

The boys dismount, sweating from the sprint. The horses nuz-
zle, the stallion roughing his nose along the mare's back.

The boys rest on some rocks covered in mussels. Vassilis dips
his hand below the waterline to touch them. These rough, indifferent little creatures amaze him. Where would a mountain boy
like him have seen them before?

Wasim's hand is not far away. It too runs over the mussels
and reaches Vassilis' fingers, covering and squeezing them for a

moment. Vassilis doesn't know where to rest his eyes. Then he notices that the stallion is very much at attention — the mare must be in heat.

"Who has a better time? The stallion or the mare?" asks Vassilis, pulling his hand away to mime the act. His gestures are unmistakable. Wasim laughs and stands up, his feet in the water. The dent in his tunic makes it obvious that he too is at attention.

Vassilis feels a strange tingling in his groin, as if he needs to relieve himself, and blood rushes to his head. Wasim pulls him down and falls on top of him. He bites Vassilis on the shoulder, then more tenderly on the neck, then on the mouth. Shoulders meet chests as tunics get pulled over their heads. Taut nipples scrape. Vassilis is not sure what is going on and turns away.

Then Wasim pushes him down, onto the sand, and shoves his groin at Vassilis' mouth. Vassilis is strong for his age, but Wasim is bigger — he rolls Vassilis over onto his stomach and pins his arms down.

Vassilis yelps with pain as his arm twists at a strange angle, but his protests are ignored. He resists Wasim tugging at his britches, then freezes with terror as they are pulled away. First a lick of river water, then a cold breeze slaps at his bare backside.

Sudden agony scalds my beloved, forcing a howl from him. His clenched lips rub the sand as Wasim thrusts into him. Images flash through his mind of when he and Father chanced upon two older boys in the alley behind a neighbor's home: the naked torso of one cupped itself so neatly around the slender buttocks of the other; their britches half-way down to bare, dusty toes curled up in pleasure; their faces frozen in shock as Father lashed out a thick arm at them.

Now Wasim tenses up and stiffens, before collapsing on top of Vassilis, pushing his face further into the sand.

You needn't be shocked my little ones, though I do not think you know of this side to the man they call your father. But this is nothing. What I have seen as he writhed against my body will shock you no less!

Thundering hooves echo off the cliffs. Suddenly Wasim is on his feet, Vassilis clambering up after him. Back on their mounts they race across the heady green, toward the camp.

Here Vassilis finds the same iron-breasted horsemen that chased him from home, their braids zigzagging across the tents, overturning pots, kicking aside cushions and grabbing sacks and rolls of silk. Could they show him the way home?

But my young Vassilis decides quickly that these are enemies, not friends. He dismounts and leaps into the fray.

The Bulgar must be confused by the spectacle of a mere boy racing at them without even a weapon in his hand. Vassilis leaps onto a marauder's horse and disengages a short sword, stabbing it at the rider's back but nicking himself instead. Blood drips over their legs, making the horse's back slippery. The fury builds inside my brave little Peasant and must be let out, the terrible rage that has always driven him forward and that I have come to fear. The rider falls to the ground, taking Vassilis with him.

Another joins in, trying to pin Vassilis down. He rolls and writhes. From somewhere inside himself he finds the strength to resist them, but then a third piles in. He feels a sharp pain as a sword hilt meets him in the temple. The darkness is not welcome.

4. Absolution

The main hall of the Gynaeconitis is a vast chamber of marble floor relieved by fine Abbasid rugs scattered in all directions. Little Michael crawls on tiny knees, clearly oblivious to the cold that spreads like a fine skein of icicles through thick velvet boots, in spite of braziers dotted around the room. I suspect the Regent doesn't really want to deal with her son right now — there is too much to think about and do. If only his sisters would leave him alone!

"Girls, girls, that is enough!" Theodora calls out. "He is much smaller than you. Let him be." The three older girls run circles around Michael, then throw a large cloth over him, ignoring their mother. Some women pull the girls away as he bursts into tears.

The Augusta takes him in her arms and speaks softly to him. "My little Emperor, today you have come into your own. Your world. Our world. Your father has left us forever and we must fend for ourselves." The little one gurgles. How blind he is to the real implications!

Theoktistos arrives in a perfumed tunic, cloak over his shoulder, placing his arm on hers in his usual supportive fashion. "The mourning procession will take place in one hour. Though we have the full support of the Senate, there are soldiers who are ready for any sign of weakness."

"Have you summoned the Patriarch?" she asks.

"I have. Is the, er ..., Emperor prepared? The ceremony will be long. It would be easier if he didn't burst into tears every so often."

"We have agreed," Theodora says, pacing. "It is essential that the people see Michael, and they see that we hold the power. But more importantly, how close we are to having the new coins minted — the ones that show Michael alongside me?"

Photios is there as well, no doubt a reluctant guest to this womanly domain. "I am pleased to report," he says, "that not only are the new molds prepared, but also that existing coinage is being gathered and will be melted down and recast within the week. The Palace Guard is in full complement for both this and for the ceremony − anything could happen."

"Guards!" comes an indignant roar from the doorway. "To protect you from what?" Vardas erupts into the room, waving a helmet accusingly. Barely visible behind him lurks Petronas, a sinewy pack of leather and muscle. It would be hard to recognize that these two are brothers, and Theodora their sister, unless one chooses to notice the flattened features of the Paphlagonians, the way the broad forehead buttresses a fierce gaze and, I confess, a rather bulbous nose.

Everyone knows that the Eunuch can't stand Vardas. And Vardas must be uncertain of his future role, left undecided by Theophilos. Theoktistos, always a cautious servant of the Throne, lives to smooth things over. He is the very antithesis of Vardas, who desires to provoke.

"Naturally, there will be absolutely no need with your protection . . . " Theoktistos says, slipping between Vardas and the doorway, with his usual caricature of a bow.

Vardas holds out his arms. Theodora drops Michael in the lap of a woman and allows Vardas to embrace her. Petronas joins in.

"Dear sister," Vardas says. "Theophilos will be missed by some, less so by others, but we are well prepared for what may come our way, thanks to your hard work and foresight."

"Missed or not, he is not to be remembered as an Icon hater," she replies, escaping his embrace and straightening her cowl. "By his own will he kissed the Theotokos as he lay dying. Several of us witnessed it."

"Did he now? It must be a miracle," Petronas ventures. "Was he perhaps too far gone to realize. . . " he starts, but goes no further. No point in stating the obvious − Theodora's devotion to the Icons was always a thorn in Theophilos' side.

Vardas takes the infant and gently hoists him into the air, catching him on the way down, to giggles and chirps of delight. But there are important questions to be answered. Even the Augusta knows that some talk of business is necessary, especially with her kin right there, wanting to help. This isn't going to be easy for her.

"I hope you have not forgotten Theophilos' intentions in all of this," Theodora says, "following Michael's crowning? You were there, at the meetings with the Senate, the Generals, and the Patriarch."

Petronas and Vardas exchange glances. They probably weren't expecting to get to the point so soon. The mettle of their sister never ceases to surprise them, or me, even to this day.

"Then you know," she says, "that we have decided to act in accordance with the Emperor's wishes, on the little one's behalf. By we, I mean me and the Logothete."

The brothers look at each other.   Then Petronas takes Theodora's soft hands in his lean fingers. "Dear sister, know that we are yours and this young Emperor's. Just let some danger stand in his way, and we shall cleave heads from shoulders."

As they embrace, the window panes behind Theodora glow in the sunlight, lending the appearance of a halo to her cowl. But she is no saint, I assure you.

† † †

As much as I grew to hate Theodora the Augusta, I understand why she did what she had to. Though I will refer to her from now on as the Regent, for that is what we called her ever since I can remember.

This is why I tear out Photios' pages and pollute his fine script with my crossings out, and my unpracticed, womanly scrawls. I don't deny that he fills in the story for those who will not have heard of these events, and that he does so in a manner infinitely more accomplished than I could ever hope to achieve.

But the women in this tale belong to me. For what would a solitary man like him know of us and of what makes us persevere when men would undoubtedly fail?

They say the Regent had a dream. She stands bathed in golden light, reflected from marble looming all around her, rising to the semicircle of bronze bars that form the top of the Chalke Gate, the entrance to the Palace. Framed in these bars is the great image of our Savior, hewn in stone and made holy by blessed, golden mosaic, the harsh late morning sunlight transformed into a beacon by His piercing gaze. At least this was how the gate looked before our Iconoclasts had their way with it.

Perched high on the bronzed bars, a figure daubs plaster over our Savior, covering up the eyes with sticky white. The figure turns to look at her with vacant sockets and slips. A skeleton tumbles to the ground. She hears herself screaming.

Now she looks down to find herself clothed in a white toga with the black trimmings of a juror. The courtyard swims around her; on steps in front of the arch, jurors stand in similar attire — only these are grizzled, pompous graybeards, rolls of parchment in their arms.

Sounds of harsh clanking and screaming ring out, followed by the slaps of a whip. The gate swings open, a crimson glow suffusing the entrance. She peers into the brightness — a machine is being dragged through the gates. In its wake, a crew of pale, dirt-streaked Thulians drives a bloodied sod forward. They are naked, save for giant wings that caress the darkening air as lightning flashes from the sky. The source of the man's pain is evident — the blood drips from wounds covering every inch of his pale, sinewy body.

Theophilos! Theodora recognizes her ravaged husband's body now, a body she once knew and longed for. Part of her rejoices that he has returned — that, finally, she has the chance to save him. Another part is aroused by the pain he is in. But mainly she bristles with rage. Who are these fools to do this to her charge?

She shouts out in indignation but other words slice through the air at her. The ground buckles with thunderbolts. The graybeards drone as one.

"Theophilos of Amorion, you have been brought before with charges of blasphemy and heresy. You have destroyed this image of our Lord — as you have wrought destruction in the hearts of Romans everywhere."

He is dragged to the rack and manacled to it. But who are they to do this? She and God are his only rightful judges.

"He has repented!" Theodora tries to scream above the thunder. "Did he not embrace the Icons as he lay dying?"

The voices boom back at her. "His actions were vain and weak. Did Bishop Euthymios not die at his hand? How many monks and priests suffered at his command?"

The rack is drawn tighter. Theophilos screams and weeps, his splintering limbs and torso tearing beyond their limits.

She wants to rush over to him but cannot move − her limbs are like lead. "His actions were great and noble," she shouts back. "Look at how he has built up your great City, heaven on earth."

"His cruelty was greater," their booming voices respond.

Christ has returned to this world − at least here. Theodora weeps with joy and awe as the plaster covering the mosaic glows and begins to crack away, flakes spattering like rain onto the pavement below.

This gives her the strength to shout back. "Only because he believed what your priests told us − that we were worshiping idols. But all who walked the streets of Vyzantion knew that he loved the people."

Lightning crashes, or is it the sound of their voices? "So say you, woman. But did he not try to crush you when you conducted your own affairs? When you sought to enrich the state through your own pursuits? Did he show you affection then?"

How do they know this? Who are they? Theodora rages. "He did not mean any harm!"

Theophilos gags as blood seeps out of his mouth.

"Did he not have your own brother whipped? Why do you plead for him?"

Theodora's throat is raw. But she still manages to speak out: "This is not justice. His heart was great. His name must be praised, and will be as long as I live! You must absolve him. Or to hell with the lot of you!"

The Christ sculpture has softened into flesh. Its hands reach out to her with young Theophilos' hard face smiling in eternal youthfulness. Its gaze, no longer stern, but inviting, seductive, blinds her, leaving her convulsing, sobbing, her groin strangely damp.

"Take me, Lord − but absolve him!" she screams, and rolls over on her bed, sweating and tousled, her heart thudding with the dark realization that her husband has left her forever. She is now truly alone, the pillows strewn on the floor her only consolation.

† † †

Theoktistos the Eunuch comes to get the Regent from her bed. That morning she seems to be exhausted, but it would not be appropriate to ask why. After a hasty breaking of her fast, she agrees to leave the comfort of her quarters for a stroll.

"You will have to get used to starting early," Theoktistos says. "I think we will have to move you to the Emperor's chambers, close to the Throne Rome. The business of the day waits not even for a Regent! Of course, I will do what I can from now on to smooth this path for you."

I am sure his mind is racing with ideas. Together they walk along the dew-covered pavement, up gleaming steps, and then through the passage lined both with trees and columns that leads to the Magnaura.

"We will have to deal with yet more bickering today between the abbot of the Stoudion and the bishops," he begins.

"Of course," Theodora replies. "There is much anger to be overcome. Those who abhorred the Icons now find themselves accused. But let those who are without guilt cast the first stone. And let us not forget that I have forgiven the worst of them."

Theoktistos must be moved at her conviction. What she says makes perfect sense as usual. Which is why he seldom feels compelled to disagree with her, and neither did most of us, at least most of the time.

"It is not so much guilt, as fear," he continues, "fear that those who once persecuted, or did not stop the persecution, not only deserve to be punished, but must be punished."

"So what do you suggest?" she frowns, her eyes dark. They have arrived at the doors to the Magnaura. The guards stand aside to admit them. This is another drafty place which never seems to warm up, even on the hottest summer's day. The cold of the night barely has time to yield to the sun before the latter disappears, in spite of the windowed dome that hangs heavily above.

"I think ... that we might need to call together the bishops," the Eunuch says. "We might want to consider some sort of a conference, but include others as well as those in power. I am referring to their followers as well."

"To ensure that everyone is in agreement? Like the Councils of old? I see. But what would we hope to achieve?"

"We keep it very simple. No issues of doctrine. No statements of position. We reconcile."

Theodora is nodding. "I agree," she says. "We look to forgiveness rather than accusation. We do not judge whether they have sinned and neither do we allow them that luxury with each other."

"Absolutely, Worthiness, no harsh punishment or retribution — only ways to redress the balance."

Then the frowns return as they leave the building. "Who would lead it?"

The Eunuch's silence says it all.

She smiles thinly. "But," she pauses on the path back. "You know how hard it will be. I must act as an Emperor would ... and more; with the clear, demanding mind of a man — but the robes and forgiving heart of the Theotokos herself."

† † †

How is my fine young Vassilis? Tossed this way and that, does he curl up like a worm and await the final crushing footfall? Hardly! It takes him a moment to realize that the stinging pain reaching inside him is sheer cold. He lifts his head and sees sticky scarlet oozing into the snow, but his temples ring with such agony that he drops back into the snow.

A door creaks open and Vassilis tries to look up. A shaft of light silhouettes a craggy shadow, from which a cautious eye peers out. The shadow reaches out to touch him. Then someone is leaning over him, muttering.

"Water," croaks Vassilis from between frozen lips, gesturing.

"Who are you? Why are you here? Let's get you in," the shadow speaks.

Vassilis imagines he hears a foreign tongue. He feels himself being lifted toward a fire. Then he hears someone speaking Greek. Has father returned to help him? Or perhaps his brothers have found him. He invokes Saint Vassilis. The blackness swims across his eyes again.

He comes to his senses in warmth, a strange, old man beside him. The man reaches for a bowl and lifts it for Vassilis to drink. He tries to sit up but collapses back onto the bunk.

Then he wakes up to find the old man rubbing rags across his face. A woman stands behind him and comes closer. She touches her fingers to his mouth and droplets moisten his lips. But the blackness returns.

Vassilis comes to, yet again, with a burning bowl brushing against his cheek. He gulps down some hot broth. Eyes now wide open, he looks at the space around him, comfortable but simple, just like the home he once knew. A fire burns under a bubbling pot, wood lies stacked in the corner, and colorful rugs cover the floor and a wall.

The man leans over him, white bristles erupting sparsely from his marked face. Vassilis wonders why he mistook this man for his Father. Earlier days flood into his thoughts, the time spent with his brothers in the forests, amid mountain springs.

The woman returns. She is so beautiful, just like his mother. "Are you an angel?" Vassilis says.

"Greek!" she says. "The child is one of ours!"

The old man carries on in Greek. "The riders left you here, didn't they? I wonder why?"

"They probably want him for something," she says, "and will come looking for him again. But right now you need someone to take care of you."

Vassilis reaches for the old man and tries to embrace him. "You have helped me. I won't forget this."

"Come now, sit back," the woman says. "You must rest, you are in safe hands. My name is Maria, and this is Tervel, my father."

"I thought I would never hear Greek again," Vassilis manages, though his throat is on fire.

"We lived in Thessaloniki for many years," she says. Her words caress him. "But where are you from? Anyway, you must rest now."

She pushes Vassilis gently back down onto the bunk as he tries to answer her and moves over to the fire to stoke it more.

As Vassilis drifts off, his father, or perhaps it is Saint Vassilis, appears over him. They embrace. He hears the words "unless you have me in you, you will never know what you are." The words quench his frustration like a deep draft of wine from the altar. He need not fear — Father and Mother are right here beside him.

5. Oh, Fortuna!

c. 843 AD

John the Grammarian will be patriarch for only a little while longer, and he knows this. He deflects the contemptuous stares and hard looks as he enters the antechamber of Theoktistos' home, striding through to the main hall with great dignity, his robes billowing, his features set as if in plaster — not unlike the plaster he ordered laid over our beloved Icons!

Photios is here, as is Leo. Not you, little one! Your namesake, Leo the Mathematician, former Metropolitan of Thessaloniki, one of our greatest teachers and a close friend of Photios, though his Iconoclast sympathies are well known.

John chooses not to take a couch. Instead, he moves to a pillar at the far side of the hall. In the middle of the room, Theodora stands in intense conversation with Petronas, Vardas, Photios and of course, the Eunuch.

Theoktistos leaves them, moving back to the antechamber, this time to welcome the obvious candidate, the wizened Methodios, in most deferential style. Bishop Ignatios bursts through the curtains and struts toward a brace of Stoudite monks on the other side of the hall. John is probably worried that he is about to humiliated by the Iconodules. Surely Ignatios is not a serious contender?

Theodora calls the meeting to order. Photios writes that Michael fidgets and shuffles, his hand clasped in hers, such a little rascal already. The ritual obeisances are waved aside — her free hand rests on old Methodios' arm.

Theodora speaks calmly, but her hands quiver, not quite hidden in their drooping sleeves. "We have decided that the Chalke must shine as before. It came to me in a dream. The face of our Lord will return to its former glory."

She pauses, obviously expecting a response, but the Iconoclast bishops are too afraid to utter a word, and the rest of us are wondering what the judgment will be.

The Regent steels herself. "First we must thank our noble Patriarch John for his devotion, and for his acceptance to allow others to lead the restoration of our faith from the patriarchal throne.

This must be a shock for John to hear it spoken; to hear the public confirmation that his work has been for nothing.

Then Ignatios' high-pitched tones ring out. "All praise to Your Worthiness — but that is not enough! The heresy must never be allowed to happen again. Need I remind everyone that your great predecessor, the Augusta Irene, has trodden the very path you take and moved to turn back the Iconoclast heresy? But her actions came to nothing when the hard hearted soldiers chose to ignore her. What actions will you take to prevent this from happening again? At the very least, surely, we must remove all the Icon-haters from office, not just the Patriarch!"

Sandals shuffle apprehensively.

"I turn to the forgiveness of our Lord," Theodora begins, "as you must." But she blushes as she says this. With Ignatios anything is possible, and she knows it. Wasn't all this already agreed? Why does Ignatios choose to rake about in old wounds?

"We should look to the noble actions of the heretics themselves," calls out Vardas, perhaps too casually. This gets a buzz, but he continues regardless. "It is true that they expressed contempt for the Icons. And that we have suffered many defeats over the past years. But let us not forget how the Iconoclast Emperors after the Holy Irene led countless armies in turning back the Bulgar and the Abbasid, and preserved our City as a result — with the Theotokos' help, of course."

The monks are now in full protest. Ignatios glowers in indignation. "How dare you speak to us in this way — you have no right to discuss religious matters!" Turning to Theodora, "Your Worthiness — why do we have soldiers here — especially those covered with the filth of their deeds before the eyes of God? They have no…"

The Eunuch cuts in before Theodora can register indignation at the slight to her family. "That's enough. We are not here today to wallow around in the misery of the past, but to restore the natural order of the Kingdom of Heaven. We must rise above the past, or risk sowing the seeds of misery and resentment that will grow into more suffering for all of us."

† † †

What did Photios think? That we would simply overlook his feud with old Rome? That Vassilis would use his tale to convince those generals whose support still wavered, who still held their breath in the hope that someone somewhere will have the courage to usurp the Usurpers? Photios' plan was to show that my Peasant's origins are noble, that his path to us was ordained by Christ, that his rightful place was on the Imperial Throne. But what did he expect in return? A place on the patriarchal throne once again? But I am once again too far ahead in my story.

Appointing old Methodios had been a particularly good move, according to Photios. His moderate position kept the hard-line, Icon-worshiping monks at bay, and excommunication of the former Iconoclast bishops became less of an issue. Methodios' proposal, to extract long penances instead, had been grudgingly entertained by all, but they had accepted it finally. It's always difficult to maintain a position at the center of the balance. This is the role of the wise. Only fools live life in extremes. But Methodios was never a ship firmly at its moorings; one day he drifted away in his sleep. Theodora blew into mourning and withdrew for months.

Photios writes about the feast day of the Great Constantine, five hundred and thirty years since the founding of our City. He arrives, late as always, to join the Imperial procession late at the Forum of Constantine. The imperial family waits, with Theoktistos and Vardas ready to argue over who will carry Michael when he tires. The broad cobbles of the forum have been swept and covered in fresh sawdust, and the statue of Constantine-Poseidon radiates blue light on all those dwarfed beneath it. The Regent glares at Photios — he is being judged for his tardiness.

"Your Serenity," he says, bowing deeply. "The reason I am late is that I have been following up my latest research on the Iconoclast threat. Some marvelous new volumes have arrived. I can confirm that the Paulicians come from Crete originally, the followers of Paul of Samosata. But they are Romans — having fled east a century and a half before and relocated many times before reaching the coast of northern Anatolia."

The imperial party gathers at the head of the procession. "What difference does all that make," Theoktistos says, "when it is clear that they prefer the proximity of the Abbasid?"

"Yes, but there is a perfectly good reason for that," Photios says. "What else can Paul's followers do, when living among the Abbasid, but play at being good neighbors?"

Imagine it is one of those breathtaking summer days in which sunshine glints off the armor of the guardsmen, bathing in a warm glow the olive branches that the people are holding up high. The houses along the roadside seem to tremble as the laurel and myrtle draping them rustle in the sea breeze, the pungency of these herbs mixing with the comforting smell of horses. The Imperial entourage glistens in purple and white silks.

Vardas speaks. "As far as I can tell they sit there, quite out of the way, a simple peasant people, working the land, safe in the heart of Anatolia, albeit in the very bosom of the Abbasid. What difference does it make to us? Leave them be!"

Theoktistos and Vardas face each other squarely. The procession comes to a halt.

"That is true in principle," Theoktistos says. "However, you know as well as I do that the monks, fired up by Ignatios, have begun calling once again for exile of many of the old bishops."

"Brother of mine," Theodora stands alongside the Eunuch, "with old Methodios no longer here to mediate, we face the establishment questioning our authority at home. The only answer, especially in matters concerning the Icons, is to exert our authority abroad."

"It's very simple," retorts the Eunuch. "The Paulicians and Abbasid are Iconoclasts alike, and therefore both are enemies and traitors. We cannot appear weak in this regard."

Theodora cuts off further protest with a wave of her sleeve as the procession arrives at the entrance square to the Church of Chalkoprateia.

"Enough bickering, both of you! We will decide in due course. I suspect that a show of force is the only answer, but we will make plans another day."

Events have a way of deciding themselves, and what followed in the months afterward was easily one of Theoktistos' most humiliating defeats, though it could have been a Roman victory for the taking. It began with the Abbasid taking the Roman fortifications in Crete most bloodily. The Logothete jumps at the opportunity; he rushes preparations for a campaign. Hundreds of ships fly to that beautiful but bedeviled island and there is a terrible onslaught. Then, at the peak of the battle, a messenger brings him news of rumor: that Vardas and Petronas are taking power with Theodora. Everyone suspects Vardas' hand in this, of course. So Theoktistos scurries back to the City to challenge the usurpers. The troops see it as desertion even though he leaves General Nicetiates in charge. Unfortunately, the General and his men do not last long.

† † †

Vassilis finds himself in an arena in Pliska, balancing on haunches, wiping the fine sand off his face. The stallion in front of him skitters toward and away from him, disdainful, yet mesmerized by this quiet young man. The Bulgar court assembles around the yard to watch the spectacle.

The many months in Pliska have changed him. No one had come looking for him. Instead, Maria had encouraged him to join the stables. Here he works very hard for a boy used to playing and running around in the mountains. Everyone has to work here — life is demanding and dangerous if you did not find your place. The daily grind of horse feed and clearing up horse droppings teaches him much about patience. He recalls Father telling him about Job, how God had tested his faith through trials such as these. He never understood how God could do this to those he loved. Now he knows that God demands patience, though what he gives in return is not always clear.

It had been a bad night for him, as happened sometimes, tossing and fighting the blanket, dreaming of being held by his mother, waking up in anger to realize that he didn't know where she was, only to find Maria hovering over him, caressing his curls and singing gently in Greek to soothe him back to sleep.

Then the Chief Equerry turned his scarred snarl on him and the other stable boys with a mocking challenge to break in a horse no one else can, in return for some vague reward. Vassilis does not realize that they are being used as fodder for a spectacle. He does not even think that the Equerry might be trying to put him in his place. For Vassilis it is simply a chance to prove his strength, by doing something no one else would dare, even if it means breaking a limb.

Now, Vassilis springs into action, landing on the young stallion's back. Human and animal flesh press against each other, sandy thighs scrape on damp coat as it flails about, desperate to rid itself of this parasite.

Vassilis indeed slips off, though with a leap he is back on, his limbs trapping its neck and torso in as hard a grip as he can muster. But in his thoughts he lets go. He imagines that the body fighting to shake off this unwanted weight is his, that the hooves which tear at the dust are his own. He feels the anger of this creature, lost from its mother, just as he is. Vassilis tosses his head and feels as if it is his mane that flies in the wind, as if his throat neighs in indignation.

The stallion snorts to a stop. Whispers of amusement crack along the surface of the gathering.

Vassilis reaches with a single, smooth motion across the creature's neck and slips a rope bridle over its nose, hugging its neck as he does so, and relaxing his body into a gentle hold. He slips off, panting, but too proud to let his exhaustion or his pleasure show. Let them think he does this every day. Father and Mother would have wanted him to keep some dignity among the pagans.

Vassilis raises a hand. The stallion backs away from him, head bowed. Holding the rope loosely, Vassilis turns and walks forward to guarded cheers, the stallion following meekly behind him.

Vassilis looks around for the leader but it is difficult – they are all ugly. Perhaps the tall fellow with the hardest chin and the thickest braids? Ah . . . the one with the fine cloak. He knows, with the instincts of a caged survivor, that he must judge right, or he will lose this chance forever. He dismounts and leads the stallion to the side of the ring. A young nobleman inclines his head and takes the reins, raised eyebrows contrasting with a half-grin.

In poor Bulgarian, Vassilis mouths, "Your mount, my lord."

Boris, son of Presian, Khan of all the Bulgars, clasps Vassilis' shoulders and shakes him. "Bravely, bravely done," he says, gesturing to all those around the ring. "He is the only one to have tamed the wild Asparukh!"

Grudging cheers fall like welcome rain on Vassilis' young heart, parched for acknowledgment. But the moment is brief; the throng takes off, forgetting him. He watches them leave him behind and wonders what to do, whether to follow the crowd or to return to the stables, before the stench of the Chief Equerry's breath hits him in the face.

An ugly mixture of broken Greek and Bulgar pours out of the Equerry's mouth. "You think you're a fine one, don't you, you un-finished piece of Greek shite. One of the mares is about to foal. Let's get some blood and dung on that smart tunic."

Back at the stables Vassilis is pulling off his tunic, his arms over his head as the Equerry comes up to him. He lands a sharp punch to Vassilis' stomach, causing him to double over onto the ground. Several lads appear from the shadows, pinning him face down on to the cold floor, and ripping away his britches. Blows land on my Peasant from all directions, hard knuckles and bare feet, as he struggles to break free. His nose is pouring blood, and his fingers slip in it. Dirt cakes under his fingernails as he tries to pull himself up. He feels a knife at his neck and the Equerry's great bulk on him. The tearing pain of being plundered, though more familiar than before, seems never to end. He cries out far too many times, in spite of himself.

6. The art of war

It was a dangerous time for the City then, only three years after Theophilos' passing. We were at arms on all sides, fighting the pagan Bulgar in the north, maneuvering against the Abbasid at sea and on land, to the east and south.

The Bulgar look only for immediate reward and seem barely worthy of mention. The Abbasid, dare I say it, are our rivals in culture and learning. Yet they are weaker in battle, thanks to our Roman blood, true to the spirit of our ancestors, able to meet the Abbasid's persistence with steel and cunning.

The Black River travels deep into Cappadocia, in the rugged heart of Anatolia, where our men often find themselves maneuvering against the Abbasid. Now the Paulicians, with their hatred for the Icons, stand alongside them. Fortunately for us, our Akritai here were once our soldiers, now rewarded with land for their years of service in the Imperial legions. Unfortunately for them, their retirement is less about savoring their dotage working the fertile lands than they would wish. Some reward! They must fight to ensure their own survival.

Why would anyone choose to live in the country, far from our wonderful City? Some say it is better to live in the bosom of Anatolia, either in the fertile northern shores of the Black Sea, or the verdant Pontic forests, or even the forbidding Taurus mountains to the south. I suppose that the Akritai are there partly in return for the land, but also to escape the uncertainty, the petty intrigues and the in-fighting that are our daily bread back home. I am happy for them to stay where they are, for without them, where would we be?

Photios writes that Vardas' steed is foaming at the mouth after the fast gallop from camp, according to the gossip he heard from some of the commanders later. He doesn't look very happy either. His orders to be awoken for morning drills were deliberately ignored, presumably at the Eunuch's interference.

Vardas arrives at the head of the battalion, a formation of a thousand or so footmen, infantrymen, and archers, which is in the process of coming to a halt on the south bank of the river. The archers are taking up position. A small contingent of Abbasid troops, stationed on a neighboring hill, must surely be out of range. The Eunuch rides up and barks the order to fire. A swarm of arrows floats out in the shimmering heat, only to expire far short of its goal, at the foot of the hill.

Drumming follows a billowing yellow cloud — the Abbasid are on the move! The Eunuch's white stallion looks even more skittish than he does. The surrounding commanders exchange worried glances. If Vardas doesn't do something he knows it will be a missed opportunity.

"What is this?" he retorts, his gaze sweeping over everyone present. Then to the Eunuch, "Why, noble Logothete, alert the Abbasid to your presence and then fire out of range, both guaranteed to produce no effect? Get the infantrymen marching now."

Vardas surveys the situation with exaggerated care. The enemy is apparently not that bright either — they are deserting the high ground. He barks orders to the commanders. "A variation on the standard maneuver: send cavalry central division straight ahead, to the count of fifteen, then fan out around the hill to let the infantry through. Meanwhile bring up the infantry, another ten counts, then both archers and infantry wings advance."

A moment of uncertainty all round, then "Move, you lazy pricks!" he barks at them. The commanders turn about, visibly relieved, orders flying.

It is the Eunuch's turn to shout a counter order into the noise. Then he is saddle to saddle with Vardas, the two horses engaged in a bizarre dance, the Eunuch trying to get Vardas' attention.

"How dare you!" shouts the Eunuch. "This is my command!"

Vardas keeps one eye on the advance while circling. "How often have I stood at the eastern frontier, falling within inches of my life, only to rise again ... while you have ... softened the Palace cushions." Now their mounts are almost touching. "You and I know you have no place here."

The battle is off to a good start. Vardas can afford to be smug. He has the Eunuch off guard. The latter seems to be struggling to find his breath. "Perhaps I have been in error," says Vardas.

"What is your plan?" But he waits no more than a moment and charges off to follow the advance.

Infantrymen drop, their beards and hands thick with blood, spears serrating their sides. Even the many cavalry can barely hold their own. Vardas storms back, commanders trailing him.

"It is no use!" he bellows at the Eunuch. "We outnumber them but have not decided a proper strategy. We must retreat!"

"No! We will defeat them with numbers. Reports are that there are no further reinforcements."

Vardas rides up to Theoktistos and reaches across to grab the latter's reins. "I cannot see our men thrown away like this." He lives for his men. Well ... for them and power. But you need men to acquire and maintain power.

"And I cannot take this insolence any longer," says Theoktistos the Logothete. "You will answer to me, General, or you will no longer play a part in this command. Return to the battle!"

The two circle each other. The nearby commanders watch in amazement. Or is it amusement?

Vardas makes his move. Loud enough for the nearby commanders to hear he says: "You leave me with no choice. Let us see what our loyalty to good common sense and the Regent have to say about this."

He pulls to and makes a show of riding away from the battle. The commanders hesitate for no more than a minute before following. They call to their deputies — the message burns across the formation. Weapons are retrieved and men turn on their heels. The Abbasid cheer. But many Romans lie injured or dead. It is neither a defeat nor a victory. A price will have to be paid, as Vardas must have realized.

What I have learned as Empress is that the veneer of order on which statehood prides itself comes at great cost. Ambition and lust for wealth bubble underneath that veneer in a thick, venomous brew that poisons all who spare no effort in tasting it.

The Eunuch was a source of misery to me, so I cannot write well of him. It is unfortunate that his soft, cultured ways lacked the gusto of a true soldier, and his strange collection of young men did not inspire confidence overall. Little wonder that many at court grinned behind raised sleeves while whispering his court moniker — Dickbreath!

So ... the Eunuch succeeds in convincing the Regent that Vardas has planned the mutiny at the Black River. This is a subtle twist on what Photios relates above, which is what he heard later from the soldiers. Their loyalty to the Logothete was exceeded only by their loyalty to the Imperial Throne. Vardas' quick anger, coupled with Petronas' unquestioning backing for Vardas, mixes with the subtle logic of the Eunuch's silken words in the mind of the Regent. The stubborn old sow feels she has no choice but to avoid her brothers and take decisions in their absence, keeping counsel solely with the Eunuch.

† † †

Clouds of pungent, pine-fueled smoke wash over Vassilis as he enters the castle hall. Bright flames from a log-strewn hearth cast shadows on a long wall as men and women move around, drinking, talking and sprawling on dark rugs. A wealth of roast meats, earthenware carafes, and thick loaves of bread line tables alongside the opposite wall.

Maria has arranged for my young Vassilis to come to the Bulgar court today, to celebrate the midwinter festival. For my young Peasant it would have been a time of quiet joy with his family, in preparation for his name day. But as he has no family, he is grateful for the diversion.

Keep your place, he thinks, as he jostles with the crowd. Some of the men he recognizes, and nods in return, not quite sure what to do. He is trying all he can to cover up his delight at being here, after all those months of trying to win the favor of the Equerry and finally bowing down regularly to the foul creature's needs. He is also very intrigued by the delicate female faces that peer at him from beneath gaudy headdresses, given that he sees few women in the stables.

Vassilis observes that the Khan keeps his people well. The crowd quietens and nods respectfully at Presian's arrival. The Khan moves in sprightly fashion for a man well into old age, his broad shoulders and sharp chin betrayed only by the expanse of long white hair that cascades past his shoulders as he embraces many of his lords in greeting.

"So Asparukh's tamer is here!" the Khan has spied Vassilis.

"Your courage is to be praised. He has proven a worthy mount. My son is very pleased with him."

Vassilis is surprised that the Khan has even heard of him. He half bows at no-one in particular, fumbles at a table, tearing a hunk of bread and taking a mug of wine. He mimes consumption somewhat warily.

The hubbub resumes as he moves into the shadows, where he discards all suspicion and drinks deeply. The bitterness of the brew combines with the pine smoke to make his head swim. Maria swirls into view out of the darkness, the fire making shadows of her chiding eyelashes.

"I see that you have quite an effect on our women!" she teases, although he can sense she is only half-joking. She has begun looking at him quite strangely lately, especially since the wound on his forehead healed and he has begun to walk taller.

"But you are my favorite," Vassilis whispers in her ear. He was always able to say the right things, though sometimes the loathing lurked behind his eyes when he was with me. He never forgave me for losing her, his first woman, even though I did everything for him ... and for my sons.

Vassilis pulls Maria toward him and drags her back into the shadows. He tastes the brew on her breath as their lips brush each other's cheeks.

Maria stands back, all sternness, but the laughter in her eyes is unmistakable. "You are suddenly very bold! Not quite a year ago you were like a cringing babe in my arms. Can you not wait at least until after the feast?"

"I can wait forever," he whispers back at her.

Maria reaches out to take a sip from his mug as the pipers begin wailing. The crowd surges around him and picks up a rhythm that moves him too. The women twirl around in the center as a circle of men leaps and dances around them. Vassilis finds himself joining in.

"I see you know more than just horseplay," Maria teases as she twirls into view. Meanwhile, Boris has arrived. He signals for Maria's attention. Maria raises a finger to her lips to suggest that he should leave her to do the talking.

"Ah ... our Roman friend has joined us." says Boris. "Asparukh has given me much satisfaction — you tamed him well.

Yet your people seek to tame us, do they not?"

Vassilis hesitates. Maria tries to respond but Boris continues.

"It was my great-grandfather, Krum," he says, "who took much pleasure in destroying your armies."

"My people had no part in these battles," Vassilis says. "We are not from the City of the Romans. We too had our homes destroyed by them, many times."

The Khan ponders a moment then reaches out to a shelf behind him. "We have not always been as lucky with the Romans as Krum was. But certainly he took great pleasure in this."

With a grand sweep, Boris produces a small human skull that has been splashed with molten silver. He pours the contents of his horn into it. The skull seems to bleed wine. "This is ... was ... Nikephor — an Armenian who once led the Romans."

"Nikephoros," Vassilis says. "I have heard of this Emperor. I too am Armenian — a noble house, my parents led me to believe." Yes, this certainly fits in with the myth Photios has invented!

"I want you at the hunt tomorrow, at my side," says Boris. He turns away to greet someone, but not before glancing at Maria. "Just make sure he is able to ride a real horse in the morning," he announces for all the company to hear.

Maria drags Vassilis outside the tent, into the snow. "The Khan's son is already making jokes at your expense. That is a good sign."

Snowflakes drift between them as her tongue thrusts at his, her kisses singeing his lips. Part of him lets her take him, then plays with her, then against her. It was from Maria that he learned how to play with women, how to capture their souls by giving in to their demands, before taunting them afterward by holding himself distant from their hopeful joys.

Vassilis presses his face against her warm cheek, surprised at how easily he finds himself hardening at her soft, inviting embrace.

7. The art of love

ABOUT A YEAR LATER, C. 846 AD
There are things that seem similar yet should not be compared; even though you might think it natural do so. For example, summer and winter. Night and day. Rain and sunshine. Youth and age. A person's laughter and their anger. Black and white. Love and hatred. The red-purple porphyry dye from the coveted murex snail that colors our finest robes, and the rare blue-purple indigo dye that merchants bring in tiny vials from the east in exchange for a bag of silver. To someone with no good taste, these are simply reflections of each other, yet to the discerning eye they are seas apart. For instance, the porphyry dye improves with age, whereas the indigo fades with time.

It is the same with love. A man can love one woman in one way and another completely differently. But usually men do not change the object of their affections once they have decided. Whereas it is possible that a woman can stop loving a man, because she feels that he has become someone else — even though he is still the same person.

I want you to learn about the ways of love, my little Leo, as you grow into life, and all its pains and joys. Certainly my feelings for your father waxed and waned, whereas my soul continues its constant sighing for my Peasant. As for him, he clung to Maria's indigo even as it crumbled in his hands, even when my porphyry offering was laid, ready sewn and folded neatly in his arms, his to use as he wished.

I forgive Maria for being Vassilis' first woman. I have to forgive her, for her loss was my gain. But I will never forgive her for teaching him this womanly secret that I am about to relate, one that he used against me whenever he could. Oh, Vassilis pretends to know much about books of learning, such as the laws, the Novels of Justinian, which I introduced him to first, but in reality he works through his scribes and uses other scholars from the University and, lately, even Photios to help him find the right words and ideas. But in knowing how to use people, especially women, he has a natural talent. One Maria fostered. But one I have also delighted in.

Maria related the following to me, as we grew more intimate. On the way back from the Bulgar court, the chasing and snow fights between Vassilis and Maria had become rowdier, the kisses longer and more profound. Back home, it had only been a matter of time before the old man, drinking bowl in hand, slid into snores, helped along by Vassilis who drank the evening away with him.

When Maria comes to Vassilis' bunk he experiences a momentary hesitation. He has never been this close to a woman before, other than his own mother, of course. But Maria's warm body dispels all doubts. Maria tastes the beads of sweat on his forehead, somehow both sweet and salty, as he addresses each of her nipples in turn. If only we could still discover these simply joys in our couplings again!

Then she lets him inside, where he feels as natural as day. Why then does she suddenly push him away, just as he is about to succumb to his passion? "Women take a little longer, my dear," Maria says. "We are not like the mare who wishes for the stallion to be done quickly with his work."

She directs him downward, to the seat of her fire. Vassilis has described it to me as a third nipple in rare, poetic moments. He is happy to torture it into firmness, learning when to be gentle, when to tantalize. At first, he backs off at the sounds she makes, but then he responds to them, riding her with his tongue until she takes him in again and lets him writhe to their mutual delight.

"You are a brave lad," she nibbles at his ear as he lies panting. "And you have learned quickly. Let this be the first lesson: the path to happiness for a man is to make the woman's happiness the most important."

Indeed!

†††

I have told you something about the Eunuch, as he appeared to all of us. But whom did he embrace, in whose bosom did he hide his secret sobs, the tears that rise up in the lonely night hours? With whom did he rejoice when his heart sang? For a singular man like him, who is there to share those moments when success has risen, eel-like from the depths, ready to slip out of one's grasp when reached for? Do not be astounded, my little Leo, by what I am about to relate, or even that I relate it at all. I have warned you before that no experience is new to me. So do not cringe at my telling of this.

From the little I knew about the Eunuch everyone spoke about how the young Cyril was the joy of his life. Apparently, Theoktistos discovered him and Methodios on the doorstep one day with little more than the clothes on their backs.

The plight of the young orphans touched Theoktistos immediately. Their father, an official in Thessaloniki, had died some time back, and while Methodios was happy with his lot of meditation and supplication in an Athos monastery, he felt there were other paths for his bright younger brother. With the great Theoktistos' care, surely Cyril would have a much better chance in this rough world? The Eunuch was reluctant at first, but how his mind changed when the young man began speaking.

So let's imagine that Theoktistos has returned from the Palace today, eager to bring good news. Let's say that his arrival is the signal for unspoken pleasures to begin — but let me speak of them anyway!

The Eunuch had fine quarters, appropriate for a most senior official. Not for him the public baths of Zeuxippos, or a rinse at the seaside. I can see him reclining in a fine marble basin, the kind that seems to repel water, its waxy surface cushioning the drops. He is the kind of man who might fill such a basin with hot, salted water, letting it caress his tired muscles.

Imagine him sighing with pleasure as he rises out of the water and pushes aside the curtains, only to be surprised by hands over his eyes and soft lips on his neck. He doesn't turn around when the hands descend past his nipples and belly, at least not until they find the prize. Now he gazes at the milky skin and dark beard in front of him. He wants to dive into the soft hair, to feel the smoothness of their skins rubbing against each other.

The bed is ready. They draw each other into the sheets and Cyril's hands alight on the Eunuch's firm insistence. I imagine it is not inconsiderable — he was a tall man! Perhaps Theoktistos responds with a sigh of anticipation. Perhaps he just kisses this young creature gently, ardently wanting to claim this symbol of what he might have been, a fertile man. Who can tell?

Theoktistos produces his gift for the day as he leans on an elbow and runs his eyes and a hand along the slender frame next to him. "I have secured an audience of sorts with the Regent for you next week," the Eunuch says. His hands travel slowly over Cyril's lean ribs and down to the hollow of his stomach.

"You are very dear to me," says Cyril, his beard rubbing the Eunuch's shoulder.

Theoktistos turns onto his back, letting the young man invade his arms and lie down on his chest. He sucks gently at an ear lobe. "It's not much. We will be discussing the Bulgar problem. I think your understanding of them may be just what is needed."

"So what must I do?"

"I have shared some ideas with Photios. Talk to him about the possibilities," Theoktistos says. "He will present a proposal to the Regent. All you have to do is be seen. There is no need to speak unless spoken to."

"Of course, Your Thrusting Munificence," grins Cyril. "I love it when you are so much in charge."

"If all goes well, we might be sending a message back to your brother to come visit us."

"Yes, General!" quips Cyril, then instantly regrets it. His disarming grin returns. "As it happens, my dear brother will be visiting the monks in the Stoudion monastery next week. May he join the audience?"

The Eunuch nods back, all smiles, then laughs out loud as Cyril buries kisses in places that even I dare not write about.

† † †

There had been no sign that Tervel's departure would happen quite so suddenly. Always a quiet participant in what was gradually turning into Vassilis' and Maria's household, his silence should have spoken volumes. He seldom left their quarters and would grit his teeth when the need to eat was unavoidable. Maria has not forgiven herself for missing what was taking place. But distraction was everywhere for the excited couple.

Vassilis, as with all young men, had failed to realize the consequences of the joyful acts he and Maria performed, and that even
for an old woman like Maria, with some thirty-five years behind
her, it was not inconceivable that her womb would bear fruit. The
preparations for a child's arrival bring confusion to my Vassilis'
mind, as does having to deal with Maria's unwelcome awkwardness. Like all young fathers, Vassilis is at first more of a hindrance
than a help. After all, a man beginning his twenty-first year is little more than a boy, even though his shoulders are nearly as broad
as a cypress.

Fortunately the Chief Equerry has lost interest in humiliating
my Vassilis, whose calm indifference is a powerful weapon to those
who hate him. He takes time to discover new things when he is
not in the stables. For a man with no education, he is happy to
learn how to work wood and how to tame metal grown soft in the
furnace. But he learned early on how to talk to power. Serving
the future Khan allowed him to see what it was to be a real man,
strong-willed and clear-thinking, but able to laugh as well. I never
met Boris or Presian, but they don't sound too bad, at least for
barbarians.

Then one morning Vassilis awakens to shrieking, a sound that
chills him to the bone when he realizes its source. Maria has always been the calm sort, not given to unnecessary displays, so
Vassilis falls over everything to get to her. Tervel lies frozen on
his mat, his arm curled under a drooping chin, his flesh icy to the
touch. It takes several hours for Maria to stop weeping at every
thought of her father, made worse by the fear that her grief will
harm the child within her.

Now Vassilis never leaves her side. Not only does he take part
in digging the grave, but he is there to help her move her ample self
about, to bring their food to the table, to wipe the tears from her
cheeks, to bathe her tired limbs in warm water, drawn from a pot
above the fire that he keeps lit. All the favors that she performed for
him he returns tenfold, without them being reckoned in his mind
as such — or so it seems in both Vassilis' and Maria's telling of
events to me much later, the latter in quiet moments of womanly
chatter in the Gynaeconitis. How good it is to have such a man at
one's side!

The night before the birth she is convinced she cannot bear

much more. She prays for release, and sees a dream. A sparrow flies in to perch on the table among some crumbs. As she reaches for it, it flies out of the house, and she finds herself running lightly to follow in its path. The sparrow alights on a great tree, but then flies off and away as she approaches. Then suddenly rain pours down, and she awakens to find her legs drenched and a strange pain in her belly. Vassilis finds the midwife who issues him with two clear instructions. He is to gather the women and to become scarce ... until summoned.

Maria wanders around her dwelling looking for some corner which will offer relief, stopping occasionally for the midwife occasionally to massage her with oil. Back in the stables Vassilis keeps to himself, whittling a new stool for Maria to sit on when feeding the child. Then he starts on some toys, though the silly thing does not realize the child will not play with these until he is much older. Vassilis expects a boy, naturally, and Maria hopes she will not disappoint him.

Then Vassilis sets aside his handiwork and rides out to the forest, where he can find closer companionship with his thoughts. As he wanders he prays, in the manner his parents taught him long ago — for he has not seen a church for many years and can barely remember what one even looks like. He prays for his parents, that they are still healthy, and that they may live one day to see their grandchild.

In a clearing he crosses himself repeatedly while gazing up at the heady blueness above, praying with all his might that the archangel Gabriel — the only angel whose name he can remember — might guide his little one into and through this life, and that he may never know the disappointment, on coming home, of finding no father and mother to take him by the hand to the evening table.

8. Each unto his own

From before he could walk, it was obvious that Michael adored the Golden Tree, that marvelous machine built by Leo the Mathematician as a gift to Theophilos. Like all children he loved real birds and real trees too, but the golden sparrows twirled and chirped exactly when he wanted them to. This made all the difference to the spoiled little brat that he was. In spite of his foibles, my brave Leo, you should know that I cared greatly for your father at one point.

Photios writes that on a warm, late winter morning Theodora has had Michael brought to the Pavilion in the gardens, rather than leaving him in the Gynaeconitis. The young Emperor must learn that life is not all play — he has duties to perform. But right now he prefers slinking around labyrinthine geometrical hedges, stalking the squirrels across flower beds, racing like Hermes around the mosaic-studded walkways, or simply collapsing on his knees in front of the Tree as he orders the servants to turn the mechanism.

"Uncle Vardas!" Michael shrieks with delight as he suddenly gets pulled up onto his feet, then thrown high into the air.

Vardas grunts, "You're getting a bit heavy for that sort of thing, you scoundrel!"

Hand in hand, Michael tugs him along in a half-run. Vardas briefly gives in, an ungainly scramble for such a big man, then draws the child back gently into a stroll.

"I hear that you nearly struck out your trainer's eye with a sword," Vardas says. "Just like a real warrior!"

"Yes, Uncle, but I really didn't want to hurt him," says Michael.

"That is right," Vardas says. "After all, he is there to teach you. But a real Emperor must learn to do more than just hurt people. He sometimes has to kill them."

"Why? When they want to hurt us?"

"Well, people want all sorts of different things. You can allow some things when it suits you, but some you must stop, especially when they take something that is yours or belongs to your Empire. People often don't stop until you hurt them. They usually only understand pain."

Vardas is often in didactic mode around Michael. He believes the lad needs to be told things like this. After all, who is there to tell him? The Empire's dominions need steel and cunning.

They walk back to the Pavilion. Ignatios, perspiring in his black robes, presents a mess of hair, sweat, and crumbs. Weren't the clergy supposed to observe the fasts occasionally? To lead by example? Bathing would help.

Theodora and Theoktistos are speaking with raised voices, Methodios and Cyril in attendance. Michael wriggles. Ignatios bends down as if to address the young Emperor but the little one runs away.

"No, I won't play with you. Smelly grandfather. Just go away!" pipes Michael, hiding behind Vardas.

"Now, is that the way for a young Emperor to behave toward the Holy Father?" Theodora's sternness is at odds with the twinkle in her eyes.

Suddenly, Michael charges at the shadows. He grabs Cyril by the hand. "But I will play with you!"

Bishop Ignatios withdraws, glowering, though everyone pretends not to notice.

With Michael in hand, Cyril bows deeply toward the Regent. "With your leave, Worthiness?" Theodora assents with a nod. Cyril lets Michael drag him off into the garden, Methodios trotting behind them.

"Let us discuss the Bulgar again," says Theoktistos, "now that the Archbishop has left us in peace. They are once again causing us no end of trouble, attacking outposts, in particular in the recently regained Macedonian Theme which, as you may recall," with a sarcastic glance at Vardas, "I engineered shortly before Theophilos' passing. They do not harm us, but cause great losses to the Macedonians and Thracians who are still not sure where to turn. It is vital we exert our authority."

Vardas shuffles. He bristles at the war talk, which should be his domain. "The Bulgar listen mainly to their Boyars, who often don't often work together. Though they listen to the Khan when they have a mind to. No matter how many times we beat some of them, there will be others who attack from a different quarter, and of their own volition."

"May I..." stutters Photios. Heads turn in surprise — he seldom takes part in deliberations, preferring to do simply what is required and to leave others to the agonizing decisions. He always found it safer to show too much deference at court, rather than too little, until he became Patriarch. "In all humility ... this is not really my ... it is clear to me that we need to approach this differently. What if we were to bring one of the Khans, say Presian, into the fold?"

Theodora hides her skepticism behind a question. "How do you mean? Our laws and culture mean nothing to them."

"They would think nothing of emptying their bowels on our Hippodrome if they felt the urge," says Vardas.

Theodora shakes her head at this remark.

"With your leave," says Photios, "a plan would be to make them ... to convince them that we are ready to give up all aggression ... in the name of faith."

The silence is filled by bird calls and the spray of droplets from a nearby fountain.

"Indeed," begins Theoktistos. "My messengers tell me that the Franks are already at the Bulgar court. We should move."

"If the Bulgar were to befriend Louis the Frank," Vardas says, "then we would have a worse problem on our doorstep — the bishop of Rome.

"So we talk to them. But do they even understand Greek?" says Theodora.

Michael tumbles into the room, the young monks breathless behind him. He tugs at Vardas' elbow.

"Uncle, these men speak magic to one another. When I whisper to one, the other can tell me what I have said after they grunt at each other," the child giggles and grins.

Does Theodora kneel down to stroke his soft curls with a smile? If so, it would be a rare gesture — surely he see that he is so like his father in so many good ways?

Cyril bows. "Your Worthiness, noble ministers, it is nothing. My brother Methodios and I have been fortunate enough to live with the Bulgar in Thessaloniki. We speak their tongue."

Haughty coughing all around. A commoner addressing the Regent without leave! Theoktistos says, "I think that the young Emperor has already guessed that the Chief Secretary and I would like to send this young man and perhaps his brother to the Bulgar, to learn more about them. We might even get them to hear that our message is one of peace and prosperity, not war."

"Then I can have many new friends to play with?" Michael asks hopefully, turning on a leg.

"As you know so well, Your Worthiness," says Photios, "the Treasury has the means to send several of us to the Bulgar court with a small retinue and sufficient gifts to interest the Khan. I would be happy to lead it."

At least Vardas is nodding. Far better to avoid battle when the victory is not certain, when diplomacy will work better.

"Well decided, little one," Vardas pats Michael on the head. The little one smiles at the praise, though not quite sure at what he has done right. But no one is listening to Vardas when he says "I see no reason not to support this." Theodora and Theoktistos look only at one another. It's not clear what has been decided.

† † †

I have jumped too far ahead in the telling of this tale! So let me go back, my already wise Leo, and tell you how it was for me when I first went into Her Worthiness' service. Imagine me as a mere kitten of seven or eight years, with so many different things embarrassing me that I can hardly even reckon them up yet.

The months pass, during which I do my shy best to avoid the Regent's disdainful eye, like hiding behind a curtain in the Imperial quarters whenever I can. Of course, as I grow older I realize that I am there at her indulgence. I am delivered each evening to my mother on the verge of tears, making her wring her hands in despair. But Father persists in sending me to court the next day, and I must say I don't regret it now.

I remember one day — I am almost ten by now, and no longer quite the kitten that I had been — when the Regent's heart must have melted, for she brings out some drawings and shows them to me. I am so disturbed at this sudden gesture of kindness that I can hardly stretch out my hand to take the paper. She points to one picture after another, explaining what each represents. She starts off with what she claims is a mountain picture: a forest, with birds flying above it, and a picture of a river.

Then she shows me sketches of clothing. She explains that these are soon to arrive for her wardrobe; they are still with the seamstresses. My eyes grow in wonder at the complexity of their design and the lavishness of their ornamentation. At times like this I gaze at her in amazement. As a child I am still unaccustomed to the idea that a person could be adorned so richly. I begin yearning to wear such clothing myself.

The women in the Gynaeconitis are not unkind. They laugh at the things I do, like losing myself looking out the window at the trees, or playing for hours with the collection of threads, getting them all into knots. Observing how experienced they are in their duties and how easily they carry them out, I cannot help but feel envious. There is not a trace of awkwardness in any of their movements as they deliver robes or notes to Her Worthiness, or rearrange the coals in a brazier on a chilly evening.

I also remember the first time I encountered the Eunuch in person. I am helping to dust out the Regent's bedroom and change Her Worthiness' bedding when suddenly I hear loud voices outside ordering people to make way. "His Excellency, the Logothete, is coming," says one of the women, as everyone hurries about to remove scattered belongings and clothing. As instructed earlier, I move to the back of the room behind a curtain, from which I am able to look out of the window at his approach. I am in awe: the purple of his cloak and his golden robe look magnificent against the marble pillars and the white snow, the last of the season as I recall.

"I should not have come," he says, stamping a few remaining flakes of snow off his red boots, "since both yesterday and today are days of abstinence for Lent, and I have been taking care of my estate to the north. But it has been snowing so hard that I felt bound to call and find out whether all is well with you."

"How did you manage?" Theodora asks. "I thought all the paths were buried."

"I managed," says the Eunuch, "because it occurred to me that I could move your heart."

"Your concern is very welcome," Theodora glows as she gestures to a couch and for one of the women to lay a bowl of tea and some preserved fruit before him. "Please refresh yourself."

The two of them sit and begin exchanging small pleasantries. In my young, foolish way, I am utterly amazed. I wonder if anything on earth or in heaven could surpass this simple discourse, and the sheer beauty of it. Next to Theoktistos and his handsome garments, the Regent is dressed in a brilliant white damask robe over which her long hair hangs down loosely in the back, with two more layers of purple damask over her shoulders.

Then the Eunuch spots me peering out from behind the curtain. "Who is that back there?" he exclaims, and the women roar with laughter. They drag me out in front of him. I had been embarrassed enough when I had been looking at him from a distance with the curtain between us. Now that we are actually facing each other I feel extremely stupid, and can hardly believe that this is happening to me. I keep my head lowered and try to cover my face with my little sleeve.

"So," he asks with a wicked grin, "are you fond of your mistress?" I blush, at first not sure what to say. But it quickly dawns on me, in my childish way, that this is one of the first lessons of court life: absolute loyalty to the Regent.

"Your Serenity," I say with a deep bow to Theodora, recalling the alternate form of address that Father had drummed into me for special occasions, but which I had not had opportunity to use until now, "how could I possibly not be fond of you!"

And just then one of the women sneezes loudly.

"Oh dear," says the Regent, "so you're telling a lie. Well so be it!" she dismisses me with a wave. I am stunned.

What utter rubbish, to think that the Regent believes I am lying because of a sneeze! I had even grown a bit fond of her by then, at least as fond as a young girl can be of being ordered around by someone who is not her mother. The real liar is the sneezer's nose, and their poor timing. But I am still far too young to know how to make good, and since dusk is approaching quickly, I am whisked home in some confusion.

I am present a few weeks later when Photios enters the Gynaeconitis, amid several deep bows. Michael is once more at the mercy of his sisters. The girls are giggling loudly. Thekla, the oldest, grabs his arms while two of the younger ones take a leg each. "We buried your soldiers in the moat," they chant. "Now come and dig them out or they will die, they will die." They drag Michael, trapped and wriggling, from the hall. Theodora nods for a woman to follow the children while Theoktistos smiles politely, albeit thinly.

Vardas arrives right after Photios. "I should say," he blurts out, with no introduction, "that the time has come to … get rid of the Bishop. There is no love lost on Ignatios in this court even if he always revered the Icons as we do. Even Michael knows this."

Theodora knows her brother's maneuvering well. She wants to ignore him — but he is right to some extent and courtesy has not left her completely.

"I agree," she begins, with feigned patience, "but the anger of many — for example, the Stoudite monks — if he were to disappear? You do know that, while he is not as loved as old Methodios the Patriarch was," the Regent's lip trembles then tightens, "there are those among the monks of more extreme persuasion that still heed him."

"But he does not have to disappear, although I wish it were that simple," says Vardas. "Do you recall what our ancestor the Augusta Irene did? She simply replaced her Patriarch with her Chief Imperial Secretary. Ignatios will be quite harmless then, although perhaps a bit annoyed. And I do believe Tarasios was your great-uncle, wasn't he, my dear Photios?"

Photios blushes and grins at the same time. Even the Regent appears amused at his delight and embarrassment.

She nods. "I agree. But not yet. As always, Imperial Secretary, you have shown that your modesty is exceeded only by your pragmatism and insight. All in good time. Right now I have summoned you for a different reason. We have decided that your mission to the Bulgar must go ahead, but that you should send others to represent us. Those young men that were here last time will suffice. We desire that you do not accompany them. I have greater need of your presence."

But she has not completely dismissed Vardas' point. "Brother, you are right to raise this issue. The patriarchal throne has been vacant for too long. But you must see that I have no choice at present. We need someone who has the right support with the extremists to fill it, someone exactly like Ignatios." She exchanges a smile with the Eunuch, who nods his agreement, then bows and vanishes.

I can imagine Vardas burning with irritation at his suggestions being pushed aside yet again. From Photios' writings I see that this is not the first time.

"Brother," she starts, taking him by the hands and looking at the floor. She appears to be steeling herself to look him in the eye. "You have always been a vital source of strength to me. But perhaps it is time to take a rest. You have been very out of sorts these last months."

"I see," Vardas says, "though I think you need me here more than ever before."

The Regent brightens. Perhaps she expected more resistance. "Why don't you visit Athens? I lament never having done so myself, especially since Theophilos restored it to the fold. They say it is filled with inspiring churches, and you would be attending on our behalf."

"Indeed," he says, a touch bitterly, bowing his way to the exit, and out of our lives. "Though I would prefer to spend more time discovering the legacy of our ancestors, such as the remains of the great university."

9. The natural order

Bird song winds its way into the stillness of the Imperial apartments, threatening the clicking of a small loom. I watch Theodora out of the corner of my eye. She sits erectly, her gown spread out in an orderly fashion around her, like an enormous cushion. The fuzz of the soft cotton rubbing along her wrists, even as it threatens to cut her fingers when drawn tight, is a familiar and welcome sensation to her. I wait, as instructed, for a command — perhaps a call for some needles, a drink, or to rearrange her footrest.

I have been chosen to attend this week on the Regent, just as I have waited at her pleasure more and more over the past three years, first a few hours a week, then a few a day, then whole weeks at a time. I would much rather be sitting at home weaving, or with the other girls in the Gynaeconitis sharing silly stories of handsome courtiers, but Father will be pleased to know I am here. I'd even much rather have Mother nag at me about learning my letters and reading the old Greek texts with her. We prefer the stories of antiquity to reading boring homilies of the saints and their lives. Mother still finds it hard to bow down to an Icon. She would say that she doesn't like kissing the false paint. I am indifferent, but something in me tells me that it would be much more amusing to bow down and kiss a man where he most longs to be kissed, at least if the stories of the older girls are anything to go by.

I can see that the Regent's mind is tucked away in its own boll of quiet, sweet memories, perhaps back in Paphlagonia, her father coming home with everything she needs to create the rich patterns with which she orders her everyday life. Everything must be in its rightful place — even her feet are arranged neatly on her footstool. This can be very tiresome for the rest of us, though.

Presumably working on designs of this kind empties her mind of all other designs, especially those she endures as Regent. Back then, I was too young to know the burden of the Throne. But now

I can imagine that Theodora curses the daily struggle of pitting faction against faction to achieve her goals.

I enjoy listening to the debates and arguments that rage in the Gynaeconitis, especially when she provokes them. Monks from the Stoudion visited her today to discuss the Bishop of Rome who now refuses to recognize Ignatios' appointment. I didn't understand it then, but Photios' words in this volume have taught me that the popes of Rome had refused all along to countenance the Iconoclasts. Now, even with a born Iconodule like Thunderguts in place, the Pope has taken issue with the Regent on a point of procedure. No doubt he means to test the resolve of a mere woman! At any rate, I still think it strange that a pope should be so ignorant of the internal affairs of Empire.

To this day I cannot understand why men always look at things so strangely, why they need to argue about who is first, who will follow. For them it always comes down to who is topped and who is the topper. Surely it is not that difficult to understand that it is people who matter, and life, and the begetting of it. Surely we should fight only for peace, so that our children can just grow!

As I write these pages, some thirty years after the events they portray, I can sing Her Worthiness' praise for realizing how important it was to keep the Pope on our side, given the gradual loss of lands in Sicily to the Abbasid and the rest of the western territories to the vicious Franks. Tall, hard men, they say, with murder in their hearts and the minds of ghouls. The Abbasid have advanced around Syracuse in Sicily right up to the river Magro, where they say a thorny plant called a cactus grows, and then on up to Leontini. The Regent sent General Vryennios on a mission of reconciliation to the Abbasid administration in Leontini, but this seems, so far, to have not borne fruit. On his return she will send him with official letters to the Bulgar Khan instead, where Cyril and Methodios have been hard at work.

But right now Michael stretches on a white rug at his mother's feet. His mind seems to be far away, racing through the Hippodrome on the miniature chariot he pushes along, spewing imaginary dust from his wheels as phantom steeds churn away in front of it. I confess that I find him intriguing; more manly and leaner every day, I muse that perhaps one day his arms will embrace a woman. Little did I know then who that woman would be.

Theodora indicates that I should leave them alone. I hurry out of sight, but not out of earshot.

"Your father was a wonderful man," she begins, somewhat absentmindedly. "He could make people do things for him, through fear or love. He wielded great influence and demanded much. I knew I was for him when he gave me the apple. And he knew it too."

Why would a child even be remotely interested? I peer around the curtain. Michael is graciously accepting the laurels from an imaginary Emperor, perhaps even himself.

"The apple? What did you know?" I hear him murmur.

The loom shudders into stillness. Cicadas strive to outdo bird calls as the twilight descends.

"Your grandmother," Theodora says, "gave your father apples as gifts for his favorite women at the Bridal Show. The other girls thought it was very odd for an Emperor to hand out apples when he should have been giving us jewels instead. But I knew he was testing us. I was the only one who did not eat mine. I kept it safe instead."

"I've heard ..." Michael begins, "my friends say that Father meant to give an apple to another woman, Kassia, but she said something horrible and made him angry. So he married you instead."

I chuckle to myself. Michael probably has heard the rumor that Theodora was second choice. Everyone knows that, except perhaps her.

"No," she chides him gently. "That's not what happened. Your father told her that women are the source of all evil, and she told him that life also springs from us. She insulted him!"

I have heard how Kassia became a nun after this, and withdrew to the Stoudion. Her writings still circulate among the women, and frequently scandalize us.

"Was he brave and strong?" asks Michael. "Did he ride with the charioteers?"

Later I came to enjoy how Michael spoke out abruptly and with abandon, in a way which none of us were allowed. Even now I marvel at how children, even you, my precious little ones, do not forget the oddest things, and repeat them guilelessly at the wrong times. Michael would be heartbroken to find out that Theophilos thought it beneath himself even to enter the Hippodrome, or so I heard.

Theodora lectures. "He fought many battles, he even won some of them, but his life was tinged with sadness, especially when he lost our homeland of Amorion to the Abbasid. And when he learned that we still loved the Icons..."

Michael says, "Was that when we all still used to visit grandmother Euphrosyne in the monastery?"

I realize now that Michael's sharp mind was recalling distant events, when he was still barely a toddler. I've heard that he and his sisters would play in the walled gardens of the Blachernae Palace with Euphrosyne, Theophilos' stepmother.

My own mother would never fail to remind me, with that sharp contempt that was her specialty, how Euphrosyne was the most tireless of Iconodules. She even defied the Emperor, her very own stepson, and would teach his daughters to "play" with their "dolls." Those days died a harsh death when Theophilos found out that the dolls were nothing less than Icons of the Forty Martyrs, or images of Saints Raphael, or Nicholas and Irene, depending on the season. Theophilos raged and sulked for weeks.

Michael has more questions. "Mother, when can I have another father? Why will you not marry again? Why haven't I seen Uncle Vardas for such a long time?"

"No one can have more than one father!" the Regent retorts, her anger cascading needlessly onto the innocent child. Or is she thinking that his guile runs so deep that he sees through her?

"I already have too much to think about and do. We have an Empire to govern and people to take care of." I'm sure she has no interest in another snoring beast in her bed with soiled britches.

I peer through the curtains separating us. She embraces him rather awkwardly, as if she cannot decide whether to be affectionate or stern.

"More important is that you marry!" she says. "You will soon be Emperor in your own right. Every Emperor needs an Empress to rule the court and to bear more Emperors."

"Rubbish, Mother, I don't believe any of it," Michael pulls himself away, the scorn on his face like a slap to hers, his eyes narrow. "Girls are disgusting and this is boring. I want someone to take me for a ride."

I let the curtain fall back as he runs toward it, shouting, "Get the chariot ready and find someone to drive it for me."

The Regent is right behind him. She can move quickly when she wants to. She grabs him with a rough shake.

"Never forget, silly child, that you are God's chosen!" she shouts. "If you do the right thing at the right time in the right way, all will be well in our kingdom, just as it is in the Kingdom of Heaven. If you do not ..."

But Michael twists from her grasp before she can finish, runs back to grab his toy chariot and races from the room, leaving such noble expectations halting far behind him.

† † †

Vassilis is surprised to see two tall, well-mannered young men, roughly his age, ride in one day wearing dark tunics of fine cloth. He is even more surprised when, as he takes their horses, they curse in Greek at the bitter cold. Vassilis greets them in Greek, to their surprise, and then thinks nothing more of it.

One day the younger of the two, Cyril, comes down to the stables to chat with him. He does this every day, just a few minutes at first, but each time for a bit longer. Vassilis burns with shame as they speak more. Cyril uses many big words that he has to explain or replace with easier ones when it is obvious that Vassilis can't follow him. He feels even clumsier when Cyril chuckles at this, although he does it in the friendliest of ways. But he is amazed that Cyril, who is so young, seems to know so much.

Vassilis used to tell me that his time working in the Bulgar stables was one of the happiest of his life, once the Chief Equerry lost interest in him. Especially the time spent in the smithy. He loved coaxing the grudging iron into shoes for the horses while the blazing fire burned his cheeks. Forging confidence in men is much harder, as he found out later. Blows do not work.

Vassilis walks to the entrance, his bare toes rasping on the rough stone floor, the dry heat glowing against his uncovered back. The sunlight is pale, the wind cool on his face. He wonders if it will rain. Suddenly Cyril appears in front of him.

He wants to know if Vassilis can spend time in his quarters today to help with some work. Indeed, Vassilis is almost done with his morning's duties, and would be able to slip away soon.

His nose is greeted by strange, musty smells as he enters the brothers' gloomy hut. Then his eyes grow accustomed to the candlelight, and images burst out at him from all sides. There are Icons everywhere — the likes of which he has never seen before.

Instinctively, Vassilis begins crossing himself and kneels to pray. When he opens his eyes he finds Methodios and Cyril standing over him. Methodios pulls Vassilis to his feet.

"There's no need for that, my friend," Methodios says, a smile playing on his lips. "After all, none of these have even been blessed, and some are still far from ready to make their first trip to a church."

Vassilis has grown accustomed to the shyness Cyril and Methodios always bring out in him, perhaps because their eyes always seem to sparkle with a gentle joke just beyond his grasp.

"So," Methodios says, "if you've quite finished standing there, rooted to the spot like some timid sapling, why don't you come over here and do something useful?"

"What are you doing?" Vassilis asks, as he moves closer, and then instantly blushes at the stupidity of the question. Their paint-stained fingers and nails should make this obvious, as should the half-finished image in front of them. "I mean, what church will you fill with these?"

"Hmm . . . hopefully, one day, your Khan will build a real church here, and these will fill it. But for now, they will fill the Khan's castle. He is fascinated, you see, by us Christians."

"The problem we have right now," Cyril continues, "is that he wants something my brother has done for no one before, something huge to cover the wall of his castle that will impress his recalcitrant Boyar lords."

Words like "recalcitrant" mean nothing to Vassilis, but he gets the idea of painting a giant Icon to impress and is eager to help.

Cyril pulls out a scrap of parchment. "Here are the directions. The eggs are over there. You will find red clay, animal skin, and honey in the urns in the far corner. These will need pounding. Oh, the clay is special — we have had to bring it all the way from the City, so be careful with it."

Vassilis peers into the corner where urns and wood are piled up. "I have no idea what to do," he says. He had seen the priests and monks at his church as a child, painting simple Icons, but had never been involved.

"Start by mixing the egg tempera for me. It's all here." Methodios shoves the parchment under Vassilis' nose again.

When Vassilis begins to mouth the instructions, syllable by syllable, Methodios grins again. "I see. You can't really read, can you? Then we will have to teach you." They look at each other in the eye. After a moment's pause it is Vassilis' turn to laugh.

"What's so funny about that?" ask Methodios.

"Father taught me to read the scriptures a bit, but ... you are not much older than me. Are you to be my teachers, then? I am a bit old to learn, I think. I already have a son."

"You do?" says Cyril, starting in surprise. "Well, it's never too late to learn something new. Of course, if you're not interested in reading then we will show you what needs doing, or get you to cut and smooth the poplar planks that will be needed for the panels. Actually, why don't we get going with that? It looks like you have the right arms for it."

Cyril places a hand on Vassilis' shoulder. He runs fingertips along Vassilis' muscles, along a vein that lies across his bicep, and down to his wrist. He rests his hand on Vassilis' waist. *A man has never touched my Peasant in quite this way before.* Something flickers to life in his britches, leaving him a little confused.

"So!" says Cyril, whipping his hand away. "It's time to work!"

† † †

This is the first time Michael saw me properly. As a woman, that is, and not as a faceless servant. Later, in gentler moments, he would tell me how he recalled events like this. Then we would laugh, and tease each other. But usually all we did was ... embrace. Or he would weep in my arms. It eventually became tiresome.

Michael and the other boys have had a good afternoon racing around the polo stadium and he has forgotten mother's silliness that morning. But in spite of the good sport and the mild breeze cooling the wintry sun, the black horse that lives in his heart champs annoyingly at the bit. *The black horse, I maintain, that dragged him to his death.*

So he decides to race back to the Palace, to prove to all the others he is the fastest. He ignores the ancient rule that this is generally forbidden due to the danger to those walking, and pushes his mount to excess. After a few blocks, his mates close behind, the horse slips, and he smashes into the ground, right in front of the entrance to my quarters.

He musters all his will to stop the tears from erupting. This has been such a horrible day! But he is fine, apart from a very painful elbow and bloody scrapes across his knees where they grazed the cobbles. The boys swirl around him but cringe at the sight of blood, admonishing him instead to be brave and to act the part of an Emperor.

Several hours before this, the Regent had dismissed me more curtly than usual. She had been summoned to confer with officials, so I decided to stroll through the gardens, finding fresh parsley and wild origanum for a stew, as well as some rosemary to freshen up the couches. I was planning to spend a quiet afternoon, cooking and reading with Mother.

Turning the corner to our quarters reveals a heap of sweaty boys piled around in front of my doorway. I am no older than the oldest boy there, perhaps thirteen, though I chance a very adult, all-knowing shake of my head, my braids swinging widely.

"So, children, are we playing nicely at being idiots?" I announce, pretending not to notice the young Emperor at first. Silence ensues.

Then, "Ah, Your Worthiness, my apologies," I say, though I don't let my eyes show any sign of humility to this ten-year-old. "Let me help you if, as it seems, your friends are unable to."

I settle myself down on the steps, dig around in my basket for a cloth, and poke one of the boys. "Hey, green eyes, why don't you run into the house and get me a bowl of water for your Emperor."

I confess I both relish the gaze of these sweaty creatures and despise them for it. But it is clear that they can't decide if they should be shy or scandalized by the attention that I lavish on Michael. They must be wondering what part girl, what part woman I am. If they were several years older and a bit cleaner I might be happy to let them find out.

With a filled bowl of water obediently placed on the ground next to me, I produce my herb knife and use it to tear the cloth neatly in three. With one piece I rinse the wounds. Michael does all he can not to utter the slightest sound although this costs him effort. With the other two pieces I bandage each knee in a neat knot, giving the last knot an extra squeeze for good measure.

"There you are, Your Worthiness, ready to ride again." I pull him to his feet.

The poor dear – he mumbles some word of thanks. But everyone, including me, is stunned into silence when I plant a kiss on his forehead. I quickly pull my things together and rise to go inside.

The boys twitter and moan, half teasing, half amazed. I can see Michael trying to hide the burning red rising across his face by leaping onto his confused mount, reining it in, and trotting away as fast as he possibly can.

I head up the stairs and think no more of it.

Part II

Ignominy

853−856 AD

10. Messengers and missions

To protect our modesty there are several long curtains along the gallery of the Gynaeconitis, and when we open some of the windows to let in fresh air they blow carelessly about, which I find very agreeable. This also lets us hear footsteps, or men's voices.

Courtiers arrive to bring their wives or daughters, dispatching the eunuchs with them up the stairs to the main room where the Regent is usually waiting. Today I am here before everyone — having been charged with spending the night in attendance on Her Worthiness. I find it pleasant to look down on these men lining up on the veranda, discouraged as they are from entering the main hall upstairs. They stand invitingly in a line after giving up their charges, their backs against the wall, some of the younger ones with their outer robes folded casually back under their beards so their chests, peering out from the gaps at the top of their tunics, can scandalize us.

Yesterday flew by. We held a rehearsal for today's procession to the Pege monastery, arranging and brushing our head gear and robes and garlanding herbs and flowers, as the sunlight and warm breezes sailed through the curtains. Then some pipe players came by and stood outside practicing their pieces for the procession. It looks like the weather will be as uplifting again today, and I am looking forward to baring my cheeks to the breeze, not to mention the gazes of the young sailors on board the Imperial barge.

Theoktistos arrives amid a great rustling of silk robes, and looking quite unkempt, which is unusual for him. We fall over ourselves in haste to make way, hardly finding time to announce his arrival. Behind him is the strangest thing any of us have ever seen, judging by the silence that descends.

"I have brought you a special guest today," he says, standing aside, and displaying a handsome woman, though a dun-colored outer robe and a strange variety of britches mar her appearance.

I would almost think she is a nun, were it not for her bearing, especially the fierce darkness in her eyes and her thick black hair.

To our astonishment, Theodora goes up to this strange creature and takes her gently by the hand. "Come sit with us," she says to her, "we will arrange your toilet in a moment."

"Martinaka," Theodora uses my family name, unable to resist an opportunity to put me down by reminding me of my Iconoclast ancestors, "bring us a fresh cloth to wipe the lady's hands."

A lady? We all stare at each other. We have no idea who this is, and it is obvious that she doesn't understand what we say. One of the women titters that her coarse sounds are that of the Bulgar.

"A somewhat irregular foray," says the Eunuch, "by troops stationed in Adrianopolis, deeper than we would normally go, uncovered this prize. What she was doing traveling so far from Pliska, we can only imagine, perhaps heading for the sea to take the waters?" He permits himself a chuckle.

"We should take good care of her," Theodora says, "she is, after all, a woman, not some scoundrel or thief. We can't just throw her into chains. At least until we know exactly whom she represents. She may even be of use to us."

As far as the Eunuch is concerned, the subject is closed. He is back to business, pacing about. "There is bad news from the borders. The heretics are on the move again."

"What do you mean?" Theodora asks absentmindedly, gazing with a broad, inviting smile at the Bulgar woman who clutches herself more tightly.

"It appears," says the Eunuch, "that the Paulicians have moved even further into the heart of the Abbasid, and are regrouping in a place called Tephrike, my sources inform me, on the shores of a great river."

"Oh," she responds, "surely there is no need to concern ourselves about this right now. They are far away, and the sun and our hearts shine with joy."

"We must respond if we are to be consistent in our approach," he says, "or they will see it as a sign of weakness."

"Of course we will," she says firmly, "but not today!"

I am quite amazed at this lack of interest in affairs of state, which is so unlike her. She is obviously pleased with something, beyond the distraction of the new arrival. I knew nothing of it then, my interests centered on little more than my loom, my burgeoning cleavage, and the rather sumptuous hand-me-downs from Her Worthiness' wardrobe. However, reading Photios' notes here, I guess that her satisfaction was at a woman's work well done, not to mention at how our coffers brimmed over. Thrift is the cornerstone of a successful state!

Shouts and steps echo from the stairs as Michael bursts into the hall. Eunuchs and the young Emperor are the only men allowed unfettered access here and Michael makes full use of this privilege, reveling in our consternation even as we are taken in by his boyishness. Today he leans against a pillar at the entrance, showing off excellent britches of light green silk and a short scarlet tunic. His hair falls in black waves to cover the neckband of his cloak which he loosens. His eyes come to rest on me while he begins to chat with one of the women.

"Is the Emperor ready for the procession?" asks Theoktistos. "Surely you don't intend to lead the worship at the monastery in garments fit for the Hippodrome!"

"You are quite right, noble Logothete," Michael says in mock seriousness. "I will have to redress myself in much the same fashion as you seek to redress me!"

We do all we can to hide our smiles at this masterful rebuke, but Theoktistos ignores us. "Find the Master of the Wardrobe," he spits at me.

I try to slip past Michael but he reaches out a hand to take my elbow, touching me accidentally on that part of my outer robe covering a breast.

"Worthiness," I say, smiling, "please do not trouble yourself."

I rummage quickly around for a decent pair of pale cotton britches that I know will be cool in the midday heat. Here is a muted long purple under robe with gold thread cross-hatching from left waist to right shoulder, a thin cream cloak, and dark red felt boots. I present these, bowing deeply to the Eunuch and the Regent, being careful to show the bindings of my dress.

"Perhaps these would be more appropriate," I say, somewhat officiously. The Regent frowns in grudging approval.

"Of course they're not," Michael chortles wickedly. "They're no fun at all. But I will put them on if it pleases the assembled royalty." We cannot control our giggles at all now, and I would receive more pleasure from Theoktistos' angry departure if Michael's bright smile, aimed straight at me, does not strike me in the heart.

"Oh yes," Theodora says, spotting our little exchange. "Someone will have to look after our new ... guest while we are on procession today. We could hardly take her along; she is not only tired but quite ... unkempt. Martinaka," she says, looking me straight in the eye, "I am relying on you to be a caring and considerate hostess in our absence."

† † †

Photios ponders on my Peasant's origins. He writes that Vassilis must be a descendant of the Arsakids, the ancient house of Tiridates the Armenian king, who embraced the message of Christ long before the greatest Constantine of them all.

I read that, with Vardas and Petronas in exile, Photios passes the long hours with his books and his gardens, broken only by his brother Sergios dragging him away to visit his family. And where have the brothers got to? Rumor had it they traveled to southern Greece, to visit their cousin Theophilitzes, some said they roamed Athens endlessly, some even mentioned Ravenna.

So Photios is delighted to sit down with Cyril, freshly returned from Pliska for a short visit, at Photios' behest. They had not spent much time together before he left, most of it on the practicalities of the visit to Pliska.

"Master Photios," Cyril begins, "I must thank you for making me come back. I have not lived here much but it feels like I am home." The lad had been torn between staying with his older brother and leaving, though it would not be their first time apart by any means.

"What is your take on the pagans?" Photios asks. "How do they respond to the Word of Christ?"

"It is not as if I have not known them before," Cyril laughs. "They are a good people, a bit rough, but very loving to their friends and families. They have no recourse but to be warlike, their land is not as abundant as ours. They are a plague to our farmers because what livestock and grain they have is quite pitiful."

"I see, but what of the problem I have posed?"

"With the greatest respect, Master Photios, why should they care to be told about the scriptures?"

"I think you know what I mean," says Photios. "Have you tried to explain Christ's message?"

Cyril perches on the edge of Photios' desk, a smile on his lips. "The Boyars want land and food. The Khan wants peace; because he is wise enough to know it will make his life easier. Scriptures are rather . . . irrelevant. Granted, there are indeed some who know Greek and who could preach the message of the gospels. I believe our brothers from Bavaria are already trying to do this . . . in Latin, no less!"

This was when all our troubles started. Cyril goes on. "The Bavarian monks are feared less than we are. We have warred with the Bulgar for too long for them to think of us as friends. How can forcing them to learn our language possibly convince them?"

"What should we do?" Photios fidgets on his stool.

"Well, we could try to tell them about the scriptures in their own language," says Cyril, somewhat dubiously.

"Surely the whole problem is little more than writing it down for them? It would be easier than getting them to acquire an understanding of thousands of years of Greek."

"Indeed! If only they had written language. But I could try to use Greek characters. There will have to be many concessions — the noisy 'sh', 'zh' and 'ch' sounds are not in our native tongue."

"Your quarters are satisfactory enough, I hope, for this short stay, and for you to begin work immediately?" Photios says, but then realizes how rude this must appear. "Perhaps we should take a meal together — the beginning of many hours spent discussing this, I am sure, before you return. Let's find Theoktistos. I am sure he will be glad to join us."

††††

The Bulgar court doesn't stand on ceremony, unlike us Romans. The Khan demands simple obedience but little else, at least that's what I hear. He governs through skill and tact, not like some well-bred stallion, chosen by birthright for the fastest chariot races. He doesn't require acclamation and veneration after passing through several prostrations, as the Regent does, when conducting business in the Throne Room. And woe betide a general on campaign who fails to dismount and kiss the ground in homage when the Emperor arrives. Whereas the Khan expects none of this.

Vassilis leaps at the chance to accompany Methodios to the Khan's private castle, out on the Ticha River, where he invites only his most loyal Boyar lords. The wood and stone interior, with stone columns at its corners, in contrast to the bright sunshine outside, is a strange world to my Vassilis. A fire thunders in a brick enclosure, scattering light off an array of swords, maces, and bows on the adjacent wall. A raised floor hides beneath a dark-woven rug that spills over the sides.

"This was built by Omurtag, Boris' grandfather," whispers Methodios to Vassilis, indicating the walls around them. "In imitation of what he had heard about our Throne Room, it is said, although I think the tale has lost some truth in the telling."

There is a throne, if one could call it that, that is little more than a squat stool. It raises the Khan a head or so above the throng of fifteen to twenty bearded men, most of whom appear to be as old as his father.

But this is still all wondrously new to my beautiful Peasant. After all, he is still an ignorant youngster with dirt under his fingernails! Where would he have seen even such primitive luxuries before? In some dung-spotted hillside back home? Who would speak about the kinds of things he hears at court while following Methodios around? He marvels at how the monk engages in all sorts of complex topics with Grozdan, one of Boris' most senior courtiers, and also one of the fattest men Vassilis has ever seen.

Boris lifts his head and summons the council with a single word. The Boyars step up and seat themselves cross-legged on the rug.

"We have been affronted by the Romans," exclaims Boris, "yet again!"

"Are you referring," responds a young Boyar, "to your sister? What happened? Did a stroll in the forest turn into a trip to the seaside? Unfortunately she did not pass through my lands, or I would have taken much better care of her." The gathering explodes in raucous laughter.

"You may view it as of no significance," Boris says, gesturing for silence, "but where does that leave us with the Romans?

We ... I ... have given them something to hold us to ransom with, which was not our intention. All we can trade with is our loyalty."

A Boyar speaks out. "We will take from their wealth when and as we need it, as we always do. Nothing changes. Your sister's plight is not our concern. It is a family matter."

Dead silence. Boris continues. "It is all too easy to be content with taking — but what if we want something they do not wish us to have? Such as an alliance?"

"What alliance would we need," retorts another Boyar, "from soft skinned, perfumed women who don fighting gear only when they are not kissing each other on the backside?" The gathering roars appreciatively. Boris shakes his head and waits for quiet.

"I tell you," Boris says, "even now, the Franks are on our doorstep. Our treaty remains unsigned though we have worked hard to convince them." He nods to Grozdan to step forward.

"Oh great riders of the steppes," Grozdan says, "would you bend the knee to other peoples, to foreign kings? Kings whose steel glove lies heavy across the rich lands of Frankia and Germania, to whom dukes and princes show obeisance, and who would not think twice about pissing on us in return for the rocky crags we command?"

"Exactly," says another Boyar, "we have nothing to offer them — why would they bother with us? Even the Romans do not worry us any longer. Who even remembers the other treaty, the one your father signed with them?"

"What if they seek to play us against our Slav brothers in the east — Rostislav of Moravia comes to mind — to weaken both us and them?" Grozdan says. "Surely it is easier to talk to an indifferent yet powerful ally, one who seeks neither tribute nor lands, only peace of mind."

Fists are being shaken, they cry out against Boris, against us Romans. This is not to their liking, especially because they understand, deep in their hearts, the truth of it all. Morons! I imagine Methodios tugging at Vassilis' arm, nodding to the door.

"Enough!" Boris booms above the gathering. "I warm to your loyalty. In fact, the real issue before us today is something quite different. It is time for war again. Surely there are those among you who would like to take a stand against the Franks?"

Warm nods and cheers greet this suggestion, apart from Grozdan, who retreats from the gathering, shaking his head.

"As it happens, Prince Rostislav, who we thought might be an enemy, has suggested we join him in an attack on Louis the Frank. Just as we did with the Romans, let us show the Franks that we are not to be subdued easily!"

The Boyars rise as one — clasping each other's shoulders firmly, the swell of voices ringing out through the hall. Perhaps even Vassilis feels his heart lift at the idea of fighting for one's land, one's people, and of joining arms for a noble cause.

I doubt it. For though my Peasant lacks education, he understands, perhaps for the first time in his young life, how words chosen properly can move hearts, even those of oafs and ruffians. I have known this to be true since my first days in the Gynaeconitis — although it took me many years to understand how to use it to my advantage.

Poor Photios learned it too late, in spite of all his great knowledge of past writings, of events, of people. Truly great men know that one must speak to hearts, not minds. For the latter are usually small and easily compassed, whereas the conquest of hearts is a labor before which even the gods quail and falter.

11. Endless possibilities

ABOUT TWO YEARS LATER, IN THE SPRING OF 855 AD
Photios writes how he, the Regent and the Eunuch became a
steadfast trio in those thrifty, eye-watering years. How they held
their gaze fast to the prize: prosperity and peace. I am moved.

One clear but cold day the sun shines more brightly than usual,
melting away the last of the winter snows. The three of them wait
inside the Treasury, amid columns of marble towering both over
them and over a crowd of senators outside, in the courtyard of the
Augusteon. The senators jostle for space near the closed bronzed
doors to the Treasury. Many are elderly, many indignant. They
fume at the oddness of the time of day, wondering why they have
been called to assemble outside, and why here when they should
be in procession? They are not afraid to muse openly that perhaps
another war is to be fought. Perhaps it is true that the Eunuch is
not content with the capture of Damietta, that he now wants us to
rule Egypt again as in times of old? The conversations skirt over
inanities, conniving, vicious gossip of philandering and conquests
writ large, while the failures implied are even larger in reality.

Let the creditors cry now, Photios is thinking to himself, as
they lose their interest when the bonds get paid back in full. Everyone else will be laughing – the coin they will pocket today will
buy a lot more than they expected, at least in the beginning. The
Regent basks in the rising anticipation. Let them stew a bit, she
must be thinking, picking at a plate of walnuts and figs.

Suddenly she laughs out loud. When last did she do that?
The Eunuch comes over to her, his eyes bursting with pride at her
satisfaction. The financial statements are ready to burst out of
their ribbons, thanks to the hard work of my staff. Newly minted
coins glow in vast bags that bulge over teak chests. Next to them,
rolled up in pregnant heaps, lie jeweled cloths of purple-dyed silk.

Theodora nods at Photios and he thumps the ground to give
the doorman his cue. She touches up her gold-lined head scarf,

then strides out as the bronze doors growl open. Treasury curtains are drawn back as an orange sunrise pours into the room behind her. Complete silence reigns.

Michael is there, is at the back of the gathering, with some other young bloods in tow. He looks confused, even annoyed.

This is Theodora's moment. "Venerable senators, you will notice that I have broken with convention and brought you to an unusual place at a time that ill suits many of you. Lent begins today, and with it a time of ritual hardship — symbolic, in some ways, of the greater hardship we suffered for so many years. But that hardship has now been relieved by our faith, even as we worship freely, and to our hearts' desires, the images of the saints and fathers of the church."

Michael's companions, ever ready to abuse his lack of dignity, cast jibes at the young Emperor. Birdsong descends into the expectant stillness as everyone else tries to ignore the young men.

Theodora speaks out over the noise. "How long did we labor under the misunderstanding that our love for the Icons caused our suffering? I hope I have shown you, over the last twelve years, that this is nonsense. Instead, we have grown stronger and more prosperous. God wishes us to worship Him with all our hearts. How we remind ourselves of His greatness is irrelevant. So I have asked the Patriarch to consult his brothers in the east, and to agree with them that this Sunday be remembered in all our prayers forever."

Soft boots and robes shuffle, but there is no protest. They have become accustomed to a woman dictating religious policy. This is the precedent she bartered for when appointing Ignatios patriarch — the monks would never have stood for it otherwise, neither would have old Methodios, I suspect.

"As proof of how the Theotokos has smiled upon us, we have taken account of all that we have gathered in, through tribute and taxes, and through our own industry since the great Theophilos left us the kingdom. There are those who would consider us weak and womanish and not worthy of government. But we would make it clear that our stewardship of your wealth has been exemplary."

This is the Eunuch's cue. Photios has prepared all the accounts for him. He steps forward, chiseled features in deep shadow, his imposing height in contrast to his high-pitched tones. "Here, then, is the state of our coffers: currently 184,510 feet of finest silks, 191,743 pounds of gold, and 328,291 pounds of silver all held in the City. Further amounts are owed to us in tribute of . . . " the drone is swallowed up as cries of amazement ripple out across the gathering. Theodora smiles broadly into her cowl, hiding her pleasure behind a stately gaze. She can leave this to the keepers of the books and turns to leave.

Michael catches up with her. "Mother, you told me nothing about this. Could you not even have included me in your little announcement?"

"We were busy — it was nothing — I did not expect this reaction from the senators." She must be surprised and a little afraid at how forceful he has become.

"That's good — because Uncle Vardas should have also been here to take some credit for the good news."

"My darling, we have been over this many times. I had no choice. It was one or the other. The Eunuch is generally much more useful at court. We have many commanders for our armies — but who can help me with this pack of thieves?"

Michael always hated it when people did not listen to him, when they saw the boy, not the Emperor. But the Regent usually ignored nearly everyone, except the Eunuch. Michael never realized how powerless we all are before our mothers!

† † †

I insert these pages here because I want you to know, my dear son, how I nearly wasn't part of the Bride Show.

I remember the morning clearly. The Bulgar woman sits spinning in a corner. Rumor was that she was some kind of barbarian princess. At any rate, she is not much use at the best of times, having not mastered enough Greek to converse meaningfully. The Regent insists on teaching her prayers, which the poor woman recites, even though she clearly doesn't understand their meaning.

Dickbreath — by now I was old enough to have heard the Eunuch's court moniker, though I didn't understand quite what it meant — has come around for one of his usual briefings with the Regent before the day's proceedings. The resident officials of the Wardrobe had been dispatched in the early hours of the morning to retrieve some new items — something the Regent had ordered made up from a recent shipment. We are fussing around with her hair and arranging space for her to try on the new items as the bags arrive.

Envious breaths are drawn as armfuls of soft, creamy silk pile out on the rugs, and a majestic lavender-and-brown brocaded dalmatica is spread on the table. A veil as gentle as spring rain emerges, presumably to augment the cowl she usually wears. The heavy, tapestry-woven brocade on the dalmatica scandalizes us. It has been done up in a very manly style, with complex patterns running up and down the sleeves and with bold outlines. The pile of silk turns out to be her under robe, the softest I have ever seen.

The Regent tries them on but casts the dalmatica aside. She calls for her usual outer robe, one with scenes of deer in a forest scene, embroidered at the front and back. The dalmatica is a bit much, at least for regular use, but she will wear it soon, she says, when the Bulgar envoy arrives. I am instructed to order some brocaded gloves to accompany it. I will confess to you, my little Leo, that I learned much about good taste from your grandmother.

The Eunuch indicates that we should vanish. She nods us off. Little did I know then that they were discussing what could have been my future. But we girls had our own conversation, if you could call it that. We go off to the "cathedral," as we women jokingly call the towering, many-domed cabinet that houses the perfumes and makeup.

"So they won't be after what you have to offer," Gemma taunts me, quickly smearing a fingertip of the Regent's favorite lip balm onto her own lips. "I have heard our future Augusta is already arriving by sea, one of Her Worthiness' distant cousins sending more of his stock to market!"

"Do I care?" I reply, dipping into a jar of perfume oil. "The Emperor has pledged himself to me. Michael is so much more than you could ever wish for."

"How could he have pledged himself to you?" she hisses at me. "You are such a fool. He is just a boy and has no idea what he is saying."

"Anyway he has assured me that I will be part of the proceedings," I counter, sullenly.

"Part of the proceedings! Holding the Regent's gown off the floor while she wipes her nose is what he meant, I imagine."

I throw one of the Regent's boots at her. "At least his heart belongs to me. Let's not talk about your young Spatharios — what is his name? Theodoros. Or should I call him Oedipus. Seems to me he has not even left his mother's embrace. They will be together until Christ's return, I am sure."

"They will not!" She hoists an empty perfume jar at me. "You are wrong. He wants me, and can have me more than you will ever have the Emperor! Live in your dreams, you snake!"

"Scorpion!" I scream, and lean over to smack her. We fight as only girls can, in the worst kind of way, with unfair scratches, slapping, and a lot of noise. Suddenly the Regent is towering above us.

"I should have known it," she says, fixing me with one of her fiercest stares, her lips drawn tight. "The Martinaka girl, causing trouble again, just like your mother. Your family was the bane of my existence before... I don't know why I endure you now."

She suddenly grabs me by the shoulders. I am astonished into silence not only by the fact that she has never touched me before, but by her strength, as she shoves me in the direction of the Eunuch. He pulls me along by the ear and pushes me ahead of him down the stairs. The shame flares in my cheeks, before collapsing into the smoldering realization that I am being thrown out of the Imperial quarters.

"You do not carry yourself admirably," the Eunuch pipes in my ear, "and now I have every reason to explain to your father that we don't need you at court for a while. I don't know if he will mind, but I do know that Her Worthiness won't be disappointed."

I know Father will understand. He always understands me. He knows I don't care for stupidity, for empty words. I will tell him exactly what happened and he will believe me, and then chide me in his adorable way.

That's how it began, my sons. Your mother is not and has never been one for groveling. Or for keeping her mouth shut. Let them be damned, the pig eaters. Let them know now that the melted ice of Thule that runs in my veins, in your veins, keeps my heart pure and my mind clear.

12. The brave and the fair

A MONTH OR SO LATER, IN THE SPRING OF 855 AD
Here comes young Constantinos, bounding across the floor, leaping effortlessly into my Peasant's arms. His son's supple frame hints at great strength for someone only six years old. He'll be just like me, Vassilis must be thinking, his pride hidden behind typical Macedonian gruffness. Pride is something he knew little about before he came to the Bulgar, before he had a wife and child.

This simple, daily happiness – caring for the lives of others – has made him understand life itself. Meanwhile, at court, he has crept closer and closer to the heart of the Khan than he would have dared believe possible. Watching a powerful leader at work, pitting himself against big ideas and small people, every minute an act of survival, and then coming home to the warmth and love of his wife and child, has changed him.

No, I didn't get all of this from him. I got this much later from Maria, the woman who watched him grow ... in fact, helped him grow up ... and then stole his heart with her motherly embrace.

I wouldn't say Maria and I became close, but we confided, as women do, especially when there is nothing else to pass the time but wait for the men to return. Or rather, I pretended to listen as a young woman would to an older one, respectfully, with an ear for precept and understanding. Except that she did not know then, when she told me this, that the man we longed for was one and the same.

My Peasant has an inkling that today will be one of the days when hearts will be broken. He has been dwelling on his choices for some time now, while thinking back to the daily struggle, with his brothers, on the hills outside Chariopolis, catching live animals to sell in the marketplace. He was lucky, he knows this, not to have been killed by the pagans who took his childhood away.

But right now the child leaping on and off his lap distracts him. Constantinos is almost too big for this sort of thing, so Vassilis mock wrestles him down to the floor, proudly feeling the young muscles straining in response. Each day the child tests himself against his father. Each day he looks more like his mother – sad, slightly moon-shaped eyes, clear, milky skin, and a toothy grin all his own. Maria flops down next to Vassilis on the rug.

"You are quite distant today. But you know this makes me even more eager for you!" Her lips consume his.

Her love is there, perhaps stronger than he has ever felt it before. His adoration also knows no bounds. He lets his hands wander across her face. They vanish in her hair. He marvels at the ways of the heart, that his fondness for her has grown so much.

"The Khan takes me into his confidence a little more each day," he says. "Years of just taking care of his horses – and now learning about the ways of the court."

"In some ways they are not that different from one another," says Maria. She is happy that he is happy. But Vassilis desperately wants to soften the blow. He squeezes her shoulder, feels the warmth of her neck beneath his fingers.

"You know how we have been getting many visitors from Constantinople? I am friends with one of those, a monk from Athos, a painter. His name is Methodios. He is very funny. He and his brother, who left some time back, have helped me improve my reading."

Maria gets up, moves to the hearth, rescues a bowl of soup, and returns to the pillows and into his warmth.

"Of course I know about Methodios, who doesn't! I am glad you have Roman friends – they must be much more interesting than us barbarians," she says. Teasing him like this still thrills her.

"The people still can't stop talking," she continues, "about how you chanced to overhear that plan to kill the Khan while helping Methodios put up the Icons in the castle, and that your words in the Khan's ear may have saved him."

She burrows into his arms. Constantinos has gone for the moment. Vassilis tries again.

"Methodios will tell me soon, for sure," he says.

Alert but timid, like a wary fox, she sits up. "Tell you about what?" she asks.

"I think he wants me to visit the City," Vassilis whispers softly. "To help him. The Khan is sending an envoy to – what is the word he uses? — negotiate with the Romans."

He knows this will be hard for her. But if there is any chance that he might find his brothers, he knows he must take it or forever believe that he didn't try hard enough, that he had let them down. The fire sputters away, the bowl hangs, forgotten, in her hand.

Then it shatters on the floor. She plays ferociously with his hands, then pulls his face to hers. She tries to memorize the smell of his beard. She pulls at his tunic. But there is nothing to say. She can see that his mind is already on the dusty road, on the trails through the hills, leaving the green forests far behind. She realizes what she always knew — that one day he would have to pick himself up and take off. That he was always a visitor.

Maria asks herself if her more than three decades in this world revolts this young man so much? She once told me that the attraction to younger men is because one needs them, rather than the converse. This puzzles me. When they need something, is the return currency that of a favor, rather than an honest gift?

Standing up suddenly, her elbow catches him in the chest and she almost tumbles back to the ground. She pulls the blanket to cover her shoulders as the tears creep out from under fierce lashes. Constantinos peers in from the doorway, confused at the noise.

Vassilis is up at once, reaching for her, but pulling back as her anger sears his eyes.

He looks away. "There might be a chance," he whispers. "This is the one place I haven't yet searched for news of my parents, for Marianos and the others. Please understand that I must do this."

She nods as she turns away, her shoulders trembling. "I will prepare a bag for you," she says. When she looks back her lips are firm, as they carry the unspoken question: Will you ever return?

† † †

The young Emperor is at his studies. Michael tries his best to keep his mind on the parchment in front of him, in anticipation, no doubt, of another angry session with Theoktistos if he doesn't copy the exercises that Photios has set him. The Eunuch went to Photios for guidance on what Michael should study, though he insisted on delivering Michael's instruction himself, when he had the time, that is.

Michael always complained that Latin was abominably dull. Who can understand how to share jokes, or have fun, in a language which sounds like the scrape of scythes on the lawn? Photios nevertheless encouraged Theoktistos to teach it to him. Every Emperor should know this language, he maintained, though he was no expert at it himself.

Michael is thrilled that Damianos, son of the Leader of the Greens, has brought him something quite scandalous, partly translated. The Eunuch would reprimand him severely were he to discover that, instead of working on his Latin exercises, Michael has been translating this Latin text into Greek, using the lexicon that Photios had devised for him. That the text purports to have been written down by Saint Jerome of Stridonium would have not impressed the Eunuch at all. But Michael would love to believe that a saint could write this sort of thing.

He is eager to crack the puzzle. He slides the scrap of parchment into view. The words of Piglet's last will and testament spring into view.

> *On the sixteenth day before the Calends of Lamplighting, and in the consulship of Oven and Peppersauce, when the cabbage greens are plentiful, Magirus the cook said, 'Come here, you runaway piglet! You have wrecked the house, you have burrowed endlessly. Yet you have failed to bury your parents. I will put an end to your life today!'*

> *Corocotta the Piglet said: 'If I have done anything wrong, if I have broken any pot with my little feet, I beg you, Lord Cook, I beg you for my life, grant my petition.'*

> *Magirus the cook called a boy: 'Go and bring me a carving knife from the kitchen so that this piglet might shed his blood.'*

> *Thus Corocotta was grasped firmly by the slaves and led off, in the consulship of Oven and Peppersauce. When he saw that he was going to die, he*

*requested an hour's stay of execution to make his
will.*

*Here begins Marcus Grunter Corocotta's last will.
He was not able to write, so he had it written down
to his dictation.*

To Hoggy Lardy, my father, I grant thirty bushels of
acorns.
To my mother, the breeding-sow Veturia, I leave forty
bushels of Spartan winter wheat flour.
To Quirina, my sister, whose wedding I will not be
able to attend, I give thirty bushels of barley.
Of my flesh, I grant my bristles to the cobblers, my
brains to the quarrelsome, my ears to the deaf, my
tongue to the litigious and garrulous, my guts to the
sausage-makers, my thighs to the stuffing-makers,
my loins to the women, my bladder to the young boys,
my tail to the girls, my cock and ass to the old pederasts and young jerk-offs, my ankles to the postmen
and hunters, my hooves to the bandits.
To the unspeakable cook, I leave the pestle and mortar which I brought with me; he may hang himself by
the neck from a rope anywhere between Thebeste and
Tergeste.
And I want a tombstone to be erected for me engraved
with gold letters as follows:

Here lies
MARCVS GRVNNIVS COROCOTTA
Had he lived for another half-year
he would have scored a thousand

You who have loved me best and have been my coun-
selors in life, I ask you to treat my body with respect,
to season it well with the best condiments of nutmeg,
pepper, and honey, so that my name may be known for
all eternity.

My lords and cousins who have been present at the making of my will, order that it be sealed thus:

Bacon-Fat signed.
Meatball signed.
Cumin stew signed.
Sausage signed.
Pork Rind signed.
Celsinus signed.
Wedding Pig signed.

Over his chuckling, Michael can hear footsteps, the sound of sandals rather than boots. From this he concludes it is neither the Eunuch nor Photios, but Damianos returning to marvel at how wonderful his translation is, and hopefully other things — perhaps he has found out whether I have been permitted to take part in the Bride Show?

†††

And indeed, I have! Father had successfully wormed his way back into the Regent's dubious affections. Theodora wants to keep him in good favor, no doubt. He has functioned more on her behalf than he has for his real masters in the north, especially in bringing us news of the other barbarians. Thanks to him my Thulian cousins have started bringing shiploads full of coarse but wholesome wheat, in exchange for our cloth and spices.

The day of the Bridal Show is glorious; a summer sun fills every shadowy spot in the gardens with warmth, and I am anxious to know if I have been chosen. It is in the gardens that the fateful theater plays itself out, even as the breeze sings around the chiseled hedges, their Abbasid design luring the mind away from the evident to the tantalizingly hidden.

Sometimes the stupidity of the Regent and the Eunuch leaves me dumbfounded. The whole court knows how Michael continues to squander attention on me. So why, Holy Theotokos, subject him us all to this farce? Why summon the Empire's greatest beauties to lure young Michael to more noble aspirations when we all know where his heart lies?

In one corner a lute springs into view, plucked at by hands of silken marble, underscoring a fountain of dark curls and a clear voice. I can see that Michael is amused — she is very lovely — but I am sure she is not what he wishes to share his bed with, let alone the double-seated Throne.

In another corner, apples as red as lips find their way into a golden basket, held by petal-washed fingers. I imagine Michael shuddering at the timid, pleading gaze of Dekapolitessa — his wife-to-be, if the Regent and the Eunuch have anything to do with it. A sweet girl, for sure, but how she pales next to me.

The heat settles in the late morning on a third young delight, arranging different kinds of purple silk in an open chest. Her red hair burns like the sand on a sun-drenched beach, her perspiration the vaguest hint of surf as it retreats. She knows she is very fair, and ... unwanted. At least she made it this far, she must be telling herself, having come across the sea to Constantinople, like the Regent Irene before her, after much petitioning from her father, the Eparch of Athens. No doubt her mother will be pleased if at least some young courtier will have her. But it won't be Michael. From my seat in the shade, I can see his gaze shifting out of focus, beyond her... to me.

I wonder what the rumors are. Do they know that Michael and I have moved beyond kisses? Even Damianos, soon to be appointed Companion of the Bedchamber does not know this, I suspect. I have chosen my seat wisely, right next to Michael's favorite — the Golden Tree.

I watch Michael's eyes widen at the sight of me. I have left my hair to cascade over my shoulders and past my breasts. The lightest silk gown hugs my waist. And why not? Even Photios writes that the soft rolling consonants and clear vowels of my court epithet, Ingerina, sing of conquest and adventure!

13. New encounters

ABOUT TWO MONTHS LATER, IN THE SUMMER OF 855 AD
Days without deep sleep have left Vassilis invigorated. The many
hours on horseback would have knocked out most men, but his
arms and shoulders tingle from the cold dawn breeze, as if his
nerves were thin, hot wires, like the kind he pounds out in the
smithy to reinforce saddle seams.

The plan is to sue for peace, in return for the Khan's sister.
Next to him rides Methodios and, in front of them, Grozdan the
Envoy. A small group of knights and attendants ride behind them.
The Envoy complains constantly, which annoys Vassilis, though
Methodios' good humor lightens the mood.

The scraping of rustier bits of Grozdan's chain mail are somewhat muffled by a wide cloak draped over his shoulders. He rides
off-balance, which Vassilis despises, so Vassilis canters ahead. At
least dear Methodios knows how to move with his mount! Vassilis
wonders if the Envoy's abuse of their beer supply will be evident
when they meet the Emperor. That is, if they get to see him in
person. The City rises into view as he nears the top of a hill.

They start down a long slope. A change in the breeze, now
salty and warmed by the hot morning sun, blows across them. The
horses' footfalls awaken wonderful smells form the damp earth.
Huge buildings of marble sprawl in the distance while, at the bottom of the slope before them, the bright sunrise reveals walls the
size of which Vassilis has never seen before. The sea glistens
beyond that, specks of silver on an azure arm stretched along
and around the walls, luring these land-trapped peasants from the
gloom of their somber, mountain world. Vassilis can hardly draw
breath at the splendor of it all.

† † †

A king castles behind a row of pawns. A chessboard teeters on
a pile of books, maps, and geometrical drawings, the kind that

typically bore Michael. He much prefers the sea view from these rooms, and the way they seem to hover above the water. The Bucoleon Palace has always been one of my favorites as well, especially the way the sea laps at the feet of the marble lions guarding the walls.

The Eunuch and the Regent are receiving the new Envoy, so Photios has been left to pass the time with the young Emperor. He hopes earnestly that Michael doesn't start whining to go out and tries to hold his attention even further by talking about some of his latest reading in the subject of mathematics.

"So the need to denote 'nothing',"says Photios, "when one calculates, according to the Indian number system, in fact, any number system except for the Roman, requires the invention of a cipher that is called 'zero'. Has it ever occurred to you that we do not have a cipher to represent the absence of quantity? King's knight to bishop four. Are you following, Your Worthiness?"

"A good move," says Michael. "You are in close quarters to my King. Supposedly he is hiding away in his palace of pawns. Queen's bishop takes pawn. A weak move – but you leave me starved for choice."

Then he yawns, and his gaze wanders to the new drapings, covered in birds and flowers – the product of Abbasid weavers.

"If only I could visit the Abbasid lands, and conquer them as did the ancient Alexandros, as did my father!" says Michael. "Can we talk about something else? Algebra is so dull. Why should an Emperor bother with it?"

"Queen to queen six takes pawn. I'm afraid it's checkmate in two moves."

Michael fiddles with a map. But then he is up, looking out over the bay, his eyes scrunching up at the bright sun which has taken on an eerie brightness. "So why is mother talking to the Bulgar?" he says. "Who cares about them anyway? Aren't they just a wild old lot?" Then another yawn, ill-suppressed.

Photios sighs. "A lesson in political history, I see. Where does one begin? Who does not yearn for our great City, settled by Constantine, enriched by Justinian, and set, as the brightest star in the sky of nations, at the very center of Empire, by the great Heraclios. Need I remind you of these things?"

"Of course you should, I'm a complete idiot, don't you know!" he smiles mischievously. "We will talk more about your algebra soon. But why the Bulgar?"

"Worthiness, we have been struggling with the Bulgar for more than a hundred years. They plunder our Themes and attempt to thrust at our great City. But, even worse, they flirt with the Franks, who, while not being our enemies, are not our friends either. It is the Bulgar, in particular their Khan, Boris, who tries to play us against Louis of the Franks. He woos us both, as a man might woo women, although of course . . . in your position . . . this is hardly an issue, now that it is all decided."

Photios pauses. "Nevertheless, it was your, let's see, great-great grandmother, the great Irene, who first wooed the Franks, that is the great Charles, and was refused. No, that's not right. Irene was Augusta Euphrosyne's mother. Euphrosyne was your father Theophilos' stepmother. I'm not sure if that means . . ."

"Augusta Irene!" he interrupts. "Why does no one talk about her? She brought the Icons back to us, did she not? Why will no one ever say a word about her to me?"

Photios busies himself with the maps, making distractions, searching for something to say. But Michael's eyes are shining with interest.

"Well, it is indeed time someone told you. Irene was a worthy holder of the title of Augusta, actually the first woman to rule as Emperor. But that's only because she took the title for herself."

"And . . . ?" says Michael.

"And she indeed restored the Icons, if only for a time. But it was very difficult for her. She had to convince the court. To make it worse, the Franks invaded our lands in Italy. Then the Abbasid Caliphs Al-Mahdi and Harun al-Rashid humiliated us by forcing her to pay tribute. Finally, Charles crowned himself Emperor of the Romans, or at least the Bishop of Rome did it for him. What was she to do?"

Now Michael is confused. "Was there no one who could be Emperor? Did she not have sons?"

"Yes, she did. She had a son — Constantine — who was . . . not up to being Emperor. But I suppose that is a story for another day." Photios rises as if to leave.

But the young instinctively know deception. Michael gets up as well. "You simply must tell me." he says. "Please, Master Photios. You know I have no one else I can talk to about these things. Mother is always too busy to talk and his Excellency, Lord Dickbreath," in mock falsetto, "is ill-suited for chatter."

"Your Worthiness, as you get older you will come to realize that people rely on what they have seen, what they have done, what others have done, to tell them what should be done. This is often very wrong. Less educated people fear the future because they fear the past. Perhaps learning, even algebra, will one day help them to move from this way of thinking but until then... Do you follow?"

"Yes ... until you started on about algebra again. What is it that they fear?"

† † †

It was at the Palace of Blachernae that I must have had my first glimpse of Vassilis. The Palace stands amid the walls at the very edge of the City. It has become my favorite. I think all Empresses must love its beautiful windows, perfect for treading warily with unknowns. Like the lidded gaze of a cautious virgin they peer out, not quite ready to reveal any inner charms to a visitor, but sufficiently inviting to those with some curiosity ... or ambition!

Her Worthiness had reluctantly let me back into her retinue after Father had woven his usual spell over her. But it had not changed her mind one bit about me. So I am demoted from the "cathedral" to maintaining the Imperial footwear. The smells are horrid, and one can only have limited admiration for boots, no matter how finely worked the leather is. Not to mention that I have to work directly under one of the Master of the Wardrobe's officials, which I find very humiliating.

None of this stops me from wandering over to the windows. I want to see the foreigners. It has been some time since I have been able to see brave men, and, even though these are barbarians, they are so much more interesting than the empty-headed youths or over-opinionated graybeards that seem to make up the court.

The Regent and the Eunuch peer down into the sparse courtyard below, conscious that they are largely invisible behind a pane reflecting the afternoon sun. The guards clatter to attention. I lurk behind the curtains.

Theodora appears amused. I am disappointed. The riders seem fewer and less grand than I expected, not to mention a bit rough around the edges, possibly from their long ride.

"So your plans have borne fruit," she is saying. "The Bulgar are here to discuss tribute and allegiance to us, I assume? Will they ever tire of battle? God knows that we have. How can we find common ground with such barbarians?"

Theoktistos looks away from the window. He knows he can't answer that. "It would be a welcome peace, after so much struggle. But it is too soon to tell. We still need to find out exactly what they want. Methodios and Cyril have not been able to tell us much that we didn't know already."

The party has dismounted and is being held in the entrance chamber beneath our feet. Even though they are barbarians, the Regent has insisted that they be greeted with the usual cool wine, spelt cakes, and soft couches that any visiting patriarch or dignitary might receive. This way they can go back and tell those at home of the special hospitality of the Roman court.

"Whatever happens, I insist we do not let them farther into the City," she murmurs. "It is enough having strangers here in my place of rest and worship." She beckons to the maids. There is still time to finish her makeup and to compose herself. She calls for the brocaded dalmatica and the new gloves, and I am to find some jeweled boots. Digging around in the dirty footwear. How annoying!

14. Old friends, new friends

Photios abandons all etiquette and looks deep into Michael's eyes.

"It happened some eighty years ago. Irene was a remarkable woman. She had taken great care of the Akritai, as well as those of us who lived in our City. She had instructed the army to fight the Bulgar and others, and even tried to marry one of her daughters to the Franks to keep us all safe. But her attempts to give up the Regency to her son failed, at least in her eyes. She grew tired of his ... weakness, his mistakes, both in battle and in court. Oh, and his lack of interest in having children. She loved him very much. But she felt it was more important that somebody strong was in charge of her people." He pauses. There is no response. "Is all of that clear?"

The lapping of the waves is audible in the gloomy, gray sunlight. Michael nods.

"So, ...she ...diminished his capacity,". Michael raises an eyebrow. "In the very room in which she bore him, the Purple Room, where you also flew into this world. Oh, how proud your father was finally to have another son, one who would live on and carry his name. Of course your mother was too."

"What do you mean by saying she diminished his capacity?"

Michael needs to know how deeply unfair life can be — it is far more than simply a quest for comfort and satisfaction. But telling him this is a duty few others seem to want to shoulder. Photios, as always, is a stickler for duty.

"An emperor blinded is not worth much," Photios says. "She had hot irons melt his eyes. There, I can't say anymore."

Michael's frown vanishes, his cheeks pale.

"Do you understand now why everyone ...defers rather than speaks straight to you about it?" Photios struggles for words. "She wept too. After all, she loved him. But she had shown him mercy through this act. She could have had him killed."

He rustles papers, maps, anything he can find, and makes as if to leave. But then Michael reaches a hand out to him.

"Thank you, dear Photios, for this honesty and the courage you have shown me today," he says. "May the Almighty absolve you. I think it is time for the Emperor to make some arrangements of his own."

† † †

They must wait several hours for the first audience, though they are well refreshed with food and drink. Grozdan is restless in spite of Methodios' pleasantly irreverent remarks to pass the time.

Guards arrive and march them down a passageway beyond the antechamber. There is barely enough time to take in the size and splendor of the vast bronze doors in front of them before they are thrust into a large hall.

Grozdan's beard bobs with nerves. He drags silver-ringed fingers over a close-shaven head and pulls at the chains around his neck. Vassilis extracts from under his cloak a small wooden cross which he holds on to, partly in fear, partly out of habit, his coarse woolen stuffs contrasting with the dark silks of Methodios and the rather too elaborate spectacle of Grozdan. Come to think of it, Vassilis is not sure why he is there.

They follow Methodios' lead and kneel. He whispers to them to lower their heads, but Vassilis sneaks a look.

They are in a large hall with open windows. The wind whistles around them. Vassilis marvels at the array of purple curtains, held up in wooden frames, before them.

A horn sounds. "Her Serenity, the Restorer of the Ages," intone voices from the left hand side of the hall.

"The Wise and the Bountiful," chant deeper voices from the right hand side. Attendants appear and slide the curtains out of the way.

The towering, slender frame of what must be the famous Eunuch appears, encased in a white senatorial toga and scarlet cloak. Another set of curtains stands behind him. He waits.

"Hand over the gifts," whispers Methodios, nudging Grozdan.

Grozdan moves forward, head lowered, pushing a large bag of furs in front of him. The Eunuch nods to an attendant who takes the bag away. The second set of curtains is shifted away to reveal the Regent on a backless throne, perched on a raised dais that disappears into a shadowed apse. She is a study of elegant, veiled authority in deep purple, green, and gold.

The Eunuch adopts the usual pomp. "Welcome to our court, Envoy. Be at peace, we are here to use words not swords."

They climb to their feet, and Vassilis lifts his head to look up. "Keep your eyes averted!" Methodios whispers fiercely.

"Your welcome warms my heart and ..." Grozdan responds, struggling for the right phrase, "... and gives us leave to feel at ease." A glance at Methodios reassures him.

"Her Worthiness will deign to discourse at her leisure." the Eunuch says. "Your Greek is most impressive. I see you have made good use of our scholars."

Methodios lowers his head further, in acknowledgment.

Grozdan decides to risk a compliment. She is, after all, a woman. "But my command of your language is humbled by the beauty I see around me."

Methodios is now shaking his head. Her Worthiness is not the slightest bit interested in hearing this sort of thing, especially from a barbarian. In her position, I would have been offended.

"Then ready yourself to be greatly humbled," she replies.

This is not quite the answer Grozdan expects. His eyes flash in anger as he raises them to look at the dais. "Your welcome is as warm as that of the great Louis of the Franks and the Bishop of old Rome. Do you know our cause?"

"You do not address Her Serene Worthiness," Theoktistos retorts, "unless you receive a direct question. Enlighten us. We will hear you speak of it at length."

The Envoy has memorized a small speech. "We seek commerce with wealthy peoples, a union of strength against the northern and eastern threats. Louis has been crowned Holy Emperor by the Bishop of Rome, as was his father, the magnificent Charles. He would have us bow to him in return for a presence at his court."

Theoktistos frowns. "We do not recognize this title for Louis. The holiest of Roman Emperors has always been here in the City, in a long line since Constantine. The barbarians you mention were crowned without authority."

Grozdan expected some resistance to this. "We have it on the authority of the Pope, your spiritual brother, that Constantine gave authority first and foremost to him to anoint kings and emperors. Do you deny this?"

Theodora speaks. "If you refer to that ridiculous fiction, the Donation of Constantine, then the Franks are as gullible as children. It is through Constantine himself that Rome came to Vyzantion, and not through the fabrications and plots of some bishop — even if he calls himself Pope — that we, and none other, can claim the right to the epithet of Holy Emperor."

Vassilis is in new yet welcome territory. "Then where is this Emperor, Lady? Is it true that he is a child still?"

I can imagine the Regent is not sure who addresses her, or whether she cares for this young brute, but she feels compelled to answer. "We rule in his name until he is of age. No authority is in question here."

But as she says this, the doors burst open and Michael stands before them, decked out in full chain mail, with a helmet under his arm, and a purple cloak hooked over his shoulders.

"Indeed, Holy Regent, our authority is not in question here." Michael strides up to the dais where his wiry but short frame succeeds in towering over his mother.

"We acknowledge the presence of the Bulgar envoy," announces Michael, perhaps a touch too loudly.

"We are aware of our brother, the King of the Franks, and his attempts at dominion over you." This comes out in a more regular tone. "Have you yielded yet?"

Grozdan's drink-dulled nerves combine with surprise to leave him struggling for words. He lifts his gaze.

He turns to Methodios for help, then back to the dais. "No, Your Worthiness, we have not, but it is not a question of yielding. It is a question of ..." he leans over to Methodios to confer — then turns back to the throne, and then to Michael, and bows, "...embracing as brothers."

Theoktistos is shaking his head. With a raised hand and rings flashing, Theodora checks him. No doubt she wants to see her son perform. As I will want to see you perform one day, my darling Leo. After all, a young Emperor should learn how to do this sort of thing.

Michael's grin fascinates Vassilis. He has never seen an expression quite like this before, like a young wolf before the pounce.

"An interesting proposal," Michael says, "but hardly appropriate. You are fortunate to be in the presence of the Chosen of God, the one who represents Christ on Earth, and has power over life and death. Yet you talk of brotherhood!"

Vassilis sees that Michael is even younger than him, perhaps by as much as four years. Is this who leads the Romans? My cunning Peasant senses that Michael lacks authority. And he wonders at the slender limbs, the elegant, ancient features.

"But your dominions are smaller, are they not, mighty Emperor," says the Envoy, "as others occupy more of them?" Vassilis recalls the fascinating discussions with Methodios and Cyril of lands and people far away. No doubt Grozdan has had similar conversations with Methodios. The Envoy continues. "The Franks and Lombards have all but taken Italy. And I believe that Sicily and Amorion are now the domain of the Abbasid."

Michael must be aware that the experience of his opponent outweighs his. "I see you and your companions have an excellent knowledge of history and geography, Envoy, but you will find no greater image of God's power than here," Michael responds. "For our strength lies not only in our dominions, but also in the very embodiment of all this, our City, the greatest in the entire world."

"Where does that greatness come from, your Worthiness?" Vassilis says, proud that he is using the correct form of address.

Michael smiles at Vassilis' accented Greek. "Our defenses have never given way," Michael says, "thanks to the protection of the Theotokos, who bathes her people daily in her glory even as they worship her and her Son."

No doubt Theodora allows herself a brief moment of motherly pride. I would have felt this way. But she is also critical of him. He should soften up the Envoy even more.

But I know Michael. He always tired quickly of just talking. He was always driven, constantly, to do something, to provoke someone, to be involved in some new adventure.

"We feel the time has come," Michael says, "for you to see the real City. You and your aides are welcome in our Daphne Palace, where we shall discuss this at our leisure, after my wedding."

He shouts for his mount, and steps briskly from the hall, his retreating footfalls leaving behind silence, then confusion.

† † †

There was Michael, after the wedding and the processions, pacing impatiently along the Balcony, with no clue as to how much I wanted to be up there with him, looking down on the scatter of chariots and horses that would start the races in celebration of his wedding. While I sit hidden in the back rooms, waiting for the Regent to summon me, chafing at the bit, bored to the point of idiocy, Michael frets, watching the mob elbow each other in the ribs while jostling for stone seats.

I understand him well. He wants to be running down the track of the Hippodrome toward his teams, swapping jibes and mock praise with his drivers, slipping a hand over a sweaty horse's back, breathing the acrid smell of horse droppings drying on the hot sand. Instead, he must gaze across at bronze steeds glinting greenly in the high sun, far above the chariots trundling into the stalls. The games must follow the wedding, and then there will be the banquet. Protocol dictates that the people must see the holy couple on the day of the wedding.

The Balcony itself is still cool and relatively empty — he stole here right after the ceremony to be rid of the pitiful cow. He swears that they will keep separate beds. The late summer heat, mixed in with her perfumed sweat, the airs from a flatulent Ignatios, and the overwhelming frankincense, made him gag.

Surely there is time for some wine! Michael beckons a servant — but the courtiers have already begun filing in, in the middle of which are his new Empress-to-be, as well as the Eunuch and the Regent.

The Eunuch comes up to him, placing a purple cloak on Michael's indifferent shoulders and a tiara in his hands. The new wife sidles up obediently, her tiara already at attention, her pitiful eagerness to please Michael adding further to his scorn.

An array of horns sounds a long note. The noise subsides. "The Viceroy of the Most Holy does greet his people," the acclamations begin.

The salute swells up from the crowd, "Worthy, worthy, worthy!"

Michael knows the appropriate formula. God knows he has studied protocol all his life. "Citizens of our New Rome, we greet you in all humility, that you may know that my wife and I serve the most High, the King of Kings."

I am sure that what is foremost on the Eunuch's mind is how genuine the cries and clamor of approval sound, thanks, as always, to the coinage which rubbed its way, in little skin bags, out of the Treasury.

Horns sound again. The chariot stall gates snap open and horse flesh ripples into action. The Greens' laps, counted by twelve granite dolphins on the top of a scoring tower on one side of the stadium, fall away more quickly than those of the Blues, denoted by twelve granite eggs on the opposite tower.

The crowd draws a collective breath as a chariot wheel belonging to one of the Blues falls away. The rider topples overboard, narrowly escaping being trampled by the other steeds, but the crowd prepares to cheer as the final dolphin is removed.

Michael springs from his seat and claps with his hands high above his head, yelling "All praise to the Greens!"

The outpouring from the crowd buoys the Green charioteers across to the steps in front of the Balcony. Michael is all grins to his mates as they bow deeply. But it is only the start of today's races. The Balcony settles down to watch the rest and expects the crowd to do so too.

Cries of indignation and amazement erupt into the settling silence. Two hooded figures climb down, out of the stadium, and onto the sand. Theoktistos screams at the guards. Could this be what the cryptic messages his men intercepted were about? Is this a nightmare turned to reality?

The men walk to a spot below the Balcony and lower their hoods. Two grizzled and dusty faces peer up at the Balcony and salute, even as spear points surround them. Their voices rise over cries of amazement from many in the crowd who recognize them.

"Great Emperor of all that is in Christ's dominion, humble greetings," the men shout in unison.

"Vardas! What trickery is this!" the Regent is up and in a rage, hands twitching. The Balcony chatters in confusion.

Michael leaps to his feet. "Uncle Vardas, Uncle Petronas! You made it! Make way for my uncles, clear the Balcony, everyone out. Now!"

Courtiers stand frozen. The Eunuch screams above the rising noise for the chariot stall attendants to start the next race.

"Come on you pricks, out, out!" Michael bellows at everyone around him. Confusion as people scramble for the exit. Michael must be enjoying the taste of commanding. These last few days he has had more than ever before.

15. Celebrations

Hunters poise, ready to spear a grazing deer nibbling delicately at a bush. Lions and wolves stalk in myriad poses. Water pours endlessly from a half-tipped jar, held by a peasant in a tunic billowing tastefully in the wind. Poseidon roars soundlessly as he rises from the waves, his trident raised to push back the attack of a murky, black cloud.

I can't imagine what it must be like for a village lad whose eyes are accustomed to fields of grass or, at best, rough stone beneath his feet, to see the floor of the Hall of the Nineteen. Vassilis stands, waiting for orders. He cannot stop swaying as the mosaic sparkles and ripples around him. A bright braid of green, blue, and gold tiles winds its way around the edge and corners of this long hall of windowed apses.

His gaze returns to the gilded oval tables set up over the mosaic, encircling the largest raised table at the far end. Each table is surrounded by a half circle of couches, their armrests angled toward the table. My Peasant is not sure where to look first. Oil lamps shimmer and reflect in a film of gold covering the walls. But Michael, already reclining on the first couch, fascinates my Vassilis far more than the glitter. Vassilis follows Grozdan and Methodios to their table, facing Michael's.

Does Vassilis yearn for that lean face, which I, too, have not found unattractive? Does he admire Michael's high cheek bones and girlishly slim frame, the pale skin, the deep black curls descending into the matted grayness of a shallow beard.

Vassilis cannot escape the waves of envy that flood over him, that this is what he should have been by now, what he should have had, if only he had been born in the right place, to the right parents. But regret has never been something my Peasant has dwelt on for very long. And he sees that Michael's attention seems to go no further than his goblet.

Courtiers and family members shuffle in, knowing exactly where to position themselves. Vassilis takes in, with a sharp eye that sets him apart from his brothers and cousins, that rank dictates one's distance from Michael's table. I agree with Photios at least on this: Vassilis' relatives, or at least the few I have met, are as simple as old cloth that has never been dyed.

Vassilis wonders at Michael's disregard for his surroundings, indifference displaced only when the charioteers stumble in. Methodios and Cyril must have told Vassilis of the famous Greens and the powerful Blues. Charioteers of the Green faction have indeed been wildly successful today, but their dignity has already succumbed to the wine. A table nearby receives their sodden frames. To Vassilis it is a mystery that such finely dressed men can get so drunk. Oh, my Vassilis still had so much to learn about the court — to the rest of those assembled these were just charioteers, hardly respectable men at all! But to Michael they were everything, until my Peasant came along.

The short swords and garments of the entrance guards also fascinate Vassilis, but their colorful Abbasid dress brings back memories of the caravan, and images of Wasim come back to taunt him, and perhaps arouse him as well.

From where I stand in my usual spot behind the curtains — ready to respond to Her Worthiness' command — it sounds more like a bazaar than a stately gathering. The buzz is deafening. I am not used to such events, which lie in stark contrast to the sobriety of the daily processions, the long prostrations before the Icons, the ritual chants and acclamations, the endless waiting, only to be prodded into action by Dickbreath or one of his minions.

The hammered dulcimer and lute barely rise above the hubbub of the charioteers. They are loud enough to make some elderly courtiers scowl in disapproval. Prissy oldsters are never far away!

A loud pounding heralds the arrival of the Imperial women: the sun with the moon in tow. Theodora looks magnificent in a full-body gown, silk sleeves billowing out, her hands ablaze with glowing rings and bracelets, beads radiating from her tiara. I should know. I helped her dress for this.

As if to add insult to injury she insisted that I should be the chief woman in attendance. If one didn't know better, it would appear that the Regent was the new bride today. Forgive your mother this moment of chagrin, little Leo, but behind Theodora comes Michael's new wench, a simple, pale white gown and small tiara, silver rather than gold. I'm sure her lithe boyishness appeals to my Vassilis, though he has never admitted it openly to me.

To Vassilis, the first impression of the legendary General Vardas is that of a pompous soldier. But his instincts are already pricked — he wonders if Vardas is foe or buffoon. Could this be the famous general that Methodios told him stories about?

When I peer out again from behind the curtain, Petronas is heading for his place, close on Vardas' heels, thin and purposeful, a man who is everything Vassilis and I imagine a soldier to be. A tough man to those who do not know him, I heard he was a pussy-cat in private. I confess I have longed for his embrace. But no one knew who warmed his pallet at night. Many say he occupies his free hours with prayer and meditation, and little more.

The swaggering prelate arriving next is our beloved Thunderguts, Patriarch Ignatios, who leaves his acolytes trailing behind him, no doubt thrilled to be officiating at the first wedding of an Emperor in living memory.

And this is where Photios comes into my story — this is where Vassilis first saw him. He is slightly late, as usual, and fumbles to arrange himself on his couch.

"Worthy, Worthy," resounds from the gathering as the wedding party arrange themselves around the main table after Michael and Dekapolitessa: Vardas, Petronas and Photios, on their right. Ignatios squeezes his perspiring frame into the space beside Theodora, who takes the other end of the table. Vassilis does not realize it, but it is indeed rare to see men and women dining together in the Palace. It is only the special nature of the Emperor's betrothal that permits this. The Eunuch is not present, which is also strange.

The buzz resumes as the platters arrive, laden with battalions of roast flesh and carcasses of fowl. Armies of fish lie in formation alongside skewered suckers of octopus, halos of squid and naked shellfish. Leafy dark greens trumpet sauces of tantalizing shades, while the fragrances from baskets of hot loaves and bowls of herbs make his mouth water. Of course he cannot partake yet, as he is required to stand in attendance.

Peering out from the curtained pillars I spy the confusion at

the second table as Grozdan fingers the cutlery. Vardas is showing off, a mean grin glistening over his beard as he chews. I inch
closer, in order to pick up what is being said.

"You hold onto the thin part," Vardas demonstrates, "and lift
the food with the bowl-like part to your mouth, like this."

The Envoy blushes, clearly flustered. He balances some meat
on the flat end of a pronged spoon, and then drops it. Vardas continues, apparently oblivious to his embarrassment.

"You might prefer to use the sharp end for that." He spears a
braised chunk and drops it neatly into his mouth. "It is a delight
to be back, dear sister," he announces, raising his goblet to the
Regent.

I can see that, under her makeup, Theodora is annoyed to the
point of exhaustion. Not only has all protocol been abandoned
to the winds, but she has to deal with unwelcome barbarian visitors and, worst of all, her brothers! But her self-control is superb:
dark-ringed eyes and pursed lips are the only clues to her anxiety.

'Your servant speaks Greek," says Theodora to the Envoy. "He
must be one of ours. How did he come to the Bulgar? Did you
capture him?"

"It is not ...," Grozdan begins, "...a tale that would be to
everyone's taste."

Vardas is in the mood to taunt whenever possible. "Oh, I am
interested as well," he says.

"He was once from Chariopolis", says Grozdan, "...near Adrianopolis," he adds when he sees no recognition of this village
name. "He had been left to die. But we took him away and gave
him a life when he thought he had none."

Everyone seems to be waiting for him to go on, except for
Michael, who evinces complete boredom.

"The Khan is a generous man," says Methodios, trying to return to business. "He is interested in his people and how he can
lift them from their misery. They are kind to all, if that kindness is
returned." Grozdan nods gratefully at Methodios.

The others listen but I gaze at Vassilis. He hasn't said a word.
I wish that he would be given leave to speak.

"My young friend here is very modest," says Grozdan. "The
Macedonian cast a special magic over our horses and, once our
Khan's eye fell upon him, the court wanted him for much more."

I can sense the neighboring tables are restless. The young ladies and men mutter and smile behind long sleeves, their eyes on Vassilis. Then slow, rhythmic music rings out. It is the cue for the women. Lifting bracelet-laden arms high above their heads they rise and weave between the tables.

Michael takes in a sideways, pleading glance from Dekapolitessa, to which he responds with an absent smile, raising himself wearily to head for the charioteers' table. There it is exaggerated toasts all around, arms draped around shoulders, sinewy frames bouncing off each other in cruel mirth. I am pleased that Dekapolitessa's eyes are lowered, tears creeping from them at the slight. She has been given a hard path. But there is much for her to take comfort from. After all, she now has the Emperor in her bed. Who wouldn't want that!

Amid all the stateliness, the ugliness that suddenly affronts us is a shock to all but the charioteers, who roar with delight.

A miniature, misshapen patriarch launches himself onto the table, feet landing neatly between the piles of food. It is the dwarf Gryllos, renowned for his cruel antics.

The creature grabs a bunch of parsley and a flagon of wine from one of the platters, pulls out his member, and makes as if to piss on the parsley, but some wine does it instead. He shakes it over the charioteers in mock blessing which gets guffaws, clapping, and shaking of fists in approval.

The parody is obvious. The real Ignatios blanches and eases himself out of his seat. Grisly beards in nearby tables grimly shake their heads and rise to follow him out of the hall ... all to groans of mock disapproval from the charioteers.

The music changes to one of my favorite tunes. Ignoring my responsibilities to wait on Her Worthiness, I swirl with the younger women into the space around Michael's table. I have chosen a pale blue gown today, and my braids are raised into thick rolls on either side of my head, the copper bracelets on my arms showing above my sleeves which I have pulled back as far as possible. When I look up, I find Michael's hungry gaze feeding on every inch of me.

Encouraged by the bawdy cries around him, Michael takes another goblet and emulates my movements. Someone shoves him toward me. He staggers, spills, and then straightens to loud guffaws. Everyone else cringes. The dulcimer rises above the silence.

Theodora is completely silent, listlessly spearing a piece of bread in a bowl of sauce. Vassilis is amazed. The bride is present but no one seems willing to address the affront to her! How do the Romans govern, if they cannot govern themselves, he wonders?

Michael jumps up onto the charioteers' table, slightly less nimbly than Gryllos a few minutes ago.

"Quiet, everyone. That's enough!" Michael says.

The music dies down, as does the buzz.

"Enough ... festivities," he slurs, then slips off the table and walks over to face Grozdan. "We have decided to accept the mission of this Envoy, whose message appears to be one of peace. He has brought gifts, and so it is fitting that we return a gift to him. We would have him take back one of his ladies sister who, we imagine, will be most welcome to the Khan." He beckons toward the curtains, and she emerges, the Eunuch behind her.

Theodora looks furious. It is exactly what we had all guessed: the Bulgar woman who had been idling time away in the Regent's quarters was highborn, or whatever passes for that in barbarian terms. I learned later that this was the Khan's sister, and that these negotiations took place right before the wedding, between Michael and the Envoy. Michael was finally showing some mettle.

He continues. "I have also decided, as the Thirteenth Apostle, to accept Khan Boris into Holy Mother Church. I am prepared to adopt him as a son, indeed to baptize him myself. Take this as our real gift to your Khan, Envoy."

Everyone looks around, uncertain as to what to do. Vardas stands up and starts clapping.

Then people start to rise, hand on hand in unison, leaving the Envoy and Theodora frozen on their seats. Methodios pulls the Envoy to his feet.

Theodora gets up and swirls off, the Eunuch and Dekapolitessa in close formation. I should be following Her Worthiness but I slip behind Vardas' table instead. I want to hear what Vardas and Photios are saying to each other.

"This young one has come a long way since I left," Vardas says. "Why is he still under my sister's thumb? Or is he?"

Photios says "It is a very politic move, indeed. But I wonder how the Envoy is taking it?"

Vassilis told me later what happened at Envoy's table. "This is ridiculous," Grozdan whispers furiously to Methodios. "The Khan is perhaps twice his age. What am I supposed to say to either of them?"

My Vassilis understands what has happened. It is like cajoling a wild steed to do your bidding.

"You should agree," is Methodios' response. "The Emperor has just called your bluff."

16. Diptych

Vassilis staggers slightly, and not just from the wine he has taken on an empty stomach. Theophilitzes, all bracelets and oily wiles, has draped his unchaste hands around the arm of my young Peasant. He herds him toward a divan in the gardens. Flushed cheeks cool under the suspicious breezes of the early autumn evening while torchlight cascades over the fountains, the most distant torches highlighting Michael's shadow, and mine.

Michael and I have slipped away into the gardens together. The celebrations have aroused our desire to the point where reason falls prey to abandon. All those late night embraces by himself have taught Michael to stand to attention at the sight of me. Yes, little Piglet, struck down in the calends of Lampshade and Ovensauce – you have used your muscles well! Father says that I am foolishly brave – but it has always held me in good stead. In the darkness of the late evening, with the celebrations continuing in the background, my legs have crept around his, our limbs entwined in a flagrant mockery of the day's holy rites.

"So," I say, "you have a wife now – what am I to you?"

Michael runs the tip of his tongue along my face and sucks at my fingers as I reach for his cheek. "I dream of your smell," he says. "You are too much for me – and always will be." He is obviously drunk, but still quite delightful.

"I am yours," I say. "Nothing else matters."

While we are locked in embrace, Theophilitzes arranges himself nearby on the bench right next to Vassilis, his eyes everywhere, a ravenous expression on his face. The honeyed tones, the scents of patchouli and tea-tree, the twitching smiles, tactics still unknown to my Peasant, nevertheless awaken strange desires within him.

"Your master's mission to us is flawed," Theophilitzes says. "What would we do with barbarians like the Bulgar – unless there are more like you among them?"

"But surely there is something to be gained from peace," Vassilis says, thinking back to conversations with Methodios.

Theophilitzes places a jeweled hand on Vassilis' leg. "I am sure many women have known peace in your arms."

Vassilis is startled at such forthrightness, and hesitates.

But in my arms, Michael is much bolder. "Shall we play?" he asks, moving his lips down to my neck. When I do not respond he pleads, "Let me take you here, right now!"

"Would you be man enough, Worthiness?" I taunt. I spread my legs, pushing his hands down into the soft fabric of my robes. Let the court know who holds the horns of the bull. My skin tingles. The night air is marvelous.

Gryllos' arrival breaks the magic. "What have we here! The evening is not yet upon us and the night is almost over?"

I am never sure if Michael is amused or annoyed by the jester.

"Gryllos, why are you torturing me?" Michael moans but does not stop what he is doing. "Piss off! Get to the feast. Keep them busy — we still have a task to perform."

But this is Gryllos' function — being a nuisance. "I am here to bless the marriage. But which couple should I bless? I shall leave you in peace — or in pieces. I might even sing the mass later — and perhaps feed them a verse of two of the holy union I see here."

He vanishes.

Vassilis sees the logic now. "I am yours to command, noble sir," he says, smiling at the older man.

"Well said, my Bulgar emissary, you will go far," Theophilitzes flashes a hungry grin. "But this is not the time nor the place. Tell me about your home." His fingers slide up and down Vassilis' arm.

"Which home would that be?" Vassilis says. "I have had many. I know no place as home, except the hearth of my father, which I left many years ago. My mother died when I was young. I have lived in the forests, lived with strangers such as the Bulgar, and even journeyed with the Abbasid. The Bulgar … gave me a wife, and a child. Perhaps that is home?"

"It sounds like you should come to visit me someday and see even more of the world. What do you know of the sea? Of the city of Patras? I would have you meet my patron and her son, a close … friend of mine. He could learn much from you. He knows nothing of the hardships of the world. He still needs to learn how to survive, to be a man amid danger."

"Why, of course," Vassilis says, perhaps a bit too quickly. "I am sure it will be a meeting well made." Theophilitzes raises an eyebrow at this — but the Jester bursts in upon them.

"Blessed be him and him in the name of the father, a holy duality," Gryllos announces as he crosses himself.

Then short arms tuck themselves in at the waist in mock indignation, while he circles Vassilis at a safe distance. "My, what have we here?" Gryllos says. "A broad chest, thick arms, a bold chin, a fine leg. No doubt someone big in all respects."

A frown on Gryllos' misshapen brow contrasts with a wicked grin aimed at Theophilitzes.

"Could it be, my lord, that there are many such men among the Bulgar? If that were so, I would travel far abroad and leave this miserable hole, giving my hole . . . person to them at every opportunity . . . for my betterment of course!"

Vassilis is tense, as if to spring. Theophilitzes places a hand on his shoulder.

"Don't be offended," he says. "He's just a fool feeding at the scraps of our table, there to make us laugh at ourselves, as long as we enjoy him more often than not."

"Not your table, good lord," smirks Gryllos, "which I believe you left behind in Patras, though not your behind, from what I see. My table. The Emperor belongs to me. But I see there is a man here who will belong to no one. And the Emperor's real Empress is behind us as she is under him. Majesty surrounds us!"

He bows to the ground and makes as if to kiss Vassilis' feet. "Your servant, worthiness. But I wonder if I should bend lower while we are all taken from behind?" Tiny buttocks spring into view as the tiny patriarchal habit lifts. Vassilis jumps at him and locks an arm around his crooked neck.

But Vassilis knows he must appear to be in control. So he lets Gryllos slip away to a safe distance.

Gryllos pulls his habit back down, makes the sign of the cross with parsley which appears from nowhere, and cocks an ear as they become aware of our distant panting and moaning.

He turns to face the men. "I bless you, in the name of the most high — in the name of the Archangel Michael who — even now —

is nearing the gates of heaven."

Then he scampers away before Vassilis can land a fist on him.

† † †

The Throne Room is seldom abused in this way. Michael and the men have stolen here after the wedding banquet. Several of the younger Generals have also been invited to drink late into the night to the Emperor's health, as well as some older, supposedly more distinguished courtiers, who seldom let on how much observance they give to Bacchus. Photios is not one of them. He writes that he there only out of a sense of duty to Michael.

They sit at the end of the hall, that is, not near the Throne. Michael has draped himself over one of several couches which he ordered dragged in this evening. Vardas and Petronas recline nearby. The Envoy stands nearby, looking nervous, Methodios right behind him. A eunuch enters, pushing a golden trolley of fruit, its wheels scraping.

Michael's eyes water, presumably from the tartness of an apple he bites into. He seems very pleased with himself, and relaxed. "Your success fascinates us, master Methodios," he says, his mouth full. "You have turned every misfortune into good luck. And brought us this opportunity to deal with the Bulgar."

Grozdan's weary eyes peer out from behind his goblet. "Knowing this man's modesty in all things to do with himself, I will say this much. The Khan asked for an image of the most terrifying thing that Methodios could paint. The result was a vision that could easily strike fear in the hardest man — that of ... what do you call it? ... the second coming of your Christ."

Photios turns to Methodios. "They say that you assisted the Khan in more than just providing Icons for him to gape at?"

Methodios looks embarrassed. "We ... that is, the young man who attended us at dinner and me ... were putting up the image. It was made of twelve separate panels that had to be laid next to each other to achieve the full effect. Of course this meant we were speaking quite loudly in Greek to one another about the spacing of the panels. Then we heard several of the Khan's Boyars talking nearby. They must have thought that, as foreigners speaking Greek, we had no hope of understanding them."

"And does the young man paint as well?" Michael slurs, looking for something more to hold his attention. When no one understands quite who he is referring to, he continues. "The one who accompanies the Envoy. What is his name?"

"On the contrary, Worthiness," Methodios says, "Young Vassilis is an equerry and a fine rider. As you know, the Bulgar love their horses more than anything else."

"How is he at the chariot?" says Michael. "Though surely the Bulgar have little use for chariots in their rocky domain."

Grozdan spots another opportunity to play the diplomat. "No, but they have need of you, Your Worthiness. I mean, this court and your city."

"In one way or another," says Vardas, "our ancestors have ruled since the first Roman republic and its founder Lucius Junus Brutus, thirteen hundred years ago. Or perhaps we should date our lineage to Octavian Augustus, the first Roman Emperor who lived five hundred years later, after the Republics fell. My point is that the Bulgar cannot understand us in a day, let alone have us."

"Uncle, it is good to have you with us again, but you sound too much like Photios, who must fill my ear constantly with facts and figures. I would have our guests enjoy their stay with us while not being bored shitless."

Michael turns to the Envoy. "We must get this young man in one day. I want us to ride together. I am sure he will find himself at home in a chariot."

Grozdan struggles to stand upright. Exhaustion perhaps? "Great Emperor, noble Romans," he says. "My gratitude knows no bounds. I thank you for bringing us to the heart of your City and for your hospitality. I will take back your message of brotherly love to the Khan. But now, I beg your understanding — it has been a long day and I would prefer to retire before morning."

Michael swings his legs to the floor. "Call it brotherly love if you will, but remember it includes submitting his tiara to my crown. In return he gets peace, prosperity, and protection, something no Frank or pope can give him, with the Abbasid never ceasing to play at being a neighbor."

"Understood, Your Worthiness." He retreats, bowing deeply, his braids lolling forward over his shoulders.

Michael reclines again. He nods off. Everyone waits respectfully for His Worthiness, exchanging amused glances. Should he be taken to bed? But he starts when a log falls over in the fireplace, and stretches. Petronas has joined them.

"It is excellent to see you again, Uncles. But why did you take so long?"

Vardas and Petronas look at each other, and chuckle. "We needed an excuse," Petronas says. "You forget your mother did not want us around! With the damned Eunuch keeping control of everything, as always, one has to tread with care."

Michael sighs. "He is owed favors by half the City. This is how he has us all — like an ungelded bull by his intimate parts."

Everyone roars, perhaps a bit exaggeratedly, at the joke.

"Very good." Vardas takes the lead at a nod from Petronas. "But I hope you won't mind if I say that it is obvious that you have let your situation move out of control."

Michael's lips twist. His eyes churn. "Uncle, don't chide — especially not today!"

"My boy, my boy, I do it because I love you, and because I see in you the hope of our Realm. You must not cave in completely to your mother and the gelding. Women, both of them. Now, granted, women are the most powerful force in the cosmos, but the reputation of the Romans abroad ..."

He waits for this to sink in. "Reputation ...do you understand? A City, no, an empire ruled by a woman and a eunuch. Do you not wonder that the Khan is in two minds about which court to play to? You've shown the right strength today. But you need to take control even more!" Vardas slaps the couch suddenly.

"That's quite enough, Uncle. I find this ...discussion quite annoying. This was supposed to be a fond re-acquaintance. I did not expect that you would return to taunt me."

"Dearest nephew, we have returned to help you." Vardas is feigning calm but his neck has turned bright red.

"So what do you suggest?" the Emperor says.

"It's obvious. You exert your presence."

"And if they resist?"

"Come, come, my boy, think! You fight back. Or you remove the opposition. You simply don't cave in to it!"

Michael dips a finger in the wine in his goblet and rubs it along the rim. "I have no qualms about getting the two of them out of the way for a bit, although I am not sure quite what that means. But how will I control this nest of scorpions without them?"

Petronas weighs in. "How have our armies and navy performed while we were away, nephew? We know, as does most of the world. Give the Court a victory, with you in control. Show them your mastery of the field. Inspire them with leadership. The poison in their tails will dry up."

"I really have never understood what passed between you and my ... mother, but she is, after all, the womb that bore me. I cannot wish her harm."

"And neither do we," Vardas says. "After all, she still may be useful to us. But we have to strike at her most powerful ally. Do you think they have bedded each other?"

"By all that is holy, Uncle, I never knew your penchant for such talk!" Though I catch him suppressing a smile.

"Then just leave him to us. It's not the first time I have thought about it, and perhaps the solution is simple."

Vardas stands up. "I am not as young as I used to be. It is time for me to retire too, and wish you many happy years in your rule over the ... domain of your new empress. I wish I could slough off all these ugly old years and take her to my chamber."

Michael stands up and puts his hands on Vardas' shoulders. "You can have her if you wish, Uncle, this marriage has all been Mother's doing. I grew tired of resisting her. It seemed as if giving in would silence her, once and for all."

We wait respectfully for the moment to pass. Vardas extracts himself from the embrace.

"One more thing," asks Michael. "The young Greek. Vassilis. What did you think of him?"

"The servant?" Vardas replies, a little taken aback. "He is just a rogue, I am sure!" He doesn't know yet that this is always Michael's way, like his father, someone who does not see rank as anything of real importance. Perhaps this is how it is when you don't have to earn that rank.

Michael curls back into the couch. Then jumps back up. "I am off to the stables. Bring me my blanket."

Off to sleep among his horses again, no doubt. The gathering exchanges looks of resignation – surely there is a better choice for a first night of nuptials!

††††

Images of the banquet weave through my Peasant's thoughts as he stumbles through the docks. Is this wantonness and debauchery the City of Christ on earth? This is not what he had learned from Father, and, more recently, Methodios.

He is also confused: why are people taken in so much by his appearance? He thinks back to Theophilitzes, not to mention many of the women and some of the men at the banquet hall who looked as if they were ready to devour him. He remembers Father telling him that it was not what he was, but what he did that counted. Father had always said one's strength was nothing to be proud of since it was no more than a gift from God. Yet how often do we forget that what we are speaks so loudly that it is sometimes difficult for others to hear or even notice what we say or do? Vassilis longs for peace tonight, the kind of peace he had enjoyed out in the hills of Thrace. And he longs for Maria too.

He has walked far this evening, or so it seems, having been dismissed rather absentmindedly by Methodios after the banquet. His steps have taken him out of the Palace gates to the harbor, past stinking men crooning in pools of filth, past rag-torn children, some of them hobbling on one leg, begging for a coin. A woman squats to relieve herself in a gutter.

At the dock side, strange images ripple across the waters in front of him as boats of all kinds jostle against each other. This is his first view, close up, of our Golden Horn, and the vessels that travel across it and onto the sea. He has never felt the breaths of so many unknown people on his skin, their bodies bumping him out of the way with complete disregard for his aimless milling about. With the instinct of a caged animal that longs for escape, he knows that no peace will be found here, among the strange tongues, the sharp voices, and the rough calling and chattering.

He pushes out of the throngs and beyond the harbor walls, and lets his feet take him farther along the grassy shore that weaves in and out of the bay. Gradually a soft blanket of stars descends. He sees a bright glimmer in the distance and walks toward it. The light transforms into a bright cross, carved out of a large doorway, filled with golden light from some unknown source. Then he notices the people lying around, in front of the doorway, curled up in rags, most of them fast asleep.

He peers into the light and sees an altar and oil lamps beyond. But the door does not open, so he kneels on the steps to pray.

After what seems like only a few moments, he wakes up to a rising sun, his arms and legs cramped stiffly beneath him, foul smelling people moving around him. But hands are shaking him, forcing him to look up.

"What in heaven's name are you doing here, my boy?" asks a deep voice. A clean-smelling beard and bushy brows thrusts its way into his face. "I have just got back. You can come inside if you want." He looks around and raises his voice as the others pick themselves up. "The rest of you can wait out here."

On a seat inside, he accepts a cup of hot broth from the dark-robed man — a priest, he quickly realizes. The man waits patiently for Vassilis to gather himself but his eyes seem to be dying for a chance to speak. Vassilis looks down at the man's hands and sees they are trembling. He then looks down at himself and is embarrassed at how dusty his feet and clothes are. Father always wanted him to look clean, even after a day out in the fields.

"You are not from here," the priest ventures, "that style of worsted looks Bulgar, if I am not mistaken." He rubs Vassilis' sleeve between his fingers. "I weave for a living. And I should have said that they call me Diomedes. You find yourself at the Church of the Mother of God Valinou."

Vassilis stares dumbly at him. He has lost his voice.

"What is your name?" Diomedes asks softly.

Then the words tumble out. Vassilis talks about the wedding celebrations, the Emperor's marriage, the court. He somehow feels comfortable and refreshed. And there is the opportunity for shared silence, so valuable to my Peasant, and something none of us ever understood — no doubt a yearning for the fields.

The day passes, and Vassilis helps Diomedes with taking care of those less fortunate who often spend the night outside, sheltering from the rain and snow. The two of them carry out various tasks around the church, and prepare a late afternoon meal to-gether. By evening they find themselves walking at the waterfront.

"I should be getting back to court," says Vassilis, though he doesn't want to leave. "Methodios will be wondering where I have got to."

"Which Methodios would that be?" asks Diomedes.

"A monk, the brother of a scholar called Cyril," replies Vassilis.

"Cyril!" responds Diomedes, his features softening in recognition of some special memory. "Do you mean the young student who ... attracted the attention of the Logothete and the Imperial Secretary? Is he returned from Pliska?"

Vassilis responds with a dumb nod, then a shaking of his head to explain that Methodios is back, not Cyril. He is amazed that even out here someone would know his friend. Diomedes puts an arm around him.

"Why don't you stay the night" says Diomedes, "and I will send word to him in the morning that you are safe?"

17. The heart is a lonely mistress

Poor creature! Dekapolitessa has drawn the curtains and emphasized her intent with Persian incense – so much more comforting to her the orange blossom and rose fragrances of the Abbasid than the heavy spices that are customary for many of the women at Court.

But the cloying airlessness stifles Michael. Her delicate frame, like a moth resting on the softest white linens the wife of an Emperor can command, is not enough to quell the sense of duty that gnaws at him. He settles at the end of the bed between the curtains and caresses the slender limbs that lie before him. They are not unattractive, he supposes.

Michael's new wife has tired herself spending another day fretting over her husband's constant absence. The gossip with us women was once a source of joy. Well, if not of joy, then at least of solace. But now it annoys her. Everything has changed for her since her ascension, uncrowned, to the Emperor's embrace. The rewards are few, the loneliness great. Words normally bandied in pleasure and gentle jibing within the Gynaeconitis are now bitten back when she sits down among us. She knows very well that we talk about her endlessly when she is not there.

From what I have heard, her yearning for Michael knows no bounds. Perhaps if I had felt the same way about him he would not have been so interested in me. Perhaps that was what gave me the power to do what was necessary?

She does not have at her disposal the luxury of not loving him. I imagine she wants him to take her in his arms, to feel rose petals fall on her breasts from his hands, to cradle her cheek on his shoulder. She craves his vigor, his passion, his lean boyishness, the paleness of oyster skin against black curls. She wants her lips to be tickled by that beard — to wince and rise as it brushes against her nipples.

The pillow hides her eyes and hands as she senses him lingering ... at her feet. She fingers the small Icon pendant hidden within the goose down. She has never felt so alone in her life. Daily devotions with the Regent and her daughters do not seem to fill the hours well, partly because the Regent distances herself from everyone, even from her, on whom she once lavished affection, presumably because of the weight of the affairs of state.

She feels as if she has failed them, and him. It is as if her life has been displaced, as if her rich garments carry her body through the required daily rituals, but cannot lift her soul, which is only moved by her new husband.

Michael's lips begin their cautious descent — a meek sparrow pecking gently at her cheeks, her shoulders, alighting fleetingly on her breasts, before swooping down. I know well his favorite parts. But she is both ravished and scandalized by this attention — she cannot stop herself from twisting and crying out as his tongue finds her tender spot, though her mother warned her against making sounds or acting out her feelings. Men like the Emperor might be disgusted at anything that smacks of whorishness. She has been instructed not to move, not to distract him from his pleasure in any way, not to imply that anything is for her benefit. Everything in total submission, went the lesson.

Poor thing! I am sure she is content to possess a few moments like this, however short. But if I were her, my mind would wander. Does he sample other pleasures: the women who wait for trade in the filthy market, or possibly the barbarians who clean the kitchens? If she had the slightest ability to think I am sure she would have realized, as everyone else did, that nothing aroused Michael more than his horses and me. Until, of course, the wine took place of precedence.

I would happily have set her mind at rest, if I could have been bothered to spend much time with her. I imagine her giving voice to a rising wave of pleasure. Here she is pulling his mouth toward hers, feeling his hands on her shoulders, her neck, her sides.

But why will he not take her? With gathering impatience, she reaches down and lifts his tunic only to find that her hope was in vain. His sad face hangs over hers, his eyes are hidden. A further kiss is exchanged, a whiff of wine left in its stead. He does not linger. She lies, cold and naked in the semi darkness, the sheet shrouding her spread limbs.

Does she stab impatiently at herself, finding the source of the fire which glowed but is fast dying? Do her fingertips mix the shame of the pleasure she finds there with the pain of being left alone? Does she drink deep from the wretched, tortuous brew that wells up from her disappointment, hemlock and syrup that swirls hot under her palm and bubbles up, along her arm, through her breast, into her quenched heart – now cold with despair?

But she is not me. So how could I ever know?

† † †

Letters are ordinary enough things, yet how splendid they can be! When Father is far away and I am worried about him, and then a letter suddenly arrives, I feel as though he is suddenly right in front of me. It is a great comfort to have expressed my feelings in a letter even though I know it cannot yet have arrived. If letters did not exist, how miserable life would be! But when a reply arrives, it is as if I have taken a drink from a mountain spring.

Some time has passed since Father journeyed to attend to matters in the court of the king of Denmark, matters in some ways not that different to what we encounter here, it seems. He writes that ten years ago the king had exiled his sons, Rorik and Harald. These brave men went on to fight the King of the Franks for a place called, quite strangely, Friesland, after which the King befriended them. Then a new leader arose and Rorik and Haraldfell into disgrace. Rorik escaped imprisonment, turned against the Franks and returned to the Danish court to assume the throne. But now he has died, killed in battle. Father has no idea what will happen next.

How good it must be, I wonder, to be in the arms of one those bold Thulians, men who can love a woman by means of strength and simplicity alone, without recourse to seduction and intrigue. I yearn for such a man to take command of me. Rather than the sweet but ineffective little mother's boy whose ways are charming but more and more . . . predictable.

Silly girl! What will I think of next? Such men are like Father's bodyguards. My desires are instantly curbed. Imagine them opening their mouths. What foulness might pass their lips! I haven't even mentioned contending, at best, with a creature who only bathes at the end of the summer or, at worst, was not opposed to sharing his body with small insects.

I try to imagine what it is like to be one of those wives who faithfully serve such husbands, holding not a single exciting prospect in life, yet believing they are perfectly happy. This fills me with scorn. Often such women are of quite good birth, yet do not try to find out what the world is like. At least Michael is fine smelling, gentle and cultured, and not that unadventurous. If only the Eunuch had not persuaded the Regent otherwise.

How I miss Father! I long to nestle in his broad arms, my brow being tickled by his thick beard, to breathe in his smell of soft leather and clean metal. I enjoy teasing him about his developing girth that, in its own way, is quite comfortable for a daughter to rest on. I would love to listen right now to his travel stories, his tales of strange peoples and mountain passes, to succumb to his quiet but vicious joking about the goings on at court, both here and in the north.

I throw myself in desperation onto my bed. What will become of me? I have not seen Michael since the night of the banquet, and the Regent has stopped calling for me. Word has probably gotten out about what Michael and I have been up to. The way Mother has tried to comfort me, with gifts of flowers and sweet cakes, suggests even she knows what has happened.

If Father were here he would immediately have sharp words with me for endangering his position, then roar in approval at the idiocy of it all, and then rush off to see the Regent and make amends. But right now, until he returns, I can do little but wait.

† † †

While I ponder these rather gloomy thoughts, at least for me, the steps tumble past Michael's feet. The gardens are a welcome relief. He nearly shamed himself by retching in Dekapolitessa's chambers. Or so he told me later, when he would try to convince me that she was of no interest to him. I don't know why he bothered — I believed him.

His feet pound the pavement, as if to rid his blood of her, and the Palace gates open before him. Can she ever guess how much her simpering shyness brings him no pleasure? He descends into the market place, shaking his head to clear it, only to breathe deeply the clouds of cooked meat and burned spices. His feet splash in water reeking of fish. He has seldom been here before, and never knew that there was a huge statue of a wild pig just visible over the heads of the traders, next to a column covered in tasteless images over which someone has draped a blanket.

Most courtiers would consider themselves better off dead than to be seen here, among shoppers and sellers — in short, scum. Syrians, Persians, some even more foreign, their lidless eyes peering suspiciously over heaps of cloth at him, continue to shout at each other in languages he does not recognize.

He must find something to drink. He weaves through the spices and fruit, the rows of sandals and cloth, the swinging joints of meat, the piles of honey cakes and peppers, when his elbow catches a basket of eggplants, sending the dark globes tumbling to the ground.

Long, dark hair turns in rage and words swipe at him before the woman sees the scoundrel for who he is and drops to the ground in obeisance.

Michael is all apologies. Her tender cheeks tremble with tears, her lips with rage reined back. Kneeling down next to her, he is a clumsy hand at collecting her tumbled wares. She tries to stop him; their palms embrace at an unsuspecting vegetable and tug in opposite directions before she slips and falls in front of him. Michael's grin greets her as she climbs back to her feet.

"You are in bad luck today ... I am not myself," Michael says. "Let me help you put this back together. I have no right to be a nuisance to you."

"Your Worthiness, it is not your place to concern yourself with these things." She gazes, now not so humbly, at the young visage in front of her. "You have your father's eyes and ways. The Emperor Theophilos came to the hospital where I was recovering when I was a young girl. He held me in his arms. I remember his eyes and smile, just like yours."

"I am sorry that you suffered. And glad that he was kind to you. I wish I could remember him."

"I thank the holy martyrs that I have seen you today, Worthiness. This ... has been our Lord's way of reminding me what I need to thank Him for daily." She gathers herself and her vegetables in a broad sack and moves hastily away.

"Why ... why are you leaving?" Michael wants to know. "Are there no buyers today?" When she ignores him, he fights through the throngs to reach her. "Stop. Let me help you carry that," he says, finally reaching her and pulling on her arm. He gently takes the sack from her shoulders as she waits obediently.

From a speechless trot that has left Michael breathless, they burst into an eating hall. Michael sets the bag down gently and calls for wine and food. He notices nothing of the stares and raised eyebrows.

Michael leads her to a seat and arranges the plates and bowls the keeper brings before them. "No cutlery I suppose," he jokes as he sits down. She doesn't understand this. He smiles sheepishly.

"We eat with metal in the Palace," Michael says.

"I am not from the Palace, Worthiness, as I am sure you know. This is where I work and live. The keeper has no idea why you are here. He probably fears some kind of trouble." She looks down at the table. "You should ... feel to free to leave, Worthiness."

An awkward silence unwinds. Michael fumbles with a spoon, pours some wine for each of them, and drains a bowl. "It seems I am no end of trouble to those around me," he says.

She looks up. He is drawn by the decades hiding behind her gaze, in the wrinkles that clothe her eyes gently, and in the compassion that they guard fiercely.

"Then you must become happy with yourself," she says. "For it is only when we love ourselves that we can love others, and be loved by them."

The words buffet him like a tempest on a lost bark, flung about by the waves. Can a simple one as this have so much understanding? That she can see straight through into his soul?

Anyway, what was there to love? Michael didn't tell me, but I know that this humble mistress of the market had forced him to look inside, to the rising panic that made him want to discard everything, especially the things he loved more than life itself.

What is there left to say? An urn of soup arrives and a ladle dishes out vegetables and broth. With a muttered, "Yes, yes, you are right. I must go," Michael is on his feet again. "God absolve you, my child." The empty platitude escaping his lips echoes deafeningly within him.

18. Hints and suggestions

A WEEK LATER, IN THE FALL OF 855 AD
Torches burn a way through the stifling darkness as Photios, Vardas and Petronas descend the steps. Or so Photios writes. The march of soldiers fades, to be replaced by echoes and dripping water. The entrance to the Cistern of the Forty Martyrs lies right beneath the broad, busy road that is the Mese. The entrance is so neglected one can hardly see it on the roadside — hundreds must pass it daily and not be aware of it.

Vardas is bursting with good charm. "It is good to see you in private again, old friend," he says, slightly out of breath. "How have they been treating you? As you can see, we have come here so we can speak freely."

"You know I don't care what happens as long as they leave me to my work," Photios says. "Although the atmosphere of ... conciliation is sometimes a bit stifling — the Logothete and the Regent are too eager to keep Ignatios on our side. We have to tread warily with the monks. One never knows when one might put a foot wrong."

"Little has changed, eh?" Vardas says. "We are gone ... what is it ... nearly ten years? It is as if we had left only yesterday."

"The wounds are old, time will heal all," says Photios.

"I'm not so sure. What are we to do with the situation?" Vardas is shaking his head. "It requires much more than time."

Squeaking, slithering and dripping fill the silence.

"Well, it is clearly untenable," Vardas continues. "My sister has Michael squashed into a corner. The Patriarch is throwing his weight around, and the Eunuch fumbles on. How long can this go on?"

Petronas fixes Photios with that quiet, steely look of his, one he has used often, I am sure, on disobedient officers.

"My only concern is for Michael," Photios replies. They nod, furiously in agreement.

"What progress with your students?" says Vardas. "Any thoughts about that academy we once considered setting up?"

"An academy? What a wonderful thing that would be if only I could free up the time. In addition to my normal duties, and dealing with a Patriarch who does not cease engaging my staff in pointless pursuits, I am now preparing an embassy to Baghdad. When can I find the time to debate with students?"

They chuckle politely. Vardas points a finger at Photios. "We need to talk about this," he says. "I learned something in Athens, of both how and how not to maintain a school of learning. We must discuss this in more detail when the time is right. But what is old Thunderguts up to these days that you are so beside yourself with aggravation?"

"The court is riven by disagreement over what our stand should be regarding the followers of Paul of Samosata," says Photios. "Although I fundamentally disagree with their beliefs, I say let them alone, they do nothing to worry us, the few that are left. But the Patriarch will have no living Iconoclasts in his see, and claims the Pope's backing in this. I think we should have more practical concerns. And the Regent is forced to listen to him. The monks of the Stoudion are right behind him."

"I had no idea that it was quite that bad," Vardas says. What a liar! He must know how bad it is, or they would not be meeting in this way.

"We will take care of Ignatios in due course," he says, placing a broad arm around Photios' slight shoulders. "I see that now. But first let me ask you to consider the source of our problems. Who has led the expeditions? Who carries out every whim of the Regent? Whose command do you all follow?"

"What are your plans?" asks Photios.

"A little ... boosting of morale," Vardas says. "The Paulicians are as good a foe as any. I trust I can rely on your support. I am also relying on you to make sure that the anointing of the Spatharoi that will be held in late November will take place outside the City. Only take care that the Eunuch is not invited. It is arguably too minor a ceremony for him to be involved in."

"That is unthinkable," Photios responds. "It always has taken place at the Ayia Eirene. What do you suggest I do, relocate it to Ephesus?"

Vardas chuckles. But the flames reflect in his eyes. "All you have to do is make sure it happens away from the Palace. How about at Blachernae? In return, I promise that we will find ways to ...

simplify the situation with regard to the Patriarch. This will make your life a little easier, I'm sure."

"That can be done. I will do my best to arrange for my trip to Baghdad to be brought forward."

"An excellent idea!" Vardas says. "Yes, do what you can. We will take care of things while you are away."

"But I want no bloodshed," Photios says. "The days of sacrifice are over for us. You do not know what hardships we have endured while you enjoyed yourselves abroad. We are in good times now. I would like to keep it that way."

This gets an exchange of glances and staged nods. Clearly a decision has already been made. Perhaps it will be nothing more than a public humiliation.

"Are we done?" says Photios. "Surely we can find a more amenable place to talk in future. I hate the skulking. And the mortar looks quite rotten to me — I wouldn't be surprised if it all drops down on us at any moment." This gets another chuckle.

They traipse up the steps. "One more thing," Petronas says. "We'd feel ... safer if you assigned us some guards, say a unit or two. Could that be arranged?"

† † †

At the service in the local parish the previous Sunday, Diomedes had reminded his flock of the story of David against the mighty Goliath — meaning the Iconoclasts. And in the midst of warm embraces that night, Diomedes had explained to my Vassilis that Patriarch Ignatios had instructed all priests, both within the City and out in the border lands, to weave the anti-Iconoclast polemic into every sermon. Battle could resume at any time. The people's hearts needed to be ready to support the Emperor with their prayers and their bodies if he were to go on campaign.

Perhaps this is why my Vassilis finds himself where he is today, in a wrestling hall, fresh sand especially laid for the occasion. He has agreed to pit himself against a Paulician prisoner for the sport of it — something Theophilitzes arranged. The Paulician is nearly twice his age and size. How do they get so big, I wonder? I suspect their land is more abundant than ours. Are they big in all ways that one might find satisfactory?

The Imperial trio arrives. The gathering quietens and makes way for Vardas, Michael, and Petronas to take the only couches in the hall, right at the edge of the wrestling floor. Theophilitzes navigates his perfumed mass between the throng of charioteers to hover behind Michael and Vardas. Vassilis is reminded of his first time in the ring in Pliska. Perhaps I would not even be putting my pen to parchment if the Khan hadn't noticed him that fateful day all those years ago.

The myth of Goliath, at least from the point of view of my Peasant, seems painfully obvious right now. Though the Paulician is a good head taller than him, Vassilis is counting on the fact that he will be weakened by months in captivity. He recalls quite clearly some of the Bulgar's wilder tricks. He plans to tire the big man out, and then use his waist as the grapple point.

Of course I wasn't there to see all this — but he told me about it later, much later, and he told it to me quite often, whenever it matched my pleasure. I would have been thrilled to see these fine specimens, their bare limbs oiled, ready to spring at one another.

But my Vassilis' beauty was by far the greater, of that I am not in doubt. Back then, he wore his twenty-five years remarkably well. Neither tall nor short in stature, his long, brown hair he often dressed Bulgar-style, in a rough tail, hanging mildly tamed over well-muscled shoulders. The finest dark hair lay scattered across his arms and legs. Pale cheekbones, roughened slightly by years of living much of the day outdoors, indulged my lips, as did the skin of his chest, stretched over tight ridges. And dare I point out my fascination with his shining light, either erect or flaccid? I enjoyed it often enough then, though now I have that opportunity much, much less.

Sometimes when we made love, his arms pinning mine to the bed, his body cupping mine, I imagined this scene. The men lunge at each other, their sweat mixing with the oil on their skins, making it impossible to hold on to anything. I can see their bodies slipping from hold to hold, their corded muscles straining for release, and with mounting tension, the final, convulsive, throw. Amid my hoarse cries for more, and his steady passion burning within me, I became more acquainted with this scene than if I had actually been there.

The final throw sends the Paulician tumbling back so his head hits a pillar. The audience sits frozen, unsure, until the first groan is heard. Then they are all around my magnificent Peasant, clapping him on the back and showering him with praise. Vassilis begins the ritual prostrations as the crowd parts for Michael and Vardas, but Michael quickly stops him and lifts him to his feet, his eyes shining.

Need I say that Theophilitzes is right behind my Vassilis, taking every opportunity to touch this gleaming treasure wherever and whenever possible.

† † †

Photios writes that the clutter in the map room is unimaginable. Just days away from his trip to Baghdad, Photios is not himself, rushing to respond to a special audience requested by Patriarch Ignatios.

Vardas' return has many people on edge. He has already had words in many quarters, and pledges of support for an academy have reached Photios' desk. This through Vardas' preferred approach — agreements struck through shared meals and promises of favor at court.

The Regent, to her credit, is in favor of an academy. She has allowed Photios to take funds from the Treasury for the refurbishment of the Magnaura, and has also approved a very handsome provision for his trip. In turn, he has promised to take charge personally of the restoration of the Icons in the Ayia Sofia, on his return. Now Photios must listen to the Patriarch's illogical insistence to pursue the Iconoclast Paulicians.

Vardas paces the map room along one side of the long table, scattering scribes and servants out of his path. The Regent occupies the center of the other side of the table, Ignatios stands next to her, the Eunuch behind them.

"Explain it to me again," Vardas says. "I am not clear on where this is going, and why we should concern ourselves."

"It is crystal clear!" retorts Ignatios. "What I don't understand is your involvement in this decision."

There is no response to this. Ignatios continues. "You promised you would reconsider, Worthiness. It is appropriate that we move once again to rid ourselves of the festering heresy in the east." He stands up as if to deliver a sermon. "Why, Her Worthiness' own homeland is in danger! How could we not take a stand?"

"But in danger of what?" asks Theoktistos. "We are not dealing with the Bulgar, or Pecheneg savages. There are no raids for livestock, no displays of aggression on the part of the Paulicians. I fail to see the real issue."

"We are all in terrible danger of the Iconoclast heresy. The specter looms!" hisses Ignatios. "Even Pope Nicholas has expressed his concern."

"Now that is hardly an issue." It is Photios' turn to be indignant. "I fail to see why these matters would concern him at all."

Ignatios is sweating. "There is real risk that the Paulicians will find common cause with the followers of Mohammed. They have been of little concern lately, but in time we will face danger from both our own people and the Abbasid."

"I agree, holy Patriarch," replies Vardas, to raised eyebrows. "Sister, I see the logic here. I advise action."

"It is not clear who gave you the authority to advise us," Theoktistos' slightly tremulous tones pierce the air.

"Indeed," says Ignatios. But we can barely hear his next words. "How dare an adulterer inform the most holy Regent on matters of which he knows so little."

Glances dart around the room. Vardas blushes, though not out of embarrassment I'm sure.

"If Your Worthiness will agree this," says Ignatios, "then do it as a mother caring for our Holy Church."

Vardas smiles. "I am an old man — you must allow me my pleasures. They are few, and when they cross my path I do not decline. They are not the issue here."

Theodora has been silent all along. Her fingers move to the Icon pendant on her breast. Then she speaks. "I am open to all advice. From what the Logothete informs me, we have the resources." Then she fixes her dark eyes on Photios. "You yourself have written in protest against the Paulician heresy. Do you advocate teaching them yet another lesson in power?"

All eyes turn to Photios. He blushes. "Indeed I have written, Worthiness, and much on this topic, as you well know," he replies. "While I abhor the shedding of blood, I am able to take a stand in principle, and it is one over which I have no doubt. I recognize that if we leave the Paulicians to their own devices we do them a disservice. Our Lord will be a far more ruthless judge of what is right in this case than our blades."

Vardas looks pleased. Theodora frowns. Reading Photios' words, I am glad that she disagrees.

"I find it hard to believe my ears." Theoktistos' says harshly. "Do you dare to advise Her Worthiness so poorly? Are you all completely bereft of sense? We all know that the last campaigns did not achieve the decisive blow we intended. Let us not forgot that diplomacy with the Bulgar may yet bear sweeter fruit than combat. Perhaps it is time for us to try this with the Paulicians."

"Diplomacy?" sneer Vardas and Ignatios almost as one. Vardas goes on. "It is a question of discipline! How could you know — it would be like using diplomacy with ... children. We all know that they require a proper, harsh lesson. Even Photios agrees."

The Regent is on her feet. The others move deferentially aside and lower their heads. Lately, she has insisted on ceremony.

"I find it hard ... " she begins, "to understand the reason for another offensive against the Paulicians. We have already moved against them most decisively. The result? They escaped farther afield, from Crete to where they are now, deep in the heart of Anatolia. In short, it did not work. I see no reason to squander our resources trying again."

"It did not work, dear sister, because you had the wrong people in charge." Vardas throws this at Theoktistos.

"You dare again to question my authority?" Theodora faces Vardas directly. "I insist you do not forget that you are in this court out of my ... sense of duty to kin. Now that you are returned, I had hoped that you would be a friend to your nephew, not another cross for me to bear."

She sweeps from the room. As she leaves, I send Vardas a questioning glance? He gestures casually, as if to say that all has turned out as expected.

Ignatios brushes past Photios. "The Bulgar are still not ours," he smirks, "though our brothers from Rome have been making some progress. Remember this, the Bulgar too will need a show of force in good time. Just as you say."

19. The enemy within

How wonderful to be able to travel abroad, to the east. It is years since I have ventured anywhere, and one tends to forget that people's lives, often very different to one's own, exist outside our City walls. I devour Photios' words of his trip to Baghdad. He writes that the day begins uneventfully for him and Cyril, though damp and wet, as they board the ship to Bithynia, to embark on the long trip along the well-beaten roads and tracks.

They plan to take the roads across Anatolia rather than the sea route via Damascus, as the passage thereafter would have been too risky. But they have decided on as few stops as possible, partly because every day wasted is another day when brothers suffer in the hands of our enemies, and partly because this is not the right time for the Emperor's emissaries to be abroad, even if their mission is to the Caliph of Baghdad. Letters have been sent well in advance to smooth their passage as much as possible.

Photios' first opportunity to act as Imperial ambassador to the Abbasid both intrigues and dismays him. Records indicate that there are at least forty-five Roman soldiers being held in the Caliph's cells. He is to sue for their release, and to use all his powers of persuasion. Perhaps he will even get to see his old friend Leo the Mathematician again.

One day, my curious Leo, I will show you what he wrote of that week and a half of travel. But nothing captures his eye more than the magnificence of their destination. They take most of the afternoon to cross the sweltering streets of Baghdad, over bridges and vast gardens, and through as many crowds milling about on them as one can find in our own glorious City. The main difference is the absence of those refreshing sea breezes.

The Caliph's officials do not impress Photios, though the Palace steals his breath away. He can see why Theophilos had the Vryas Palace built the way he did, though it is but a humble replica. The

Abbasid have a softness of line and a taste for space that Roman buildings cannot match. Next to them our courts seem harsh, angular, and far too large.

The officials are most polite and hospitable but, alas, the Caliph is not in residence. They direct Photios and his party north, to the new capital of Samara. He discovers that Leo is also in Samara, and an official at the House of Wisdom provides him with the names of people to contact.

After another day's travel they arrive at the Caliph's new residence.   The audience lacks any ceremony.   His Highness al-Mutawakkil waits for them in a small, peaceful chamber surrounded by doorways beckoning out to greenery on all sides. The trickle of water from both indoor and outdoor fountains is like balm to the ears. His white robes and turban contrast with the gleam from a polished wooden seat, while his slippered feet rest on a dazzling rug of indigo, black, and white covering the floor of the entire chamber. He is very old and soft-spoken, though it soon becomes clear that this gentleness hides a much more cynical heart.

It takes Photios a while to broach the subject, as the conversation always seems to turn to construction. Has Photios seen the new mosque? What does he think about the network of irrigation — is it anything to match the Roman aqueducts that feed our City? At the risk of being bored long before his mission is complete, Photios plays along with the Caliph's obsession with order. This brings up a subject that makes Photios uncomfortable.

"The women from the west have a special place in the order of things," says the Caliph. "We find them very desirable indeed."

"I am delighted to hear it," says Photios, modestly inclining his head.

"Whoever wants a slave girl for pleasure, should take a Berber," announces the Caliph. "Frankish women are very hard workers, though no one can beat us Persians at nursing children.' But Roman women are widely known to be the most desirable. This is why you keep them in veils, is it not?"

Photios and Cyril are at a loss for words. The Caliph continues. "In fact the King of the Romans must be the king of all humans because his subjects have the most beautiful faces among humans, the best-built bodies, and the most robust constitutions. And Roman women are known to be the best at keeping precious things safe."

I read with horror what Photios writes about the number of Roman women the Caliph has enslaved in his ranks, many of them mere girls. Photios is wise enough to see where the conversation is heading, so he moves quickly to dispel all doubt as to the benefits to the Caliph of the release of our men. Would a one-time donation to the Caliph's building projects help, he suggests? He must tread carefully — this could be taken as an insult, given the wealth all around. Indeed, currency does not seem to interest the Caliph much. If not money, then goods? The Caliph smiles at this. Clearly he is not lacking in anything. Then he mentions Abbasid warriors captive in our City.

The deal is clinched when Photios promises to provide several hundred rolls of purple-dyed silk for the Caliph's personal use, in addition to an exchange of prisoners. Photios and Cyril are rather pleased at this result, particularly because it means that that they can use the far quicker sea route for their return, with Abbasid warriors escorting them, via Antioch.

††††

Let's get back to my Peasant, who is curious to know why he has been called to the administrative offices. Apparently, there is a request for him, says one of the clerks. Does he know Master Theophilitzes? Why yes, of course, he nods.

The clerk repositions a pumpkin seed in his mouth, showing yellowed teeth and ink-stained fingers. "Well then, he wants you to visit him in Patras. He has mentioned your name, and wishes you to meet the Lady Danielli and her son. Considering the gift of hospitality you owe us, is that too much to ask? You will accompany one of her caravans which returns in a week." The clerk disappears suddenly and Vassilis wonders if he has been dismissed.

Vassilis has no wish to leave his new life. The last two months with Diomedes have been restful. The priest's wordless gentleness has been a relief from the daily shock of the court, the excess of wealth and ornamentation, the gossip, the harsh busyness. They've shared long talks into the night, confidences and embraces on cool walks, daily meals and ... let us say ... a hearth. He has never before felt such fondness for any man, not even his father or brothers.

Methodios, always conscious of Vassilis' welfare, had arranged work for him in the stables. He loves the fine horses dearly. He has never seen animals so well cared for to meet the needs of polo, parade and war. And he delights in learning from the skilled equerries the kind of training that turns beasts of burden into vehicles of elegant but deadly utility.

So he is lost in thought as the clerk turns to him again. "The Lady Danielli is a great source of revenue for the City, did you know that, my boy? Just don't let on that we need her as much as we do."

The patronizing done with, the clerk dismisses him by pushing a greasy pouch across the desk and burying himself in a gray codex, a fresh pumpkin seed between his lips. My Peasant bristles, but slips it into his bag anyway.

Back with Diomedes that evening he faces the priest's downcast gaze. It is the same pain that he saw in Maria's eyes, only the priest has already resigned himself, whereas she had been bitter and questioning.

So he does not resist at all when Diomedes caresses his lips and runs fingers through his hair. Their beards brush, their sighs echo like distant thunder as Diomedes' hands find their way lower and lower. The attentions are not unwelcome to Vassilis. Nearly spent, he turns Diomedes around and pushes him gently face down onto the bed, his arms splayed out like a cross.

They have lain together here for so many months without more than touching briefly, albeit tenderly. As Vassilis pulls the priest's britches down he hears cicadas in the distance. Their song must be an ode to him, the traveler. So he holds Diomedes tight to his chest as he eases inside him, intent on pleasing him the way he might a woman, on returning the love he has freely given. Does he realize that those who care for him always will be victims of his desire, his yearning for something more — he knows not what?

The priest cries out with the pain that turns to pleasure, the sundering that begs for submission, the offering that is the ultimate benediction. Vassilis decides that he prefers the giving far better than the getting.

† † †

A bloated evening sun bulges from black clouds, reddening the light in Theodora's chambers. Even though it is not quite cold enough to have a fire, the Regent has made us light one for her.

She uncoils her hair, shedding the layers of clothing and jewelry that make up her court persona. I watch obediently, wishing that the fresh robe waiting in my hands was for me instead.

The others are drawing the bath. We know that Vardas' return must be foremost on her mind. She had her reasons for sending him off before — now she has to deal also with the resentment he, no doubt, harbors against her.

A dulcimer softens the loud crackling from the fireplace as the Eunuch emerges from the shadows. His hands flutter from pocket to sleeve, then to his face, cupping his mouth in a palm, then back to his sleeves.

"They're playing a dangerous game," he says.

"Come, come. That's all in the past."

She rubs her face, gazes in the mirror at the insistent wrinkles on her brow — more like natural markings one might say. Certainly not bad for a woman of her age!

The Eunuch paces the floor. "I continue to have misgivings. I approached the Captain of the Palace Guard this morning with my usual ... gift for the New Year, but he placed the gold back on the table. He has never refused before. He looked embarrassed and left hastily, mumbling something cryptic about how this was not a Christian way to govern."

"Oh, do sit down. Vardas is harmless. He may even be good for Michael. Such chagrin at a simple soldier's return hardly becomes the great Logothete." She smiles.

The Eunuch perches at the edge of a couch. His head is in his hands. "I have no idea what is going on, and that is mainly what concerns me."

As the sun sets I am delighted to see that the lines on her face appear in greater relief.

"Sadly, dear friend, you are such a worrier," the Regent says, combing her hair. "But I thank God for it, for without you by my side, I would have not been able to bear the burden that was left me." She puts the comb down and reaches for him.

"Together we have ruled wisely," she says. "Now the Realm is ready for anything. Let us leave past disagreements behind."

Theoktistos relaxes onto the couch. I understand these two well. The Eunuch feels safe with her. She always knows what she wants, and takes care of her own, even to the death, as long as no one crosses her.

"You know I have always been yours," he gets up, arranging his tunic neatly, "since we played as children in the fields of Paphlagonia. I had a different path to follow. Mine was to lose my manhood in order to gain some standing in the court. Yours was to be the perfect wife to an Emperor. But this is also why I am concerned — even for your life." He looks down at his feet.

Christ, Ruler of All! The man who once instilled awe in me is like a terrified child.

The Regent's robe drops to the floor, revealing surprisingly firm limbs for her age. There is nothing so ready to evoke envy in me than a woman who does not show her age!

"Leave us now," she turns to dismiss me.

But her words are drowned by a loud crashing from below, followed by shouting. The guards are being ordered to stand aside! I quickly pick up the robe and drape it around her shoulders. There is no time even to straighten her hair as she heads for the stairs.

The Eunuch dives behind the couch as infantrymen fill the chamber.

"What is this? Stand down, I say!" her words are shrill.

Vardas tramples in behind them, breathing heavily. "Sister, we have no quarrel with you. But the traitor behind you is another matter. Leave us, that we may deal with it in the appropriate way."

I realize why Vardas is so respected on the battlefield. His words fall like chain mail on stone.

"How dare you, brother, walk in here and command in that voice! You are still a guest in our City, only recently returned."

"Let this go. Michael wishes it. Let us make a clean start. Take him!"

The other women and I stand frozen and astonished.

"No, you cannot! No, by the Theotokos," roars Theodora. Vardas throws an arm none too gently around her as if to restrain her. The guards surround the couch. She struggles, getting her hair in a complete mess as tears of rage and spittle pour from her.

Even I pity her. Who understands her loveless existence? Who can understand the loneliness of a woman in power?

The struggle behind the couch is even more pitiful. The Eunuch is a strong man, even for his age, and several soldiers are required to move the couch and pin him down. They rip away his stole of office and tear the silk chlamys from his chest. Slender forearms, once decorated with gold bracelets, are now strapped with rope and will soon reveal welts of a none too imperial purple.

"Christ have mercy on us!" she screams.

They drag him from the room. Only then does Vardas let her go. The rancid smell of male sweat, an odor of power, of the lust for power, of hate, hangs heavily in the air.

I throw caution to the wind, race down the stairs and peer out. The Daphne courtyard is not used to a spectacle of this kind. Courtiers have gathered on the lawn and marble paving. Michael emerges from their midst as Theoktistos is thrown to the ground, panting. A guard forces him back onto his feet.

Running toward them is a sight which hardly becomes any high born lady, let alone the Regent. Robe and hair flying, her bare feet are unused to the cobbled courtyard. The sunset light drops into amber relief at her own grim fire.

She drops to her knees and clings to the Eunuch's legs. "What has he done that you must treat him so?" she cries. "He always put you first in everything he did!"

"Mother, mother, mother." Michael is all magnanimity as he tries to pull her to her feet. "His first concern was never me. It was always your sense of order. My time has come."

He squats down beside her and continues more softly. "I need to know why we should keep him alive."

"Oh!" she spits back at him, "if you are so stupid as to ask that question then I wonder that you are fit to rule."

Such public betrayal sucks the wind out of him. He turns from her on the balls of his feet, stands and walks away. "Enough! I hope you will never find reason to speak to me like that again, Mother. As for this vile . . . insect — get rid of it."

He mimes a knife across his stomach while nodding to the guards.

Vardas move over to speak softly in Michael's ear. "That was not quite what we discussed — he may still be useful."

"No? He has saddled me with a stupid woman, and cursed my whole life with misery."

The guards look to Vardas. We all freeze.

"Do it now," Michael shouts, "or I shall have all of you whipped in the Hippodrome!"

Vardas pulls Theodora away while two guards hold the Eunuch's arms tightly behind his back. Another steps forward, his blade slices through the air, and entrails spill out onto the ground. We all gasp at the suddenness of it. The wind blows the stench toward me but I can't stop looking. The Eunuch vanishes into himself, writhing and spilling blood out across her feet.

"Finish him off!" Michael screams. Another guard steps forward and sinks his blade into the twisting bloodied mass that is all that is left of the Eunuch.

So Michael has it in himself to make such a decision! I admire that. Perhaps Vardas' return is for the best.

For once, I pity Theodora. She stretches out over the body — a sunset-burnt cushion of white seeping into purple mud, her screams piercing our souls, withering the bloodied flagstones beneath her feet, echoing off the pillars nearby and even off the distant Icons, casting their timeless judgment on our pitiful lives, willing us to repentance, to contrition, but above all, to subjugation eternal.

Part III

Imperium

856–865 AD

20. The enemy without

Travel on land — either by foot or on horseback — has never been a burden to my Vassilis. But water is not his element. Heaving the last of his breakfast into the harbor waters leaves him angry enough to break the arm of the next person to cross his path.

He feels dirty: first a storm at sea, then navigating the chaos of a busy Piraeus, and now the filthy harbor of Patras. He knows now how badly seawater can stink. The noise is deafening, and he is suspicious of everyone. These descendants of the primitive Spartans should be watched carefully, his father had once taught him — thieves and ruffians all! He yearns for some wine, and a place to lie down, even a quiet spot under a tree would do.

Familiar faces from the trip gather around and push him on. The road to the Danielli conclave is remarkably busy and Vassilis has to jostle to make his way. Then a fat, friendly beard greets him, separating him from the others. "You have been given a room in the main house, please come this way."

Vassilis marvels at the opulence before him, not at all how he imagined self-denying Spartans would live. Rugs with detailed needlepoint crisscross couches. Embroidered curtains frame silk-lined windows, keeping the hot sun at bay.

A quick dab of water and perfumed oil and he is whisked off to see the Lady Danielli. She receives him on cushions amid sweet-meats, drinks and the bustle of attendants.

Her breath is cinnamon and cloves, her perfume that of citrus blossom. "We are delighted to have such an unusual visitor. What news from the City?"

What news can a stable boy have? The horses are being read-ied for some campaign in the east. He saw the Emperor in pro-cession to the Ayia Sofia some weeks ago and he appeared well, and so on. Bulgar skirmishes continue to annoy the Romans.

"Your Greek is unusual, my boy," Danielli says. "Where are you from?"

My Peasant's instinct is that the less said the better, though frayed images of his father's home flash through his mind. "It is a long story," he says, "and perhaps not to everyone's taste."

But her smile immediately puts him at ease.

"I was once from Chariopolis," he goes on. "Near the capital, Adrianopolis," he adds when he sees no recognition.

She is not unattractive for her years. Her skin has been well blessed by the sun and glows under thick bracelets, necklaces, and silks. The only suggestions of age are hints of gray creeping out from under a loosely tied head scarf.

But it is nothing next to the appearance of her son John, a young mirror of Danielli except for the gray shadow of a lean chin. His black eyebrows and slender limbs cause Vassilis no end of discomfort.

"We were attacked ... I know not by whom ... and I escaped. But the Bulgar took me away and gave me a life when I thought I had none."

Danielli wraps herself around each of the young men's arms, drawing them together. "Here we are, my darlings. I hope you will get to know each other a bit better. My son, John, has prepared some fine entertainments for you, young Vassilis."

She winks. "I know what it's like when the men get together. The ancient tradition of symposiums lives on in our city. I am sure John will make your stay with us very worthwhile."

Vassilis' groin burns and tightens. Perhaps it's the heat, or the exhaustion from days of traveling. Or perhaps it's the disarming smile the young man gives him. Danielli tips her head quizzically from one to another, reads positive signs, and is satisfied. Her son gets a kiss on the forehead, and then she holds Vassilis' face in her hands before planting her lips fiercely on his startled, half-open mouth.

† † †

Michael has been dispatched to the field, no doubt with Vardas egging him on. Can't the men see that war is a waste of time, energy, and youth? I am convinced that by dubbing the "other" with the epithet of enemy we have obviously already taken sides. How often do we do that — use words to make us comfortable with whatever atrocities we are about to carry out? Pontius Pilate himself realized this when he ordered "King of the Jews" to be posted beneath our Lord's cross. Are we that different to our ancestors? For we also refuse to recognize the Paulicians as our own, that they are simply other Romans, whose particular love of peace and the open spaces have made them into warriors for their own cause.

Michael has had more experience of my embraces than he has had of battle, so it is good that Petronas is there to guide him. He must be enjoying the long rides, the horses pounding out the dust clouds behind him, the signing and dispatching of orders with his seal upon them, not to mention the camaraderie, the nights of drinking and singing with the men, the kind of thing Michael always enjoys.

The ground-shattering cacophony of hooves and the snapping of the standards in the open air must thrill Michael, especially as the enemy comes into view. Petronas and Michael lead a charge of Cataphracts at the Iconoclast standard of the Paulicians. Their half-armor, brown with rust, comes into view. It will be no match for our troops; a slaughter is inevitable.

A bearded Goliath topples Michael. The young Emperor is quickly back on his feet. He parries just in time to fend off a sword slicing through the air toward him.

How these unaccustomed images must burn into Michael's mind: the broken standard half-toppled nearby, the burning heat reflecting off the dark stones, his opponent's long curls erupting from under a cracked helmet as he offers the Emperor certain death.

Michael thinks this is Karveas, the Paulician's legendary leader. Michael would give a lot to be the one who deals their enemy a blow in mortal combat. But whoever he is, he is faster, and as tough as the land. His arms bulge with stony sinew. Michael could never be his match.

Michael takes a moment too long to stop his head spinning, and to catch his breath. Pain flashes in his side. He falls onto his knees, struggling to breathe, blood pouring out of a crack in his chain mail. The Paulician towers above him, rough sword ready to strike again, a vicious grin gleaming in anticipation at this magnificent prize.

Then suddenly, the Paulician crumples. A blade bursts through his chest and he topples forward onto Michael. Petronas comes into view, ripping his sword out from the victim's back. He gazes down with a proud smile.

"You have fought bravely, nephew, and now we need to get you to …" His words recede into the welcome blackness that furls over Michael like a blanket.

† † †

Patras' summer evenings are somewhat less sedate than we are accustomed to in the City. The night air is warm enough to stand on the wide flat rooftops without a tunic, and some of the men, especially the younger ones, have taken advantage of this. They wander around like lions on the prowl, their limbs golden in the lamplight. The older men settle onto couches arranged in horseshoe formation, surrounded by snacks on all sides: herbs, sheep's cheese, bread, and much wine. A dulcimer tinkles clearly over their subdued voices.

I don't much care for Theophilitzes, though I only met him once. But I despise any man who survives purely on influence and indulgence, who makes his way by being amenable, without toil of some kind. He is surprisingly agile for a man of his girth, flitting everywhere, ensuring that conversation thrives, goblets are filled, and appetites are sated.

The night sparkles with singing and dancing from afar, while cool breezes tickle bearded cheeks and bare chests. Many of the men are not much older than Vassilis but the topics of conversation make his head swim. Which is more important: traders or leaders in society? Is the rule of holy empire compatible with pagan democracy? Will the City ever reestablish its influence over all its lost territories?

Evidently, the ritual for an evening's entertainment is to follow drink and discussion with poetry. Theophilitzes silences the dulcimer with a gesture which leaves the cicadas alone to accompany the ancient verse of Homer.

Vassilis' father had taught him some of the old Macedonian stories, handed down by word of mouth from father to son since time began. But this sounds new to him — such difficult Greek, so melodic, yet in so many ways foreign. He remembers the stories of Odysseus, 'the sufferer,' — the one who never gave up, never lost sight of his goal: to reunite with his family. The young men drift to couches as Theophilitzes begins reading. John reaches for Vassilis' hand as they sit down together.

After Odysseus had contemplated these wonders to his heart's content, he entered the main hall. There he found the leaders of the Phaeacians bringing offerings of wine to Hermes, as the hour of sleep had arrived, and this was always their last ceremony before seeking slumber. No one saw Odysseus as he crossed the spacious room and came close to the king and queen, for he was still concealed in the thick mist which Athena had thrown round him. Suddenly the cloud vanished, and Odysseus threw himself at the feet of Arete, and raised his voice in supplication.

'Arete,' he prayed, 'I have come to thy husband and to thy feet through many hardships and sorrows. May the gods give thee a long and happy life. For many years I have been a wanderer from home and all I love. I beg that thou wilt give me a guide and send me to my own land.'

When Odysseus had spoken these words he sat down amid the ashes, close to the fire, and all the guests grew silent and looked at him with wonder. Then the oldest of the chiefs arose and said: 'Alcinus, this is not a royal seat for a stranger, among the cinders of the hearth. I pray thee, raise him up and place him on a throne, and order the heralds to fill a cup with wine, that we may pour a libation to Zeus, the protector of suppliants, and bid the guest welcome to our good cheer.'

Then Alcinus rose and took Odysseus by the hand. He led him to a splendid throne just a little lower than his own, while the herald placed a table before him loaded with dainty food. When Odysseus had eaten and drunk, the attendants filled the cups to pour li-

bations in honor of Zeus, and Alcinus said to them,
'Listen, ye leaders and chiefs of the Phaeacians. Tomorrow we shall greet the stranger in our palace with
honors and offer a great sacrifice to the gods. And
then we will consider the best way of sending him
home. But if we should find that he is a god instead
of a mortal, we will do what seems best, for the gods
do sometimes visit us in human shape.'
Then said Odysseus: 'No, Alcinus, I am not a god,
nor like the gods in form or looks. I am only a wanderer, and I could tell of fearful sorrows; and I would
willingly die if I could only see my home once more.'
The guests all greeted Odysseus with approving words,
and promised to aid him. Then they rose, and each
man went to his own home.

"And so should we, in due course," Theophilitzes grins. The
dulcimer tinkles again. John thrusts a goblet into Vassilis' hands.

"Try some of that special wine," says Theophilitzes, hovering
nearby Vassilis. Homer's words fill him with painful longing, a cry
for release. A traveler is always lonely. Vassilis thinks of his brothers and drains the goblet, tasting bright flowers. He feels himself
sliding into the headiness of the beautiful men moving around him,
of the words flowing around the roof.

Now John kneels over him, his slender shins nestling against
my Peasant's strong knees. Vassilis looks around to see what is
going on. The others share similar embraces. He tries to get up,
but finds John's lips on his, pressing him gently down. They draw
on each others' breaths. Fingers trace soft cheeks and taut shoulders. Vassilis pulls the young man's britches down with one hand,
while the other finds its way down to John's buttocks.

My Peasant chances another look around. Theophilitzes has
not one but two young compatriots paying homage to him. But
John is straddling his mount. His delicate hands rest on Vassilis'
chest, and then on his shoulders as he leans forward.

Vassilis no longer wishes to resist. He adds his unwitting
moaning to the choir. Time halts as John draws him deeper with
every thrust, to a blinding finish, the pleasure before pain, the little
death, the sowing of his seed, deep inside this lithe creature.

After a moment John tries to guides Vassilis' lips where they have never been before, but now Vassilis suffocates. He pushes John away and sits up, leaving the other to slide onto the couch.

Theophilitzes glances over, sees what has happened and nods to John to move aside. Dismissing his own worshipers with kisses he puts on his robe and comes over.

"So what do you think of … events?" His smile teases, not unkindly, as he sits down right beside Vassilis.

Vassilis sets his feet on the ground and pulls on his britches. He gets up but finds himself lurching, toward the roof edge. A sudden breeze and the reflection in moonlit waters of the glowing town brace him, though his thoughts continue to slide around as he catches himself swaying.

Theophilitzes appears beside him, laying a hand on his bare shoulder. "I see you have not taken opium before. In the wine, that is. It is a regular novelty among us, at least for those who can afford it. A fruit of our trade with the east, you might say. You will come to appreciate its benefits if you stay long enough."

"What I have been wanting to ask you all evening," Vassilis says, with difficulty, "is why you brought me here?"

Theophilitzes grins. "I, too, am delighted that you came. It is obvious you have rare … talents. I thought it a good time to get you out of the way, my handsome traveler. There are strange goings on in the City right now. I wanted you somewhere safe while they settle. After all, if Vassilis the Macedonian is to get the ear of the court, after coming from nowhere to wait at the table of the Emperor, we can't have him mixed up in any bad business, now can we?"

Vassilis stares straight ahead. His chest is on fire, but not from the wine. Now he starts to recognize that all the nonchalant words at court, the deferential nods, the exchanges of pleasantries, the invocations of the saints and martyrs, are all part of the games we play. The facade of piety is nothing more than a diversion. He has been stumbling around like a blind man among the sighted, without any idea at all. When will he learn!

Don't you see why Vassilis relies on anger, my little Leo? Only when he is angry can he know how strong he is, how much of his father is in him. Yes, the lust for revenge boils in his chest. But he hides it, his native caution never deserting him for a moment.

"What bad business would that be?" says Vassilis.

"I doubt you will have heard anything about it yet. The mighty Logothete has been executed. The court lives frozen in fear as to who will be next on the list. Summary punishment is all and about. Rumor has it that Cousin Vardas is involved, though we can't be sure if the Emperor himself is responsible or not."

Vassilis pales. The cicadas redouble their efforts.

"Oh my handsome hero — that got you startled," Theophilitzes teases. "But there's nothing for you to worry about. Anyway, what do you think of our local Athena?" In response to Vassilis' blank stare he adds, "I mean the Lady Danielli."

Vassilis finds Theophilitzes annoying — the man does not understand the value of silence. The courtier shrugs off Vassilis' attempt to ignore him. "Be sure that she means you no harm. In fact, I would go so far as to say you would do well to take her advice. In return all she wants is someone to give her a better ... hearing in the City."

Vassilis greets this news with another blank stare.

Theophilitzes sighs. "I see we will have to educate you a bit," he chides. "I'm sure you can tell that we are quite pleased with ourselves here, but we are too far from where decisions are made. The Emperor gives land out in the border areas to the Akritai. With this the City gets taxes and we get ... the possibility of clients. Everyone needs things, don't they, especially when they live in the outposts, far from civilization? What they can't find we sell to them. But how to get the ear of the Akritai? The Lady Danielli needs someone who can forge that link, someone right in the administration, if you understand my meaning. Find out who is who, let us ... reach agreements as to who the court deals with ... and you, and we, perhaps even the court, will be amply rewarded."

There is much to learn. Vassilis could refuse, and go back to living the clean, hardworking life that Father had always taught was the right way to live. Or he could take part in this game.

Theophilitzes finally leaves my Peasant in peace. Frustration gives way to a hint of something beyond his understanding, something fascinating. In his slow, village way, it dawns on him that his life is laughable. What does it mean to take care of parade horses in the City, when there is so much going on, so much more that he could be involved in? First, there is a debt to be paid, to his hostess for her kindness. Next he must bring Maria to the City, as well as Constantinos. How could he forget that he has a son! He must also make himself better known at court, a bit like he did in Pliska. Although on the last he is a bit vague — the City is a far more difficult proposition.

He wanders over to John, who is resting on an elbow, passion spent. The lad looks up somewhat warily. Vassilis reaches out to stroke his brow, wiping away an imaginary bead of sweat and straightening his hair. He touches John's lips gently.

"These should smile more," Vassilis says. "How are you at riding? Why don't we get some horses together tomorrow and go down to the beach? I can tell you some of the things I have seen. Perhaps then we can see what might ... befall us?"

21. Rude awakenings

AS BEFORE, IN THE SPRING OF 856 AD
One thing had led to another and Vardas invited himself to his ex-son-in-law's quarters, that is to say Symvatios' quarters, just outside the Palace, while Symvatios was abroad, facing the Paulicians most bravely alongside Petronas and Michael. Perhaps this is why Vardas sent his ex-son-in-law so far away, and to battle, especially when Symvatios is not even a soldier. But who could ever tell what Vardas' motives were, really?

First, let me tell you what a strange creature Symvatios is! A mean, spindly fellow, I often wonder if an ostrich spawned his spotted, mostly balding egg of a head before someone balanced it on the tip of his scrawny neck and nailed it in. His long nose carries a perpetual droplet that he wipes away mercilessly on his stole of office, a garment that is far too long for him. It seems as if he about to trip over it any moment. Following the briefest period of mourning after Vardas' daughter died Symvatios had secured the affections of my close friend Eudokia, although the Theotokos alone knew what she saw in him.

In the Gynaeconitis today, Eudokia is full of giggles, her cheeks flushed, her eyes twinkling with secrets. The Regent is still in mourning, hidden in Blachernae with her closest attendants. Dekapolitessa, still uncrowned and unused to her new role as wife to the Emperor, keeps to her quarters. So we girls are ready to take all the liberties we can with the daily routine. Eventually I egg Eudokia on enough to tell us what is afoot. We drop all pretense of work, drag the couches together and sprawl on cushions to hear everything.

Eudokia tells us she arranged a delicious repast for Vardas. Fine Armenian wine, crusty bread, roasted octopus in garlic and herbs, and a whole tray of perfectly ripened peaches. Symvatios has done well in marrying her. Not only is Eudokia a fine hostess, but her features and limbs resemble those that the Athenians must have used as inspiration for the Caryatids on the Parthenon, when they weren't admiring self-indulgent dolts with exaggerated musculature.

That Vardas' stomach muscles have long since vanished into the firm padding that constitutes his generous waist does not deter him from pursuing Eros with great vigor. This, and his utter obsession with women, makes him very desirable to many, though not me, I confess. It had been clear from the moment he set eyes on Eudokia at her wedding to Symvatios — which had taken place far too soon to earn the court's approval — that the attraction had been mutual. They proceeded to take every opportunity to get better acquainted.

Vardas remains a mystery to me. Surely he felt some pain at the death of his own child, Symvatios' former wife. He had once boasted that his mirthful daughter was the most wonderful creature he had ever met, so similar to him in so many ways, and over whose absence he wept bitterly while in exile. But right now Vardas must be very pleased with himself, with the Eunuch out of the way, a Triumph in the making, and an evening of Aristophanes with a gorgeous woman.

We applaud Eudokia's literary good taste: Lysistrata. Aristophanes' heroine, a powerful devotee of Athena, convinces the women of Sparta and Athens, whose men are permanently at war, to forbid their men carnal pleasures until a truce is signed.

It's a clever excuse for Eudokia and Vardas to spend time together, under the banner of learned discourse, especially since few read Aristophanes these days or would even know the subject of the play, other than Photios, who had unearthed it recently. Though I don't think he has let you read it yet, my little Leo — that would hardly befit a young Emperor!

Eudokia tells us she chooses to read the character Myrrhini, the sly young wife to Vardas' Cinesias, her over-eager husband.

'Our home is a shambles, Myrrhini,' retorts Vardas, playing Cinesias. 'Everything, your stuff and mine! And . . . and . . . you've left Aphrodite's shrine unattended for ages! When last since you performed her rites? Aren't you coming back?'

He places her hand on a significant bump in his britches.

'I don't know,' pronounces Eudokia, 'and I don't care until all you men get together and agree to end the war.'

'But Myrrhini! It's been such a long time. Let's make love!'

Vardas bites into a scrap of octopus and brings it to her lips. Her nibbling grows into a kiss, but then she directs his mouth down. He strips away her linen undergarment. She writhes with pleasure as he scatters kisses all over her.

'All right then,' Eudokia continues reading. 'Let me bring a mattress first.' She gets up and scurries around, pretending to arrange a couch.

'Don't think of it,' laughs Vardas, while trying to maintain a dramatic pose. 'The ground is good enough for me.'

She pretends to fuss around him. 'There you are! Quickly, darling, lie down and I'll strip. How awful! We need sheets!'

'Sheets? No, no, no! No sheet for me!'

'Yes, darling, sheets! It's so vulgar to do it on the bare cords!'

Their mouths find each other. Neither wishes for the embrace to end. His hands are everywhere, and she brooks no resistance. She feels herself giving way to his merciless onslaught and pulls away. She is off the couch and out of the room.

Vardas reaches for his lines. 'Oh, do be quick then, sweetheart! Get the sheets, but hurry!'

Eudokia returns with a thin blanket of Abbasid design — animals on a green backdrop — and drapes it across the couch.

'Here's the sheet. Now lie down, darling and I'll undress. Oh no! We need pillows!'

'Pillows? I certainly don't need a pillow, darling! My God! This cock is being entertained like the greedy Hercules, starving for his supper.'

Eudokia scampers to another couch, just out of Vardas' reach, and retrieves several cushions before climbing back onto him. 'Heads up, dear! Now, have I got everything? One moment, darling. I'm just going to undo my breast band ... but don't you forget the Peace treaty, now, will you?'

'May God strike me dead if I do,' Vardas says, feigning a sigh.

Eudokia undoes Vardas' tunic, and removes it slowly, rubbing her chin in his beard, and planting kisses along his neck and down his chest as she does so. Her lips tease his ample belly and continue their way down. She leaves a teasing kiss on the bump in his britches and picks up the manuscript again.

'This is to help you raise yourself, my man!'

'Raise myself? Darling, I've been risen long enough!'

'Ah! Oil! We need fragrant oil for the right mood.'

'Oh, God, no! No oils, please, my little Myrrhinaki!'

'Yes, yes, yes! By Aphrodite, you'll get perfumes whether you want to or not!'

'Ah, well, let the oils flow then, oh, let them flow!'

'Come here, my lion. Let me be your cheese grater!'

They collapse in a pile of laughter and entwined limbs.

The text no longer of concern, Vardas' tongue roves to her nipples and the sweat that glistens between them. She throws her head back. Equally without reserve, her hands grasp his firmness and they topple alongside each other, in opposite directions. Then it is the turn of her tongue between his thighs, while he finds the source of her pleasure, and goes even further beyond, she discovers, quite to her surprise.

A brief pause to let in the late afternoon sea breeze finds them panting in each other's arms and sharing a goblet, though the pause is not for long. For the nymph has subdued the bull, and Eudokia straddles Vardas, her arms on his broad fists.

I am green with envy at how she is not afraid to possess him, and at how he plays along merrily! He boasts there is no greater satisfaction than to bring pleasure to a woman. Eudokia is happy to return the favor many, many times, before evening comes.

† † †

Vassilis' promise does not materialize the next day as he would have hoped, nor even the next. The exhaustion from the trip, the opium, and the stark realization that he and his choices have been manipulated, have left him with a fever.

Several days have passed in which he has let himself be comforted by smooth sheets, softer than anything he has ever slept in. He marvels at the pillars of the vast room around him, the rugs and tapestries, sewn with dizzying designs, interspersed by the occasional servant with trays of sweet foods and meats. But every time he tries to sit up and look around he has to give up, his head spinning, with no recourse but to sink back into the firm comfort and familiar smell of the horsehair mattress.

Even before he opens his eyes he can sense the cloud of honey and cinnamon he has come to associate with Danielli. She has brought goblets of fragrant juices for him to drink and some rather sour-smelling cloths to lay across his sore head and stomach.

"How goes my champion?" she asks, kindly. "I think you have had too much happen to you lately. Even Hercules felt the need for rejuvenation at times."

"I am no one's champion," Vassilis murmurs. "I don't even know what it is I hope to find. At least Odysseus had a goal."

"To reach his Penelope?" Danielli's perfect teeth support a wicked smile. "But that is hardly much to look forward to. Women are everywhere. Those few that are special are burdened by motherhood. It is easy to make them mothers, as I think you know well."

This is a new thought to Vassilis. She is right, that queen of the south. I know it myself. The pain of birth is but the smallest part of the mother's burden, as are the daily cares. It is the fear that if you do not care for your child, no one else will. How sweet it would be to blow away my concern for you, my darlings, and leave you to drift in the water, like tadpoles, to grow where you will. Yet God has not given me the ability to do this. Know this, my wise Leo, and you too, my strong Alexander and quiet little Stephen. Know how hard it is for a mother.

"If you have no goal," says Danielli firmly, "then, at the very least, you should aspire to make an enemy of no one. I know that Theophilitzes is making sure that the court will get to hear of you."

Vassilis still feels too weak to question further. But he raises himself up on an elbow and stares at her.

Danielli soothes him back down. "Don't be amazed. I do not expect you to acquaint yourself with the Emperor himself, but what of his charioteers? He befriends all alike, regardless of office, just like his father before him. This means you can get to know his acquaintances easily, even perhaps some of his officials."

Then, with a hopeful look in her eye, "John tells me you got on well the other night. He is looking forward to spending more time with you."

"And I with him," Vassilis manages to reply. Such kindness and good advice are a disarming combination, one which Vassilis has only experienced in Maria before. He vows to do anything for Danielli, to be up the next day, no matter what it takes.

And so, for the next week or so boys do what boys must in such circumstances, especially if they are so inclined.

† † †

But now Vassilis is back in the City, clutching a leather bag of letters and coin. He feels too guilty to face Diomedes. The recollection of their warm embraces seems cloying in retrospect, though Vassilis has only a vague idea of what to do next. He decides he can always find somewhere else to sleep while he summons up the courage to do what Theophilitzes suggested.

So he returns to the stables, only to find that old Andreas, the Chief Equerry, has been sent away due to his close connections with the Eunuch. But the work with the horses never ceases and he quickly settles back into the old routine.

A particularly reluctant mare takes some encouragement to respond to him and, after a few days, Vassilis decides to try her out in the polo field. The pleasure of the ride helps him forget the feeling that he should be going to the administrative offices again, this time as a supplicant. He rides, and bats the ball endlessly around the field for what feels like hours. Then he shoots the ball into the seats by mistake. When he looks up he finds the Emperor himself catching it in both hands.

Vassilis almost falls off in his haste to prostrate himself.

"Really, there's no need for that," calls Michael, striding up. "I remember you ... from the wrestling match. And from the wedding banquet."

Vassilis is speechless. He decides to look the Emperor in the eye. Michael doesn't mind. He never did care much for protocol.

Michael says "I come to do mostly the same thing, just play around by myself for a while. You will probably get into trouble for doing it without permission. Everything here happens with permission, you know. Even I mess up sometimes for doing things I shouldn't."

Vassilis' jaw drops. This gets a guffaw in return.

"You hold on remarkably well," Michael says. "Your mount seems to know exactly what you want from her."

"She's a good one," Vassilis manages. "But not yet ready for anything serious."

"She will be just right for polo one day." Michael slides his hand along the mare's rump. "Look at these short legs, the thick muscles. Perfect for quick charges."

"I would not take her out hunting, though," Vassilis says. "Far better to ride something with a longer gait."

"You need a different animal for the chariot as well, not to mention when you ride into battle. These must be strong rather than agile. One has to pull a heavy load, the other to carry one far."

Vassilis tries to nod in a sagely sort of way as they lead the mare out of the stadium, to the entrance where Michael has tied up his mount. "I did not know the hunt until I lived with the Bulgar, but when I was young my brothers used to teach me to catch wild horses, on the plains of Macedonia."

"There are many forests between here and the Euphrates, you know, and different kinds too," Michael says.

"And what of their pickings?" asks Vassilis. "Back home, we would gather berries to brew drink for the winter."

At last it dawns on Vassilis that his boorishness must be showing — wine making could hardly interest someone with affairs of state on his mind. So Michael's next words catch him unawares.

"They are arranging a Triumph of sorts," Michael says, pulling himself up nimbly onto his mare. "Uncle Vardas wants to celebrate our victory over the Paulicians in a week's time."

He breaks straight away into a canter. "I want you to view it with me," he calls back over his shoulder.

22. Emperor to the people

Let me tell a tale of spectacle, my little Leo. One you will know little of, your preference already for books rather than sword and pomp. The throng climbs over itself to witness the Triumph, brought to its attention through harsh gongs, and dissonant horns. Not the typical round of chariot or horse races, mind you, or a bout of gladiator fighting. The latter spectacle has never even made it to the Hippodrome, banned as it was some four hundred years ago.

But first, here is my Peasant, heading along in his new outfit, purchased with money from Theophilitzes, though the money was only the smallest part of it. He had been summoned to see the same official he had visited before his trip to Patras. Rather than waiting for him to do anything, Theophilitzes had arranged it all. This time the official seemed a bit less gruff, managing to break into a weak smile when Vassilis wasn't sure how to sign the document accepting the title of Spatharios, bought for him by Theophilitzes.

"Just make any mark, it doesn't really matter," the official said, virtually pushing the quill in Vassilis' hand across the parchment for him, before rubbing a large seal in pitch and pressing it to the document. "We can't have a stable boy joining the Emperor in the Balcony tomorrow, now can we?"

The clerk at the office of the Master of the Wardrobe was a different matter. His ring-decked fingers waved away Vassilis' letters of recommendation, even the certificate of title Vassilis presented to him.

"Titles are easily bought and sold," he muttered, turning away to a pile of papers in front of him. "It is not my place to ask what you have done to deserve this, but I do not hand out insignias lightly. The Imperial markings must be earned."

A veil of blackness descended across Vassilis' vision as he fought the desire to break the clerk's arm. Then he recalled the coins hoarded away since Patras.

A quick sprint to his quarters and back, and Vassilis stumbled home again fully laden with white tunic, cloak and short sword. He held out the white cloak proudly so that its purple border and golden thread glistened in the dim lamplight. With his new station, and garments such as these, he must find accommodation that is more appropriate.

Now, all dressed up, he stops at the main entrance to the Hippodrome. The Emperor has arrived on a white mare, in advance of the procession from the Palace. He is covered from shoulder to foot in a pure white cloak, not unlike a senator, with hints of blue and gold shining through.

Michael jumps off the horse and beckons for Vassilis to follow him. They ascend the dark, spiral stairs past the guards to enter the Balcony through the Snail door. Michael leaps two steps at a time, Vassilis right behind him, doing his best to maintain a deferential mask over his immense pleasure. Michael indicates with the smallest of nods a seat at the back.

Vassilis steals a glance around the Balcony. There is a constant rustle of commentary but he can't really pick up what is being said. Then a wave of jeering from the crowd pulls his eyes to the stadium below, where men and women stumble forward, covered in filth. Their feet and hands are rough, bleeding receptacles for the riches they bear, the broken armor of the men clearly pinching, even cutting, their skin. A few wagons filled with vases, weapons, and skins drag in the dust behind them.

These captives, thinks my Peasant, are much like him in appearance. Their filthy, dark curls fall on frames bursting with stocky muscle just like his. He feels a strange flush of anger, or is it tribal pride? Could these be Armenians, his countrymen?

The Imperial Guard tramps in, splitting into double formation as it passes the captives. Each cohort stands to attention immediately below the Balcony, the captured treasures displayed between them. The chariots of the Blues clatter into the stadium with their tuneless, ritual chants. They pass to the right of the Balcony, the Greens coming in behind them, taking position on the left.

Oh, how exultant Michael must feel to be the subject of procession into the Hippodrome, even if the spoils are pitiful. How magnificent to have the Generals of the Themes inclining their heads in apparent obeisance, the Factions lining up for him. Vassilis is in awe at it all and does not realize that Michael's appearances and his utterances have been largely ignored till now.

Michael moves into the sunlight, right to the edge of the Balcony, in clear view of the crowd. He throws off his cape, and it is as if an Icon has come to life. Or perhaps it is the Archangel Michael himself. A chain mail tunic in finest gold burns the eye, relieved only by shimmering bands of lapis lazuli. Loose sleeves reach to his elbows and his knees are barely covered by a skirt of indigo silk. Visible only to those seated behind him in the Balcony is a pair of golden boots. A sword's gem-encrusted hilt reflects the overhead sun. He holds it high above his head.

Much later, in one of my rare conversations with Photios, when he had begun to appreciate my knowledge of history and had realized that I was not just a silly woman, he recalled the ancient parallel on display, and wondered who else saw it. Here was a modern version of Caesar Julius entering Rome triumphantly, he said, only the latter would have worn proper armor and red battle paint.

"Today we celebrate our might," Michael calls out. "We have put the heretical Paulicians to the death. The ways of the Icon destroyers are truly over. We have led our brave army abroad and all quake at our unmatched might."

Exclamations and cheering ring out. Michael waits for a horn to sound.

"Now that our campaign to subdue the Paulicians has ended," he continues, "our mother has withdrawn from the cares of state to serve Christ more closely. It is my duty, from now on, to minister to my people's needs."

The cantors begin chanting. Michael walks slows back to the center of the Balcony, but still in view of the people, and turns to face them. His voice carries well over the chanting.

"Though born of woman, mortal by nature and time, we now take our full and rightful place on the Imperial Throne. We have refuted the lawless errors of our ancestors, the Iconoclasts, and return to be the most pious of all, to the glory, praise, fame, and dignity of Mother Church."

Vassilis sees clearly the boy in front of him, and the man! How he yearns for the glory himself, or at least, the adoration. But such was the vanity of your fathers, dear Leo, and all men, except, as far as I can tell, you! How many know that the Abbasid are re-grouping for a bigger attack now that their allies, the Paulicians, have experienced this humiliation? How many can see that this entire spectacle is an excuse to divert the attention of our people from the real problem?

A throbbing whisper of "Worthy" gradually builds until it deaf-ens, echoing across the entire City, and taking several minutes to subside. Michael begins again. "For his excellent service at the frontier we have decided to grant cousin Symvatios the role of Lo-gothete. We can now turn our attention back to the Abbasid. They are a curse on our Levantine domains."

With hindsight I see why this has happened – Vardas is clearly putting his men in place. Not to mention that the thing he needed most, that we all need, is obligation, especially given his dallying with Symvatios' Eudokia.   How slighted Dekapolitessos, Michael's new father-in-law, must feel. As Epi tou Kanikleiou – the title Theodora granted him in return for a very handsome dowry – it would have been logical for Vardas to appoint him Lo-gothete instead. Clearly Dekapolitessos is not in the ascendant!

"Today we begin preparations for a new campaign in the east that I and our new leader of the Thracesian Theme, General Petronas, will lead. We will strike at the heart of their power – Baghdad if necessary!"

This gets a warm but not overly enthusiastic response from the crowd. Petronas acknowledges the honor with a twisted smile and a bowed head. The title of Logothete had been offered to him, but he had declined, saying that his place was on the battlefield. Thracesian was indeed still ours. But with Karveas far from dead, and forming strange alliances between the Paulicians and the Ab-basid, especially the Emir of Melitene, I am sure that Petronas knows that peace is still months away, if not years. But I am also sure that he welcomes the challenge.

Horns and gongs clamor around the Hippodrome. The guards fall to, marching out of the stadium in formation. The charioteers prepare for the races. Michael turns to face the Balcony. To Vas-silis' amazement he is summoned forward.

"And my new Chief Equerry, Vassilis the Macedonian, will ac-company us," he says, beckoning for my Peasant to step forward.

There is a collective gasp from the assembled courtiers. Michael lays a hand on Vassilis' shoulder and whispers softly in his ear. "I have a special task for you before we go on campaign. It involves ... I will explain more after the games."

Yes, my darlings, plans were being set in motion, without your innocent mother having the slightest inkling of them.

† † †

FIVE MONTHS LATER, IN THE WINTER OF EARLY 857 AD
Let's say that you are the son of an Emperor, and your name is Michael Rangabes, the first Michael of that name. Now, for a moment, try to imagine that your father, the Emperor, has been forced, through a series of humiliating defeats, to tip his crown both to the Bulgar, in the person of the Khan Krum, and to that of a barbarian, Charles the Frank. Would you not think that the humiliation was complete?

This is Ignatios' predicament. His father abdicated in order to allow his most powerful general, Leo the Armenian, to take over and save the City from the ruin of chaos. In return, his family's lives were spared. But the price of mercy was high: his father, brothers and even he was castrated and sent to a monastery. His mother, Procopia, resisted the abdication order and vanished. How is life then, for someone like him? Could he ever make peace with all those who wronged him?

Michael decides to tonsure his mother and sisters. They refuse, and Patriarch Ignatios takes their part, sensing advantage in withholding that which is being asked for. So Michael, encouraged by Vardas, decides that he must reaffirm his coronation in the eyes of the court with holy rites.

It's a gloomy winter's day. The snows have fallen lightly, but the festival of the Epiphany, following two weeks after Christmas, is upon us, a time of quiet reflection and moderate exhilaration. The Imperial family and senators gather in the Augusteon and move to the Ayia Sofia in slow procession, Michael at the head, candle held before him. The Patriarch awaits them at the great doors, ready to invite the procession inside. Within, the deacon is in full voice and the crown, chlamys, and fibula await the Patriarch's blessing. Sub deacons vest Michael with these garments while Ignatios censes and prays over the crown. The Patriarch invokes the Holy Trinity and beckons for the crown to be placed on Michael's head. Michael's eyes blaze. How much more confirmation does he need? He is the rightful Emperor, if only he could see that in himself!

Vardas and Photios are nodding to one another. Some plans are afoot. I imagine that they are glad that Michael has reaffirmed his office in the eyes of the court, and, most importantly, in front of the Blues and the Greens. He moves to the Imperial compartment, where he is divested of the crown and takes hold of an enormous candle. Emperor and Patriarch proceed together to the altar, though Michael must halt before it, at the chancel barrier, while Ignatios enters to kiss the altar. On Ignatios' return they exchange the kiss of peace — a parody under the circumstances. A small willfulness from Michael ensues: Ignatios offers him the chance to bless the altar with the censer, which Michael declines. This raises a few eyebrows and a smile from Vardas. Michael returns to the Imperial compartment and seats himself on the throne to hear the remainder of the liturgy.

The Imperial entourage advances to receive communion. There is some hesitation as to who will receive the sacrament next, until Vardas does the right thing and guides Dekapolitessa gently forward.

Then it is Vardas' turn. He kneels on one leg, opening his mouth to receive the Blood and Body, as all who have walked under this heavenly vault have done for hundreds of years. What happens next takes us all by surprise.

Ignatios closes his eyes and chants even louder, holding the chalice high above Vardas' head. The procession halts in confusion. Then the Patriarch turns his back on Vardas and the rest of the supplicants, and proceeds to cense the altar again, not offering so much as a drop of Christ for the sampling.

A ripple runs through the congregation. Vardas turns an angry red much like an unfortunate octopus as you steal up on it and pierce its eyes by surprise. He gets up, makes an elaborate sign of the cross, and strides out. Michael rises and follows him in more stately fashion, as do the attendants, leaving a sea of whispers behind. Photios is close behind them.

† † †

By the next day the Gynaeconitis is ablaze with rumors that there is a usurper in the Palace and that Ignatios is behind him. Now that the Regent is banished, many start to wonder how secure the Throne is. The court has cooked up a perfect judgment for its delectation, based on the flimsiest of ingredients: a floury shell of supposition, shortened by the lard of opinion, filled with every kind of personal injury that memory can recall, seasoned with invention, then topped with as much malice as can be mustered. A most delicious confection to the tongue, it sickens all who have to stomach it.

Vardas and Michael have leaped upon the feast and made it worse for all of us, exhorting Photios to arrange for Ignatios to be tried by jurors ... for treason! Photios writes that he cannot see any trial happening in practice, so decides to delay as much as possible. The situation is bound to change.

He escapes to Cyril's study in the Magnaura, which is far more comfortable than it has ever been, thanks to Vardas' initiatives. Cyril's quick wit and a perpetual grin are a constant source of pleasure to the old scholar. Cyril and he have been trying many different combinations of Greek letters, always coming to the same conclusion.

"It simply isn't possible," Cyril says, "and even if one pretended it was, and made do with letter combinations that captured most, if not all of the Bulgar sounds, then the resulting orthography would still be clumsy."

"So the problem is that the Bulgar tongue is much more varied than the palatalized smoothness of our native, docile Greek?" asks Photios. "It sounds like a bit of everything, doesn't it?"

This strikes a chord within Cyril. "Yes!" he says. "This suggests we should turn to some unusual devices. Let's try a bit of everything, then. For starters, the bizarre shushing sounds of Bulgarian that are totally unheard of in Greek can be found in ... Hebrew, the mother tongue of our faith."

"That is very bold," say Photios as Cyril scribbles furiously. "God forgive our immodesty in pursuing such a course but if He blesses our work then there may be a way forward."

"Then ..." Cyril says, "we need something to denote the

voiced equivalents of these shushing sounds. Hebrew won't cover them all. Any ideas?"

It strikes Photios that since they are going far afield, the Coptic alphabet might be a source for such sounds. Cyril's eyes shine with excitement.

"Exactly! I suspect we can use Greek for most of the other sounds. The resulting mixture of alphabets will look a bit strange, though, won't it?"

It is a brilliant idea, and Photios feels that he should be more encouraging. Only hard work will tell if this will bear fruit.

They talk about Leo the Mathematician's imminent arrival. In addition to teaching he has written of wanting to start some grand projects, such as a line of beacons stretching from the City all the way to Tarsus, to give the Emperor advance warning of Abbasid raids against our Akritai in the furthermost regions. The two of them chuckle at the thought, but then laugh out loud when Photios relates Leo's plans of building a rising throne, to imbue the Imperial presence with even more grandeur.

23. Guardian of the flock

I read Photios' words with great interest. So much happens which escapes us women. The threat of more campaigning against the Abbasid continues in the wake of our marginal success with the Paulicians. Pope Nicholas reaches out to the Imperial Throne once again with his all-encompassing web, fighting the only way he can: with sharp words, clothed in apparently reasonable ambitions, yet hiding fear and indignation. By whose authority did the Regent appoint Ignatios all those years ago, he wants to know? I chuckle — it would appear that Ignatios was in favor with no one.

According to Photios, the Pope is testing Michael's authority. Michael and Photios write a note to Nicholas, making it quite clear that Ignatios' appointment had been an internal one, decided by the Regent on the young Emperor's behalf as the highest Roman authority. Therefore, the case was closed. However, Michael might allow legates in to examine the matter, to satisfy the Pope's curiosity if he so wishes.

Then Michael outdoes himself. The afternoon is bright but windy, and clouds race each other across the sky. Photios and Michael are playing chess, much as they had when Michael was younger and had less distraction. Michael is playing brilliantly, which is quite unnerving for Photios, because he does it rarely and with little modesty when it happens.

"I have decided what I should do with Thunderguts," Michael says. "He refuses to hold the slightest respectable discourse with me these days. Soon he will turn all the clergy against us."

Photios nods. "The snubbing at the coronation has led to several public displays that are far from ideal for the Throne."

"Is it obvious to no one but me?" Michael says. "The disagreements are over, aren't they? The days of the Iconoclasts lie behind us, even if some bishops still harbor misgivings?" Photios nods. "Then why isn't someone more ... amenable ... in charge?"

"Dare I mention, Your Worthiness, that the Patriarch has a point?" says Photios. "The entire population now follows the bitter arguments that have raged between him and Vardas. You can thank the Blues for that. They have sided with Ignatios."

"Exactly. And Uncle Vardas doesn't need this right now. Not with so much going on, surely you can see that? All the more reason that I want you to be in charge!"

"There is the minor problem that I am, in fact, not a member of the clergy. Granted, that did not stop Uncle Tarasios before me from assuming this holy duty. And there have been others." He pauses. "But there is the rather more serious obstacle — that I am not really suited to this sort of thing, I mean..."

"I won't take this refusal lightly, dear Photios."

"I am honored beyond my ability to express in words, Worthiness, but we are just about to close off one dispute with the Bishop of Rome. This act will provoke another." He pauses again. "Of course, there is a way. I could work my way through the ranks. It could be achieved in the next year or so."

"A year or so?" Michael sighs dramatically, though his eyes twinkle. "By the Holy Trinity, that's far too long. What I had in mind was Christmas."

"Then we risk losing credibility. Are you prepared for that?"

"Checkmate!" announces Michael, knocking a bishop out of the way with his queen. It must be delightful to poke a finger in the eye of even such a remote authority as the Pope.

I can just see Vardas' hand in this.

† † †

Photios often wonders if the Senate has any function at all, other than to give lip service to tradition and the notion of consultation. Imperial decree had been the method of business since Octavian, since that four hundred year bout of democracy called the Republic that preceded him, when the old Romans shrugged off the yoke of their small-minded kings.

Nevertheless the Throne Room has everyone dutifully in place, reluctantly leaving the damp autumnal gardens and mint-strewn fountains behind to attend to the Emperor's words.

"Such sadness ..." Michael begins. "We have just received the news that there have been designs on our uncle's life, and that he succeeded in quashing these." Here Michael goes very quiet. "I shudder to say it ... agents were sent by our very own mother!"

Will they swallow it? He knows that many would never believe that Theodora would ever be capable of collaborating in such an act, although some might sympathize with her motives.

"As a result of this, we were pleased that the former Regent was to be tonsured and given the opportunity to retire to a monastery. However Patriarch Ignatios refused us this, and has gone so far as to ... threaten to excommunicate our uncle."

Some purse their lips, others frown and appear distant. They are starting to learn that being acquainted with this Emperor is to be a bedfellow with caprice itself, just like his father, though Theophilos was generally more pedestrian in his revenge.

"So I have decided," Michael says, rising and leaping to the floor, "that the Regent will be confined to the Karianos Palace from now on and will be permitted no further contact with us." A faint sigh of relief runs across the gathering.

"However, Ignatios has displeased us with this action." Michael allows himself a full measure of indignation, pacing through the assembled Senators. "How dare he treat the Anointed in this way? We wonder what other malicious plans fester in the heart of a priest who should be caring for his flock?"

Michael gathers his cloak about him and climbs back onto the Throne. "We therefore will appoint Photios to the Holy Office in due course who, like his Uncle Tarasios before him, is a man without whom the City would be much poorer."

You would expect general commotion ... not complete silence! That's where the problems really started.

† † †

A MONTH LATER, LATE IN THE FALL OF 858 AD
The first snow has melted much more quickly than anyone expected, and the winter sun falls boldly on the damp earth. Photios is off to confront Vardas about what happened. He writes that the Christ-loving Emperor has lost the confidence of the people. Surely Michael will understand why he needs to tread carefully!

He takes the short route to one of Vardas' new residences, through the market, which remains shut. Its normally frenzied stalls lie charred and trampled, while the last of the fruits drip their smashed pulp into the gutter, and torn reams of damp cloth soak up puddles. There isn't even a beggar in sight. A cat casts a suspicious eye at him while burying its nose deep in a broken bowl.

Not since Justinian's time has Nike! rung through our streets! Rumor has it that the call for victory traveled far afield, even to Smyrna and Neocaesarea. But what kind of a victory is it? If only Ignatios could have settled for a simple and graceful resignation. Not only did refuse this peaceful course, knowing it to be inevitable if that was Michael's wish, but he abused everyone in the process.

This is what happened. The riots began at the Stoudion. Or, perhaps more accurately, with Vardas, who banished the Abbot of the Stoudion to the distant Cherson, on the northern shores of the Black Sea, allegedly for his hatred toward the Iconoclasts, though the poor man had hardly made a public utterance on this subject in living memory.

Within a day all manner of rabble had tumbled out on the streets, raging and burning everything they could. Ignatios took advantage of the banishment to exhort several bishops and monks to work on a pamphlet, inciting the clergy to gather for a meeting in the Ayia Eirene.

The pamphlet asks why the Emperor has forced their Patriarch down, and why the Emperor mocks the Patriarch in so many ways. It questions an Emperor who parades in the street with the dwarf Gryllos dressed as the Patriarch himself. It asks by what sanction the Patriarch should ignore Vardas' adultery. And, thirdly, it wants to know why the Emperor squanders the state's wealth when so many of its people are starving.

In Michael's defense, I must say that the first is a fiction and the second a happenstance. Yes, there was that incident of Gryllos parodying Ignatios at the wedding, but Michael would never allow such public irreverence of a patriarch, no matter how much he despises him. On the second point, Michael is simply unable to tell the source of his power what to do. Vardas never listened to anyone.

Sadly, the last accusation has some truth to it. One of

Michael's recent acts has been to commission a new stable, decked out in finest Cappadocian marble and running water for his prize horses. If that were not affront enough, he pronounced it his legacy to the ages, comparable to the Ayia Sofia or the Parthenon!

The pamphlet succeeded in drawing a large crowd at the Ayia Eirene, at which Ignatios' followers call on the monks to petition the Pope to sanctify Ignatios' appointment. Of course this amounts to an insult to the Imperial Throne!

Photios writes that he is shaking in indignation by the time he has crossed the market and arrived at the portico to Vardas' new mansion. The servants are being dismissed from a newly-laid inner courtyard. Vardas is on a couch, drink in hand. Michael has arrived without the usual entourage of hangers-on but appears to be in equally good spirits.

"Come, come, cousin," Vardas says to Photios' glum expression. "This is what you wanted, is it not? Our Thunderguts will, well, ... thunder no more. The path is clear for you to take office."

"But this is not the message of the gospels," Photios says. "Under the circumstances, I will not be party to such violence."

Photios gets up to embrace him, grinning broadly. The two kinsmen were always too close for anyone's good.

"What circumstances?" asks Michael. "We banish him to his estate in Terebinthos, and you allow yourself to be tonsured tomorrow. On Monday we shall arrange that you are declared a sub-deacon. If I am not incorrect, this means that by Tuesday we are within our rights to give you the full title of deacon. By Wednesday you shall take holy orders. On Friday I will see to it that you are bishop, and archbishop on Saturday. That way, on Christmas Sunday, when Ignatios would normally begin the Mass, the path will be clear for the brethren to confirm you as Patriarch."

"Both of you are wildly misled," Photios says, "if you think that I want to lord it over a bunch of cutthroats and back-stabbers who stick blindly to tradition in the name of God!"

They laugh out loud. Back in his quarters he begins drafting a letter. Tradition dictates that a new patriarch must inform the college of patriarchs of his assumption of duty as soon as it is decided.

24. King of all men

It turns out that the court is to receive the papal legates, and Photios must arrange a council. Evidently, Ignatios and his misbegotten followers have already written to "that most holy, sacred, and reverend fellow-minister, Nicholas, pope of old Rome," imploring him for Ignatios' reinstatement.

Photios writes back to Pope Nicholas in the most flowery language, begging him to become the confidant of his sorrow in assuming the burden of the Patriarchal throne, reminding him that the clergy had one intention, one determined resolve — that of imposing the episcopate upon Photios in spite of himself.

Sometimes I am not sure who is more provocative. The Pope writes 'It is Our Will that Ignatios should appear before our envoys that he may declare why he has abandoned his people without regarding the rules of our predecessors Leo and Benedict. All the proceedings will then be transmitted to Us, that we may judge by Apostolic authority what is to be done, in order that your church, which is now so shaken, may be firm and peaceful for the future.'

Nicholas demands that we must give back Calabria and Sicily. It is unreasonable, Nicholas writes, that an ecclesiastical possession should be taken from him by an earthly power — by which he means the Emperor. This upsets Photios no end.

Well, I must agree with our scholar cum Patriarch! Sicily has always followed Constantinople, based on the very tradition of the Apostles that the Pope invokes. At the same time, Nicholas somehow stretches the argument all the way from Ignatios' deposition to the possession of land. This is devious logic!

Photios writes about all this to Michael. And about how much he worries for Michael, as a father would a son, because of his labors far away on campaign again, on the Euphrates. Perhaps Photios understood, as I later did, that Michael was always in the tow of a rebellious black horse which persists in dragging him down, especially when he rejoices in moving forward.

Photios' words make me wonder why Michael is this way. Who knows how God throws the dice, and how these decide the seed that, in turn, becomes one of us? No doubt Michael's heart sinks at the thought of another day of dull preparations: the tedium of planning maneuvers and setting up supply lines, interspersed with short, often deeply unsatisfactory bursts of warfare. I can see him walking out, as far as possible to the farthest reaches of the trenches, to find solace in the deep black sky, hanging like a diamond-studded anvil over his head, with wine in hand, of course. Or perhaps I am completely wrong, and he lies there in the night heat, driven mad by the endless cacophony of the cicadas, tortured by the thought of my body, warm and inviting, lying next to his.

† † †

Yes, Photios' words do make me regret what happened to your father, dear Leo. I am not as quick at putting things behind me as this tale might suggest. But what of my Peasant? Vassilis is indeed always at Michael's side, and for good reason. Right now he enters the Imperial tent and unstraps Michael's sandals. He oils his hands and rubs the Emperor's feet. There is little need to speak. After what happened today they are beyond words.

They had accompanied a small group of riders that morning on reconnaissance. Some reconnaissance! The group had wandered rather sloppily out of formation along the hilly slopes of the river. General Petronas had remained in the camp, deep in disagreement with suppliers over the costs of a provisions contract.

Vassilis had to shut up the men with a sharp hiss when he heard the first strange horns in the distance. These bored City boys didn't seem to know anything about lying low and seeking the prey — rather than becoming it!

At the bottom of their hill lay a vast encampment, dug in and surrounded by pachyderms. Vassilis had only heard about these enormous creatures in drunken storytelling, about their size and strange trumpeting noises. But the unruliness of the Romans had proved too much. One of the horses strayed into view of the Abbasid guards below. As the alarm went up through the Abbasid camp, arrows poured up at them.

Within a heartbeat Vassilis had grabbed a shield and flung it over Michael, just in time to prevent an arrow from entering the Emperor's flesh, but not fast enough to prevent a nick himself.

Then a sudden cry rang out right next to them. Damianos, Michael's drinking chum and erstwhile Companion of the Bedchamber — though he never came near the Imperial quarters — lay gurgling in a fountain of his own blood, an arrow pinning his neck to the ground, his helmet still in his hands.

Tonight, Michael cannot stop touching Vassilis. "Today you and the Holy Theotokos have saved us," he murmurs. "We are brothers in life and death."

"I am yours to command," Vassilis says. Clumsy kisses and embraces follow. "As you are mine to protect. Lately, it has become clear to me that my place is here, that my love for the Emperor of the Romans rises above all else."

Vassilis enjoys the tender touches to the Imperial person allowed him to-night, the kisses and the shared gentleness. Perhaps part of him wants the child to grow up, to become a man for him to embrace, while the rest of him simply wants to play with his new position of being held in confidence.

Michael takes Vassilis' hands in his. "Dear Damianos, his death was in vain. Those filthy Abbasid caught us unprepared, but tomorrow we will get our own back, won't we?"

Little does Michael know what awaits them. The tent flap gets shoved rudely aside, and a messenger from the City announces himself, covered in river dust and bad news. Photios and Vardas have sent letters and urgent messages. The Rus have laid siege to the City. Would the Emperor please provide specific instructions?

† † †

Back in the Gynaeconitis, we have just shared a hot jasmine infusion after a long morning's weaving, and are feeling quite relaxed. Nowadays the women seem more ready to listen to me. The Regent and Dekapolitessa live in silken entrapment in their quarters. Without them there is no one to guide us. So I have taken to directing activities, and the women are often happy to act on my proposals.

I suggest we play the game of lists, which goes down well. Sometimes the lists we come up with are clever enough to make us laugh, and the last hours of the day fly by before we go home. Usually though, we run out of ideas, and the lists get us thinking about other more interesting topics.

We agree that today's game is to list all the things that should be large. Gemma reels off a good list. "Fruit. Homes. Cloaks. Horses."

'Priests," says Theophano. That gets raised eyebrows. "Who would believe a priest who is not ...imposing?" she says. We know who she is thinking of. It is easy to laugh about Thunderguts openly now that he is no longer in power.

"That makes me think of ...candles," says someone else. We nod in agreement. Nothing is more satisfying than the appearance of a thick beeswax candle, aromatic and imposing, penetrating the darkness.

"Men's eyes," I say, suddenly. I'm not sure where this has come from, so I add, "When they are too narrow, they look feminine. On the other hand, if they were as large as bowls, I should find them rather frightening."

Others pipe in with various suggestions. Braziers. Beds. Olive trees. The petals of roses.

"And horses," I say, "horses as well as oxen should be large." The women titter and nod knowingly at one another. Gemma retorts: "I am surprised you have not mentioned your favorite subject by now."

She is just jealous. I've told the women very little about Michael and me. Then I think about the new man, Vassilis. How bizarre to have such a fine, self-possessed creature in the tow of a young pup, even if the pup happens to be the Emperor? What would he be like in close embrace? From the little I have seen he is a person who is in no way eccentric or imperfect. On the contrary, his appearance is remarkable — and I wonder if he could be that rare thing, a man who is superior in both mind and body, and who remains flawless all his life?

As if following my thoughts, the game has moved on to our other favorite subject: the men of the court. The main topic is Vardas, whose lustful advances, though old news, still cause concern to those who have not been the subject of his attention. It's now common knowledge that the old lion devours his prey when on all fours, lapping and licking it into submission, although some feel that a wild boar rooting for mushrooms would be a more appropriate description!

Just as speculation is about to overtake reality and leave it halting far behind, the daughter of Eparch Oryphas joins us. Apparently, the wild Rus have finally reached the City walls: pale-skinned, blond barbarians, with braids like women, wearing a combination of leather, coarse chain mail, and skins. Our men, the few that are not away on the Euphrates, are already marching to the battlements. Then a baby starts crying.

But by now we are in full flow. With the infant tucked at its mother's breast we all laugh at hearing about the braids — like mine, they tease? I wonder if these Rus are the people I was taught to fear as a young girl on Father's knee, our distant cousins from the lands along the river Dniepr that lie far to the east of the City. This gets me nostalgic again. When will Father return from the north? No doubt he will have heard by now of my doings with Michael. "The court has a thousand ears and tongues, but no mind" is one of his favorite sayings.

Some of the girls claim that they can hear distant thumping. They jest that Vardas must be hard at work again. A slender priest enters. We stifle nervous grins and exchange winks and gestures over our earlier discussion on the preferred size of the clergy. What is the man doing here? Beseeching us to pray while the Icons are displayed on the battlements? Who is displaying Icons? Why, the Patriarch of course. But what is there to worry about, I wonder? Our walls have never been breached before. I look around for diversion.

Vassilis' wife, Maria — the Bulgarian as we call her — had arrived some weeks earlier, in a confusion of strange, pony-tailed knights, coarse-shod women, and tears. The handsome young Constantinos is often by her side, a fine young sapling, bursting with strength and good looks. Maria mingles sparingly with the others, her provincial Greek not always up to the subtleties of the lies and innuendos being exchanged, some only half in jest.

I am of a whim to find out more about them, and, in particular, Vassilis. I decide that this is a good time to make new friends. As Maria sits, I get up to kiss her gently on the forehead. She looks relieved. I nod to Gemma to show the handsome young man the gardens, so that Maria and I can become better acquainted in peace.

25. Master of none

Photios' words amaze me as I read them now. I hang my head in shame when I think that we women don't realize sometimes quite how hard it is for our men. They come home, having weathered fear that would have frozen the blood in a woman's veins, and wait patiently for their supper and a quick embrace before bed. Though I, of course, have no one come home to me yet, though some may say that Michael is mine. I might have his heart, but it is he who possesses me. And he hasn't returned yet.

Despite the fact that the Rus had to cover so many lands and kingdoms to get to us, so many rivers and seas, they came. They ravaged the suburbs, destroying fields, houses, herds, beasts of burden, women, children, old men, and youths. They thrust their sword through everything as a matter of course, taking pity on nothing, sparing nothing, like locusts in a cornfield, like mildew in a vineyard, like a whirlwind, or a typhoon, or a torrent.

Where was Michael? Far away with all the armies and commanders. We were deprived of everything. But we were not completely helpless!

Today the priests and monks are out in full force, processing along the battlements, chanting and brandishing Icons, many of which are freshly painted images of the Theotokos. Battering rams pound against the Gate of Eugenios, at the side of the harbor, that proud legacy of the second Theodosius some four hundred years earlier. At this rate they will eventually break in. Some of the catapults, primitive though they are, succeed in launching over the walls. Gate hinges bulge and creak. Scores of Rus ladders are propped up against the walls, the invaders' coarse limbs moving up them with ease, trading shouts in apparent fearlessness as they go.

Vardas orders the bridge to the inner walls to be pulled up — from the other side of the moat, that is! So the soldiers and clergy are now on their own, caught between a moat and the Rus.

Small carts have drawn up to the foot of the gate just before the bridge was lifted. The carts contain barrels, several bellows devices, and stretches of oiled, leather hosing. Vardas orders more men down to move the barrels up the ramparts. It's Vardas' idea. There will be great risk to our men nearby, but it could work! Even if it doesn't do much ... it will at least terrify our attackers.

The men roll the barrels up ramps and then display phenomenal strength tying them up and hoisting them to the top of the ramparts. The soldiers unpack the hosing and attach one end to the bellows. Metal nozzles at the other end of the hosing are extended on long poles over the edge of the ramparts. The ends of the nozzles have wicks attached. A flaming torch appears, carried on high, like that of a marathon runner of old. Even the chanting stops as the wick is lit.

Suddenly streams of liquid fire gush out of the hoses and onto the nearby Rus. Limbs curl and roast. The men roll in agony down the slopes. The flaming naphtha licks at the wooden scaffolding of the machinery, as well as the ladders and the grass around the gate. Retreat to the water is the only choice. I am told that the chaos is both marvelous to behold and pitiful, for the pain is beyond comprehension, and almost always fatal.

Now the siege scaffolding is on fire. It crumples down the slope into the water, which steams and smokes as the naphthalene spreads across it. Men churn the water with their arms and legs, and flaming oars. Some pull out to sea in burning boats while others drag their charred limbs on board. Our men stagger, and weep, in relief.

Back in the Ayia Sofia, with all of us feeling safer thanks to watches set across the Bosporus in case they return, the court gathers to celebrate a service of thanksgiving. Photios cites the bravery of the soldiers, the cunning of our very own Vardas, and of course the protection of the Theotokos. Her final blessing was to release a downpour shortly after our defense, dousing the flames which threatened to engulf the harbor.

††††

A MONTH LATER, IN THE FALL OF 859 AD
Until Michael's return, a decision on the crowning of his new wife

is still outstanding. Speculation is endless as to what will become of her. Dekapolitessa makes little attempt to show her face in the Gynaeconitis, spending time, it is rumored, with Theodora and her small coterie in the Karianos.

Given our headless state, a visit from Kassia the Nun seems ominous. She would never have come if Theodora were here. The woman who famously refused marriage to Theophilos is a common irritation, speaking out against every perceived wrong. To make it worse, she appears to want to teach us a lesson.

"The rightful patriarch sits like a common thief in jail," she pronounces, arms on her hips as she marches along from the entrance. "While you amuse yourselves with garments and idle chatter there are those who suffer injustice!"

There is nothing I despise more than a low woman taking on airs that are not hers to adopt, especially one who smells quite so badly. I decide to speak for everyone.

"What would you have us do? Don hair shirts and beat ourselves in front of Photios' door? I don't think it would have any effect on him." This gets a titter from the younger girls.

"How pitiful," she says, "to see such hard hearts. Show some remorse, at least."

"Remorse for what?" Eudokia asks. "We are innocent, sitting here all day long, doing our best to supply our men's needs. What part can we possibly play in all this?"

"The injustice done to Mother Church bears some consideration!" retorts Kassia.

"The Emperor is away," I respond, "as you well know. Take up your case with him when he returns."

"While we all wait, a most holy minister suffers in prison," says Kassia. "He has taken a bad chill. Who will care for him?"

"That may be so," I speak firmly, "but who was standing our ground as the barbarians were climbing our walls? Where would your monasteries be now had the wild Rus entered your houses, drunk from your holy chalices, or picked their noses with the Finger of Christ? If Ignatios and Vardas were still at odds with one another, fighting on every corner, shaming our state, we would not be safe today, and you would not be here to speak to us in this way, I am sure!"

The women cheer me on. In fact, I don't care who is right or wrong, I just want the best man fighting for me.

"Very well argued," smiles Kassia, "but I still want to know which of you is ready to stand by your Patriarch ... your deposed Patriarch," she amends as I open my mouth to protest. "All I need is your assistance – to take him and those staying with him some medicine and clothing. I am planning a boat trip to Terebinthos with several Stoudites. Who will join me on this mission of mercy?"

Well, the others can do what they want as far as I am concerned. Some go over to talk to Kassia. Apart from occasional diversions like this, time weighs somewhat heavily on my hands. Of course we continue with the regular daily work, spinning and weaving cloth for our families and endless banter for ourselves, much livelier without the Regent's chilling presence. As I have said before, with no Augusta in attendance, no first lady to guide our thoughts, we are much freer to turn our attentions to other pursuits. With Michael away, I am even freer than before. The clandestine visits to his quarters before he left were tiring and not as rewarding as I'd expected. So I start to read. And listen greedily to Maria, whenever she chooses to come to court.

She tells me stories which make me envy her more and more. How good it is, she says, for a woman to wake in the warm morning air, her husband's sleeping breath tickling her ear, his body a protective cocoon around her arms and shoulders.

Gradually, I learn how Vassilis receives a regular pension from abroad. At first, Maria avoids the subject, but I wear her down gently. The merchant widow Danielli has been providing them with money, and it was she who arranged for Maria's arrival in the City. She provided them with horses and an escort for the trip, not to mention adequate cloth, jewelry, and woven garments for her appearance at court. But what could Danielli possibly want in return, I ask, quite amazed? On this Maria refuses to speak. My curiosity is piqued even more. I decide to discuss the matter with my friends Eudokia and Gemma. Eventually we are all talking about it so much that when Maria joins us we struggle to find something else to discuss.

I can't imagine what Vassilis sees in Maria. Granted, her hair is still shiny black and well dressed, but she is already in her late thirties. What a stale loaf for such a fine young man! What manner of charms could she possibly exercise that would interest him? When I listen to her I become angry about my own situation. If such a woman can have a man worship her as an equal, then why must I be resigned to the life of a concubine? I thrust aside my reading in anger, determined, more than ever, to find a proper husband, no matter what it may take!

† † †

The Throne Room is dimly lit, and the Emperor has ordered that extra lamps be brought in. An uneasy clutch of senators files into the room. Michael reclines on the double-seated Throne, finding it hard to avoid folding a knee in Christ's space.

The last years of constant campaigning with Karveas and his Paulicians, not to mention the Emir al-Aqta and their allies along the Euphrates, have taken their toll on our Emperor, not to mention an ongoing pique that he completely missed rescuing the City. Even his morning wine has left him sluggish and full of yearning.

Vardas and Photios stand beneath him on either side with my Peasant not far away. Michael gestures for silence.

"We have finally returned to respond to the great need of our City," Michael begins, to barely suppressed sniggers. "Yet the City has stood well, under the careful stewardship of General Vardas, and as a result we are all safe. Uncle, may the Theotokos bless your hands and your heart — always in our service — and now greatly in our debt."

Vardas nods in a remarkably humble way. There is general assent. It is hard to deny the truth in this. Michael continues.

"During our years in the east, the General and the Patriarch have invited men of great learning to join us, with the hopes of ... bringing back to life our university, so that it may one day rival those of antiquity, such as those that existed in Alexandria and Athens. With his careful and loving acts this past year, we are indebted to our uncle. He has done more than act as our very good keeper. He also wishes to make better men of all. It is fitting and right that I bestow on him the title of Demestikos ton Scholon."

Symvatios steps forward and intones, "Worthy Demestikos, blessed of the ancient house of Mamikonian, we salute you." This gets a reluctant "Worthy, worthy." The faction leaders are silent. Where are the ritual acclamations?

"We will hold the ceremony, in due course, to honor everyone with all proper rites and public acclamations. But today we mourn the passing of Damianos, our Companion, on the Euphrates."

Everyone is taken aback. Mention of the Companion of the Bedchamber is hardly suitable for such a gathering. They gaze at their feet. Michael clears his throat.

"So we have decided that Vassilis the Macedonian, who has so courageously protected our person on the banks of the Euphrates, is to be our new Companion, a duty to be assumed immediately. That is all."

The senators file out, muttering and shaking their heads. Vassilis moves to the foot of the Throne and lowers his head. "There is no need for this great honor. I am always yours to command. You know this."

Michael climbs down and falls into his arms. He is trembling. "I do. Yet ... I am so tired. Without you by my side, I fear that each day will be more wearisome than the one before. You are more than a companion. You are my brother and father as well."

Vassilis takes this simply. "It is time for you to rest, to get your strength back. You must not concern yourself."

Michael gazes up into Vassilis' eyes. "Travel. War. Marriage. All duty — all slavery. We should be the masters. Though what did Plato say ... that the masters are the slaves?" With his head on Vassilis' chest, he murmurs. "I want joy, love, and beauty. Bring me my Ingerina. Only her touch can restore me."

"I will do as you command," Vassilis says.

"At my chambers, tomorrow evening. I would have you both there!"

26. Knight and bishop to king's flank

Ten months later, late in the summer of 860 AD

The spicy market smells fill the room, enticing Maria out of bed, even as her gaze falls on the small Icon of Saint Vassilis nailed to the wall — to which she give thanks again for being next to the person — once a boy, now a man — who she wants to wake up next to for the rest of her life.

Constantinos is barely able to wolf down some yogurt and honey before insisting that they head out to play. The new accommodations have worked out well — Maria does not need to go to court if she chooses not to. She would rather spend the day here making new friends at the market and watching their son to make sure he keeps out of trouble.

Vassilis has had his fill of the court lately, even though they have only been back a few months. He would like to be out on campaign again, with Michael. The life of a warrior appeals to a man who has grown up with the boredom of village life.

Constantinos is still quite lonely; his poor Greek does not quite allow him to mix freely and he often suffers abuse for being a Scythian — as do all foreigners from the north. Vassilis has not been able to get him a tutor yet at court, and he wants them to spend more time together, so that Constantinos can learn the old ways: to read a little, pray a lot, and be ready for anything.

Papa has a surprise for him. They are going to spend the whole day together. But first they will go down to the market with mother to buy today's meal. The boy — a young man a moment ago, but now a child again — embraces him and rushes off to pull on his sandals and a fresh tunic.

The market is a moving mosaic of smells, arguments, and color. Vassilis really has no time for the noise and the debate over prices, but soon there is a monstrous sea bream in the basket and a fine bunch of okra.

"What should we do know, eh?" Vassilis whispers into Constantinos' ear. "A turn around the bay? Or a race to see who can make it first up the ramparts?"

The child is wide-eyed. Are they allowed up the ramparts? The Companion has the run of the City if he wishes, Vassilis proudly informs. The decision made, they leave mother behind. There is much work to be done, and, anyway, one of her new friends has come around with some honey cakes.

How you loved your boy, my darling Vassilis! I knew it, and I am sorry for what happened. But a hen's concern is always for her brood. From the condition that Vassilis and Constantinos came home in, Maria can only imagine what must have happened.

They stroll across the courtyards within the Palace complex, skirting the walled walkways. Vassilis proudly points out the Emperor's quarters but, of course, the young one is not very interested. No matter — there will be plenty of time for him later to show his face at court.

Now away from the Palace, the Hippodrome directly behind them, the stairs of a tower in the south wall materialize from behind a stretch of trees. Vassilis challenges Constantinos to a race up into the dark stairwell. Their legs and lungs burn with effort as they burst out into the sunlight. The Bucoleon Palace squats magnificently at the shoreline in front of them.

"It looks as if the bulls and lions are alive!" says Constantinos. I, too, can gaze at the reflections of these marble ornaments off the Sea of Marmara for hours.

"You beat me! How did you get to be so quick in Pliska?" Vassilis teases.

"My friends would race me to the river every day." Constantinos nestles against him. "It would have been more fun if you had been there. We climbed lots of trees — there are so many more than here. But here we have the sea. Perhaps one day you can take me out on the bay?"

Now here is the myth Photios believes he invented. It is not his at all. Vassilis believed this before he ever set foot in the City.

"Over this small sea lies Anatolia," Vassilis says. "A long, deep land, even more beautiful than what we see here. At the end of the land, on the other side of some broad mountains, is our home, the kingdom of Armenia, and far to the south of this is a great city, Caesarea, where my patron saint lived."

"Why are we here, Papa, and not there?" Constantinos is ...was a bright lad. I can easily imagine him thinking hard and questioning everything.

"Because we were thrown here by those more powerful than us. They took your grandparents from the rich lands they lived in and dropped them in a rocky place, leaving us at the mercy of everyone who was more powerful than us, like the Bulgar ...and the Romans."

"But isn't the Emperor powerful? Couldn't he have saved them?"

"There was a different Emperor then, a cruel man, who cared neither for us nor what we believed in."

"Will you be Emperor one day?" I love how children always come up with tricky questions like this. Though yours are sometimes impossible, my bright little Leo.

"I doubt it. But God's will is difficult to know. As he set up his Son, a man, to be our Lord, so he could take even the lowliest, humblest beggar to be Emperor."

"You are no beggar!" Constantinos stretches up to touch Vassilis' face. "You are a very special papa."

Vassilis pretends to bite his fingers, and then mock wrestles him to the ground. "Why, even you could be Emperor one day!"

Constantinos slips out of his grasp and they hurtle along the ramparts, one after the other, teetering on dangerous slopes, jumping to adjacent walkways, like the arrogant little Macedonian goats on whose milk Vassilis was raised.

As the child tears out of sight around a corner, Vassilis hears a cry. He finds Constantinos lying curled up on the stone floor, blood dripping from an elbow, tears flowing.

Vassilis ignores the wails, does not waste time on comforting, but pulls off his own tunic and tears it into ribbons.

"You are fast, but a bit silly, aren't you? When you escape danger, you must not allow yourself to fall into something worse. You must be fleet of foot like Achilles, but sure of step like Hercules."

The wound wrapped up tightly, Vassilis takes him in his arms. I know he adores having his son close to him. He lives for the kisses that the little one showers on his eyes and hands, especially as the tears dry. Constantinos' cheek rubs against my Peasant's chest, where I have spent far too few evenings for my own satisfaction. The boy must be getting feverish. He seems to be muttering and repeating himself.

Maria heard the child's plea many times. "Papa, you went away for so long. I missed you so much. You must never leave me. Promise me that will not happen again!"

Perhaps Vassilis hugs the little one even more tightly as they descend the steps. "You are my greatest hope. You are my life and my dreams. You need never want for anything as long as I am near."

I wouldn't doubt it for a moment.

† † †

Without me or anyone else knowing about it, the Comptroller, at Symvatios behest, consults Photios for advice. I read that Photios pities him, being new to the job and eager to impress the Throne. Or perhaps it is vanity on Photios' part, that men should consult him for advice. The registers reveal a healthy increase in the quantity of merchant ships passing through the Golden Horn, especially to the eastern Themes. However this does not square with the duties being paid. This means that the state is not receive proportionate revenue from all this shipping! Photios calls for an investigation, to which the Comptroller agrees, eager to set his men to action.

Meanwhile gossip entwines itself around the Palace, like a vine groping for sustenance yet unsure where to rest its tentacles. Why are we refusing to let the legates enter the City to resolve the issue? Why does the Emperor play with the papal emissaries, keeping them waiting on the other side of Macedonia for more than a month, professing business and distraction? Michael had been indulging in plans for rebuilding churches and had even commissioned the re-fortification of the city of Ancyra, the ancestral home in Amorion, as well as the redecoration of the Virgin of the Lighthouse chapel, here in the Palace. All this to leave his mark on history, I suspect. At least it is better than the marble stables that are only partially used.

Photios and the Comptroller press the officials for more details on the goings on at customs. Over the months large shipments of olive oil have been coming from Patras to the Golden Horn, where they are resold to merchants taking them onward, mostly on ships destined for Amisos and Trapezus, in the Chaldian and Armeniacon Themes. But the sales are happening on board ship, and transfers from ship to ship are being effected directly, thus escaping the full harbor tax that would normally be applied if these goods were to touch the shore. Photios is cunning: he advises the Comptroller to find out who is involved, but also to do nothing for the time being.

Everyone admires Michael's pluck, the way he is not opposed to toying with the Pope. The bishops and monks are angry — they are convinced that Photios is encouraging Michael to show strength in order to bolster his own position.

The legates come and go. Vardas and Photios agree that Ignatios can be brought back from Terebinthos, and can perhaps lead the rebuilding of Pilos, after what the Rus did to it. We are all convinced the storm has blown over.

But then Vardas and Photios decide to engage in a little theater. Photios now has all the evidence he needs to prove who was behind the unlawful harbor trading uncovered by the Comptroller.

The two of them enter the Throne Room from the patriarchal entrance on the left side, silently and without the usual ceremony. Rooster and raven strut wing by wing, the purple, gold-lined cloak of the Demestikos shining out against the Patriarch's somber garments. Michael's nose is deep in documents but he is no doubt desperate for the morning's work to be done.

Vardas fixes an eye on Vassilis and crows: "Don't I get even so much as a nod? Or the Patriarch, here? Haven't you learned the correct obeisance in the presence of the Demestikos, or don't they teach you that in the stables?"

Photios reaches up to hand Michael a sheaf of documents containing the findings of the Comptroller's men.

"Or perhaps the lessons are different," Vardas says, "for those who frequent the dock sides? I've heard that is where you take your instruction."

Michael peers suspiciously at the papers in his hand.

Vardas continues. "I am waiting for a decent demonstration of the honor due to my station, Spatharios. Must I wait until old age sets in, until the Abbasid embrace Christ as their savior?"

He walks up to Vassilis and faces him, arms folded. Vassilis normally stands at attendance with hand on wrist — now his arms are at his sides, fists tightening. He forces himself to bow, though his legs tense as if to spring. Vardas reaches out suddenly and pulls my Peasant's chin up.

"My, my," Michael says, cocking an eye down at Vassilis, "it is obvious someone has been dipping his finger in the fish stew. Really, I expected something a little less simple-minded, fascinating though it is..."

"The facts we have uncovered are nothing, nephew. There have always been those who try to rob the state of its due."

"Then there isn't really any problem with this ...?" Michael says, hopefully.

Vardas paces, pretending to be deep in thought. "You are being made to look ridiculous — a laughing stock for anyone with a mind to think it through. This won't go down well with the soldiers."

Michael fidgets as Vardas continues. "I think it should be made clear that you do not stand for this sort of deceit, especially not within your own ranks. Don't you recall how your father felt when he discovered your mother's business interests? He ordered one of her ships burned! When those close to you deal in underhanded ways, you run the risk of the state being despoiled — involved in petty disputes and other unseemly business."

"Alright, Uncle, I think you have made your point. So what are we to do?"

"I worry that this knowledge is already public in certain circles. I suggest we deal with it in some suitably public way."

Michael slips to the floor and places a ringed hand on Vassilis' shoulder. He whispers in his ear. "I wish you had been a little more careful, don't you know who you're dealing with?"

Vardas smiles. "I would recommend something small, say twenty lashings in the Augusteon, no invitations or announcements, just anyone who happens to be passing. How about after a meeting of the Senate? Perhaps ten would suffice. We wouldn't want to appear too harsh."

Michael paces for a minute before returning to Vassilis. "I have no choice," he mumbles. "It's about reputation. You do understand, don't you?"

Vassilis pales and appears to be trembling. "As I have said before, I am yours to command."

"Well," announces Michael, "that's all settled then. Let's get it over with, shall we?" He flashes a sudden grin at everyone. "After all, wasn't it Cicero who pointed out that the merchant classes are the backbone of society, Patriarch Photios? So it can't be all that bad."

He strides across the floor, vanishing without any escort, while guards spring forward at a nod from Vardas, to march my beautiful Peasant off to the gaol.

27. Holy trinity

JUST OVER A YEAR LATER, IN THE FALL OF 862 AD

When Vassilis told me what had been going on — much later of course — I chided him severely before I let him speak another word. It was not that he lowered himself to negotiate with scum, even though they professed to be his countrymen, but that he believed that they would keep their mouths shut out of a sense of honor. Someone had bribed them to talk to the Comptroller's men. Honor counts for nothing among thieves — unless there is a price attached. I would have thought by now that even a peasant would have learned this!

If only Photios really knew what was afoot. Indeed, catching these small fish may have been very useful, distracting Vardas and Photios from much larger prey beyond their reach. How easy it is to be delighted by a full net in the light of the moon, when the sea beyond teems in darkness. You see, my patient Leo, back in the Gynaeconitis we are hearing other things, spiced even further by news of the whipping.

Although there had been no proclamation of the event, the whole court knows about it. We women can't talk about anything else, so fascinated are we by this stable boy from the sticks, that he should draw upon himself the wrath of the Throne in this way. The confusion stirs the broth even more — some are convinced that the Emperor bears the love that dare not speak its name for the Companion. So how could he let this happen? But I know Michael enough to know that this rumor is not true, and events today prove it to me, were that proof needed.

My curiosity is piqued. How exactly will this so-called justice be served? Though it would not be seemly for women to watch such an event, the day's work is done, and it is almost time to go home, so I reach for a head scarf, throw caution to the wind, and slip out with Eudokia to the Augusteon, to peer from the shadows. This is when she tells me what Symvatios told her: that Vardas is behind this show of authority. I forgive Michael, though not by much, but resolve to harden my heart toward the old bastard.

Some senators have stopped to watch, but one could hardly call it a gathering. Vassilis is standing with feet apart, facing the wall. The paleness of his arms is a wonder to behold, the muscles in them like knots of exquisite cypress. Thick hair flows down beyond his shoulders and onto his chest, covering his face, so I can only imagine how those fine cheekbones rest against the marble. Even if he were guilty, who could not bring themselves to forgive such a wonderful being!

My heart skips a beat as I conclude that I have made a mistake in coming. I cannot bear to witness that perfect flesh being corrupted, like an Odysseus at the mercy of some cruel Polyphemus. I turn to leave before the whip arrives, dragging Eudokia away.

And what does my Peasant think of such humiliations? Well, he fumes at his own stupidity! How Father would despise him, were he to see such an abomination! How Mother would weep at the shame! He utters an angry verse of Elijah to himself with every blow, leaving scarcely a thought for the pain.

In the days that follow, the gossip turns around how Vassilis took the punishment like a stoic, and how strange it is that he was treated like a common thief. Word has it that Vassilis has played some part in even further business dealings, with buyers and sellers from west to east. That must explain Vardas' wrath! I am intrigued, though I still have only an inkling of how far this peasant smithy has come from forging metal to forging deals.

Michael has returned from his trip to investigate the new fortifications in Ancyra, so I must prepare once again for our evening games together. The whipping still unsettles me, and I am not particularly of a mind for what he is usually after. This will be my first visit to the newly redecorated Karianos Palace, taken over by Michael since his mother and sisters finally relented and withdrew, though still not tonsured, to the Ta Gastria monastery, and I fear my tongue will get the better of me.

††††

The weather matches my mood. Thunder rolls over the Palace, driving down sheets of rain. Two eunuchs from Michael's retinue arrive to escort me and I step hastily through puddles, along mosaic pathways, beneath half walls and dark trees. The necklace around my neck — a gift from Michael — hangs heavy, even as the rain weighs down my cloak, and lashes my hair to my face.

The lightning chides me; reminding me of how weak my position is, just like the man who is my lover. Michael was once a teasing, adventurous youth with enough of a man in his loins to know how to please me. But that no longer satisfies me. Our bodies sliding together over silken sheets is all very well, but there is so much more to life if only he had a mind for it.

So my thoughts circle again around Vassilis, whom I have only glimpsed till now, mostly when he has come to summon me to the Emperor's quarters. His strong frame, his steady gaze and the quiet that surrounds him all fascinate me even as the image of him crucified against the wall haunts me. My thoughts alight on his face; I wonder what it would be like to run my fingers along the deep shadow that lines his jaw, or share a kiss with the sun that has kissed his well-shaped cheekbones, not to mention the bold feet and hands, clearly happy naked or shod. He is so like the men I have longed for in childish moments.

The huge dome of the Ayia Sofia is harsh and critical against the flashing sky. I cross myself angrily in its direction. Our steps quicken as the rain lashes down even more, driving us through bronze arches, over slippery marble pavements covered in pummeled branches and soggy leaves, to what I know will become a haven of misery for me.

Servants scatter as I enter the Karianos Palace and drag myself up the stairs. Michael obsesses about light these days, so candles have been haphazardly amassed. They coat the cloth furnishings of his chambers in somber red. I know that the darkness of the nights on the Euphrates once filled him with great fear that comes back to him at times. The candlelight is his remedy for this, though it fails to soothe. He is already reclining on a couch strewn with rose petals, a goblet in one hand, his feet being massaged by a new Abbasid slave, his lean frame barely denting the soft down cushions. The soft tinkle of the dulcimer seems incongruous. I feel slightly ill at ease — I am struck by the menses and would rather not engage in any frivolity tonight, though I know I will probably have little choice in the matter. I pray that I can escape by pleasuring him in other ways.

The hunger in his eyes annoys me, so I challenge him by staring right back. I fling my damp hair forward over my breasts and instantly regret it — this arouses him even more.

He gently removes my cloak, running a hand around my shoulders and along my arms. "Come, come drink with us." He gestures to the servants to leave. "As always, it is as if I am being visited by a member of the heavenly horde."

"I am reminded of what it must be like to be led out of the stable," I respond.

"Since my return I have waited long to touch you again. Holy Mother, you are a vision of unearthly splendor."

"Are we not to be joined by your wife this evening?" I decide to tease a bit, but instantly regret the mocking tone that emerges, my usual tenor when displeased or disaffected.

"Oh, come, my darling, do you not tire of this?" Michael smiles at the game. "Obviously we have other plans!"

He takes me to the couch and, with my cloak gone, my robe shifts aside somewhat to reveal an ankle. I don't bother to cover it. It is good to have a man rubbing my hair dry. Though I am hopeful that he is not up to the main act, judging by the smell on his breath.

"So what are playing tonight?" I ask. "Chess or backgammon? Promises or pleasure?"

"Life is often both," he parries. "Why not play one now, the other later? That way one doesn't have to choose!"

Suddenly Vassilis moves out of the shadows and hands me a goblet, startling me. I thought he had left with the servants. But I hide my reaction. I pretend not to watch his limbs move like a lion's as he stands nearby. He takes a drink for himself.

I face Michael again. "As you know only too well, my body is yours. But how will you reach my heart? For without the one, the other is but a vessel."

A frown flickers across Michael's brow. Women have always pushed him around so he takes pleasure at the game.

"I thought all this time that I had both in my grasp," he replies softly, a half-smile on his face.

"You are after my sense of duty," I pretend to examine my hands. But it is futile. The more I resist, the more aroused he becomes. "But my duty to myself must come first. Your honeyed words have turned me before, but now . . . "

Unexpectedly, Vassilis joins the fray. "Michael, the time for talk is over. You wish to have her?"

I like this. But is it the drink alone that clouds Michael's eye? Surely it is hardly Vassilis' place to speak here. "You know I do."

"Whenever you wish, if I understand correctly?"

"Enough! You know I am aroused and not interested in games!"

Vassilis permits himself a chuckle but quickly resumes a deferential mask. "I know. Of course. I just wanted to be clear. So why isn't it as simple as this? Divorce Dekapolitessa. And marry Ingerina. Surely the Emperor has the power to do this."

This draws a sharp breath from me. After the whipping, I expected a broken man, not this kind of boldness.

"If only it were as easy as you think for me to . . . discard my wife." Michael gets up and paces. "Since Dickbreath was . . . removed, I have had little support in the Senate. Uncle Vardas excels at foreign policy but we still need sway with the regular officials. Symvatios is too new and lacks influence. Actually, as far as I can see he seems quite dim. Sometimes I feel like a puppet master with no strings. Without Dekapolitessos' soft words in the right senatorial ear, we would have no control at all."

Michael walks over to Vassilis and rests his head on a broad shoulder, before speaking again. "But there is something entirely different that concerns me. The Pope is now in somewhat of a rage over Patriarch Photios' appointment, or rather," Michael grins, "at my ignoring his rage over this matter."

He sits down and looks at both of us. For a brief moment I see the burden he carries, and how he can't just give in to whim.

"Don't you understand? These are not games. Pope Nicholas, though an idiot, is looking for any excuse to make matters worse for us, especially in southern Italy."

He is now in front of me, caressing my cheek. "If Photios has to approve my divorce, on no grounds whatsoever, then the situation becomes impossible for all of us."

He turns to Vassilis. "This is not like moving a herd of wild horses from one side of a field to the other."

Vassilis shows no reaction to the jibe. The hammering rain blends into a drizzle, then soft stillness.

I attempt a smile, looking deep into Vassilis' eyes. Will he understand? That I wish to play a game, to test Michael's love for me? That this might even be the right time to chance something? That I must make a move or endure forever being little more than a distraction?

"Perhaps," I say, "it would be best if Vassilis were to consider taking a new wife."

Vassilis cocks an eyebrow at me, perhaps he even grimaces, I can't quite tell in the light.

"It's simple," I continue and get off the couch to go over to the man who will become my Peasant.

"If necessary, Photios can give the Companion permission to marry again, though I'm sure he doesn't need it."

I turn to Vassilis but he seems to be staring right past me. I still have no idea if he understands, but I don't let that stop me. "You haven't even married your wench before a priest."

Michael frowns, then grins. I have seen others suffer because of this grin, so I move into action. His legs part easily as I kneel down and, through his robe, tease his member into firmness with my lips.

But then he reaches out to Vassilis. As I labor, I wonder at these two and envy them. Clearly Vassilis offers something I will never have. When I look up they are gazing at each other, Michael's fingers on Vassilis' cheek.

"That will free you to marry my treasure here," Michael says, "and then ... she will be mine?"

Michael understands nothing of what he is asking for, the way a child assumes its doting parents will give it everything, without regard to cost.

"How can I?" Vassilis manages, his voice breaking. "What of my own wife and child?"

Michael reaches down and cups my chin, bringing it up to his face. "The months away have made me hunger for such beauty. But what you ask is too much for both of us."

His hands are in my hair, his tongue invades my ear, his teeth test my nose, my lips. What will Vassilis do now, I wonder? He turns away, his eyes veiled in shadows. Then Michael sees my gaze, and surprises all of us.

"Brother, after all we have been through together, is not everything for us to share? Come, join us in our pleasure."

Vassilis hesitates. I would be furious were Michael to say this to any other man. But the Imperial arm reaches out and pulls Vassilis toward us. A sigh escapes me.

As Michael devours my breasts, I reach out with my lips to Vassilis. And as Michael thrusts himself at me, I twist my head and let my cries fall on Vassilis' tongue. His mouth is the release I have always wanted – I long for the waves of pleasure brought by the pain of knowing him in heart and body.

My gown is untied. It descends. We have left kisses far behind, the sanctuary beckons, and Michael enters to partake of the Host. To my great surprise, Vassilis follows a few minutes later like a thief, by the chancel door. My head spins and I cry out, but I cannot escape. Fixed between two embraces, the altar battered on both sides, the wine and bread of the Eucharist flow freely. The Holy Trinity is made manifest.

I vow to endure this humiliation as long as needed, if only so I can draw Vassilis more tightly to me. I clutch at his fingers, that I may forget my discomfort by consuming them, by drawing all of him into me, but his hands escape elsewhere, to caress Michael, who pounds against me without mercy.

I care not, even when Michael's violent end writes itself in silent grimaces, followed by his usual strangled howl. For I have not been able to stifle my own cries for some time, following a different liturgy: that of Vassilis' hard breathing against my ear and his chin on my shoulder, as he finds his own distant way to heaven.

Lightning bathes us we sink onto the couch. But there is no time for further embraces. Thunderclaps pierce the air, and we hear men calling in the distance. Vassilis is the first to pull away to a window where he crosses himself repeatedly. The whip marks across his back make my heart want to burst in pity. He shouts that there are flames leaping from our beloved Ayia Sofia, threatening to consume the dome. Somewhere in my mind I wonder if this is an indictment, a glowing judgment, perhaps eternal, of the sacrilege committed today.

28. Forever empire

SEPTEMBER 1, 863 AD, FEAST DAY OF THE 40 MARTYRS
The prize worth winning is always shifting. That is what I would be thinking, were I in Petronas' boots, deep in freshly-dug trenches on a broad, brush-filled field outside Poson, gazing at the knife-sharp dusk cutting into the distant banks of the Halys River. He rested no more than an hour the night before, receiving reports of regimental movements and worrying about Michael, of course.

The plans had been overturned several times. The Abbasid scourged our people more boldly than ever before, raiding further north with each campaign, even up to Paphlagonia. Reports claimed thirty thousand or more on the march. But then ibn Yahya, the Emir of Tarsus, had turned back to the south, leaving al-Aqta to return through the Cilician Gates with only about ten thousand. Nobody could work out why ibn-Yahya had done this. Perhaps there had been a disagreement. Idle speculation was all over the court.

But the preparations had all paid off in one way or another. Michael and Oryphas had taken the combined forces of the Anatolic, Opsician, and Cappadocian Themes down the Halys River and landed just north of Nazianzos, before proceeding to Nyssa. A week later they had joined with forces beyond their wildest dreams, the crack mountain militias of Charsianon and Seleucia. With Michael at their head, they had moved in to surprise the Emir, who had been preparing for a new move northward. Early reports from the battle that followed indicated the fighting was intense, so Petronas has been mad with worry. That is, until a report with the imperial seal arrives which fills him both with pride and relief.

Michael's forces have suffered heavy losses, engaging in a tremendous pitched battle in spite of his predilection not to do so. But they succeeded in pushing al-Aqta to the northeast, and toward the waiting troops from Paphlagonia, Armeniacon, and Bucellarion, as Petronas and Vardas had decided should be the strategy in the final week before embarking on the campaign. Petronas is proud that Michael has led the troops so well. The Emperor has finally come into his own, the people are saying!

Petronas estimates that the Emir marches at most a day behind the report. This means the allied forces must be ready to push the Emir farther north, all the way to the coast. With the shoreline of Amisos ahead of him, al-Aqta will have no choice but to veer west, into the waiting arms of Petronas and his Imperial troops, some twelve thousand men. There will be hand-to-hand combat, Petronas promises himself, of a kind not seen before.

With the final orders issued, I can imagine him retiring to pray. He kneels in front of an Icon of the 40 martyrs, invoking Erasmia, his special martyr, on this, her feast day. Licinius, Constantine the Great's predecessor, had killed Erasmia, Aspa, and another thirty-eight pious women for their unashamed adoration of Christ. The Empire of the Theotokos had stood since then and must keep standing forever, even if it means holy war.

I'm sure Petronas has no idea when the golden glow of the Icon fades from sight. The darkness embraces him in soft arms, much as the final mother who waits to claim us all back. Either way he gets some rest, if only for a few hours, before one of our finest moments — the battle of Bishop's Meadow!

† † †

FOUR MONTHS LATER, IN THE WINTER OF EARLY 863 AD
My eyes water in the dim light of the oil lamp. My thoughts wander further than the texts in front of me as the script crowds the page. So little has changed over the past year since the Ayia Sofia nearly burnt down. There must be more to life than this. With ample time on my hands since the Regent vanished from court life, I plan to pass the winter months quietly. It is hard enough to show my face in the Gynaeconitis given the spiteful speculation at my goings on with Michael and Vassilis.

As I delve into the histories, I read about the Corpus Iuris Civilis. The Latin words are strange to me, so I am thankful that I can read about the work in Greek although there is no translation of the work itself. I wonder who really lives according to the laws of the Emperor Justinian, if no one can read his words. The issue is not the laws themselves — these are doubtless in use, at least in kind. But how can their spirit live if none other than jurists are able to read them? I try discussing this with Michael, but he isn't much interested, wringing his hands impatiently and then switching attention to my bosom.

The lamp-lit hours bring me to a new realization — the Law is there to stop our individual actions from impacting those of others; to create a safe, even a sacred space in which to move freely. But to my mind the walls of such a space can also make a prison. Surely there must be a time when one needs to break these walls. The question is: who decides this?

Consider the walls of the City. Are these not an outward manifestation of the Law, both because they are built at the command of the Emperor, and because they create a space for us to carry out our lives in safety? The answer gradually dawns on me — someone who is strong enough to break these walls will be the right person to build new ones. To make the Law, one must first be bold enough to rise above it.

Playing through these ideas in my mind is a new experience for me. Even if I, a mere woman, can't rule through the Law, at least one day my son might. Certainly, Justinian's writings ring true with what I believe a ruler could do, or even should do, if they had the power.

Theodora is equally fascinating. Not the old woman that hates us all, forced now, with her daughters, into the monastery of Ta Gastria, despite not being tonsured — a coven of witches ready to lash out with a curse whenever one's back is turned.

No, the Theodora that holds me is Justinian's wife, relegated to the ashes of history some three hundred years before. Was she, as they said, the greatest Empress that ever lived? I get Photios to help me dig out Procopios, though he shakes his head in disbelief when I broach the request.

Procopios is even more confusing to me at first because the historian contradicts himself. According to one of his works, Justinian's Theodora was a vile-spirited, calculating shrew. According to a different volume, she was a paragon of piety and wisdom to her lord and husband. What is one to believe?

Understanding gradually dawns on me. All great leaders lie at the mercy of their historians, and posterity is all one has when one has everything — an empire, a court, even endless riches — and it is easily polluted. I vow never to forget this as I set off for yet another evening audience with the Emperor.

† † †

Nearly three years have passed since the visit of the papal legates: three years of brooding at the center of that rotten web of old Rome. Now, a full year after hearing the delegation under Theognostos, Nicholas the Spider suddenly — as Photios puts it — excretes indignation. He declares a synod at the Lateran, at which he tramples on missives from Michael in front of a council of bishops. He demands that Ignatios and Photios both appear in Rome before yet another tribunal. He is not convinced that the legates have adequately examined the breach in procedure.

Then, in an epistle containing language bordering on the ridiculous, Nicholas pronounces, or one might say commands his brother patriarchs in Jerusalem, Antioch and Alexandria, to instruct their sees that the name of 'that man' — as he refers to Photios — should be anathema! Photios is to be deprived of all sacerdotal honors and of every clerical function by the authority of God Almighty, of the Apostles Saint Peter and Saint Paul, of all the saints, of the six Great Councils, and by the judgment that the Holy Spirit has pronounced by us!

'By us' indeed! He has never been more than first among equals. On whose authority does he adopt such a tone?

Michael is in no position to respond further, although he chafes at the bit. Photios explains to him for the hundredth time that the Pope has exceeded his authority. Precedent is there for neighboring bishops to judge him and Ignatios, and so they have, in front of the elite of the City. Even the legates have confirmed this!

More importantly, for Michael to answer would make it appear as if the Emperor should heed the Pope, when in fact the Emperor should answer to Christ alone. Michael ignores all this good counsel, of course! He writes the Spider a spiteful letter in Greek, referring to speakers of Latin as barbarians!

Aroused, no doubt, by his own churlishness, Michael is all over me tonight, his hands in my hair, his tongue in my ears, even in my nose! Since the victory over the Emir at Bishop's Meadow, the games have become stranger than ever. Lately he has become obsessed with consuming that which I consume. He puts a goblet to my lips. I take a reluctant sip.

"Drink!" he insists. "I want it straight from your mouth."

I gag as he tips the wine into my mouth and thrusts his lips on mine at the same time. Some wine seeps down my neck. I let myself go limp. Michael buries his hands in my hair and pushes me down onto the couch.

"Do you know that when you leave I dream incessantly of your return?" he whispers.

"And I dream of having a husband," I blurt out. This has been my plea for so long it hardly bears repeating.

"If only you were to be fertile ground to my seed as well as to my love, and bear us the Roman emperor we need for the future ..." Michael's voice trails away.

Well, well, that is just fine! "I thought you had a wife for that," I spit back at him.

'But you know I cannot bear to see her pale, sickly face — the thought of her ...yielding up my child while pleading with me, always, for more love, more ...that I don't have."

I realize suddenly that there might be an answer to this impossible problem. "Very well, if it is an heir your want, but cannot crown an Augusta, then someone close to you, whom you trust, could take over the burden of the crown with you."

"Really?" Michael says, sitting up. "Who would you suggest? Uncle Vardas is too old to be my heir."

"You have already shared much with the Companion, including me, as I recall. Is it too much for you to share the Throne with him as well?"

Michael sits up abruptly and laughs out loud. "Surely you must be joking! Do you know what that would cost me? I barely have the allegiance of the Senate, let alone the Generals. They are loyal to Uncle Vardas, and he would never stand for such a thing. Don't you remember that I was forced to agree to Vassilis' punishment?"

I will never admit that this is indelibly burned in my thoughts. "That is for you to decide," I say, feigning resignation. "But keep

in mind that the Companion has become well known, both inside
and outside the court."

I realize that I must tread very carefully here, and not give away
any secrets, even if they are only rumors, so instead of saying more
I remove my outer gown and lie down, conscious that the this-
tle between my legs shows through the silken scrim of my under
gown.

Michael slides down onto me, his tongue tasting the line of my
neck, his hand lifting my gown and reaching for the altar while a
wet mouth baptizes each nipple and the down around my navel.

"I will be no man's concubine for the rest of my life," I remind
him softly. "Not even an Emperor's, and doubly not as the wife of
a chamberlain."

29. A tangled web

Lately Michael spends more of his time holed up with his chari-
oteer friends than with me. This suits me well, until he sends for
me. Then the afternoons are filled with anticipation. Will Vassilis
be there tonight, or will he slip past me in the corridor as he has
done lately? I have taken to wearing no more than two or three
layers, in the hope that he will take notice of me.

If Vassilis is not there, I can barely hide my disappointment.
By the time I get to Michael he has all the desire but none of
the ability, so no matter how furiously we couple it is inevitably a
lengthy affair. This is largely due to a growing inadequacy where
it is most needed; sometimes I can barely tell if the bow is ready. I
must do all I can to speed the arrow to the desired target.

One day, after another Imperial bedtime engagement, Vassilis
accompanies me to my quarters. We have scarcely spoken more
than a few sentences since the night of the great fire but still he
keeps silent until we arrive.

"Where did you get that?" he asks, indicating a wooden-
bound codex.

"From the Patriarch's library," I reply, relishing his slow way
of speaking, using few, well-chosen words.

"Listening to my son learn to read has made me want to read
more," he says.

I am astounded. "What do you read?"

"I thank the memory of my parents for teaching me how to
read a few words of the scriptures every day," he smiles, showing
small but perfect teeth.

"Indeed," I smile, "for without our parents, what would we
hope to become?"

"I know some monks as well, who struggle to help me along.
I find it harder to write, but they are patient. Usually they end up

making fun of me, especially when they choose to recite something from the old Greeks."

Do you understand, my dears? I loved him because he struggled to understand, even as I struggled. But it was much harder for him. How could one not admire that?

"Is there a book that can explain a vision to me?" he asks.

"What a glorious thing a book is!" I babble. "I might have once described the crusty volumes lying about the Magnaura as dull tapestries waiting to be unfurled. But I realize now that they are maps of the souls of others. So what was your vision?"

"My mother."

"Don't you mean your wife? Or are they the same thing?" Then I laugh again, to cover up how mean that must sound. "I have been reading a lot about mothers lately. Did you know that Leo the Isaurian gave widows full authority over their former husband's children and property in the Ecloga?"

"I don't know anything about that," he says, frowning.

"Well, tell me your dream, then. Perhaps I can find a book to explain it to you."

"It was a dream within a dream; a vision ... while I slept. I play with pebbles just outside our country hut, one that father had built in the forest so that we could spend the autumn hours together. Father and mother had few precious days of rest between the harvests. They worked in the fields then. We roasted rabbits and mushrooms in an iron pot and caught small river fish. I remember the sour apples we used to pick. I remember the sweet air, rolling about in the hot grass, and napping in the shade."

He goes on. "I wake within the dream to find mother looking down at me. I weep in thanks that she is alive again, and right there with me, and father too! But as I stand up to embrace them the ground turns to mud beneath me and I sink into it. My legs and body grow slow, thick, and heavy, pushing my toes deep into the cool dampness beneath. My knees have become stiff knots of bark and my arms ... stretch out farther and farther toward the sun and the eagles flying overhead, as they circle and come to rest in my branches. My parents are now far beneath, reaching out to me. I long to hold them again, but I can't! I weep — and sap drips from my eyes!"

I have never heard so many words from him, and such moving ones, too. They harden my resolve. Vardas must pay for what he has done! So I search for something to say, because I don't want him to stop talking to me.

"Fortunately," I say, "the Demestikos has taken to spending most of his time traveling across the newly liberated Themes in western Anatolia. He works to restore trade, they say, and rebuild the shattered towns there, now that the Abbasid threat appears to have receded."

The poor dear resumes his normal mask — I want to kick myself for talking about the man he must hate. I decide to joke my way back into his heart. "And help a few young wenches shed their virgin knots, no doubt!"

The mask cracks into a grin. "I think that I have done more to restore trade than he has," says Vassilis.

I am all ears. He tells me what has been going on, unknown to the court. He talks about the widow Danielli. Her agents buy and sell everything imaginable: grain, wool, silk — not to mention the finest linen and rugs from her workshops, many of which lie beneath our very own feet. He tells me of agreements, of deals, about how he has helped Danielli to profit through the partners and friends he has made at court, and across the Bosporus, across the Black Sea as far east as Trebizond and south across Anatolia, even to the gates of Cilicia. I learn how she has rewarded him in return, with gifts of many kinds and promises of many more.

There you have it, little Leo. This is the moment when I realized that I must make Vassilis mine. This was when I saw that all he wanted was to learn more and care for those who care for him. Patras had left him with a desire to know, a lust for that furnace of ideas in which reasoned opinion could be forged into something new and bold. But the wanton celebrations of Theophilitzes and the Daniellis boy parading as philosophical intercourse were not enough for him. Not that he minded such distractions. What hearts he broke, mine included, especially when I realized where his interests truly lay!

I say whatever comes into my mind, my thoughts reeling. "It isn't enough just to know more and be a good intermediary," I say, "even if one has some gold to show for it." He listens, nodding.

What I don't say is that I could show him how to do even more, so that his heart's desires could be forever in his grasp. And that I long to explore the world in his arms, to navigate the seas of ignorance with common purpose, to show him what my quick eye will find, what we could hope for, together, what treasures and ideas and past stories of people we could discover, of people just like him and me, who struggle to understand why people struggle.

There is so much more I want to say but, for someone of my reputation as the Regent's notoriously disrespectful servant, not to mention the Emperor's plaything, even our time together to-day will provoke unnecessary wagging of tongues were anyone to discover us. Vassilis has already stayed longer than might be considered appropriate, so I encourage him, gently but firmly, toward the doorway.

†††

THREE MONTHS LATER, IN THE SPRING OF 864 AD
With Michael's letter to the Pope the matter might have been laid to rest, as far as we were concerned, if Boris, the Khan of all the Bulgar and the Slav peoples, as he then styled himself, did not shock everyone by turning arms on the very prince he once be-friended, Rostislav the Moravian. Then the news comes that the Khan has even sent an envoy to Louis the Frank, asking him for assistance, in return for bowing to Louis' crown!

The Pope would be Boris' spiritual lord as well, were Boris to strengthen the relationship with Louis. The loss of an ally to the Frank as well as a shift to the See of Rome would leave us in a very weak position. Vardas' solution is simple, and logical. He surprises everyone with a proposal to meet the Bulgar face to face, and right away.

Oryphas doesn't hesitate a moment when the Emperor commands that he, as Admiral of the Fleet, should lay on an attack fleet and lead it through the Bosporus, along the Black Sea coast-line, and up the Danube. It takes only a week, with Symvatios' very competent help, to provision the ships and to outfit them with crews. In fact they have to fight off the many eager applicants who are unable to resist being involved in what promises to be yet another victory after Bishop's Meadow.

Oryphas is delighted to be racing across the water, especially with fifty ships behind him, drawn in a solid line across the Black Sea and carrying some three thousand men, coiled and ready to spring on Pliska. Next to him is Petronas, the hero of the month, still glowing with pleasure at the success of Bishop's Meadow. Petronas regales everyone with stories of the Abbasid forces, in particular how the Emir's son fled southward after the battle, only to be intercepted in person by Macheiras, the leader of one of our most ferocious Akritai militias, the Kleisourai of Tarsus who, true to his name, had slaughtered the Emir's son in hand-to-hand combat.

Of course, my cunning Peasant has been brought along for his knowledge of the Bulgar, not to mention his ability to hold strong drink well. On the deck of the Admiral's ship, the night before their arrival at the mouth of the Danube, and in front of the officers of the middle rank, Vassilis explains it all. He says that the Emperor and the Patriarch are locked in feud with the Pope. The latter sits like a pompous worm burrowing around in some glistening fruit, its suppurating core as yet unexposed, as the dull-minded Bulgar reach out for it.

How easy it is to fall under the magic spell of such a simple but earnest speaker. Vassilis easily gives the impression of biding time, cocking an ear here and there, standing quietly behind every conversation, while taking in every word, and only speaking when absolutely necessary. The conversation drifts on to the recent Triumph. Why, the commanders want to know, has the Christ-loving Emperor taken most of the credit for himself? Doesn't everyone know that the victory belongs to Petronas' cunning planning, and to the men he led? Opinion is that this was such a great victory, that it may forever lay the Abbasid to waste — indeed, there can be no question of it! The sheer injustice fills them with indignation as the wine sinks them all into amicable incoherence.

Apart from Petronas' satisfaction at seeing the Emir's head raised on a spear and carried into the Hippodrome, I suspect that the grandness of a Triumph meant nothing to him. From the little I knew and heard of him, Petronas was not the kind of man to feel indignation at the praise the cantors heaped on Michael and Theodora, and even Dekapolitessa. He knew, rightly, that we should always be in debt to the women in our lives, if only for the very debt of life itself. It would be a triumph indeed if Michael himself could simply acknowledge this, and forgive both his mother and his wife, not for what they did, but simply for what they could not avoid doing.

†††

TWO WEEKS LATER, EARLY IN THE SUMMER OF 864 AD
The court has been abuzz with the news that Khan Boris capitulated within hours after Oryphas turned the fleet down the Danube. Vassilis tells me that he had suppressed the urge to grin and wave mockingly at Grozdan — this time on the other side — prostrating himself before Symvatios, Oryphas and Petronas as he sued for peace.

Vardas, in full anticipation of victory, had given prior instructions for the Triumphal return of the fleet via the Black Sea and down the Gulf of Burgas. He wanted it to stop at all ports along the way home, to fly the Roman standards and to set up garrisons. New Rome had humiliated the Bulgar, and all must know.

As much as I hate to admit it, we all have no choice but to acknowledge Vardas' brilliant take on the situation. A special set of chariot races is called to celebrate the victory, and Michael makes an announcement from the Balcony that stuns everyone.

"We wish to honor our most noble Uncle in a special way. To the prosperity of all men and the fall of malevolent enemies and barbarians, we have decided to invoke and bestow upon him the ancient title of Caesar, not only to represent us in our absence, but to rule on our behalf."

Vardas moves forward in senatorial white. He bows to receive a crown of laurel from Michael. The crowd roars and stamps its feet in approval for several minutes.

"To fill the position of Demestikos ton Scholon and to lead us in the war against the Abbasid we call on our brave Uncle Petronas."

Petronas steps forward and Michael passes the sword to him. Petronas turns to face the crowd and holds the sword out at shoulder level. The Imperial Guard raise their swords in a similar fashion. In one voice they cry, "Allegiance to Petronas!" and snap the swords back to their sides.

While not even a sword had to be lifted for the Bulgar to surrender, we are even less prepared for the events that take place after the crowning of the Caesar. Of course, we have none other to thank than that troublemaker, Photios.

After a long session in the Throne Room, Photios switches subject from the usual course of business. Symvatios is standing in for the Caesar who is not at court today. All the women chuckle when Eudokia tells us this. Symvatios confides to her everything that goes on in the Throne Room.

The little bookworm's deferential tone is bolder than normal when he speaks to Michael. "There is little … benefit," Photios says, "in pretending to the court that your wife is of any interest to you … or that the unwed Ingerina … is of no interest to you."

Photios' words get a raised eyebrow from Michael. No one, apart from Vassilis, has dared broach this subject with Michael before, so I realize this must be costing the old man some effort.

He ventures further. "Your Worthiness, if I say this, it is only out of concern for you and the easing of … events in the passage of time. Without an heir we have no choice but to regard every passing moment as filled with danger for the court's future."

Michael's lips purse beneath a frown.

"I suggest that you arrange for an heir soon," Photios says. "I can even make … suggestions for how to achieve this if the, er… conventional approach is not to your liking. But whatever happens, Inger's daughter must be wed in such a way that, regardless of your, er … personal attachment to her, the court and the City can have some faith in their future."

The storm clouds arrive briefly on Michael's brow. "I know all this very well, and have no need for reminders. I listen patiently only because you, dear Patriarch, are and always have been my conscience in most matters. I would bear it from no one else." The grin is back. "So I have decided that the daughter of Inger is to be married to the Companion. I'll leave the arrangements to you and her. Obviously, you will officiate."

With this news buzzing around the Gynaeconitis, I choose to clear my mind the next morning with a visit to the Ayia Eirene. It is dim and empty this early in the day, and I wonder what draws me here, to the home of the great Icon of Maria the Theotokos, our mother, whose celebration has been the center of the City's strength and success since the days of Emperor Heraclius. Can you feel her reaching out to you even now, my little Leo, you who have always been shy around women? Can you feel the stolidity of her measured silver-clad smile that both remands one yet guides one to eternity.

I am amazed to find Vassilis praying. At first, he doesn't see me, but then he looks up, his expression worried. "Why have you come here?" I whisper.

He says nothing, his deep brown eyes searching me out. I continue. "So you have come to find yourself. Is that it? Now that Michael has decided that we are to be wed to one another?"

"I am determined to learn ways other than those of muscle and steel," he says.

I laugh. "I know nothing of muscle and steel. After all, I am just a woman."

"There are many scholars," he says, "who come to the City hoping for learning. All men must search, in hope of finding."

Indeed! If only I had had the chance to talk to them myself, what I would have said! But that is empty dreaming — there is no place for a woman at these discussions.

He goes on. "There are so many people in the world — the Romans and the Greeks, the Abbasid and the Umayyad. It is like those maps you once spoke of, how the mosaic of the world fits together. What do you know of my own people, the Armenians?"

"What of them?" I say. "They were the first people to embrace Christ's message in its totality, and now stand freed from Abbasid rule since Petronas' great victory."

My poor Peasant! How he must burn with shame at his lack of proper learning. He can sense that others think him quite dull, especially at court. He sees it in their veiled looks, their lip-less smiles, especially when he frequently overlooks some subtle protocol.

"Well," I say, "what do you want from the Theotokos?"

He says nothing, but looks away.

"I seek ..." his voice breaks, "I seek forgiveness because I am parting from my ... from Maria again."

It takes me a moment to understand what he means. "You mean just as an infant cries when it does not see its mother again. Well, you cannot get away from that. Are you Maria's infant as well, do you wish to suck on her teat forever?"

I curse my sharp tongue, which often responds unbidden, but he just turns away. Then I take his arm and push him gently out the doors of the church. Now I am in front, racing across the stones, my breath stolen both by my speed and the excitement. I hope no one sees us, though we almost run into an old man around a corner, some court official, who registers astonishment.

I drag Vassilis to the entrance of the catacombs, where I hope to find some privacy in the passages, but he leads me down the stone steps and into the darkness. I almost trip over my robes, but his hard hands are there to hold me up. I want him, and he knows it. I place my hands on his face and my lips on his lips. His hands find their way to lift my robe.

Yet, there is something distant about him, something that makes me even more eager to feel his arms around me. Does he serve my need because he is a good servant, because he feels he has to, rather than because he wants to? What lies before him as we couple? An image of Michael flashes through my mind, his delicate bones showing through sparse sinews and a slender waist, his narrow face a portrait of painful release. Is this what Vassilis sees, as on that evening and many times since the Ayia Sofia erupted in flame? Perhaps he sees how he could be Michael, how he should be him — how he might never be him!

I writhe within his strong grasp, his gentle thrusts driving me out of myself and through the dark space, against the pillars that I know watch silently in the darkness, bumping against the ancient stone walls, suspended over the vast basin of water beneath us, rolling silently, swelling ceaselessly, to the point at which it must surely rise, burst and flood over all of us.

Part IV

Infinitum

865−867 AD

30. The godfather

NINE MONTHS LATER, IN THE WINTER OF EARLY 865 AD
Michael shifts restlessly on the Golden Throne. Vassilis is on his
left, taking in everything, learning how to work the court, and His
Petulant Worthiness, to get results. Photios is seated below them.

Michael, dripping sarcasm, jumps carelessly off the throne and
berates me: "Is there no end to the day's business, Patriarch? Is
this what my uncle has to endure every day?"

"Rostislav, the Moravian prince, is envious of the attention we
have paid to the Bulgar," says Photios. "He wonders why we do
not visit his realm to bring God's message."

"Does he? That a barbarian prince calls for our monks is interesting," Michael says. "Though the question is more about
whether he seeks favor with us or with God. Surely the Pope's
men have already settled in? So what would Rostislav want of us
unless ... it is to shore up his position against the Bulgar. No
doubt the few remaining survivors of the Rus have passed the
message to their Scythian brothers that we are a force to be reckoned with."

He throws himself back onto the Throne. "Now tell me about
Pliska — when is the big event?"

"It is imminent," says Photios. "The preparations for the
Khan's baptism are nearly complete, and will take place at the
new year festival of Saint Vassilis, a most auspicious time. I leave
within the week. There is even better news. The Khan has requested to be granted the Christian name of Michael."

Michael's delight knows no bounds. "Excellent!" he exclaims,
leaping off of the throne once again and almost embracing Photios. These outbursts are both charming and annoying to the Patriarch. In his better moments, Michael always was such a child.

Then Photios changes topic. "On a different topic — I need
... guidance." The sarcasm is lost on Michael as he preens. "My
brother patriarchs have divided opinion as to what to do about the

Pope. His words and actions leave me with no choice. Clearly, we are no longer in communion. If he cannot accept Mother Church, we cannot accept him."

Vardas strides in, saying "What's this I hear?" Photios explains again. "Does it matter?" says Vardas. "Why do we need the old fart?"

Michael nods in emphatic agreement. "I am tempted to join you in Pliska," he says, the subject already dismissed. "No need for any special escort, either!"

"What about your safety? We will be in enemy territory!"

"Nonsense," Michael says. "I'll take the Companion with me. What can Boris, er ... Michael possibly do at this stage?" He grins at Vardas' confused expression. "We're going to baptize another Michael!" he explains.

Vardas smiles back thinly.

"If I could just remind you of the main issue with the Pope," Photios tries again, desperate to get him to stay focused, if only for a minute.

"That's your problem," Michael says. "You're our Patriarch. You decide. Either way you'll have our full support."

Vassilis and I do not approve. But this is not the right time for us to protest. Not yet.

† † †

Steam curls gently out from a rough marble basin resting on stone blocks, a small fire burning beneath it. Photios is in Pliska with his monks, giving full voice to the liturgy over the mumbling and shifting of a gathering of thirty or so Boyars, a somewhat rough crew by our standards. Not even the Icons propped up against the gray stone walls subdue them, or perhaps they are much quieter than normal, Photios can't be sure. He walks the hall, censing them with frankincense, while trying to avoid suspicious gazes. Here comes the Khan, dressed in a white robe. Photios takes him to one side and prays over him.

I wonder what the Khan must be thinking, as he prepares for the sacred water to wash over him? Does he regret calling the bluff of the Romans, or was it a calculated move? His people understand fear and little else. Or does the Khan feel that, with this act, we stake our claim over him? That we are there now, and probably will be forever?

Boris processes to the basin and lets his robe slide off, revealing a loin cloth and fine sinews. His body glistens in the candlelight as the monks pour oil on him.

"As you enter the life of Christ, how do you wish to be named?" I imagine Photios intoning.

"I take the name Michael, after my father in God, the Emperor of all the Romans."

"May our Father grant Michael everlasting life through our lord Jesus Christ," Photios chants. "God have mercy on us, Christ have mercy on us, God have mercy on us."

Boris steps into the basin and crouches down, the abasement, no doubt, alien to his nature. Perhaps even as the water tumbles from Photios' hands the Khan cries out to God in silence, wondering if He exists, admitting that he too will have to pay for his choices, as we all do. As Photios pours water over him for the third time, he springs up, throwing his head back. Water spills in all directions, the droplets cascading like shattered glass into the dark before vanishing on the uneven stones beneath their feet.

† † †

As soon as Photios returns from the Bulgar I thrust myself into his study.

"You have come to discuss the wedding preparations?" he says. "Could this not wait? There is much ... business at hand."

"Your All Holiness," I say, bending forward to kiss the patriarchal ring about to slip off a bony finger, "I thank you for asking about that, but there is something that concerns me even more."

He nods toward a stool, but I prefer to stand. "I think you know exactly why I am here, and the difficult place in which I find myself. Imagine for a moment that I, as the Companion's consort — blessed in the eyes of the court and the church — were to bear a son. How would he stand with regard to the Throne?"

The Patriarch waits for me to continue. So I do. "You know as well as I do that the Emperor wishes to have an heir and that the Empire would be better for it. But you also know that I have no right to bear a child in the Purple — unless my husband were Imperial himself and could demand it."

"Yes, but surely all this is still . . . hypothetical," he says. "What is your point? Are you with child?"

"I am not! But given the extraordinary circumstances I face right now, that we all face right now, I would have you . . . conduct the ancient ceremony of Sergius and Bacchus." There. It is out.

His eyebrows shoot up. "Surely you jest! I have never even witnessed it, let alone learned the rites."

"The central question I find myself struggling with is: who would crown a Companion's son unless he was part of the Imperial family? This is only the way to guarantee it."

"I am sure something can be arranged," he mutters. Then he looks me in the eye. "Though I must stress that I will not consider the request unless I hear it from the Emperor's own lips as well." He turns back to his papers.

I leave, pleased at what I have achieved. But just what is it that keeps Photios so busy? I find out later, from Eudokia. The Bulgar Khan, just days after the baptism, had used his spies among the western Boyars to unearth another uprising. Faced with close to a thousand peasants, and with Boyars from ten districts at their head, he moved boldly and swiftly.

It is late at night, after an unseasonably warm evening, and the peasants are feeling light headed. Several Boyars have fanned the peasants' spirits into full flame with abundant meat and drink, and with loud speeches and dancing. Most tellingly, they rail against their Khan, now a new apostle of the strange Christ. What manner of man, they ask, would embrace the Christian god, with his cannibalistic rituals, and his monks with their women's gowns?

Now the peasants gather together, pitchforks held high, scythes at the ready, tramping down the mud-filled streets of Pliska toward the Khan's palace, a score of Boyars in the lead. Some wave firebrands, perhaps others simply call out, drawing strength from their numbers and the drink that rumbles in their stomachs.

But here comes an army of Photios' brave monks in procession from the castle gates, holding crosses and Icons above their heads, lit up with tapers, the Khan and his men behind them. I can just see the spectacle moving before those dim peasant minds. A god has appeared, bewildering them with the light reflecting off the gold of the Icons. They stand transfixed. The Khan's men have easy pickings, capturing no less than fifty of the rebel Boyars and their kinfolk that night. Photios confesses to some pride at how his godson — which is how he refers to the Khan — has carried this off. An apostle of fire indeed!

By sunrise the next day the Khan orders that the captured Boyars be slaughtered and thrown in the burial grounds outside the town, in front of their wives and children. The pale spring sun is left to wreak its slow revenge on their miserable lives, vanishing into the soil with each drop of their rebellious blood!

31. Syzygies

THREE MONTHS LATER, EARLY IN THE SPRING OF 865 AD
Snow melts beyond the window panes, reflecting the light of a meek spring sun into the chapel of the Virgin of the Lighthouse. Michael has seen to it of late that the chapel is well endowed. Gold tesserae cover the walls, gilded cornices edge every imaginable surface, and silver plaques or veined marble perch in those rare spots where the builders have pitied the viewer enough to let the gaze have some respite from the shimmering glare. It is excessive, but Michael likes it that way. There are even some new icons.

Eudokia and I watch from the Chapel entrance, conscious that we should not enter. This is a ceremony for men. Photios has done himself up in considerable finery, more befitting an empress than a patriarch, I would say!

The Master of the Wardrobe arrives bearing a wooden box. Michael and Vassilis enter in simple white, with two large wooden crucifixes hanging around their necks.

"God have mercy, Christ have mercy, God have mercy," the cantor intones. "Let us pray for our Patriarch..."

To which Photios replies, in chant:"Let us pray for your servants, the holy Emperor and his brother Vassilis. Because Thou art merciful..."

Smoke pours forth as the censer swings to the antipodal chant: "Let us pray ...to the Lord". Vassilis leads Michael in a bow before the Icons. Photios approaches to face them. Vassilis is familiar with the motions. After all, I wonder how many know of the rites he shared with Diomedes.

"For the servants of God," sings Photios, "who approach to be blessed by him, and for their love in God ..."

And the response of the gathering is "Let us pray ...to the Lord."

"That they may be given full knowledge of the apostolic unity."

"Let us pray ...to the Lord."

"That they may be granted a faith unashamed, a love unfeigned."

"Let us pray ... to the Lord."

"That they may be deemed worthy of glory in the honorable Cross."

"Let us pray ... to the Lord."

"That both they and we may be delivered from all affliction, wrath, and distress."

"Let us pray to the Lord."

"Help us, save us, have mercy on us and keep us, O God, by your grace."

"A ... men."

Photios continues in spoken voice, somewhat louder than usual. "Our Lord and Master, who made man according to your image and likeness, who deigned that your Holy Apostles Philip and Bartholomew become brothers in the Holy Spirit and in the way of the faith, who deemed your martyrs Sergius and Bacchus worthy to be called brothers, bless also your servants here, binding them with a spiritual bond, not in the law of nature, but in the way of faith and love. Make them love each other, allow them to be blameless and free of scandal all the days of their lives, protect them from every demonic influence, in order to glorify the most holy name of the Father and the Son and the Holy Spirit. Amen."

The two of them embrace. Vassilis' mouth is on Michael's — the "exchange of breaths", followed by an exchange of crucifixes.

Now at arm's length from one another, Michael is calm and collected, but Vassilis appears to be trembling. He runs his hands up and down Michael's arms, touches his shoulders.

The chanting ends. Only drops of melting snow on the outside panes break the silence. The ritual over, I am not sure what should happen next.

Then an inferno erupts. Maria arrives suddenly and charges past me, dragging Constantinos behind her. Shouting, "Papa!" he tries to leap into his father's arms but is clearly too big. An awkward scramble, they embrace, and then Eudokia and I draw the young one back to the entrance.

Maria bows toward Michael. "Most holy Emperor," she intones flatly.

Vassilis receives no such courtesy, only the sharp sting of her nails across his face.

"I know, yet care not anymore, as I am lost and soon to be cast aside. Lost in heart, lost from light, Lord have mercy on us." Maria's words lacerate the air.

She turns to the Icons, crossing herself frantically, and then back to Vassilis. "I thought our heaven was for eternity. But you ... your passion for yourself, not your loved ones, will be your fate."

She swings out at Vassilis again but he steps aside. "Why does all this matter more than those who love you?" she crumples to the floor, tears streaming down her cheeks.

Vassilis kneels to embrace her but Eudokia is there first. She lifts Maria to her feet, then takes Constantinos by the hand and leads them both out of the chapel.

Michael's lip curls mischievously as he beckons. The Master of the Wardrobe opens his mysterious box. "It seems as if your love for your Emperor will soon be your fate, my Magistros." He takes the clay tablets of this senatorial office out of the box and hands them to Vassilis.

"A double honor it is for me today," Vassilis says, "to share both you and this new office."

"This will be my small gift to you," Michael says, "for you have given me so freely that which I could have taken." Michael removes a band of gold from the box — the Golden Girdle — and places it around Vassilis' waist.

Then he lays his hands on Vassilis' shoulders. "It is conceivable," Michael says, "that there may be positions of even higher responsibility in the future." He turns to me. "But more importantly, we must begin preparations immediately for the wedding."

Photios suddenly comes out with: "This ... casting aside of Maria will not be taken lightly by Khan Boris were she suddenly to appear at the Bulgar court again with this news. I will speak to the envoy at length, to convey a message of appeasement."

"Think of something," Michael says. "I am sure some gift will smooth her return. Send the Khan some of our best stallions if you think that would help."

Vassilis turns suddenly toward the entrance. "Take the child from her!" he cries out. "My son stays with me." But he hesitates, and backs away from the entrance, rather than following them.

"Surely," says Photios, "you don't mean for the wedding to take place at the Feast of the Triumph of the Icons?"

"Indeed," Michael's smile returns. "It would be fitting for our mother's achievements to be celebrated as well. Of course, there is no need for her to be there in person."

† † †

How did that strike Master Photios, that union he was called to bless? It's a special treat to read his very erudite words — especially after he has written them, and without his knowledge. But what did he make of this ceremony?

Leo, I understand full well your loathing of the always inscrutable Patriarch. Pragmatic to a fault, perhaps he harbors some secret envy at this holy duo? Could this be something Photios himself longed for, to have such a blessed union, say with a student? I wonder if he is more of a follower of Plato than he will ever admit. Is there a part of him that wants to reenact the ancient roles of puer and senex, of Socrates and Alcibiades? One would never guess from what he has written.

The union between two men is not unheard of, but such a union between an Emperor and a peasant has not happened before, at least as far as I know. Yet how my soul sank when I saw the look on Vassilis' face during the ceremony! I feared then that, with both Maria and Michael in his affections, there would never be place in his heart for me.

Maria is safely back in her quarters, still raging and weeping, so I return to the chapel. Michael is leaving, with Photios in tow. I run to Vassilis and clasp his strong fingers in mine. I plant kisses on his beard and his eyes, and cup his face in my hands for what seems like an eternity.

"When are we to be betrothed?" I ask, perhaps too boldly.

His eyes narrow at this. But my girth, obvious even under the layers of clothing, doesn't seem to mean much to him.

"When next we celebrate the Icons ... three weeks from now. I think he may wish for your child to be born in the Purple."

My plans have come to fruition. I cover him again in kisses.

How hopeful this makes me! There is nothing more exciting for a young woman than to know her future is certain. How I pity those girls not lovely or smart enough to ensure they have a man at their beck and call. Their lives must be dull and hopeless. The passage from dusk to dawn must be empty for them, filled only with longing.

Vassilis suddenly turns me around and looks me in the eye. "Is it true that Vardas slept with you those many years ago when Michael and I were away on the Euphrates?"

I permit myself a disbelieving snort. "Who? His Flaccid Munificence? Sleep is all he can do, I hear. Such rumors are hard to stop and I do not try."

"Then, the child … will be Michael's?" Vassilis begins.

"It is yours, my champion, yours! Given all that Michael and I have done in the past nothing has ever come of it. What makes you even think that he can give me a child?"

He smiles at this. Perhaps he is warming to the prospect of having me as his wife?

"Anyway, you know nothing would please me more than to be rid of the Pork-Eaters, all of them, and to be in your arms always, my one and only true Emperor."

He grimaces, then smiles. "Vardas' shadow is cast long over all matters. I hear his fury at today's union knows no bounds. What will he think when Michael announces our coming betrothal?"

As if I am not aware of this! But I too have some news. We leave the chapel. "Have you heard that Petronas has been seeing Theodora again? The women say that he may not have much longer in this world. Without him, Vardas will be that much weaker."

"I will be ready for Vardas. I will make a move," Vassilis says, walking close behind me. I like it when his mind is made up even though it's far from clear what the next steps might be.

"What will you do?" I say. "Think back to the victory over the Bulgar; how important it is to appeal to the senses, to threaten, to cajole into stillness, to weaken one's prey through terror, before making a move of any kind."

He stops and looks me in the eyes. "How do you mean?"

"Look for weakness, and then exploit it. Vardas is truly a master at this. His reports told him that Boris was struggling with famine as well as war with the Moravian, and the Boyars were in revolt. The Khan could not have had much by way of men at his disposal near his capital, and so there was little chance that the Roman fleet would even need to engage. The threat of force was more important than the use of force itself."

Silence as he digests this. I go on. "There are already as many that hate Vardas as are in debt to him. Use every friend you have to feed that hate. If you don't have the right friends, make new ones. I must be crowned if this child is to be born in the Purple."

"You fly too high," he says. "Like Icarus, your wings will burn."

"I'd rather they were singed a bit than cursed by not being able to fly at all. Accuse Vardas directly to Michael. Say that Vardas, though old, is as ambitious as ever, and there is little more left for him to achieve, except the Throne."

"Michael trusts him completely. He will never accept that. He will say that Vardas has the Throne, after a fashion. Why would he want more?"

He is right. I reconsider. "Work on Michael. Tell him I carry Vardas' child! You know how easily misled he is when angry."

Vassilis frowns, and then nods. If I am right, this is how he will come to see how I can work to his advantage, to our advantage.

"But," I say, "we must time this ... revelation well!"

† † †

So here we stand in the Ayia Sofia. A vault of dark marble soars like the wings of a gigantic eagle above a forest of pillars, buoyed to eternity by the chant of a choir of cantors. The thrumming, drawn from ancient depths, makes me think that this a temple to the goddess Athena, just as the nearby colossus of Constantine, our founder, resembles another Apollo or — dare I say it — Christ Himself! Blasphemy perhaps? Or just the thoughts of an idle woman.

The cathedral reminds me that our bodies are almost irrelevant, like sand on the beach of the cosmos, and that my soul is nothing against God or his angelic or diabolic agents.

We face the altar, my garments uncomfortably tight around the waistline. I notice, not for the first time, the scale of damage to an obliterated Icon above the altar. I hear that cunning old Photios has found both the money and the artisans to fix it.

I can barely stand from exhaustion. Fortunately, the ceremony is almost over. Vassilis wears laurels, as do I. For me they are a joy — symbols of our race, our marathon together in Christ. And for him? I fear they are more like a noose for a wild horse, tamed little by hardship and life. He continues to suffer from his break with Maria. I resolve to show him how determined I am to be an even greater source of strength and inspiration to him.

Michael's gaze bears down on us from above. He decided he would observe from the upper level of the cathedral rather than the Emperor's usual place on the Throne at the chancel side, as if he has already bequeathed some authority to Vassilis. Or perhaps that is just my interpretation.

A chill touches me. What will happen if Michael decides suddenly to drop us back where we were? Vardas and Photios are behind him in practically everything, and this recent breach with Vardas over the rite of Sergius and Bacchus will soon be smoothed away unless I can find more reason to harden Michael's resolve. I see how vital it is that I deliver a healthy child. I must sew any protests behind closed lips with the toughest thread, especially around Michael, or I could lose everything we've gained so far.

The more I read Photios' books the more I understand that, although we would like to think otherwise, most events happen due to forces beyond our understanding. It's little more than a myth that we control the cosmos around us. I marvel at the gall that Epicurus displayed in moving the center of the universe away from mankind, not only physically, through his claim that we move "in the wake of the sun's exhalations," but also spiritually, when he asserted that a true leader was not the center of his cosmos. To put it more simply, how it is not so much the help of friends that makes a leader, but the confidence of that help in times of need. I now start to understand Vassilis. He relies largely on his strength and appearance. Yet how to find those that really matter who will stand behind him?

We kneel together in front of the altar. Photios intones as he censes us, his scrawny limbs pinning up a gray beard and long robes. He seems not unhappy with the arrangement he is blessing. Reading his pages, the ones I amend as I go through them, I see pride and care bursting through his pompous words. He must have been pleased for Michael and hopeful that this would bring some peace. I resolve never to forget this.

The procession takes us with it through the south exit of the Ayia Sofia, the great bronze doors usually reserved for the Emperor and his immediate family. The sea breeze dries itself on our faces as the sun settles, warm and welcoming, like the softest cape imaginable, on my tired but content shoulders.

32. Into the darkness

The Holy Spirit moves when you least expect it. While passing through the Palace complex one day, on his way to attend to Michael, Vassilis stops to listen to the gossip of some visiting regimental commanders. One of them sees Vassilis and comes over to tell him a tale about a man claiming to be his brother!

Vassilis had not thought of his brothers for some time, although he often told me that he wanted to try to find out more about them. But it appears that Vassilis' reputation has traveled farther than he would dare to think possible.

The commander mockingly relates that this supposed brother of Vassilis had taken it upon himself, some five years ago, to join the main regiment of the Thracesian Theme. As it turns out, the man is an excellent soldier and has made it to the rank of divisional commander. What does Vassilis think of that?

The joy on Vassilis' face as he tells me the story is remarkable. I love it when he smiles, his teeth sparkling delightfully through his dark beard. He instructed the commander to take back orders that the soldier should dispatch himself to the City immediately.

As far as I was concerned, if this man was indeed a brother, then he would be coming at the right time. But the nostalgia for Vassilis' childhood seems to play so much on his mind that it disturbs me. I sense he misses the simplicity of a time gone by. I imagine him as a young child among other strong boys. This makes him more delectable to me than ever before.

So we wait together. It has been a warm but long day and it is growing late. Vassilis stops pacing and sits, head in hands. I sense that silence is best, and have turned myself back to the crackling pages of one of Photios' books.

Then a rough voice calls. Vassilis leaps into the air and I look up. I am instantly disappointed by what I see.

The two men halt several paces apart, both wrapped in awe at the gift before them. As far I know they haven't seen each other for twenty years. Marianos' chestnut curls, just like Vassilis' are streaked with black and gray. They cascade around a coarser version of Vassilis' bright smile. Then the men fly into each other's arms, the clasps and kisses insufficient to make up the time apart, the struggles endured without each other, the unspent, wasted waters that have flowed since the river of time separated them.

"By the Theotokos, you have grown far better than I would ever have imagined," pronounces Marianos, his rough hands resting on Vassilis' broad shoulders. Tears shine on Vassilis' cheek.

"You are a dream come true!" Vassilis says, trembling. "You have done well to find me." They hug for what seems like ages. I start to feel somewhat slighted.

Then Vassilis takes my arm and pulls me gently alongside him. "This is my ... wife." The pause does not escape me. Marianos inclines his head toward me. Though similar in appearance, it is evident that age and hardship have not treated Marianos well. His skin shows the ravages of disease only too clearly. There are several slash wounds on his face and arms. His fingers are thick, his brows jut over deep-set eyes.

"And what of our brothers?" Vassilis says.

"Do you remember them at all?" Marianos says, smiling. "They were on the road to Thessaloniki when the Bulgar attacked, so were fortunate to escape the confusion after you vanished."

He places an arm on Vassilis' shoulder. "Where did you go? I spent months searching every town in the area. That is, when I wasn't helping to rebuild our homes."

"The stallion we caught ran for what seemed like hours. I held on the whole time, just like you taught me." He speaks more slowly than usual, smiling all the while. He won't really want to share all the details with Marianos yet, the discovery of himself, of me, of his desires. This man is practically a complete stranger to him. No doubt all will come in good time.

Vassilis continues. "In fact, my limbs seemed to be chained around it. At some point I must have fallen asleep and slipped off, because I woke up alone."

"You look a lot like mother," Marianos says. "But that was many years ago." The tears sparkle in Vassilis' eyes. Perhaps he regrets not having made the effort to find them again — I never heard him speak once of them!

Marianos reaches out. "Come now, my boy, you are a famous man. The reputation of The Macedonian, who sits in the lap of the Emperor, is known to many."

"How is that?" I ask.

Marianos looks me straight in the eye. "Everyone speaks of a man with the bravery and courage of Achilles, and how he led a fleet that forced the Bulgar to surrender."

Vassilis does not react. Marianos turns back to him. "They speak your name with great awe, and know that you guard the Emperor's person day and night. You have been blessed!"

The silence is relieved by the mocking caws of seagulls. It is true that Vassilis has done something. But he is still basically a servant, whether or not he cares to admit it.

"What do they say about the Emperor?" asks Vassilis.

"They say many things. That his Worthiness is troubled, that he finds it difficult to muster his forces, to direct his ministers."

"Really?" I say. "Especially as I wouldn't have thought they cared much, living so far from civilization."

Marianos raises an eyebrow at this. I guess I'm being a bit obnoxious. "Yes," he says, "perhaps not so much in the villages."

I go off to fetch wine and apples. I offer these to the men.

"What is more important," says Marianos as he munches, "was that, after you left, we didn't see much of the Bulgar for quite some time again. The people said that it was because a full garrison had been stationed in Adrianopolis and the barbarians were afraid. So we were able to rebuild our town. After I joined the garrison, I heard much of the goings on at court. Sometimes that's all we soldiers talk about. Oh, that, and ... various distractions."

He grins at Vassilis knowingly. I am not interested in their "distractions". I have learned something useful. My Peasant is well known even in the villages! Now he must use that fame to win the hearts and minds of the soldiers, not just of the City folk. Why hasn't Vassilis done all this already? He has served alongside them on many an expedition, albeit it as the Emperor's footman, but now he needs to move in different circles.

Then I see too clearly the problem — the senior soldiers are in the sway of Vardas. I know I must do what I can. In my new position as consort of Vassilis the Magistros, I command more respect in the Gynaeconitis. Every woman knows her husband's unfulfilled desires, his secret dreams of power. I must listen to them more, and listen with understanding.

"I need to ask you something," Vassilis says abruptly to Marianos. "I want you to go Pliska for me. Your nephew is there. I will explain. Let's go for a walk."

Marianos replies with a broad grin, and they embrace again. I let them go without a word. I fear that Vassilis is planning something involving Constantinos, when he really should be thinking more about me and the child I carry.

† † †

Freed from another long evening of servitude rather earlier than expected by the wine goblet which holds the Emperor's hand, I run home and collapse into Vassilis' naked arms.

"I have been thinking about Vardas," I say, running my hands over the thick hair on his chest. The usual silence follows; his eyes are shut, but I sense he is listening.

I continue. "He is far too powerful for anyone to approach him directly. Though many still remain in debt to him he has incurred the wrath of a good many others. I know many wives and daughters who have let Vardas taste their sweetmeats."

Vassilis chuckles. "No doubt you have someone in mind," he says, turning onto an elbow and facing me, his eyes in shadow, the lamplight playing in his tousled hair.

"It is not hard to find victims. What about Symvatios himself? I am amazed that he is still the only one who appears not to have figured out that Vardas was the spark that lit Eudokia's flame!"

"So do I tell Symvatios about his wife?"

"Do not speak to him about that whatsoever! Leave these matters to her and me."

"Well, what do you have in mind?"

"We need to find a way to appeal to Symvatios. Whatever we decide on, we must find out what moves him. Is it ambition? Perhaps if he were to find himself in a more elevated position?"

"How is that possible?" asks Vassilis. "He is already the Logothete."

"I know that. But Petronas' health is poor. Who knows, the position of Demestikos could be vacant soon? Suggest to Symvatios that he might be a logical choice, even though I have heard that Vardas is more keen on appointing his son, Antigonus."

We kiss, and I know he has grasped my intent. He embraces me tightly, turning me gently over. Somehow, he knows exactly how to work my pathways of pleasure. The furnace brightens, now crackling hot under the breath of his bellows, my body an anvil to him. His chest pins me down, he molds the resolve of my flesh into softer, glowing metal, his hair raising sparks across my neck as drops of sweat fall from his brow.

Afterward, his is the first voice to break the silence. "But that doesn't explain what we will do with Vardas."

I caress his forehead. "All Symvatios has to do is to persuade his former father-in-law to think of him as a more able commander. Perhaps if he got Vardas out of town for a while. With some distance between the old man and his supporters he will be much more open to reason."

So let me leave us lying there, my little Leo, and tell you more of Symvatios, strolling about his new quarters with deep satisfaction. How does he come by new quarters, you may ask?

Theophilitzes and the Lady Danielli did not need much prompting to realize that their interests would be well served with the Logothete in favor. Fortunately for all of us, a fairly new residence, just at the edge of the Palace grounds, has lain dormant since its former owner, an elderly, widowed senator, fell ill and died shortly after its completion. It was a simple matter for Magistros Vassilis to acquire it, with the help of funds from Patras.

Eudokia tells me that the place thrills her even more than when Symvatios had been made Logothete, some nine years earlier. She had grown tired of his constant moping since his former wife's death, his misery from years of dedication to the administration without much to show for it — apart from debt and a grand title. Fortunately, Eudokia, like practically everyone at court, either wants more or wants to do more. They sometimes just need a way to make it a reality.

Symvatios has not yet acquired enough rugs to cover the floors, and lacks the right number of couches and ornaments to make the main hall as attractive as it might be. But he will be able to fit it out in grand style with his new, larger salary, which he will receive from the Magistros Vassilis' hands at the end of the year. Tradition

dictates that the Emperor should reimburse the senior adminis-
trators himself, but Michael has delegated this task to Vassilis,
more out of boredom, I suspect, than anything else. Fortunately,
this comes across as a sign of immense trust to everyone else.

So I feel the time is right to approach Eudokia with all sorts of
suggestions. I explain that the possibilities might be endless, with
someone like Vassilis to advise the Throne. She listens avidly,
nibbling at a honeyed oat cake. Here at last, I say, is someone who
knows how to inspire through his actions and careful decisions.
She seems to agree, though perhaps without fully understanding
why. I do like the silly thing, even though she is not that bright.

Then fortune throws the dice in our favor. Apparently, Symvatios feels that his years of struggle, bringing about change for
the better in a solid way, in tiny steps, might be brought to the
Emperor's ears via Vassilis.

He believes that delegating more power to the Themes means
more funds would be available to prime the small force he dreams
of as the standing army. Such a force, he argues, would be prefer-
able to the thousands of soldiers that currently occupy the garrisons in distant rocky outcrops, or that move at the whim of the
Emperor in expensive campaigns against the heretical Iconoclasts
or Abbasid to the east. Given the Emperor's recent successes,
there doesn't seem to be much need for the garrisons anymore.

Poor Symvatios! He should know that talking about this sort
of thing is certain to make any woman, let alone Eudokia, yawn
more than usual. Symvatios' children were probably the only ones
at home who paid him any attention — Eudokia tells me she does
nothing to encourage him to warm her bed.

I suggest to Eudokia that perhaps Symvatios feels let down by
life; perhaps he has lost his spirit? Why not invite him to her bed
for a change, why not make him feel more like a man again! We
laugh at the face she makes.

Then I mention that the office of Demestikos might be something for him to look forward to, and much sooner than he might
have dreamed possible. I egg her on. The Admiral Oryphas is always eager for more battles — why not get his wife to talk to him,
and suggest that Symvatios is not only good at arranging campaigns, but also at leading them?

Eudokia agrees, reluctantly, and so we wander through the Gynaeconitis, to find the Admiral's wife busy at the spindle.

† † †

It should have been a fine autumn, but the birth of a new son had not brought the pleasure and pride I expected.

I remember proudly holding up my darling, fresh from the birth, already bursting with vigor and loud demands, to Michael and Vassilis, and reminding them that this child had been born to a mother who was not yet part of the Imperial family. How were they to resolve that?

Neither said a word. We all recognized the dark brown, wavy hair and the broad face that was so much like Vassilis'. We all knew this was not what had been agreed. So we took our time naming him. The Theotokos punished me for this mistake, I am sure. Several days later he whimpered for the last time. My baby no longer fed at my breast.

I have never known such exhaustion, nor such emptiness. The Gynaeconitis circled, sympathetic, but unsure as to how prudent it would be to show too much concern.

Vassilis became less open with me after this terrible event, but his feelings — always hidden beneath a calm surface — still bubbled within hearing of my heart. No doubt he wondered, as I did, what the worth was in continuing to endure the endless misery of the court. But he had, indeed still has, a choice. He could leave at any time, unlike me. A woman is a prisoner of others' choices.

To make matters worse, Marianos' mission to Pliska is successful. Finding Constantinos and his mother isn't difficult, though removing him is trickier. Now Vassilis has his son back and even affords me the occasional smile, though I am responsible for caring for someone else's child when I should have been raising my own. The men do not seem to understand the multiple insult.

Michael raises no objection to young Constantinos' return, even managing an encouraging smile, though his eyes are dark. I, of course, am livid.

So I am glad to be rid of Vassilis for a while. He and Michael decide to go on a hunt. Though why anyone would bother to go hunting escapes me — the tables of the Palace bulge with fat pheasant, parchment-thin plaice, deer flesh bathed in pork drippings, and all the herbs one could imagine padding out succulent omelets and endless other means for interspersing conversation and drink with sustenance.

After many hours on horseback, but with barely a feather to show for it, a family of boar appears, snuffling in the safety of the dim light. The hoary matriarch shuffles her squeaky offspring along with thick hooves, snouts of all sizes thrusting hopefully into the earth for a good crop of roots or eggs, or perhaps a small nest of snakes.

The hunters submerge themselves in some bushes, their arrows ready to take the mother out and make off with the dim youngsters who don't know enough yet to get away.

Vassilis savors the alertness and tension in Michael's body. It reeks delectably of leather and somehow of ash, as I recall. Perhaps Vassilis feels pleasantly discomfited by this. They have said little while out today, sharing a closeness Vassilis has not felt since he shared a hearth with Diomedes — which now seems long ago.

Michael lets loose a careless arrow. It sings through the air, pinning a piglet down by mistake. The hunters suddenly find themselves scrambling over roots and branches to get to safety above the ground, in the branches of a vast cypress, as the sow charges at them.

Now they hang, still dangerously close, but too exhausted from laughing to get any farther for the moment. The sow screams and races around the tree. Then she turns to her offspring, lying in a pool of its own blood, and tries to pull out the arrow. It shudders into stillness.

Michael continues to stretch and shake with mirth, the veins on his pale neck barely visible behind black curls, still bobbing with the effort of the climb.

"So this is what life comes down to, isn't it?" Vassilis drops a jest into the panting silence. "Hanging in the strangest of places to prevent your nuts being ripped off by some mad old bitch."

"Usually, that is all it ever has been to me." Michael murmurs, and then perks up. "When mother was around, that is. But now that she is out of the way, you know I can concentrate on more important things."

Vassilis hides his exasperation under a quiet nod. As always, Michael seems only to have revelry on his mind.

Perhaps this is when he begins to see Michael more clearly. The tiredness of the ages has crystallized in this creature — young in body, but old in an old office, with little but misery to its name in living memory, except perhaps very recently. How could Michael not be what he is? His yearning for me is nothing more than a yearning for new blood!

But now, my Vassilis' predilections are exposed. Such a fool! So convinced was he that the prey was his for the taking. His gaze follows Michael's sharp cheekbones down to the small mouth, the sinews of his arms and his slight frame. Is that why Vassilis leans over slowly to kiss him, a hand tracing his beard from ear to chin? I imagine their lips meeting and lips engaging, but only for a moment before Michael pulls away.

As the sow noisily herds the remnants of her brood away, I imagine Michael's eyes transmuted to gray-silver in the dim light, shining quizzically at Vassilis, as they hang in the branches together.

"That was fun. The boar, I mean. But perhaps we should get going?" Here is Michael turning away from Vassilis, slipping to the ground, and then breaking into that annoyingly grin of his.

Vassilis burns with shame as he slides down the smooth bark to the ground, a throbbing black veil descending over his vision. This was what I came to know as the calm before the storm; his famous fits of fury were what exasperated me in the end — so dangerous that he became a threat to me, and to you, my dear Leo. But that is a tale for another day.

Then suddenly Michael takes Vassilis' face in his hands and kisses him. Their tongues flick and entwine, their arms lock around each other. Vassilis holds him even closer as the moments pass. But Michael pulls his mouth free, though his breath is still hot against Vassilis' chin.

"Is this what you want?" he whispers. "You know we are sworn brothers. Two men cannot be closer. You have given me a great deal. I need you so much. Just not in this way. Do you understand?"

Ah ...the snub — a terrible, unfamiliar feeling! Vassilis has always been the one to decline favors, to tease, to mock with his hard body the lusts and desires of those who long for him. Not this one! Michael only has eyes for me. Vassilis had always vowed to be in control of his emotions around Michael, to study disinterest — even hate — and not to give in to his own whims. Why, then, did he open himself up to ridicule on this fateful day?

Michael lays a hand on Vassilis' shoulder. "If my appearance is the source of your fire then you must look to my older sister — I have told you before she is yours to do with as you will — just give the word and I will ensure she is brought back from the monastery. They tell me there is more than a passing resemblance."

I know Michael well enough to know that he completes the insult with something like, "Anyway, why don't we get back now and hunt down my own sweet sow?"

Vassilis' gloom is as dark as the vanishing dusk, the sudden wind rustling coldly through the leaves, the sound of distant thunder, all heralding what appears to be an intense storm.

33. At what price vanity?

FOUR MONTHS LATER, IN THE WINTER OF EARLY 866 AD
When the weather is not too cold Vardas prefers to conduct business in the inner courtyard of the Daphne. I hear from Eudokia that Vardas loves the sparkling marble beneath his boots, bordered in red, green and blue mosaic. As is usual of late, Vardas has been hard at work since early on. Today, Photios is there to tell him about yet another letter he is writing to the Khan.

Michael arrives, quite early in the day for him. The scribes bustle around him, heaving documents in leather straps. I'm sure he won't stay long. Probably the next step will be to round up Vassilis for a game of polo before a long lunch.

Then Admiral Oryphas strides into the throng, with Symvatios in tow. Oryphas is an impressive man, his fit frame and tanned stolidity belying a man well into his fifties. Only the gray-flecked beard and tough, parchment-like skin give away his age.

Oryphas turns to Michael. "Worthiness, Symvatios and I were just saying to your uncle here that it has been some time since we journeyed abroad together. The lighthouse signals have been quiet for many months — no threats arise from our Abbasid foes to the east and south. We subdue them, even in Egypt, where our early raids were successful."

"Are we talking about Crete?" says Michael. "Surely we are ready to take it again? We have built ourselves up since the Eunuch attempted it all those years ago — with your successful campaigning no less. I suspect our soldiers must be quite hungry for distraction."

"That is exactly our point," exclaims Oryphas, with Symvatios nodding. "Now if only we can convince your uncle here to lead us. The Logothete has already started on the arrangements."

"This would have been just the thing for my brother to lead …" Vardas' voice vanishes to a whisper. He looks away into the distance. Oryphas lowers his gaze, but then places a hand on

Vardas' shoulder.

"I am too old for this sort of thing," Vardas brightens up. "But I think it is the perfect campaign for the Emperor to head up. Our forces are in good shape. All you have to do is give the word."

"You and I know that is no excuse," Oryphas says. "There is nothing stopping old warhorses like us from teaching the young-sters a thing or two."

"The Admiral is right," Michael says. "I would be honored to go on campaign with you, Uncle — for one reason or another we have not done this before."

"From what they tell me it is best that I stay in the capital for now," Vardas says. "Anyway, I doubt we can afford such an expe-dition." Vardas is a wily old boar. He knows something is afoot, and I'm sure that Symvatios' constant pattering does nothing to allay his concerns.

Glances are exchanged. Vardas paces, reading documents, giving orders to scribes. Then he takes Michael aside, none too gently. Though Symvatios can't quite hear what Vardas is say-ing he can hear Vassilis' name repeatedly. Something about ru-mors. Then Michael leaps back in horror. "By the very hand of Christ Himself," Michael says, as if making an announcement in the Hippodrome, "which is stored in . . . where is it stored, Patri-arch Photios?"

"In the new altar in the Virgin of the Lighthouse, Worthiness," says Photios.

"By that most holy relic," Michael says, "how could anyone countenance harm to you?"

The courtyard has grown silent. The scribes wait, confused. "No doubt," Vardas mutters, "it is as you say. But, I believe it is time for the morning procession. Away with business." He scat-ters the scribes with a gesture.

† † †

Everyone seems to be going on about the new university. All I seem to hear is how Vardas and Photios are working hard to ar-range it. A wonderful thing, but hardly what the City needs as far as I am concerned. I still want to know if the laws really work, and how people could be driven to follow them more closely. For

Vassilis the question is why there could not be more worship, and more churches in which to carry it out. Churches are fine, I say, but laws are much more important.

Vassilis and I had not intended to hold a symposium, certainly not of the purely academic kind, nor even of the more libertine variety he sampled in Patras, but simply a gathering to find out who might be like-minded "friends"; to sound out everyone's position on matters of state. My Peasant still needs to learn that politics and domination are the favorite topics of the young, especially those who feel as though no one listens to them. We have discussed this at length — he must show that he can find ways to help further those who haven't made it high enough through their own intelligence or good looks.

Persuading Eudokia to host the gathering in their new home was not too hard — with a prize in sight who is not willing to run the race? So the inner courtyard of Symvatios' home is filled with young commanders, many of whom easily release their otherwise captive opinions when assisted by a pitcher of wine. Vassilis has come to know many of them through his reunion with Marianos, whose return had been a gift for which Vassilis had endlessly given thanks in prayer and supplication. They had already sent out word to locate his other brothers as well.

The hearths blaze merrily, beyond which the servants draw back curtains and enter, laden with plates of bread and meat. Most of them are young Paulicians, not unattractive, some born in captivity since the successful campaign against Karveas. They should be grateful for the attention of the Demestikos and the new Magistros. Fine complexions, brightened by bathing and pomades, have transformed them into very fetching distractions. But this is not the time for debauchery. In fact the opposite is required — a show of piety and strength.

Now an argument is raging, albeit a somewhat specious one. What had happened to the free bread? The commanders know enough history to recall a time when Africa, from Tunis to Egypt, had bowed to the might of Rome, turning over grain supplies on command, so that even the lowliest beggar could receive a loaf every day, even if he had not a coin to his name. Now the people have to make do with coarser, thick loaves baked from northern wheat, bought at a steep price!

Indignation flows, fueled by the liquor. Why is it that days go by when the common folk rely only on vegetables for sustenance, even going without porridge! Surely this is what the administration should be worrying over, not expanding the university? What is that old buffoon Vardas thinking of? They spit out the names of the men of so-called learning that have come to the City: Theodoros the geometrician, Kometas the grammarian, Theodosius the astronomer, and those others from the Levant, who have turned from a Christian path to self-indulgent Abbasid ways.

Discontent has found more of a home in their hearts than we could have dreamed possible. Rumor has it that Vardas not only lavishes the scholars with endowments and attention, but also spends large amounts of time debating with the students and teachers. When does he spend time with simple soldiers like themselves, they wonder — men who are the very backbone of empire?

Then Vassilis decides to enter the fray. "So what do you say, John of Chaldis? Are you man enough to take on the Empire. Do you have the stomach for change?" Shocked into silence at this sudden outburst, the men exchange frowns and share glances at Vassilis'. He has picked on one of the youngest, but also one of the sturdiest.

"For when you speak so harshly of our current state," Vassilis continues in dead silence, "you criticize the Imperial rule of it as well. With what authority do you do this? Are you sure of what you say, or should our noble and kind host, the Logothete, feel embarrassed that he is entertaining fools that despise their Empire . . . if not the Emperor who rules over it in God's name?"

Vassilis fixes Chaldis with a piercing glare and lets the silence grow. The musicians stop playing.

"I think it is time for you to show me what you believe in. I want to see actions rather than listen to drunken slander," announces Vassilis in apparent seriousness. He seldom smiles or raises his voice so it is always difficult to know when he is joking or serious. A great asset, one that he learned to use wisely, except on those rare occasions when he boiled into a torrent of rage at me, or even you, my precious Leo.

Vassilis crosses the floor and pulls the stunned young commander to his feet. The silence is complete.

"Come on, you ass! Think straight. I challenge you to a

wrestle, in Spartan style." Vassilis grins broadly, and begins to disrobe, taut muscles and sinews rippling. "But because I do not believe you have it in you to best me, I will ask our host to tie one hand behind my back, to give you some small advantage. Will someone attend to me!"

The smiles break out; they roar in approval at the game, and quickly descend on Chaldis, ripping his robes from him, and running rope around Vassilis, pinning his arm behind him.

The two men face each other, roughly the same age and build, but Vassilis' greater experience is obvious, in spite of his handicap. To the sound of cheering and jeering, Vassilis suddenly leaps at Chaldis, knocking him down and onto his back. A moment later his knees straddle Chaldis' chest and his free elbow pins the young man's thick neck to the ground.

But Chaldis is not to be beaten so quickly, in spite of being well into his cups. He manages to whip around from under my Vassilis, toppling him over. Sweat pours from body and brow as he pushes Vassilis' face down into the grass.

Chaldis grabs Vassilis' free arm with both of his, presumably to keep Vassilis pinned to the ground. The spectators draw breath as one when Vassilis twists his arm away, and leaps to his feet, before suddenly throwing Chaldis over and onto the ground.

Vassilis is back on Chaldis, pinning his head between his thighs. Now he has Chaldis' right knee in his free arm and twists it around. The sound of the joint cracking gets a wince from the onlookers who nevertheless cheer them on. The roars drown the young man's moaning. Vassilis releases him with a broad grin.

Then the noise empties out of the courtyard. All faces turn toward the entrance. Michael has chanced upon them, arms folded, brows twisted. "Seems like you are having some entertainments here, brother? Why was I not invited?"

"Not at all," says Vassilis, standing up. "We are simply indulging in rather childish pursuits, a sign of how much wine we have taken this evening, nothing more. Why don't you join us?"

The guests look down, pretending to converse with each other. Someone unties Vassilis' binds. Vassilis dons his britches and goes up to Michael.

"I had come to talk of plans." Michael reclines on a couch and gestures for a drink.

By now the guests have regained their couches and Chaldis his clothes. Marianos calls for more wine and does his best to get the conversation to pull itself up by its bootlaces.

"Perhaps this is not the right time," he says, downing the goblet's contents and swinging his feet to the floor.

Vassilis stops Michael with a deferent hand on his shoulder. "I am glad you are here," Vassilis whispers into his ear, their cheeks almost touching. "Indeed, we must talk."

He beckons Symvatios over. "As the Logothete is my witness, we have learned some news about the Caesar. And his plans for ... the future."

Michael reclines again. General conversation resumes. "We are convinced that there are ... problems," Vassilis says softly. "Rumor has it that the Caesar has gone too far."

"Really?" Michael smirks. "Lately all I hear is rumor! First from the Caesar himself and now from you. What is one supposed to believe?"

Vassilis knows he must tread warily. "Now that Demestikos Petronas is no longer there to check him, we have heard that the Caesar would like to take future glories for himself alone."

"I have never come across so much horse shit! In heaven's name, what is everyone on about these days?"

"The rumors are everywhere among the soldiers, Your Worthiness," says Symvatios.

"Let's think it through, shall we?" Michael is impatient. "To what end? All my glories have been his. He would wish me no ill. I have heard nothing. If you mean the plans to move on Crete — that is not news. He doesn't even want to go."

"Doubtless," Symvatios continues, "you know how the soldiers keep to themselves, Worthiness, and would never betray one of their own, except by drunken error. If the Caesar can return Crete to us then our wars in the Aegean are over. He might even be able to restore the grain supply from Egypt again. And win the eternal love of the people. Who knows what else ... might be his for the taking?"

"If Christ wills it, of course all this could happen," Michael retorts, after a moment's hesitation, "and especially with us at his side. My uncle is brave beyond words, as was Uncle Petronas, and you — still an upstart in this court — can say nothing to the contrary." He shakes with fury as Symvatios lowers his head.

An awkward silence settles once again across the gathering. Vassilis notices Marianos watching him very carefully, ready to pounce to his assistance if needed. With the slightest toss of his head, Vassilis indicates that Marianos should do nothing.

Michael jumps back on his feet. "Brother, I am dismayed at your part in this." he addresses Vassilis. "You know how easy it was for me to raise you. I can raise anyone here in the same way if I choose." He paces the room and halts in front of a bearded and bulky olive-skinned man in his early forties, a Syrian and newcomer to the court. Vassilis is not sure why this one is here but he has not asked many questions of those present.

"Who are you, friend?" Michael inquires.

Vassilianiscus is the response.

"How fascinating," Michael muses. "Vassilianiscus, Vassilis. The similarity is quite suggestive, is it not? Perhaps either could be Magistros? Or neither?"

Vassilis ignores the throbbing pain in his brow, the fury clamping hold of his chest. He takes Michael aside. "You say he is a brave man," Vassilis says, "and you are right. But are you content to know that the Caesar has been talking to the old Regent again, and that he is considering making someone close to him Demestikos without consulting you?"

A sour expression flits across Michael's face. "He can appoint the Demestikos, he can appoint anyone. I have given him that power. It is a bit strange that he and Mother are speaking again, as I cannot imagine what they would have to talk about these days, but I see no issue here. He knows best. And what is best for me too, I am sure."

Vassilis decides to risk all. As with having to choose the right man all those years ago when breaking in Boris' wild colt, Vassilis realizes he must follow his instincts. *Oh, my divinely inspired savior — for that you is what you are!*

"Perhaps more importantly," Vassilis whispers for only Michael and Symvatios to hear, "we have recently come to hear how this famed bravery of his extended to ... guarding Ingerina's chambers whenever you were not around. Did you know about this?"

Michael frowns. His eyes narrow. He staggers, a specter of paleness, and collapses back onto the couch. "What cruel jest is this? I thought I had dispensed with Gryllos some time back. Surely you don't mean that the child ..."

Leaving Symvatios to attend to a quaking Michael, Vassilis turns to the gathering. It is once again very clear what he must do. He must reach out to them. He is not afraid to speak boldly.

"What is our kingdom to be based on?" says Vassilis, turning to the gathering. "On lies, or a return to greatness? On filthy pursuits? Are we to gather dust in the codices of history, as a forgotten people, like the ancients whose stories live on only thanks to those members of the university many of you question? Or can we leave a mark through strength and righteousness?"

Striding between the couches, Vassilis makes sure that he touches each guest somehow; with a clap on the shoulder or a clasp of warm palms. "Let us make sure that whatever we decide to do, that our lives are in the right hands. And that we build on the glory of the past ..." His words are greeted with roars of approval and raised goblets, led by Marianos.

"Then," he says to the gathering, "are we together on whatever may need to be done?"

† † †

The ignominy of the Amorion! Surely their willfulness is to blame for their downfall. As I write these last words I know no limit to my fury at the abominations we have suffered because of them. I am tempted even to destroy this book, so that their name may be wiped from the pages of history, if only you were not one of them, my handsome Leo.

What happened next is why, dear son of mine, I have never forgiven your father.

To Vassilis' surprise, he is called to the marble stables the day after the feast. Michael is there, attired in the white cloak usually reserved for ceremony. He embraces Vassilis casually, with that gleam in his eye that suggests something unusual is afoot.

"You disturbed me greatly yesterday," Michael says very quietly. "I did not expect news of that kind in front of such rabble. And you know that it is not the first time I am surprised in this way. What other news do you keep hidden from me?"

"Worthiness, the servant can offer only himself up to the master, there is nothing more to give," Vassilis says.

Michael reaches out and touches his face. "We are brothers, are we not, and I have given you so much. Why, then, do you not bare your heart to me?"

"I wanted to be sure before I caused you unnecessary pain."

Michael turns away with a frown and a sad smile. "You have failed at that. And you must never do so again. You must bear this ... temporary discomfort ... so that you do never forget this."

This is clearly a signal. The guards step forward before Vassilis can move. They throw him over a nearby horse, binding his arms together around its neck and stomach. He does not struggle, nor does he cry out.

Michael dismisses them. He frowns, then smiles. "I must mark you, as a sign of honor between brothers," he whispers. "They teach that sort of thing in the villages, don't they?"

Vassilis fights the anger. The distant clanking of hammers on anvils brings him to his senses. "You can do what you want with me. Everything I have is yours. But let me stand free."

Michael produces a short sword and slices through Vassilis' binds. Vassilis slips down, back on his feet.

Michael touches the tip of the blade to Vassilis' skin. "You must bear this for me, to remind you that you must tell me everything. Otherwise, who can I trust?" Blood seeps from a cut. But Michael pulls away, tears in his eyes. The hammers ring out.

Vassilis grasps Michael's hand and pulls both it and the blade to his breast again. "Do what you must," says Vassilis. A crude Chi-Rho sign is wrought — the mark of Christ! The blood runs down Vassilis' side and down the blade, onto the floor.

It takes much to move my Vassilis, but when his spirit is fired, especially at injustice, a mountain cannot stop him. Oh, if only I had known that he would be so reckless, I could have warned him of the danger he was opening himself to. But I only learned of this much, much later.

Vassilis staggers away from the stables, his tunic striped with blood. He strides to the servants' quarters. Beneath the Palace the darkness peels back to reveal stacks of rank, sweat-ridden mats. No doubt these arouse him. Especially in the state he finds himself, the wound on his breast itching and coarse. What are the servants' lives like? Contemptible sleeping and eating, probably little more. And, I'm sure, copulating mindlessly to while away the few free hours. Even his home with Maria near the market was much better than this. He ignores the wave of whispers that greets his arrival. After all, he is a high-ranking visitor, and is free to move among the chattels.

A eunuch servant who became mine much later told me how he heard a man bellow. How he looked up to see Vassilis standing over a man little older than him, bony and curled up on a mat. His chin is covered in stubble, yet he is, no doubt, as slender and beguiling as he was those many years ago on the Maritsa River.

Vassilis pulls the cringing mass to his feet. "What — can't you speak properly? Don't you remember me?"

"I remember you, lord," says Wasim. The words barely escape a trembling chin. Vassilis gropes cruelly at the sunken cheeks and dark limbs, their girlishness lost and replaced with lean, wasted features, the soft eyes now spun tightly into points of fear.

Vassilis rips Wasim's rags from him. I'd suspected all along that the naked vulnerability of a man stokes Vassilis' groin even more than the simple pleasures of a woman. When I heard this I knew it to be true. Vassilis pushes the slave down onto his naked groin, forcing him to gag. The rest take the bobbing, shaved head as their cue to become scarce.

Yet this is just the start. Vassilis throws him onto his back, bites his mouth fiercely while pinning him down, gnawing on his arms, his shoulders, then his nipples. Feathers of blood from Vassilis' chest smear onto the slave's body. He thrusts Wasim's bony haunches into the air, then crushes his knees into his breast.

Vassilis carves him out with deep thrusts, his veined blade lading the young man repeatedly, the pummeling continuing long after all desire has been exhausted. Pain must teach arrogance its lesson — this is Vassilis in a fury beyond fury.

Several moments of stillness follow. Then, to my servant's surprise, Vassilis leans tenderly over the young man, straightens him out, and sucks hard at his stubbly upper lip. "You are mine now, you know. I will repay handsomely for that service."

"Of course, lord," murmurs Wasim, his eyes shut.

"I will send coin and clothing for you. I will take care of you." How could he choose a piece of Abbasid scum like this rather than me to satisfy his lust? Is it because he knows what it was like to have been in the dirt, trodden on by the indifference of those in power?

But who will ever know for sure?

34. For our rewards await us in heaven

How do I paint an image of your grandmother, my little Leo? Imagine a proud woman, swirling in black silks and disbelief, her parched eyes softened by a thick mourning veil, with only a tiny Theotokos on a chain around her neck to comfort her. For I am sure that Theodora still can't believe that she is to see Vardas today. They had seen each other only a few times since she left the Palace some ten years ago, but apart from a formal embrace and a few words at Petronas' memorial service, no real sentiments had since been exchanged, as far as I knew. I wonder if she has some pleasures again these days, since Vardas had her relocated to the relatively nearby Saint Mamas, just along the northeast coast.

My old friend Gemma stayed with her mistress. She tells me that Theodora sleeps little, praying at all hours, mourning the passing of many. Petronas' death was the greatest blow for her, coming so unexpectedly. Now, Gemma follows Theodora on a slow stroll down the path. She is amazed to see an imperial procession arriving, an hour before it is expected. Vardas' bulk is obvious from afar, but it is only as they ride up to the entrance that Gemma recognizes Vardas' son, the broad-shouldered Antigonus – a shining light in the army, according to the rumors buzzing around many quarters.

Vardas climbs off his horse, grabbing painfully at his back. Gemma stands back, slightly unsure if she is still needed, but not really wanting to be dismissed. The animosity between these siblings is legendary. But, instead of bitter words, tears creep down Vardas' face.

"You are early," Theodora calls, approaching the gate with slow, proud steps, as always.

"I am here, am I not?" he calls back. "At least I made the

effort. Can we not . . . " He struggles to speak.

Is he drunk, Gemma wonders? Theodora reaches out as if to take his hand, but instead lifts it to touch him on the cheek. He draws it to his lips and kisses it. She is trembling. Surely that dried out old heart, like mountain herbs on a sun-washed stone slab, is not damp with pity? The pleading in his eyes is obvious. Who would have thought such a thing possible?

"How could God have taken him from us?" Vardas weeps.

Even Theodora struggles to hold back the tears as she allows herself to be held. "How, my brother, how indeed?"

Antigonus follows behind them as they move indoors, with Gemma in tow.

They seat themselves in a simple inner courtyard lined with graying marble, brightened only by an urn of budding crocuses in its center. Vardas feels recovered enough to broach business.

"I mourn not only our dear brother's passing," Vardas says, "but also his absence. He never said much, but he was a vital counterbalance to the forces at play."

Theodora nods in what appears to be exact understanding.

"I cannot control them any longer," Vardas says, sighing. "I worry about Michael's lack of direction, his strange moods, and the new situation with Vassilis and Ingerina."

Hah! I never said that Vardas was dim, now did I?

"It has always been painfully obvious to me that the Macedonian is nothing more than a lowly opportunist," Theodora says. "It is a tragedy that I raised a blind child to be Emperor, that he cannot see further than his own desires. I felt hopeful when Petronas came to see me after Bishop's Meadow — you know we never really stopped talking all these years — to tell me that Michael had finally come into his own. But from what I hear . . . "

Antigonus decides that his opinion can wait no longer for courtesy. "It is very clear to me that the problem is not the Emperor, but the new, so-called Magistros. He whistles and my cousin dances." His voice is pained. "Without the Macedonian, the Emperor would have no recourse but to see sense."

Well, now, that is a useful piece of information!

"Sadly, dear nephew, you mean well, and I wish it were that simple. But I am to blame."

"How can you be?" Antigonus raises his voice in exasperation and rises. Vardas lays a hand on his arm.

Antigonus tries again. "It doesn't matter why this set of events has transpired — we must cure the disease that faces us now."

"Yes, my dear," Theodora says. "But you must understand that you do not cure the disease by curing the symptom. If I had let Michael have that Thulian vixen from the beginning, then none of this would have happened. He would not have resorted to weaving such rich tapestries of lies in order to have her in his arms."

I never said that the old sow was dim, did I? At least she understands the misery she has brought upon everyone, including herself.

She rises with some difficulty and moves over to touch the flowers. "I have spent the first five of the last ten years understanding this, and the last five praying for forgiveness, that we may all be absolved from the error of my mistaken choices. I fear the worst price is yet to be paid."

Antigonus speaks softly right behind her. "I am here to ask you something that my father, as Caesar, could never ask you. I would have your permission, or should I say approval, to ... be rid of the Macedonian."

"My permission!" Theodora turns around, smiling bitterly. "Here I sit, a poor widow in a drafty, ruined palace, on a forgotten side of the bay, being asked for approval by, if I am not right, the future Demestikos. What difference can my permission make to you or anyone?"

Her response scatters off the surrounding walls like ice in a blizzard. Vardas hangs his head. Or so Gemma tells me. I find it hard to imagine.

"Sister, you are, as always, painfully right," Vardas says. "But what we are really after is your advice. We cannot touch the Thulian. She has seen to that by making sure that she is with child again, who knows, probably Michael's. So what choice do we have?"

Exactly.

†††

The name of the Meander River in Attic Greek meant just that: a river weaving to and fro as it arcs across the gentle Anatolian hills. An inviting isthmus stretches from island to shore as the warships glide and stop at the outer reaches of the mouth, wary that the tongue of land is also a sign of depths too easy to plumb.

Vardas is also wary. Michael and Vassilis arrive on shore first, shoulder to shoulder, captaining the first squad as it leaps out onto the sand. Vardas and Symvatios are on the next boat behind them, with the new Demestikos, Antigonus, all sweating and swearing in the hot light. Seagulls, riled but soon indifferent to the unwelcome guests, weave in and out of the sails.

How our plans bore fruit! Michael persuaded Vardas himself to lead the expedition. though the encouragement from Michael had had exactly the opposite effect that Vassilis intended. The sly old bastard had immediately smelled a rat. Or perhaps, because of his own plans to harm my Emperor, detected plans within plans more readily.

Photios, good-natured and a bit foolish as always, had cheerfully stepped into the fray, and suggested that Vassilis, Michael, and Vardas take a vow before leaving. On the day of the Annunciation, at the Church of the Theotokos in Chalkoprateia, with the handmaidens of the Theotokos in attendance, these three had taken the blood of Christ from Photios and sworn that Vardas would be safe outside the City. How unsuspecting were the Pork-Eaters — of their own flesh and blood!

Back on the Meander, the soldiers are already well into digging the trenches and nearly have the Imperial tent and the Caesar's tent up and in full regalia. Gemstones sparkle on holy reliquaries set up as standards in the late afternoon light. Vassilis leaves Michael, Antigonus, and Vardas in conversation, and strides off to confer with his brothers who joined the Palace guard recently, bringing with them some cousins and even some new friends.

Michael is sitting rather casually on silk trappings when Vassilis enters the Imperial tent, a leg thrown over the armrest of a portable throne. Vardas has been relegated to a couch and has not had a chance to remove his chain mail. He reeks.

"It is decided," announces Michael. He is in excellent sorts. "We leave tomorrow for Crete. There is no reason to linger here a day more than is necessary."

Vardas is tired and probably decides it would be better to discuss this in the morning rather than argue. But Vassilis has arranged for the troops to stop digging the trenches, and have placed Vardas' tent slightly higher than that of the Emperor. I imagine this leaves him feeling strangely unprotected as he settles down for the night. Perhaps he assumes that, given that they are leaving tomorrow, he will let it pass.

† † †

Photios writes that he is driven to call back the brothers to be at his side. His ears pricked by the turn of events, he fears to tell them outright, in a letter, of his fear. For what if his missive were to stray into the wrong hands?

Instead he decides to send them some of his notes on Candidus, whose "History of the Romans" was written some four hundred years ago. Photios claims that Candidus' style is not suited for history. Photios complains that the writer makes use of poetical expressions that are insipid and childish; that his composition is harsh and discordant, inclined to dithyrambic bombast or degenerating into carelessness and inelegance. He introduces new constructions that do not, as in the case of other writers, lend additional smoothness and charm to the work. Instead they make it disagreeable to read and utterly unattractive. While here and there his style shows improvement, his history is obviously a medley of unreliable materials. Well, Photios is a fine one to criticize!

The second book of Candidus' history relates how Patrikios the Magistros, who had carried on an intrigue with Verina, was slain by her indignant brother Vassiliscus. Apparently Verina conceived a hatred of Vassiliscus on this account, assisting a man called Zeno with money to recover the Throne, but was then persecuted by her brother. Photios is cunning. He hopes that, by using a name so similar to my Peasant's, Cyril will grasp his hidden intent.

Photios writes of how he looks for solace in some of Cyril's past letters. Against stupidity even our Savior must contend in vain! The Moravians are refusing to learn Latin or Greek to hear Mass. They are a proud people — they must hear the message in their own language. And yet, the Bishop of Rome's men block the brothers at every turn. There are far more of the Spider's men than our Greek monks. This is very much the same problem that they faced with the Bulgar.

But then Cyril writes that the new alphabet will prove invaluable in translating the scriptures for the Moravians, and after only two years the New Testament shines forward in bold, albeit strange script, from new parchment. Such a fine boy, indeed! He writes that Methodios is taken with the Moravians, with how they have learned to survive in their lush lowlands — in complete indifference to whoever uses their land as a path to someone else's territory, or in spite of whichever prince decides to think that they can be subjugated.

Photios reminisces about how the brothers worked in Khazar, that distant land of warm waters and kind people which lay on their journey from Baghdad. About how Methodios and Cyril struggled to explain, in incredible detail, to the Khan of the Khazars and his followers, that the faith of Moses is past and the faith of the Abbasid is just another distraction from the Truth. Unfortunately all their work had absolutely no effect. The Khazars converted to the faith of Moses soon after the brothers departed.

So Photios writes also to encourage Cyril and Methodios. He reminds them that there are two things they should not forget. Firstly, all of their work is God's work. Everything happens for a reason in His eternal plan. Secondly, they need to find friends in high places to help them. And perhaps they will not find such friends among the Moravians. How ill-fated that advice was to be for the Patriarch. Rather than bringing them home, it drove them into the arms of the Pope himself!

35. Trials and tribulations

Vardas gets tapped awake by his dresser the next morning, or so Photios writes. The Caesar is soaked with sweat, having barely slept a wink all night. He decides to skip breakfast and ignores the advice of his dresser to wear his peach-colored travel coat, even though they will be traveling today. Instead, he puts on some light armor, and is pleased when he emerges to discover that the brigades are breaking camp.

He bursts into Michael's tent. Michael is back on his portable throne, with Vassilis right behind him.

"I still fail to see why we are here only with infantry," Vardas says. "You know how important this campaign is to us."

Antigonus, the new Demestikos, enters the tent and begins to make obeisance, but Vassilis takes him by the arm and whisks him out of the tent before any conversation can ensue. The plan is for Vassilis to get Antigonus as far away from Vardas as possible. Marianos has arranged a diversion for him: a hunt has been called, in order to catch some rare pheasant for the Imperial table this evening, on the excuse that the poor birds spend their summer on the banks of the river.

Vassilis returns to the tent where Vardas is pacing furiously. "It's still not clear to me what intelligence you have that the Abbasid are planning to invade Samos? My original plan was to reinforce Crete! So why have we come here?"

Michael seems calmer than ever. The dark curls of his beard are more carefully trimmed than usual. The dim light within the tent lends his face a skull-like pall. "Uncle, Uncle, do sit down. Let us talk about intelligence. The information we have had is quite ... disturbing."

"So the situation is worse than I thought. We appear to be badly prepared. What are the plans?' 'Vardas flops onto a couch, his tousled appearance hardly becoming a man of his stature.

It is Michael's turn to pace. "A different intelligence concerns us, one which we learned of more recently. It appears that our debt to you is more than can ever be imagined. The way you looked after our most prized possessions, when the Rus attacked and Vassilis and I were ... toiling away on the banks of the Euphrates — and ever since — is truly remarkable!"

Vardas' brow furrows in confusion. The authority of age tries to reassert itself. "Michael, I am growing tired of these games. We have come a long way, apparently unprepared. What are you going on about?"

"Rumor has it," begins Michael, "that your love for us extends so far that ... even our most prized possession has been fortunate enough to benefit from it."

I imagine the silence in the vanishing dawn, the hot breezes blowing in through the flaps, hinting at a hot day to come. Certainly, where I was involved, Michael had more guts than most would ever have given him credit for.

Vardas speaks cautiously. "If I actually knew what concerned you so much — I would remedy it immediately."

"Oh, but think, dear Uncle, think! Search your memory. There we were, Vassilis and I, charging and sparring, endangering our lives, as you have done very bravely before, while you ... "

He suddenly sits down on the couch next to Vardas and slaps him rudely on the back. Vassilis slips behind them.

"Oh, how was she?" says Michael. "Did you enjoy skewering her with your leaking cock? Wasn't it enough that you had to have a go at your son-in-law's new wife, but you had to wage war on my sweet Ingerina as well!"

It is Vardas' turn to look the death's head, paling visibly. Sweat drips like tears from his forehead.

"You make false accusation here, my boy," Vardas stammers. "No, no, I have done nothing to affront you in this way." His attempt to embrace Michael is too slow; Vassilis pulls him back.

And here the ancient tragedy of Cronos is performed. "Your reputation, old man," Vassilis says, "is more than you can imagine. That alone is enough to demand justice. But do you dare to deny that the child that clung to Ingerina's breast for but a moment was yours? Small wonder it lived so briefly, born out of such ignominy. What about the one she bears now?"

For Michael, the need to show he can commit to something is what has always plagued him. "I think the time has come, has it not, brother Vassilis, to wipe out the stench of foul lust? Perhaps Mother was right all along in sending him abroad. Where to now? Perhaps Africa, where he will find many a young wench to satisfy himself."

Vardas fights back the bitter tears. Treachery is a knife in one's back at best. But from those you love can there be any worse pain?

"I am a little old to be pushed around by you, nephew, even if you think you are God's chosen. You forget about the loyalty of the men under my command. Do you dare risk their wrath? Not to mention that the Treasury is looking decidedly empty of late. How are you going to pay them? You have given the Greens enough gold to buy half the City with little to show for it. How, in fact, can we afford this expedition? Have any of you given a thought to this!" He is on his feet.

"There is nothing to worry about," says Michael. "Cousin Theophilitzes has become acquainted lately of our need, thanks to the Magistros here, and has supported us in this venture."

Vassilis and I agreed beforehand that today had to be decisive. It it wasn't resolved properly, then Vardas would take it out on him. How I feared then for my Vassilis, though I knew his resolve!

"I think Africa is too good for him," replies Vassilis. "It is time for much more drastic action. We are bound by duty to do what should have been done a long time ago."

Vardas tries to slip toward the door. At a shout from Vassilis, Marianos and Symvatios enter and block Vardas' way. I can't even imagine Vardas' horror at seeing his ex-son-in-law in front of him as Vassilis flings him back onto the couch. Together the men work quickly with some rope, trussing Vardas to the point where he almost cannot breathe.

"That's enough nonsense," Michael spits. "I too am tired. Tired of being told what to do. Tired of the way you have taken over the City. I now understand why everyone comes to you for consent — seldom to me. Why do you refuse to admit the constant insult to the imperial pride!"

Marianos gags the protests boiling out of Vardas with his own cloak. He tears off Vardas' leggings, pulls a short sword out of his belt, and exposes Vardas' member. A moment later the short shaft, covered in frayed, bloody skin, drips from his upheld hand. Vassilis told me that Vardas emitted no more than a grunt at this.

"What have you done?" Michael screams, clawing at Vassilis. "This is not what we agreed!"

Vassilis stops Michael reaching Vardas. "Courage, brother!" he hisses. "It is done and cannot be undone." He turns around. "Is that all? You have probably missed something. Try again. Logothete, bring his shield."

Marianos swipes at Vardas again. The whole package is disengaged but the depths have been sounded — a skirt of blood spews from his groin.

Michael cries out as they heave Vardas off the couch. He crumples to the floor.

Michael sways. Vassilis' hands steady him, and set him down on the throne. A goblet finds its way into Michael's grasp. Symvatios brings in Vardas' shield. Vassilis runs it through with a spear and impales Vardas' bloody apparatus on the tip.

Suddenly Michael is back on Vardas, clawing at the ropes. "He only needed a lesson," he sobs, doubling over, bile spewing out of his mouth to join the rich mosaic of blood forming between on the canvas beneath his knees.

Outside on the river banks, the cohorts line up in formation. The day seems cursed. Before them stands a strange spectacle in the growing darkness of a storm — a shield on the end of a spear, with blood dripping off it. Word runs through the lines: Vardas in shame! A trumpet sounds a single note, its tones more chilling than the rising breeze.

A standard bearer holds the dripping shield and spear above his head and marches up the slope. Vassilis strides behind him. At the top he turns to look down at the soldiers, the sun behind him.

"Today we have dealt with a traitor in our midst," says my Vassilis. "In spite of his professed love and his many good deeds in favor of our City, he sinned against my wife, and the wives of others, and continued to do so without remorse. The Emperor meted out this justice with great sorrow, but the love of our Lord extends to all. For those who wallow in filth must be helped from their sin, or be judged accordingly."

Vassilis' voice carries over the rising commotion. His words seem to be blown along by the wind. "We have news that the enemy no longer presents us with difficulties. This campaign is over. We camp tonight and return to the City tomorrow. That is all. Dismissed!"

They will not understand, at least not yet. But now we will see who Vardas' supporters really are.

† † †

TWO MONTHS LATER, EARLY IN THE SUMMER OF 866 AD
Vassilis dreams. Praise be to the Theotokos! His heart sings with pride, as Constantinos pants ahead of him, his rapid steps matching Vassilis' longer gait. They are soon at a forest which looms ahead. Then a clearing lies beyond the trees, and beyond that a dizzying cliff edge, purple thunderclouds overhead. Behind them distant neighing signals a rider emerging from the forest. A Cataphract halts in the distance, stretching chain-mail covered arms out toward them.

Vassilis does not recognize the rider at first. Then the Cataphract breaks into a canter. A sudden gust knocks Vassilis back. Vassilis shouts to Constantinos that this man might be the Emperor — they must act quickly to save him from riding over the cliff. They wave at him to stop, and struggle to get closer, but the rain joins the wind to thrash across them, pushing them to the ground like dolls. They crawl on hands and knees. The Cataphract stops suddenly, dismounts and walks toward them.

Vassilis reaches up to touch the Cataphract's face. A rusting helmet crumbles away in his hands to reveal a decaying head. Its rotting sockets gaze back at him in the darkening light. It is his father! Vassilis wants to cry out, but then cringes as his father slaps claw-like nails across his face. The wind blows painfully right into Vassilis' ear. He reaches up a hand to cover it ...

... and touches something cold: a pipe! He is in pitch darkness, in his new quarters, he remembers, prepared alongside Michael's. His arms flail for a moment before coming up against a man's face. Driven by instinct, Vassilis locks an arm around the man's neck.

This is what unfolded that near-fateful night, or so he related several hours later, when he came to me, still shaking with rage. Though he did not tell me quite everything that took place.

With one arm pinning the wriggling creature down, Vassilis feels an arm slipping down his torso. Something sharp cuts him in the ribs. Vassilis flips the man over, pinning him face down on the bed and twisting his arm. There is a crack as his shoulder dislocates. The man yelps and shakes violently.

"You feeble piece of shit! What did you hope to achieve?" Vassilis leans on him heavily, relishing that he struggles to breathe. But his smell is familiar. "You have one chance. Talk!"

"Kill me, lord, I am yours," says Wasim.

"Kill you? Why are you here?"

"I am nothing. Kill me, or she will."

"She? Not Dekapolitessa, surely?"

Wasim babbles as Vassilis squeezes his neck tighter and feels the bed dampen beneath them. "Ah, you mean the old witch. What in heaven could she possibly offer you, eh? Future service? Freedom? After everything I have tried to do for you and your kind!"

Now he cracks Wasim's limbs this way and that, testing the limits of pain. Wasim weeps.

The old anger rises — Vassilis has done nothing to harm the old woman personally — so why does she persist? But the rancid sweat from the man and the sense of relief at being alive move Vassilis to action.

He recalls some meat left over from the previous evening and gropes for the plate with one hand, rolling it in the leftover grease. I wonder how much the howling of this treacherous creature, and the arching of his slender back against the first light of dawn, satisfy Vassilis. With conquering member in fist and blood slipping down his side, Vassilis pushes deep down into Wasim's bowels, pummeling the frustrations of many years, now the miserable creature beneath him, now the women that rule his life, now the cruelty of a sworn brother, sleeping a few yards away who manages to rip his heart apart with every wicked smile, now even New Rome itself. No, he didn't tell it to me in these words, but I could sense it. I knew where I stood with him. I knew how this bitterness turned him into what he is today.

The release is fitful though Vassilis' emptiness cannot be compassed. His offending hand emerges and joins its mate around the young man's sunken head. A simple twist and the young man's chin rests on his back.

Michael enters, rumpled, candle in hand. His wicked grin lasts only a moment before he notices the corpse and kneels to examine the poison darts on the floor. "By the power of the Godhead, what is going on here?"

Vassilis peers down at Wasim's twisted expression. "A very clear example," Vassilis says "if one were necessary, of the dangers that both you and I face. Do you still doubt that we need to act soon?"

† † †

Finally, both my men are forced to confront their pasts.

Vassilis' near-fateful encounter fills me with even greater resolve. I throw caution to the winds and decide I cannot wait any longer to move Michael to act. In his quarters the following evening he tries to joke about what happened, but I am not amused.

"It is time to take this seriously," I say. "I have told you before. Both you and your brother are in danger. Your Uncle is no longer with us but his plans bear fruit, with your mother cultivating them from afar. Meanwhile our son awaits the dawning of life in my womb. What will his future be?"

"Vardas' son!" he mutters. Do I imagine it, or can he not even look me in the eye?

"It doesn't matter who planted the seed, does it?" I say. "To the entire world his father is Vassilis. You need to anoint both him and me, that we may bear an Imperial scion before it is too late!"

He shakes his head. But checkmate is in the offing and he knows it. "What about the Senate? What do you suggest I do with them?"

"You must show who is in charge once and for all by dealing with your mother. If you do, you will find many more behind you than you would ever imagine, many who are in favor of Vassilis." Not least of which is Danielli, but I don't say this, of course.

So Michael rides unaccompanied to the district of the Stoudion to face his mother. What a struggle it must be to return to the womb, and quarrel with it! One has no recourse but to feel like a child again.

The dilapidated walls of the monastery of Ta Gastria depress him as does the gloomy entrance hall. Can't they light a fire to fight the cold a little? Even the old couch chills him.

The Regent rustles in, his sisters behind her, barely recognizable in black, their heads covered in perpetual mourning, with Gemma bringing up the rear. There is not a loving word. How could there be?

"So, my dear ones," Michael announces. "What have you brought me to now? I should have you all executed."

"We do nothing more," Theodora says, "than mourn the passing of memories. Prayer and worship are our staples. But what you have done is another matter entirely!"

"Christ in his kingdom, you live like peasants here. Get me some wine."

Theodora stares past him. Sister Thekla shoves her bony cheeks and a raw finger at him. "What do you want? You have taken everyone from us already. And undone everything Mother has worked for."

"Dearest sister, don't fool with me. We all know that Mother is behind this latest ... debacle. Do you think I am a complete idiot? If I don't do anything about it the court will certainly perceive it as weakness."

Theodora brings herself to sit next to him, but her hands drop on his shoulders in a stillborn embrace. "Michael, that man is Satan incarnate. Listen to me. He will destroy everything we have built up together, even you."

He stands up to get away from her, his eyes wet. "Oh Mother, you are ... deeply, deeply wrong. As you have been about everything in my life. How would you understand!"

He paces. "We were once taking a small boat down a river with Vassilis when it smashed on some large rocks. We were dragged down by the current. How I struggled to rise, until my chest was about to burst. I managed to grab hold of the boat but could not muster enough strength to pull my mouth above water, if only to take the smallest breath. Whose arms pulled me out, when I thought it time to bid farewell to life? You have never understood what I needed, always despised everything I have ever wanted, and then done things for me I did not ask for. How can I listen to you, how can I trust you?"

Theodora, unfailingly, misses her cue. "Michael, he is a peasant, not even of Roman blood. How can he wish anything good for you?

The tears have burnt away on hot cheeks. "And Ingerina is not entirely of Roman blood either. But I need them, both of them. I also need you to leave us alone."

The glances fly back and forth between the women, like bats across a cave.

Theodora tries again. "And what of my family. I mean my grandchildren, bastards though they will be? I never saw the . . . first one. But surely the next one who is soon to enter this world should know his grandmother?"

This is too much for Michael. "Your 'grandchildren,' you say! 'Nephews' would be closer to the truth! I was no part of the child that died! I am not even sure what the next one will be to you. Don't you understand anything that has transpired?"

Theodora pales. As a mother, can she not feel the pain that Michael endures, or see that her brother might have gone too far?

"You must not resist any longer," Michael continues when he has stopped shaking. "I will have you removed by force if necessary. The Vryas Palace, on the other side of the Bosporus, awaits you. Its rotting walls will enjoy your scheming company."

"I will not miss my life here," she says. "At least your sisters and I will have each other . . . and our faith."

Michael stands up and slaps his hands together. "Not quite. Since Vassilis gave up his family, in particular his beloved wife, for me, I have been promising him some distraction. I think that now is the time to make good that promise. Sister Thekla, it seems as if your future will be more . . . elevated. The new Emperor's bed is waiting for you."

Michael turns to leave Thekla crumpling on the floor behind him, reaching for her mother, her despair echoing through the hallways. Her rage satisfies him more than he could ever have imagined possible.

The next night Michael sends for me. I am not in the mood for games. But he is more playful.

"You have asked to be crowned Augusta. I am not ready to confer this rare title on anyone. However I will agree to part of what you suggest. But only if you promise me that the child is mine."

"How can I promise anything?" I say. "I have been treated like a plaything by everyone! Even a pawn is not abused so much! Married to one man, the distraction of another, allegations of a third. Do you not understand that I, too, must face my conscience every time I pray?"

So the Ayia Sofia has had two identical thrones placed on the side, and in Archangel's garb Michael processes once again up to the ambo, with Photios in front of him and Vassilis right behind.

The courtly congregation is silent, but friendly faces incline toward me. I see John Chaldis and others whose wives I know among them. Michael addresses us.

"The Caesar plotted against me, to kill me, and for this reason induced me to leave the City. If I had not been informed of the plot by Vassilis and Symvatios, I would not be alive now. The Caesar died because of his own guilt. For this and other reasons, mainly that he is faithful to me and protects my realm and has delivered me from my enemy, I proclaim that Vassilis should be the guardian of all that is mine, to reign with me as brother Emperor."

Michael takes the crown from his own head and hands it to Photios — who hefts it onto Vassilis' matted brow. Vassilis' eyes are clouded. Is there no pleasure in this for him? I had hoped that his yearning was as much for Michael's station as it is to drink the ancient blood in his veins, or to suck the very seed from his loins.

But I am wasting time worrying about such things. There is still much work to be done.

36. Boys will be boys

Now that Michael and Vassilis stand equal in the eyes of the law and God, I am more than pleased. But Vardas' hand looms beyond the grave. Antigonus can no longer serve as Demestikos — it would hardly be fitting for the son of the dead Caesar to be in this position. Vassilis wants Marianos in this role, but Michael utterly refuses to agree either to this or to my crowning. So Vassilis takes it on himself, in front of the Gynaeconitis, to offer me the title of First Lady, accompanied as it is by the golden girdle of the Magistros. I will have to be content, for at least now my position in front of the ladies is secured and my child has earned the right to be born in the Purple Room.

But then there is Eudokia, who is very disappointed with her lack of ascension in rank. Could we have done more to soothe Symvatios' wounded pride? Probably. The first lessons in power were hard for us, my little Leo, but you can benefit from our bruised knees. Take care of your friends. For they can be more dangerous than your enemies!

Eudokia comes home to find Symvatios in a state. He cannot stop shaking. The strong wine he is swilling down in large quantities doesn't seem to be having any kind of good effect. Not normally a man given to over-indulgence, either in rage or wine, the combination is both laughable and pitiable.

"Ah, my goddess," he says, swaying as he stretches across the couch to reach her.

"Get your hands off me," she squirms. "Here you sit, drinking yourself into oblivion, while the new Emperor forges a new life for himself and forgets what he owes you. What is this I hear about Marianos? Where are all the magnificent promises now?"

Symvatios sits up and looks across at her, shaking his head. "We all have to live with promises. Perhaps you can tell me what Vardas promised you!"

"What are you talking about? You have gambled your career and our future … and lost! The nephew of the Caesar, I thought. Now there is a proper man, I thought. How could you let yourself be taken in so much? What kind of an idiot lives in that skull of yours, I ask myself? What kind of a lamp stand have I chained myself to?" Eudokia can be very obnoxious when she is angry.

"It was obvious that something was wrong when we returned from Crete," says Symvatios. Vassilis was crowned and then … nothing! I thought he would have seen sense. At least I have received the generalship of Thracesian − a title not to be sneezed at. Even though it turns out, or so everyone tells me, that I am married to a whore!"

"All you ever do is think!" Eudokia snaps. "Can't you see how humiliating it is for us! Let's imagine that Marianos is appointed. What then? You will be general under the command of someone who had served as a mere divisional commander in the Theme you once commanded! Why don't you offer your backside to him as well while you're about it?"

Symvatios collapses back onto the couch as she storms off. Does he consider ending it all right there and then, with a dagger in the bowels? His wife and daughters would probably be better off without such a pitiful creature, although I can tell you now that Eudokia would be annoyed at the bloodstains on the new rugs.

In a way I blame myself for what happened. With her constant indignation, Eudokia must have driven him to desperation. I regret not planning more of it together with her. Or perhaps if I had tried to find ways to reward her more. But one simply can't think of everything.

So even the worm turns … and quite cunningly in this case! Without us knowing anything about it, Symvatios pleads with Michael, wearing him down through obsequious fawning and endless petitions. Eventually Michael grants him, quite innocently, a few small favors. Oh, if only we had been more careful!

† † †

But by now I have something far more important on my mind, little Leo. You! Every time I chance to rest I can feel those young legs of yours eager to climb a tree or run through the stadium. You are eager to vacate your growing place and I, too, do not want to delay this.

With my new title it is right and fitting that I recline in the Purple Room. A silk honeycomb of red linen billows above me in the welcome breezes. The great bed of births and blindings is as comfortable as expected, and the women are always nearby, dabbing at my brow, squeezing my hands to comfort me, or holding quiet conversation just of earshot as they watch me with concern, some of it unfeigned!

I don't recall experiencing such profound agony before. The indignity of the first birth is a dim memory. It went so quickly. This one seems never-ending. My weight pins me down, and I long for release. My dread from the loss of my firstborn has metamorphosed into impatience as the seed within me has ripened.

So I embrace the discomfort further than I can endure. All around me are sounds of encouragement but I barely hear a thing. The pain stretches itself across my ears and eyes like a tight veil, the blood rushes to my head and I feel myself swell to bursting. I rip away the sheets encasing me, tossing away any few remaining shreds of dignity with sounds I did not know I could emit.

I am convinced I can never know pain again after this. The cosmos gushes out of me. A strange tugging inside me is followed by a hiss. The chief midwife has sunk a red-hot blade into the cord. Sounds of awe and amazement follow and are suddenly muted. A warm wetness, presumably the afterbirth, flops onto my legs.

Where is my child? I hear nothing and try to sit up. The midwife has her mouth over a ball of waxy black and purple. Then the sweetest sound in the world erupts into the silence. The women busy themselves around a marble basin, water is poured, and they thrust a little ... boy into my eager arms. Waves of joy burn through me. What is this precious lamb? His eyes wide open, an arm reaches out toward me and the little lips part. Surely the sweetest sound a mother can hear is the bleating of her newborn child.

Mutterings surround me. I do not need to look closely to see Michael's grey eyes, his nose, his raven hair. I decide that I don't care what Vassilis will think, whether or not he will descend into one of his silent rages. If this one lives, I will have proven myself a fine bearer of healthy sons.

Instead, I croon in delight as you let forth a magnificent howl.

That's my golden boy! I already know your name. I will insist upon it. For all our professed hatred of the Iconoclast Emperors, the Leos were decisive, powerful people. I vow to let that strength flow alongside my Thulian blood in your little veins.

† † †

Michael paces impatiently to and fro in the Treasury as Vassilis enters. Photios is there, as is Christoferos, the new Logothete.

"If I understand correctly," Michael is furious, "we have some figures, although we do not know how far we can trust them. You say there are about three hundred pounds of gold in the treasury?"

Christoferos bows, and picks up a document. "According to the records, when the Emperor Theophilos died he left eighty thousand pounds in the Imperial Treasury reserve fund. The former ... Regent added a further eight thousand by the time she ... left office, which means Your Worthiness began with about ninety thousand pounds."

"Are you sure you there are only three hundred left?" asks Michael nervously. "You don't mean three thousand?"

The officials gaze nervously at the floor. Christoferos ventures a nod in the affirmative. Everyone knows that both Symvatios and Michael are to blame for this, the former for giving in to the latter's whims at every opportunity.

"Well," Michael says, "does anyone have any suggestions? It is obvious that we are in trouble. And now the rumors of an insurrection run rife. I fear not only that I have no support in the Senate, and that we might have to fight our own Generals, but that now we cannot even afford to reimburse the lowliest foot soldier! What do I pay all of you for if you can't deal with this kind of thing? How much was spent on the successful campaigns, against Melitene, and in Crete?"

"Preliminary calculations," says Christoferos, "predict about eighty-five to ninety thousand pounds were spent, at most, on these ventures, primarily on weapons and machinery. Given salaries and taxes over the last twelve years, that still leaves ten to twenty thousand unaccounted for."

Michael turns to Photios. "My dear Patriarch, you see where we are. What is your assessment?"

"Worthiness," he says, "our churches are ideally places of contemplation and worship. Neither the Theotokos nor our Savior demand the extravagances that we have lavished on them recently, since the Iconoclast heresy was abolished."

"Noble Patriarch," Vassilis begins. "The gist of your suggestion amazes me. Surely you should be the keeper of the holy relics, not their merchant. Brother Emperor, I don't doubt that this is the work of Symvatios again. But I think we should have words in private. Leave us now."

Michael lays his head on Vassilis' shoulder and grins rather sheepishly up at him. Vassilis is furious that we should be in such debt that we are forced to destroy our holy treasures. Fortunately we have a Theotokos of our own — the widow Danielli, as it turns out.

37. The confidence of friends

THREE MONTHS LATER, IN THE WINTER OF LATE 866 AD
Our appeal to the coffers of Patras is dispatched none too soon, for the rumors of insurrection turn out to be horribly true. Just as soon as Marianos is appointed to the office of Demestikos, Symvatios, bitter and raging, sets tongues wagging when he sends his family secretly to their holiday home in Mytilene.

Then Symvatios himself vanishes from the court and sails off across the straits of the Bosporus, into the arms of his boyhood companion, George Peganes, the new Count of Opsician. What a fine pair! History is set to repeat itself — Opsician has always been the land of rebellion. Peganes heads a battalion and advances on the City, ravaging as he goes. If that is not enough, they denounce my Vassilis at every step, while loudly evincing their support for what they call 'the good Emperor'.

How devious Vassilis must have seemed then. Photios writes that Vassilis must be the very hand of God, his destiny playing itself out little by little, in small ways winning everyone to him. Little does Photios realize, until now, the hearts Vassilis succeeded in winning, and the minds he employed to cunning ends, including many of our young officials.

In truth, the cunning sprung from all of us. Marianos uses his acquaintances among many of the rebel troops to distribute pamphlets to the rebel commanders. I humbly submit to Photios' opinion — that the pamphlet was a stroke of genius, denouncing Symvatios and Peganes as traitors and rebels, and citing the many ways in which Vassilis — a man of humble background — had become the protector of the City, by the grace of the Theotokos herself! After all, I composed and dictated the pamphlet's text to the scribes myself!

I make sure that there is no mention of Michael, lest it appear openly like treason, although anyone with an iota of understanding can easily perceive the implications. We assume that Michael would never lower himself to lay eyes on the pamphlet itself.

Vassilis spends long hours urging Michael to crush the rebels, while the two of them gallop side by side across verdant plains, like the Greeks of old, piercing fowl or deer with one of their arrows, Vassilis behind Michael's shoulder, guiding him with wordless touches and gestures.

But sometimes fortune provides that small, vital gift that guarantees success. In this case it is a special hero — a virtually unknown commander, Nikolaos Maleinus. Not only is this fine young man prepared to defend the Realm, but he is ready to do so immediately. To everyone's amazement a small but believable force materializes. In the space of two weeks, Maleinus succeeds in capturing Peganes with virtually no resistance. A week later he comes across Symvatios himself at an inn, his rebel troops having all but deserted him.

Now the two Emperors sit shoulder to shoulder in the Balcony, taking in the punishment for treason, as prescribed by Justinian. In some ways it is like a return to the days of the gladiators, looking down into the Hippodrome, the Senate assembled obediently behind them, and the small crowd bursting with curiosity below.

The hot irons are ready. Down in the pit, the new Eparch of the City, one Constantine Myares, has the ceremonial duty of plunging them into the traitors' left eyes. Marianos is present alongside him — in his new role as Demestikos — to witness, as protocol demands, the administration of the sentence. Myares is clearly not up to the task, so Marianos moves over to take up the instruments. The crowd draws breath as one. The traitors cry out in anguish as their faces vanish in smoke.

Marianos proceeds to the second stage of the ceremony. The message must be made clear — that treason cannot be countenanced. A sharp sword appears and bloodied hands thud onto the ground. Stumps are bound roughly as the traitors double over onto their severed limbs. Their screams echo off stone seats and even stonier faces. The final part will be the worst — the humiliation of being made to stand at the gates of the Hippodrome with a bowl for alms, for at least a month.

† † †

Indeed, not even the great Photios could unravel the mystery! To him, and to everyone else, Vassilis was the hand of God. After all, how could a mere woman come up with such plans? If only everyone had thought a little harder it would have been obvious. We both understood what was needed; and bore the hope that drove us to it. For hope, in the darkest hour, is the distant candle on which you fix your gaze. It is the pinch of light that directs your stride when everything around you is shrouded with dread.

In celebration of the defeat of the rebels, Michael summons his favorites one evening to a sailor's tavern. Vassilis descends to the harbor with Michael hanging on to him, staggering and singing. They enter to loud cheers. Nicetas and Anatellon of the Greens are there, as are a party of charioteers, and of course Vassilianiscus is there, his dark complexion all grins and simpering amicability.

"Seal the doors," smiles Michael, clapping the tavern master on the back. "And bring us enough wine to last the night."

The tables are pulled apart to allow a space in the center for the Emperors. Vassilis raises a goblet "I propose a toast — to the power of the one, true, ecumenical, orthodox and catholic Throne." Sagely nods all round are followed by gulps of wine.

"And to the jerk-offs who try to abuse it!" calls out Michael, going over to Vassilis to stand beside him. This get roars of approval. "May their alm bowls be empty ...," he grimaces, hiding his hand up his sleeve, and stares menacingly around him"... and their bowels full to overflowing!" He knocks back the contents of his goblet to hoots of laughter.

Vassilianiscus says, "What of the Pope, and the Bulgar, your Serenities? Are we indeed one community in Christ?"

Michael frowns, then smiles. "Boris is not tempted again by Rome," he says, propping one foot on a bench. "Pope Nicholas is a desperate man. He will do anything to bring Boris to Rome — even if it means baptizing himself in his own piss." More guffaws from the gathering. "That way he can be amply on our doorstep — his legates eager to flit in and out of the City. Before we know it — we will become barbarians, speaking Latin!"

"Bugger the Latins, bugger the Latins, ...," the men thump the tables.

"That is one way to look at it," Vassilis says as they drink.

"But Photios' words have done more harm than good. Do you know that he has given not the slightest thought to what Boris has requested — a new Bulgar patriarch?" Vassilianiscus cocks an eye at this.

"Clearly Boris wants to have more local control," Vassilianiscus says. "I can't say that I blame him. Why doesn't he send one of our bishops?"

At this Michael makes a great show of looking around, his gaze alighting on one of the charioteers. "How about Nicetas here. I'll appoint him bishop tomorrow! He's the kind of thug who could convince a statue to shit marble!"

This gets laughs and jibes from everyone. Then Michael announces: "Come on, everyone, let's have some theater. Vassilianiscus, attend! You play me, and I'll play Photios."

The men arrange a chair on the table and push Vassilianiscus up onto it with some difficulty. Michael throws a table cloth around his shoulders and hunches over.

"I am adamant," Michael simpers in Photios' well-rounded tones, "that we do not need to send any more of my bishops to my godson the Khan."

"Why, Patriarch?" Vassilianiscus says. "Is it because you still struggle to control your priests even here in the City? Because you do not know how to keep them in obligation to you. Because you hem and haw, and would get confused by your own stole if it did not hang about your neck!"

"Yes, Worthiness," moans Michael, "How can I exert influence over someone in Pliska when I can't even stop turds shooting out of my own backside?"

The gathering collapses in mirth. Vassilis frowns, waiting for the laughter to subside. "Photios is a kind and honest man," he says, "and does not deserve this kind of abuse."

"Yes, but he is not a very political man," Vassilianiscus retorts. "What is the point in dispatching to Boris two tomes of the history of the church? What else did he write about? The duties of a Christian prince, the functions of the Ecumenical Councils. All this to someone new to the faith who worries chiefly whether to celebrate the Easter Resurrection mass in the morning or the evening before? Or whether confession should be in Greek or the Bulgar tongue?"

"I agree with my brother," Michael says, throwing off the cloak. "That's quite enough silliness for tonight. But what the Khan needs is a helping hand, not a lecture. What about our monks already in Pliska? Can't they help him out with these rather mundane questions?"

Vassilianiscus climbs down from the table. He says "These very monks are the cause of Boris' concern, Worthiness. He frets about exactly the same thing that worries you when you imagine the Latins invading the City. Too many foreigners."

"Then we should help Photios win some favor," Michael says. "At least in the City. What will do it?'

The men debate and revel into the night. Vassilis knows, as I know, that wine will do little to ease the anger he feels at his brother's stupidity. Yet plans are often borne out of that cavernous space that fills the end of any drunken discourse, and this night is no exception.

It is mid morning before Michael rolls awake on his bed. He leaps to his feet without any warning, throws a cloak over his shoulder, and orders guards to summon Vassilis, a unit of soldiers and a chariot.

Swathes of dust fill the gray airlessness of the Ayia Sofia's mausoleum as the soldiers lift corpses from discarded marble slabs. Michael brooks no words of redress from Vassilis, and before long they find themselves in a chariot, hooves raising the dust of the Hippodrome, dragging a bizarre load behind them.

A small crowd has gathered. But this is no victory celebration.

The Emperors parade two stacks of bones topped with skulls and held together with rope and crumbling tunics. Learn your history well, my little Leo. One of them, belonging to Constantine "The Shitter", has been consumed by more than fifty years of worm-cosseted dust. The other bones are newer; Patriarch John the Grammarian died less than ten years before this ridiculous event. Silent onlookers mill down the steps onto the dust as the Imperial brothers stop the chariot every so often, taking turns to smash the remnants of the corpses with whips.

As they complete a final ride around the Hippodrome, Vassilis notices the continued silence swallowing their progress. There are few cheers. Clearly the memory of the Iconoclast heretics has passed, at least for the common folk. They certainly don't care as much as we do about these matters. Michael looks a fool, though a happy one. Vassilis and I confer. We agree that this kind of thing has to stop, as soon as possible.

† † †

There is a new servant in Michael's quarters, a Paulician, and one of ours. We have made sure he tells us everything. The ranting, the weeping, even when His Worthiness vacates himself.

The tears stream down Michael's face again tonight. The many candles, the wine, even the presence of extra servants fails to soothe him. He calls for a massage. Slave hands smooth oil across the Imperial limbs while thick fingers rub deep in the flesh, to just the right point. This role was once the duty of my peasant Emperor. But now that he occupies an Imperial bed all his own, Michael, in truth, has no one to turn to.

Michael rambles, the goblet never far. "Is the child mine? Or was Vardas' lust responsible only for the previous one, the one we lost? The dark waves on its head look nothing like the lighter color of Vardas, of Theodora's family."

"Calm yourself, Worthiness" says the Paulician servant.

"Is my brother on his way?" Michael groans. "Am I to be left alone all evening?"

Michael takes off his robe and turns onto his chest. The servant oils and pummels his back.

The lock rattles — Vassilis is there. More metal on metal as he sets down his cloak.

"How could you leave me alone for so long?" Michael whines.

Vassilis lies down alongside Michael, caressing him with words. "Stop worrying. I am here. What is it? Come now! Cheer up! All is as we planned it. The court is ours, ready to carry out our every wish. Do you wish for me to arrange Ingerina?"

Michael turns slowly onto an elbow and searches Vassilis' eyes. "Vardas was a father to me. You know this. How could he touch her? Why would he wish to break my soul in this way? I have not forgiven her either. No, I wish for nothing tonight. I am tired of everyone." He drops back onto the couch.

Vassilis pulls him up gently. With a cloth he wipes away the remaining oil, with another he dabs away the tears.

"You know there was no way we could go on. You had lost all face at court. You had to show a strong hand! It is the only way with this den of slanderers and crooks."

"But what will I do without him? I cannot bear the Throne Room any more, and the Senate is a bunch of whining pederasts. Not to mention the monks and bishops who never stop reminding me of the loss of their treasures. When will the widow's gold reach us? Where are we supposed to find the money to go on if it doesn't arrive?"

The last is what Vassilis has been working at all day. The gold leaf is being peeled from the walls of the site of their sacred union, the Chapel of the Virgin of the Lighthouse, but we agreed to leave the other churches alone. Why would we incur the wrath of the bishops? Michael doesn't need to know of the negotiations with the Generals, that Vassilis is holding them off while Danielli's gold arrives.

For my part, who needs church ornaments anyway? Life is more important than golden boxes, no matter how ornate. Though one evening Vassilis terrifies me, when I use these very words to him, by flying into one of his dark rages again. How could we possibly destroy the Holy Reliquaries?

"You must help," whines Michael to Vassilis. "Will you take this burden from me, my dear brother?"

Where are the joyful times together now? The games of backgammon, the bags of wine after swimming side by side in a river, the pheasant hunts. A man who cannot control his feelings is more contemptible than a badly dressed woman — both leave a foul taste in one's mouth.

Does my Emperor seek advantage from the situation? Does he trace Michael's enduring leanness with one hand, even as the other hand eases Michael's shoulders and neck? Does his warm breath blow over the Emperor's cheek as Vassilis drinks in his smell? Perhaps thighs come to rest against each other as Vassilis puts a leg over him, the better to massage him, of course!

"I am here for you," Vassilis' breathes softly in Michael's ear. "There is nothing to worry about. You must rest and, if you wish, mourn for your uncle's passing. He was a great man — but he played where he should not have. You will be greater yet."

This time Michael doesn't seem to mind Vassilis' lips on his

cheek, a tongue lovingly exploring the line of his jaw, arms en-
folding him. As they sink back onto the couch, I imagine Michael
feels at peace the way I do when I curl up into Vassilis' frame.

Michael murmurs. "I regret now that I gave in to Symvatios' request. I should never have allowed George Peganes to become Count of Opsician." He reaches out to cup Vassilis' cheek,
but does that disarm him? Does he chance to release some of his
burning lust? No, he has learned his lesson.

"These events are all in the past, brother," Vassilis says. "Forget them. In the morning we will gather some young men and go
hunting in the countryside. I will arrange for Ingerina to visit you
tomorrow evening. We will drink, dance, and make love. Life and
empire are forever. Grief and regret are for the weak. They will
pass, as does everything in this world. Do not forget you now
have a child of your flesh. What more could you possibly ask for?"

"You are right. And I have you," Michael's voice is fading,
"that is all I need."

As Michael's eyelids droop, Vassilis feels his blade under his
feet, resting beneath his cloak. How could he have forgotten to
leave it behind in his quarters?

38. Condemnation

Photios receives the delegates of the Council at the entrance to the Magnaura. The immense main hall, now newly refurbished as an auditorium, already resounds to heated exchanges. Monks, bishops, and their attendants mill around. Arethas, one of Photios' assistants, rushes over to tell him that a handful of the two hundred and eighty delegates will not make an appearance today, not out of disrespect, but only because they have finally succumbed to the kind of illnesses travelers frequently suffer from.

Why is Photios holding a Council? He writes that he is determined that this gathering should be enumerated with the six holy and ecumenical Councils as the seventh. He wants to punish godlessness by the decision of all Sees, not just that of Constantinople. By this he means the Iconoclasts and the Paulician heretics. But we all know that what he really wants to do is reassert his authority.

Photios writes that the barbarian Rus want to change their godless religion for the pure and unadulterated faith of the Christians! They have sent an envoy, offering to place themselves under the protection of the Empire instead of continuing their pillaging. A victory for the See of Constantinople indeed!

The Senate fills the upper seats, and the Pope's legates — the Exarch of Ravenna, and the Archbishops of Treves and Cologne — take position at the center of the auditorium, on either side of the imperial thrones.

The Emperors arrive next. They process through the gathering with great pomp, Photios following a little way behind them. He separates from the procession to mount a simple lectern. And what a speech he has written!

"I thank all those who have traveled from afar to be here, and pray for those who are still suffering from their long journeys, that they will be relieved soon. Now we are ready to reap the harvest of our travails. But first I call for you to join in an accolade to the Emperors."

"Splendid to behold are our truly pious and victorious Emperors, and their feats in war, their victories, their trophies, whereof no moment of time since they have acceded to the kingly office has remained barren. The Emperors' hands did not draw the sword of the cross against one alien heresy without retrieving their enemies' defeat. Breaking up all their enemies' ranks at once, and splendidly exhibiting their own strategic feats against them all, our Emperors bestow on the whole body of the church a profound and undisturbed peace. They secure for the whole commonwealth a similar and like concord, having set up an eternal monument of orthodoxy for all generations to come."

"Time been rejuvenated, and has given birth to new and noble deeds. The cyclical motion has given way to a new flowering. A new era is beginning, and it lacks only an orator who can rise to the grandeur of the occasion."

"Prosper and reign, O admirable pair, in whom the grace of the Trinity dwells. Prosper and reign, Michael and Vassilis, because of truth and meekness and righteousness. Amen."

A Latin cardinal shouts out from the group. "By whose authority does this modest orator bring us here? You all know that our father, the Bishop of Rome does not recognize him in matters spiritual and eternal. He is a heretic and a schismatic, possibly even a charlatan."

There are some calls of agreement. But most remain silent, as do the Legates.

Vassilis comes to the rescue. Instinctively he knows that one must control this rabble. "You are here by our authority, as Regents of the Most Holy among us, and as the leaders of this earthly kingdom of New Rome which reflects the glories of heaven. The Patriarch receives his authority from us and also because he has served Mother Church faithfully and in all holiness since he was appointed to the task."

Michael enjoins. "Furthermore, you will only speak when given the opportunity to do so. I refuse to countenance petty bickering among such learned dignitaries. Patriarch, please proceed."

Photios continues, clearly shaken. "Time, it seems, had grown old, and brought forth no more the offspring of her youthful confidence and pride. Now, however, thanks to these two men, the champions of pious, new, and noble deeds, she is glorified with the birth-pangs of youth, and puts off old age with its reproaches, as if she had succeeded in showing everyone, in the light of truth, a well-born and excellent offspring shining with the grace of all good things."

The gathering stirs, but he speaks louder. "Had Time also borne a generation of orators who knew how to make words commensurate with the facts, and to elevate the power of their tongues to the magnitude of their deeds, then her prime and renovation would have been altogether confirmed."

He puts down his notes and waits for silence. "My brothers in Christ, consider that we are working at odds with one another, especially in the domains that lie between us. The Bulgar Archon Boris, known to us also by the name of our Holy Emperor, was baptized by me. The Bulgar subsequently invited some of your holy brothers to attend to his spiritual needs. As the great Constantine himself wrote to Miltiades of Rome, in 313, on the subject of the convocation of a Roman synod: 'What seems to me intolerable in those places that Divine Providence has spontaneously given me to rule and which are so thickly populated, is that the people should be split into two camps to their own damage, and that the bishops should not be able to agree among themselves.'

Silence at last. He goes on. "As the great Irene herself declared of our brother the Pope: 'We have decreed that a universal Council shall take place. And we ask your paternal Beatitude ... to acquiesce and to make no delay but to come hither to confirm and strengthen the ancient tradition as to the venerable images.' In her address to the Council Fathers, the Augusta Irene expressed very clearly, 'By God's good pleasure and will, we have brought together you His sacred priests ... in order that your decision may be in accordance with the definitions of the Councils and that the glorious Light of the Spirit may enlighten all.'

The cheers fly out of Greek and even some Latin mouths, like clumsy birds released from captivity.

He pauses for silence. "We are glad for the work of our Latin brothers with the Bulgar. However, why is it that you must contradict what we have taught them, that we must reopen the issue of the Holy Trinity, brought up at Nicea, as to the descent of the

Spirit from both the Son and the Father, with people who are not yet able to fully discern the subtleties of our differing messages?"

"This ..." the Patriarch has to shout above the rising noise, "this when our mutual goal must surely be to bring the Holy Word to the barbarians and not to dispute canonical matters with those who are but children in the faith?" The gathering is in uproar.

"Have we not spoken!" booms Vassilis. "Silence until you have our leave. We demand it!"

"Thank you, Your Serene Worthiness," Photios resumes, bowing as the silence descends. "Why do we argue about the lands between us? It was agreed at Nicea that we would maintain the Serbians, Bulgar and Moravians within our dominion and that the Roman sees would encompass the Franks and their multitudes."

The hubbub resumes somewhat. Now it is Michael's turn. He stands up and raises an arm in the ancient and correct rhetorical posture of an acclamation. "Servants of God, if you do not hold your peace, then we will be here until Armageddon." He appears to be trembling.

Then he teeters, before stumbling down the steps toward the exit, and vanishes, leaving us all frozen in amazement. Mutters and whispers begin to rise to a roar — no one is sure whether to rise or remain seated. Vassilis rescues the situation.

"Calm, holy brethren. We are close to taking a decision. Is there anything else, Patriarch?"

"Indeed, most Holy Emperor. It ... it is the very question of the source of our authority. I appeal to you, my learned brothers, that a new age is dawning, one in which our understanding has as much to say about the love of Christ as our prayers.

"Some fifteen years ago, the Augusta Theodora restored the Icons, and taught us that the pagan ways of the old Greeks and Romans had left a love in our hearts that no amount of thoughtless action, albeit Christian in name, could suppress. Holy brothers, the Iconoclasts lived through the anger of their minds, not by the love of the hearts. By the same token, let not your contempt for thoughtful learning undermine the prayer of the heart. It is with this plea to your nobler parts that I wish to make peace with our brother the Bishop of Rome."

"Very well said indeed, Patriarch Photios," Vassilis says. "Now ... we will hear the letters from the Pope, and then take discussion from all those seated at the central table. Proceed, in good order, and with dignity, or else find yourselves displaced from this chamber forthwith."

† † †

This would have been a fine moment for master Photios, and indeed for all of us, if nothing more had happened. Indeed the nature of the Trinity is not in dispute, nor should it ever be. And I am amazed that Photios went to such lengths to appeal to the Latins. I would have said that attempting to win their hearts was about as pointless as teaching a puppy to recite Aristophanes. Instead, he succeeded, only too well!

But note well, my little Leo, that Photios does not write about the sudden turn of events at the end of the Council. Was it lack of time that prevented him? Or guilt at how his arguments had twisted the Council's hearts?

That last day of the Council was meant to be a festive one. It was supposed to be a celebration of our faith, a harvest banquet for all who worship the Icons. The fruits of the feast should have been a document signed by both Emperors, and toward which even those old gray beards, the senators, had also proffered some small seeds of wisdom. Thanks to Vassilis' careful husbandry, the bickering and arguments turned the fertile ground over, and we would have been content with that, except that Photios and the visiting legates had to throw the thorns in.

Do you notice that Photios doesn't write about how he provoked his monks to pronounce excommunication and anathema on the Pope, and discovered, even to my Emperor's surprise, that many of the western bishops were right behind him, that Nicholas had so angered his own flock that the sheep could agree to support Photios in stating these damning words?

"Without a council, without canonical inquiry, without accuser, without witnesses, without convicting us by arguments or authorities, without our consent, in the absence of the metropolitans and of our suffragan bishops, you our brother Pope have chosen to condemn us, of your own caprice, with tyrannical fury."

"But we do not accept your accursed sentence, so repugnant to a father's or a brother's love; we despise it as mere insulting language; we expel you yourself from our communion, since you commune with the excommunicate; we are satisfied with the communion of the whole Church and with the society of our brethren whom you despise and of whom you make yourself unworthy by your pride and arrogance."

"You condemn yourself when you condemn those who do not observe the apostolic precepts which you yourself are the first to violate, annulling as far as in you lies the divine laws and the sacred canons, and you do not follow in the footsteps of the popes, your predecessors."

But angering the Pope is not something Vassilis or I approve of. We know how important it is to keep him as a friend. For how could anyone govern the Empire one day without powerful friends? So the outcomes of this Council do not fit at all well with our plans. Fortunately, other events took over that made this less of a problem for us. Pope Nicholas died.

Leo, aren't you curious about where the Acts of the Council are now, where these words were originally recorded? Why does no-one refer to them anymore? As our memory of these days grows dim, many even wonder if they existed.

But I will tell you a secret. I know what happened to the codex in which Photios painstakingly recorded the Acts, just as Vassilis knows. There was only one copy, hidden deep in Photios' archives. What a library he had — perhaps bigger than anything else in the world! The codex, sumptuously bound in silk and gold, was tracked down at Vassilis' orders and torn apart, its pages burnt — as requested by Hadrian, the new Bishop of Rome. How Photios wept when he found this out later!

But enough of speeches and writings! While the great assembly deliberates, a humble woman like me is outside in the beautiful gardens, enjoying the midday sun as it roasts my cheeks and hair. The air is redolent with herbs and roses. Butterflies and bees skim like flat stones thrown across a pond, while dandelion seeds escape in a sea of fountain spray when the wind blows just right. I could wander in this moving stillness forever.

Suddenly Michael staggers down the path, then moves with contrived precision, then stumbles again, before collapsing onto a bench he has had placed in front of the Golden Tree.

A servant begins to turn the handle of the Tree's machinery.

The tinkling music normally soothes Michael. But from behind a hedge I can hear that something is wrong. It seems to whine, like a dying piglet. I watch him roll his head in irritation. The burning midday light reflects blindingly off the Tree's limbs. It seems to be reaching out as if to pin him down.

"Enough!" Michael screams. "Get this miserable thing out of my sight!"

He picks up a loose block of masonry from a fountain nearby and smashes it at the Tree. The gears grind to a halt, and some of the golden birds and bits of foil crumple and fall to the ground.

He picks up the block and throws it at the Tree, again and again. Servants and courtiers rush out and then halt in confusion at the sight. I have no desire to move from my vantage point. My heart is empty. This is the man who professes to love me. Yet he can see no reason to allow my husband, an Emperor himself, to crown me.

The sobs tear themselves from his throat, as he falls to the ground, shaking, his hands bloodied. Dekapolitessa appears suddenly. She kneels over him and caresses his hair. "You are very, very tired," I hear her say in the stillness, "let me take care of you. Please let me."

He rolls away. "Get me the Logothete. Send this mess to the Imperial mint along with the reliquaries. We need the coin. And then go to hell, the lot of you." The angry words melt into another fit of sobbing. He tries to get up, slips and grasps at Dekapolitessa, before toppling into the flimsy softness of her waiting arms.

† † †

Gemma tells me that Theodora waits impatiently for every word of news from the City, her black headdress bobbing at the window panes every time she hears a boat horn. Usually the boat is destined elsewhere. Whatever is going on in the City might as well be happening on the distant shores of Thule, for few come to visit them out here on the opposite side of the Bosporus. Even when supplies come in, and Gemma bundles some letters together for the boat captain, many days, sometimes weeks pass before replies find their way back. So any news of guests is very welcome.

Photios has been an occasional visitor, though he discusses frivolities and abstractions, presumably trying not to sadden her with goings on at the Palace. He mentions how the women seem to be dressing somewhat less modestly than before — to which she frowns. I suspect this is my influence.

He regales her with wonderful stories about the Moravians, about the struggles of Cyril and Methodios in Velehrad, how they might yet reach agreement that the liturgy could be sung in Moravian, that the scriptures could be read in translation with the aid of a new alphabet. Of course, when Theodora hears the name Methodios it reminds her of her former confidant, the old patriarch who kept her company after Theophilos' passing. Perhaps it etches even deeper the bitter loneliness that follows her everywhere. Back then I was still too young to realize that the friends we make and lose along the way score our hearts forever, like figures in an ivory diptych, their gestures forever frozen in relief at the moments of shared grief or joy from long ago.

Now I understand this well. I think back to my readings of Epicurus, who teaches that the manner of one's dying is unimportant, whether alone or not. What matters are the many friendships we enjoyed, especially if they remain alive in our memories. Does Theodora know this? I am not so sure — she seldom showed much interest in the ancients ... or her friends!

But today, Theodora is all nerves. She hasn't seen the Emperor for a year. She keeps muttering how strange it is to have received letters and gifts in advance of his visit

Here approaches her not-so-little Michael, sweeping into the room, straight into mother's arms. She tries to stop herself from shrinking back, perhaps in fear or shock? For what was once a lively boy is the shadow of his father before he died — the wasted, shrunken frame, the hollow eyes, the despair writ large on a furrowed brow.

"You know how much I've always hated being alone, mother," Michael says. "I am a trial to myself and those around me. Even to you, I know now."

She smooths down his beard, wipes the tears from his cheeks, and places a maternal kiss on his forehead. "Then you must stay a while, and rest. The world will not change if you leave it a while."

Thekla and the others peer curiously from the columns, but

Theodora nods them away with a mother's instinct. She must take care of this little one, as she never has before. She knows now that she is all that he has left.

"The summer has been warm and abundant. The hunters tell me that the forest is overrun with game," Theodora says. "Why don't you take some time to enjoy yourself? Find some respite on the hoof. The countryside will feed you in heart and mind, as it does me."

She speaks warmly, but I suspect Michael has brought the cold winter chill back to her bones. She draws her cloak more closely as she shuts her eyes and lets Michael's head rest on her shoulder. She gazes sightlessly upward, lips moving — a prayer perhaps to the Theotokos, the Mother of mothers, a prayer that only a mother can pray, opening the gates to hope, to forgiveness, a plea for courage, for strength to bear the pain, in short a flood of silent pleading, of yearning, of most inexpressible sighing.

39. Like ravens against a falcon

SIX WEEKS LATER, IN THE SUMMER OF 867 AD
The banners of the Blues and the Greens fly in each corner of the surprisingly large stadium at Saint Mamas where Theodora now resides. Michael has had her brought back to the suburbs. It is surprising because I had not expected to find such a handsome palace in this forgotten corner. Clearly, Michael has many hidden resources. I wonder what else I might discover today.

Michael strides up and down the concourse in delight, clapping his favorite riders on the back. It has been a wonderful day for him, of course, because the Greens have won, with Michael their champion racer. For Vassilis and me it has been miserable, to say the least.

Vassilis is furious about Michael's latest decree – that the new beacons not be lit today. Michael insists that the people would not come out all the way to Saint Mamas to see him race today, if they saw the beacons ablaze. Yet what would happen were invasion to fall upon us from the east? As it is, very few of the people have come anyway.

Not that Michael cares. He revels in the warmth and the victories of the morons and spendthrifts he calls friends. Vassilis and I wait patiently with the other guests, constantly on our guard. Neither of us has any idea what the old witch in the balcony across from us is brewing – Theodora stares regally across at us with eyes only for Michael. Vassilis places a protective hand around mine. Wouldn't you say that this is all quite strange, my little Leo, especially as it is your birth we are supposed to be celebrating!

Vassilis can't hold back any longer. He slips away to face down Michael.

Michael brushes him off. "Wipe that frown off your brow, dear brother, this is a day of good fortune!"

"Whose fortune are we using to pay for this event?" Vassilis wants to know. "Have we not already agreed that the Treasury does not have enough to see us through the summer and we are now reliant on the good widow's help?"

"Oh, you are such a worrier, brother. Mother has kindly offered to help us out. It turns out she still has some friends in faraway places, and old favors in need of repaying."

Vassilis is nearly blinded by the throbbing behind his eyes as Michael turns away. "This will go down very badly with the clergy," he shouts to Michael over the noise from the stadium. "The monks are threatening rebellion over the loss of the holy treasures. I fear we will have more riots."

Michael strides on, saying nothing, so that Vassilis feels compelled to pull him to a standstill, wrenching him around so that they face each other. "I'm also offended," continues Vassilis, "to have seen the golden vessels removed from our holy churches, especially when it has been our duty and honor to protect them."

The banners play shadow and light over Michael's forehead and cheekbones, highlighting his painful thinness. His smile is frozen, lifeless. "Well," he says, "that is too bad. I have invited you both here to enjoy this day with me. Let's make the most of it, shall we?" He twists away and vanishes.

Back at the dinner table, Vassilis frowns. He asks me if I know why we have been seated in the middle of the table. Clearly Agalianus and Krusas should be here as leaders of the Blues and the Greens. But what does Vassilianiscus the Syrian have to be here for, and in the place of honor, at the far end, no less? Since he joined the gathering at Symvatios' house, Vassilis has seen far too much of him, usually in the wrong places. What gives him the right to lead the toast?

"To you, great Amorion," says Vassilianiscus, holding his goblet toward Michael, "you are a credit to your dynasty, and now can safely anoint the heir that we have all dreamed of for so long. May Leo live long, and may you live through him, and through his seed, until our Savior returns with the armies of saints and martyrs."

Michael nods and smiles at this pretentious little speech. Vassilis seethes, as do I. Does Michael not realize he is humiliating all three of us, himself especially, by allowing this to happen?

"And," continues Vassilianiscus, entering full stride, "we are delighted to announce, to those who do not know, that the Empress Ingerina has been blessed yet again." Michael roars with delight. Everyone knows that Michael has refused to crown me! Is this idiotic sycophant to be his confidant as well?

"That is quite enough!" Vassilis is on his feet. "You have no right to make these announcements. You have no right even to be here. Brother Emperor, what is the reason for this?"

By now, everyone has stopped eating. A fresh wind whistles through the stadium.

"The reason?" Michael says softly, the calculated coldness of that old, cruel smile playing on his lips. "Why, I should hope that were obvious, dear brother. We are here to celebrate."

"We all know …" Vassilis says, "the pleasure you take in good spectacle, of a prank well-played, brother, but why this, when we should be singing the praises of the First Lady, not taunting her in front of everyone?"

Michael swings his legs to the floor and stands up. "It's theater, my dear brother," he says. "Pure and simple theater. Which is what we all engage in, all of our lives, isn't that so?"

Vassilis stares in disbelief.

"Of course," Michael says, pacing, "you are probably right. This may be in somewhat poor taste. So I will cease … on one condition: that my brother takes off his boots."

Forks from half-bitten mouthfuls are left to drop onto platters. Goblets settle themselves onto the table. All eyes are on Vassilis.

"I asked you to take off your boots, dearest brother. The Imperial boots. The ones I gave you when I permitted you the Throne."

Is this another test, like the whipping? Will there be no end to this childishness?

"I want you," continues Michael, "to give them to my brother Vassilianiscus over here."

This is going too far!

"Most Serene and Worthy Emperor," I say, getting up from the couch and moving around to him. I take his hands in mine and kneel on the ground. "My dear Michael. This is a fine joke, but please let us be done with it."

His eyes seem to have trouble focusing. I resist cringing as his fingers play with my hair. But he shrugs me off with another rendition of that wicked grin of his.

I persist. "Do we need to bring ourselves into more ill repute than we already have? These good people know that we walk a fine line. Is there any need to make it worse?"

"I suppose you are right," he sighs. "You are always right. But our brother must learn that I am the source of all things. I am the sun in this cosmos and he is the moon. And so it will always be."

The chatter and eating gradually resume, though Michael stares darkly into space, taking neither food nor wine. I go back to my couch but clearly it is time for us to leave. As we turn to exit, we encounter Theodora right behind us, her black robes drawn tight against her thin frame, poised to take my place.

Back in our chambers I face Vassilis, imploring him with my eyes. He is as disturbed as I am.

"Have you decided?" I ask. "With the Regent in favor again, there cannot be two Emperors. When it comes to action or decision, there can be only one."

Vassilis nods. "Every decision will need her approval. What should we do?"

"Clearly we must remove the threat."

"I will not have him harmed in any way," he says, as expected.

"Well, then we are no further than we were before." I turn away. "How much do you care for me?"

He comes over and takes my hand. "Your presence has caused me much pain. But I can only blame Michael for that. And you have given me hope when I had none."

He opens his arms to me like never before. My heart throbs at the words he has spoken, the first sign of such affection I have heard tumble from his mouth. I hug him tightly.

"We cannot . . . have him removed," I murmur. "Posterity must not be polluted."

"For us to have his blood on our hands would not be Christian," Vassilis replies softly.

"Instead, let us take the advice of those that have gone before," I say, pulling away. "The words of Augusta Irene, to be precise. We make him useless."

"How?" says my Vassilis, his eyes narrowing. "I cannot bring myself to . . . even think of blinding him." His voice trembles. His beauty takes my breath away.

I shake my head. It is clear what we must do. "Steel yourself, husband. We treat him as a traitor. For that is what he has been, to the church, to the people, even to the coffers themselves. There are many among the clergy, no doubt, who will approve this act. You will cleanse the people of their sin and the state of a wastrel."

Vassilis pulls away from me, shaking his head. He paces. Will he agree? The episode with Peganes comes to mind. The punishment for treason is maiming.

† † †

What could we do, my dearest Leo? Isn't it clear that we had no choice? We had to act!

We are due to spend the whole week celebrating in Saint Mamas, so we send a message to Marianos to round up the brothers and anyone else they trust to join us. Several days later they arrive, cousin Asylaeon, Peter the Bulgarian — an acquaintance of Vassilis' from Pliska — as well as Toxaras whom you know well, and the Persian Jakovitzes.

One of them has seen to fixing the locks in Michael's new quarters in Saint Mamas while we feast. Some hours after the meal Vassilis and I let ourselves into the bath chamber, to find Michael sprawled at the side of a magnificent basin.

I marvel at how finely crafted everything is. Water trickles from the mouths of marble fish into the basin. Although it is midsummer the room is warmed by a small brazier. Firelight flickers off the eyes and claws of marble sea monsters as well as off the marble steps and the goblet drooping in Michael's hand as he lowers his legs into the water.

A remarkable mosaic lines the curved floor of the basin: octopus and squid succumb to Poseidon as sirens swirl in seaweed-strewn depths. Michael has lost even more weight than I had imagined possible, though his limbs still hint at that sinewy strength I once knew and loved. His sparse beard hides swollen lips. His cheeks are drawn and mottled.

We pace the chamber, waiting for him to notice us. Your poor father, my little Leo, this is what he has become — mumbling to himself, arraigning himself with false injustices, begging his phantoms for mercy. Perhaps he recalls the dinner with Mother —

the enormous pie made from the deer he had shot the day before, washed down with magnificent wine? Does he even know where he is? He giggles, God only knows why. "She's nearby isn't she?" he says. "Sleeping in holy chastity."

He slides himself with difficulty into the water. I watch Vassilis and am pleased that the usual calm has descended, perhaps stonier than usual. I have hardened his heart like a smithy of the soul. I have forged his hate to the point where he will forget the rides and the hunts with Michael, the evenings in the taverns.

A servant hands Michael a full goblet. He takes a sip, spluttering when he notices us. "Ah, the Emperor, and the ... Empress in all but name. What have I done to deserve your august presence? Wine for everyone, hurry."

"Michael, let's put the silliness of this week behind us," I say. "We want you to join us. Come, allow the men to dress you so we can go for an evening ride."

"An outing?" Michael groans. "No, I don't want to go anywhere! I am at peace here. In fact I have no interest in anything right now except you — my beautiful mother of mine. You shine like gold, the child is blessed in your womb where I would wish myself now."

He props himself up on an elbow and reaches around to my belly which does not yet show much sign of its new consignment.

I take him by the hand but exchange glances with Vassilis. I say quite sternly, "Come, enough of this. We have come to take you out for a ride — it is not good to be sodden all day."

"Oh," Michael says, "would that we could ride — I, you — you, me — as we have done so many a happy time before."

Vassilis shifts from foot to foot, and then looks at me. His shakes his head, mouthing "He can't go anywhere!" Then aloud, to Michael, "Do you still mourn your uncle? His evil ways are better forgotten."

I answer Vassilis soundlessly, pointing to the floor. "Then it must be here."

Michael clambers to his feet. "That's right," he shouts, "I mourn him and all good men who struggle in this world. He may have been a lecher who knew no limits — but he brought the City nothing but good — our debt to him can never be repaid. So what if he touched my precious Theotokos here! He knew what was right and holy."

Vassilis pulls the door ajar, puts his head out to motion for the rest of them who are waiting outside to enter. I let Michael hold on to my hands and speak loudly, as if to a child. "If you do not join us then we will be forced to go without your excellent company."

Michael topples gently over and lies down, almost slipping under the water. Vassilis pulls him out of the water and sits him up.

"I ... think not." Michael vomits.

Do you wonder what your pitiful father must be feeling now, little Leo? Can't he see us murmuring? The lock rattles. The men enter. Surely he must be wondering who these visitors are?

Vassilis bellows to the servants to leave.

Does Michael see Vassilis' face in front of him now? Does he see the strong, vein-streaked arms, the thick beard, the chestnut brown curls cascading down? My little Leo, what does your father think of the man who has loved him so much, and so unwisely, all this time?

Vassilis wipes the vomit from Michael's mouth and kisses him tenderly on the cheek. He lays him down at the side of the bath.

"You have become a problem, dearest brother," Vassilis says, "we cannot let this go on."

"More than a problem," I say. "This is no longer an Emperor. This is a vile, filthy insect."

Michael tries to prop himself up, probably noticing the strangers in his quarters for the first time. I push him back down with my foot.

††††

Meanwhile, Photios writes that Methodios and Cyril had wanted to return to Constantinople with the relics of Saint Clement that they had hoarded faithfully since traveling to the Khazar Khaganate.

The trip from Velehrad had started easy for the brothers, although the gloom had settled in as they traveled deeper into the worsening weather and farther away from the friendly people they had left behind in the sunny villages and towns.

But while resting in some damp inn along a Dalmatian road-side, they decided that they would return by sea, as the journey to the City by land would take them too long and also because they wanted to visit our brothers in Venice.

They had planned to step off the boat in Venice and settle into their temporary lodgings to wait for the boat to the City. But by the time they get to Trieste and take a boat across the bay to Venice, they begin to experience a sense of trepidation, barely lessened by the shining spectacle of the golden domes of the Cathedral of Saint Mark.

Bone-achingly wet, but thankful for the Venetian air, which is slightly warmer, or so I hear, than the chilly freshness of Moravia, Methodios and Cyril weather a storm of abuse on their arrival. Evidently, the Frankish monks in Moravia had given advance warning of their travels. So as they step off the boat in the pouring rain, a party of some twenty local monks whisks them off to a dark room in the Cathedral with barely a word of greeting.

Gradually Methodios and Cyril learn what happened at Photios' Council. That orthodoxy was established, once and for all. That the Council was to be numbered among the great Councils. Oh yes, and, by unanimous vote, that Pope Nicholas was held unworthy of his episcopate. The insults and accusations fly against the brothers, now seen as Photios' men.

"Does not the rain sent by the Lord fall equally on everyone?" Methodios begins, slowly at first, as the Latin words come back to him. "The Armenians, Persians, Abkhazians, the Iberians and Sogdians, the Goths and Avars, and many others. Does not the sun shine equally for the whole world? Do we not all equally breathe the air? Do you not feel shame at approving only Greek, Latin, and Hebrew for our holy scriptures and condemning all other people to blindness and deafness?"

By the time this short speech ends he can't be heard over the cries of "blasphemer" and "heretic". Cyril's sharp voice penetrates above the noise. His Latin shows no lack of familiarity.

"Dear brothers," he begins, "can I not remind you also of Paul the Apostle's words: 'I had rather speak five words with my understanding, that by my voice I might teach others also, than ten thousand words of an unknown tongue.' Many peoples possess writing, and should render glory unto God in their own words."

I suspect that they recall similar conversations while traveling through the mountains, in terrified jest, of what they might have to face. But neither had the courage to admit openly that there was only one solution. This ... attack ... and the obvious ignorance that they would always have to deal with, make it clear that there is only thing left to do: the spider must be confronted at the heart of his web.

Methodios knows this will silence them. He waits for the uproar to die down. "We are heartened to have made your acquaintance. For you have steeled our resolve. We journey to see His Holiness the Pope, bearing, as a gift, the Relics of Saint Clement. Now I see more than ever that we must explain to him, since it is obvious that none of you can, how people without scriptures in their own language are as naked as babes in a forest."

40. The lot of Job

Vassilis knows what must be done, although I can see he is having second thoughts. Marianos is right behind him, as are their
brothers. For such a large crowd of men it is amazing how very
quiet everything is. Isn't it obvious what needs to be done?

"There is no need for that!" Vassilis shouts at me as I push
Michael, who keeps trying to get up, back down with my foot. He
lolls into the water.

Vassilis helps him into a sitting position next to the basin.
Michael should have something around his waist, so I throw Vassilis Michael's britches. He covers Michael's shriveled modesty.

"You must forgive me, brother," Vassilis says. "What I do now
I do for all of us. Have another drink."

Vassilis tips a goblet into Michael's mouth and then kisses
him again, quite deeply. He lays him down carefully, stretching
his arms out and away from his sides. But clearly every movement
is an act of will for him. The grating of his sword as he draws it
from its sheath seems unnatural in the quiet. The tears seep from
his eyes. I lay a hand on his shoulder in encouragement, but he
tears away from me and turns to face the door.

John Chaldis takes him aside with a half-grin. "So! Not so
strong now, Your Worthiness? What are we to do?"

"What you must do," I say, "is clear. Here is the Christ-
emblazoned Emperor, the rightful holder of the Imperial Throne.
None other should share this title." I look deep into my Emperor's
eyes as I tear at his tunic, ripping it down the front. I turn him
around for all to see.

"The Chi-Rho," they gasp. "Truly, he has been touched by
Christ!" The men gather around, placing their hands on Vassilis'
breast, on the wounds of Michael's handiwork.

"Come," says Chaldis. "We will do the deed."

"The Emperor should not be present," Marianos says. He
takes Vassilis by the arm and leads him out. I follow on the other

arm. John Chaldis and Jakovitzes stand poised above Michael.

With identical strokes from each of the men, Michael's hands flop to the floor. He writhes and cries out as the stumps flail wildly, spraying blood everywhere.

Vassilis tears himself away and runs back, falling to his knees, grabbing a cloth as he does so. "Quickly – before he loses too much." The basin clouds with blood.

Then he is back on his feet. "Where is the physician? Why isn't he present?" he howls.

It is not fitting that an Emperor should writhe before the people so wretchedly. I surprise everyone, including myself.

"Come on you idiots," I say, "We cannot let him die." I grab his arms and try to lift them, to stem the flow of blood.

Vassilis' hands crush mine as he pulls them away from Michael. I feel the terrible weakness of being a woman. We may be superior in most things but not when it comes to brute strength. I flinch under his terrible gaze as Michael moans. Vassilis shouts at me, "We should not be here, what will you tell your son one day!"

As we rush from the room I look back over my shoulder to see Michael face gripped in disbelief. He struggles to rise, only to fall back, the stumps spurting fresh, bright blood over his face.

In the adjacent bedchamber everyone circles in indecision. "Where is the physician?" Vassilis agonizes. "His arms must be cauterized immediately!"

The men demur, their faces twisted in guilt and weakness, as Michael's cries echo next door. Vassilis calls for the servants. Then the physician arrives. Vassilis barks orders for the fire to be built up. He takes the physician by the arm. I stop them.

"Why do we need to do anything?" I say. "Let justice be served."

Vassilis frowns at me, and then pushes me aside. The sense of being released from a lifelong prison suddenly blazes inside me

"It is probably too late," I say. "The cuts were too high. He will not last long."

Vassilis keeps shaking his head. I continue. "How long has he got? A few hours, perhaps a day at most? While he suffers what is our position? Do you plan to escort a complete invalid back to the Palace? There are still those who would stand in his defense – in defense of the old ways."

"Have you forgotten our dream?" I say. "Our goals? One day our children should mount the Throne. Your children, not Michael's. What about the one I carry?"

The door to the bath chamber rattles. The men jump back. It is Michael, trying, but failing, to open the door. Blood seeps into the room as he pushes against it.

"If you love him then allow him this mercy," I say. I beckon for Marianos and remove a dagger I had hidden within my robe. I press it into his hand. He says nothing and pushes past me.

There is a strangled howl followed by a sudden splash. Vassilis rushes inside. I slowly pull open the door. Vassilis is up to his knees in the water, Michael hangs limp in his arms. The basin is a lake of red. Tears stream down Vassilis' cheeks in a way which I will only ever see one other time.

You must be wondering, little Leo, why I let this happen to your father? There was a time when I loved him. But there can only be one Emperor, just as there can only be one head on a person. Even you, who will be crowned Emperor soon, will learn that you need to make choices every day. I had to choose the man who could be the father you needed and the leader we all needed. It had little to do with how I felt about either of them.

Vassilis is once again in front of me. I feel the tears and blood on my face as he holds it between his hands. "Do not tell me the child you bear is Michael's?"

"It is not," I say. "It is yours." As far as I can tell, I know this to be true.

Marianos forces his way between us. "Rest easy, brother. All is as it should be."

I take Vassilis' arm in mine and guide him from the room. "The times have changed!" I cry out. "The Palace is ours. Prepare the boat for our return. The people will see that have done what was needed, that we are here to restore order. We must enter the Palace before the servants wake up the Senate and chaos descends. The future is ours for the taking!"

† † †

The Palace is deathly quiet and gloomy, like the overcast sky above. At first Vassilis and I worry at the silence, then relax at the absence of protest. By the evening of our return Vassilis summons the Senate to order and they, as agreeable as a herd of deer, renew their oath of full allegiance to him as the chosen Emperor of all the Romans. Not even the meekest voice of outrage or disagreement is heard! I am forced to admit the obvious: either they cringe in terror at my Peasant Emperor, or they welcome Michael's departure. Either explanation satisfies me!

So here is my Vassilis, alone on his Throne, in full Imperial robes, boots, and crown, having summoned Photios to hear his orders. Ignatios is there as well, grinning from ear to ear. Vassilis pronounce Photios' banishment to the island of Stenos. Does he finally understand what John the Grammarian must have felt all those years ago? But no, my little Leo, this was not an act of revenge on Photios, it was pure politics. We had to deal with facing down Hadrian, the cunning new Bishop of Rome.

We allow Photios a last wish, to pay his respects to Michael. Yet he still finds time for a final word, even though he has already slipped his special volume recording all these events to his brother to hide it in the Chapel of the Virgin of the Pharos. How cunning he was to instruct Tarasios very clearly not to take it to his library.

Photios writes that he takes a boat to the Palace of Saint Mamas, where he descends into the flagstone-decked gloom of the mausoleum. An old mosaic of Saint Vassilis is there, yet to be properly restored, peering out from under flaked plaster in the cross-hatching of reflected light. The Icons thrust into our world; they are not windows, but intrusions, he writes. They admonish us, but give no clue as to what ephemeral glories or darkness lie waiting behind their stern gaze. That is why those of us born as Iconoclasts never cared much for them.

The old Regent weeps, her expression old and lined from all the tears. Constant sorrow dries one out, or so I'm told.

She clasps at the cloth in search of hands that are no longer there, to hold something of her child, to comfort him as she herself needs to be comforted. Photios covers the shrunken, blue-tinged foot which has crept out from under the green brocaded blanket that usually covered Michael's favorite chariot horse before a race.

Theodora's sobs wring out. "First, a husband, then a dear friend, then both brothers. Then a grandchild I never knew. Now ... my little Michael. Oh Father God, will you never stop crucifying me!"

Photios puts an arm around her shoulders.

"Christ gave up his life," she weeps, "but I have given up six times as much!"

"You must be brave," he says. "These are difficult times".

Thekla and Michael's other sisters are there too: Anna, Anastasia, and now not so little Pulcheria. They weep too, but for their mother's pain, not the loss of their brother.

A guard strides toward them, kicking fragments of rubble out of his way. "The Emperor has commanded that the body not be left to lie in the catacombs, but be taken across the Bosporus. Leave! You will not want to witness our travails."

It is unfortunate that Michael will not be laid to rest in the mausoleum of the Ayia Sofia, as tradition demands, but, again, we cannot afford to show any leniency.

Photios writes that he tries to speak to Theodora's pain. I did not know he had such compassion in him. "Dear cousin, fear not, he will live on ... through your grandsons."

The words mean nothing to her. "My son must not be taken from me. He has every right to lie with his ancestors, near me, where I have prepared a place for him, for all of us. He will be absolved — he didn't understand — he is innocent!"

† † †

The complexity of the preparations for my coronation seems excessive, but an Augusta's coronation is even more elaborate than most other rituals. After all, women are the most important force in the cosmos, the givers of life.

The Augusteon is filled to bursting with senators, officials, and their wives. They crowd around waiting for their part in the ceremony. I process on Vassilis' left. Patriarch Ignatios and visiting Metropolitans are right behind us. The Patriarch brings the procession to a halt with several loud thumps of his staff.

He blesses the Imperial tunic, crown and pendants. Together with Vassilis, he lowers a ruby and emerald encrusted tunic over my white robe. Vassilis and the Patriarch crown me over my veil. Vassilis drapes beaded pendants across the crown. I delight in the sumptuousness of it all.

The thrones arrive, both of them simple affairs. We sit to receive the procession: wave upon wave of officials, from the first to
the eleventh rank, first prostrating themselves, then kissing our
knees. Then their wives and mothers arrive and effect obeisances
with three deep reverences, though not quite to the floor, and similar kissing of knees. But the air chokes me with damp and stuffi-
ness, and I am conscious that we have barely started.

I realize I have never witnessed such a ritual before. I suspect
few alive have, for such a ceremony has not happened in at least
thirty years, since Theodora ascended alongside her Theophilos.

We are on the move again, with the most senior senators' wives
surrounding us. A bunch of old hags, really, but I must do my
best to play along for soon I will have need of them. Vassilis leans
across and mentions that he should have arranged for Danielli to
be here. I nod in agreement. But her time will come.

The statue of the Golden Hand greets us at the portico of the
Augusteon. Ritual dictates that Christoferos the Logothete should
dismiss those gathered and before he hands me over to my new
ladies in waiting.

They accompany me to the portico of the Single Foot, at which
the elderly patricians kneel with cries of many good years.

I arrive at the Diakonikon, where an enormous curtain hangs
between the two main pillars. A group of young senators throw
themselves to the floor suddenly, shouting ritual acclamations,
startling me!

With the curtain drawn aside, banners dazzle the eye, rattling
in the stiff breeze. Fresh air, at last! The staircase to the Balcony is lined by the Counts and Generals in full ceremonial dress.
Scepters and insignias of the Themes frame a huge crucifix. I ascend the stairs with the Logothete and present myself to the Hippodrome. I have to steady myself to endure the immense wave of
jubilation which cascades over me.

The Greens and the Blues begin their endless chanting. I
could wait here forever. Perhaps Photios is right — perhaps royal
blood does flow in our veins. But I don't care about the past. The
future is what matters most, especially that of my family.

The standards and ensigns are lowered in ritual self-abasement.
The cries of "Worthy, worthy, may you live long" fall like manna,
lining the Balcony with dreams to be fulfilled. I turn back to watch

Vassilis ascend the steps toward me, a smile on his lips, arm extended, his fingers curling in anticipation of the Imperial hand I will place within it.

We turn to face the Hippodrome as one.

To contact the author or
for more information
including links, videos and
upcoming novels
please visit:

www.empireforever.co.uk

Acknowledgments

This work would have been impossible without the commitment, interest, and contributions of my parents, Amalia-Eleni and Nicholas, and many dear friends, among them Leonardo Roumieh, Adam Stevens, Laurence Lily, Nike Kojakovič, Douglas Leckie, Ray Hamilton, Sarah Ruden, Joy Hayes, Matt Edge, Lambros Bourodimos, Khanh Nguyen, Caroline Spencer, Jim Watts, Elena Jessup, Ilyas Malick, Lucy Lamb, and Barbara Lowi, who all took time out of their busy lives to read the manuscript in a variety of draft forms and comment on my handling (or otherwise!) of the material.

In writing fiction based on history one must often interpolate between the facts, and make inference where more informed minds would balk. At the same time one has a duty to make the times as accessible as possible without foisting modern norms and assumptions onto the past. Any resulting mistakes are mine alone, and not due to a lack of fine scholarship on the subject.

Concerning the latter, I am indebted to the research of Arnold Toynbee, Judith Herrin, John Haldon, John Geanakoplos, Oliver Mango, Gilbert Dagron, Steve Tougher, Benedict Benedikz, Despina Stratoudaki-White, Angeliki Laiou, George Saliba, Joachim Henning, Ioli Kalavrezou, Lynda Garland, Paul Magdalino, Maria Mavroudi, and John Boswell.

Sources of literary inspiration include the writings of two of the very few known female writers of the time, Anna Komnena and Kassia the Nun; Oliver Mango's translations of Photios' epistles and sermons; Sarah Ruden's translation of *Lysistrata*; John Haldon's translation of the *Testamentum Porcelli* fragment; Ivan Morris' translation of the *The Pillow Book of Sei Shōnagon*; and anonymous translations of Homer's *Odyssey* and Abbé Guettée.

Editorial services have been provided by Jennifer Quinlan of Historical Editorial. I am deeply grateful for her probing questions and thoughtful suggestions.

Notes

I use dates in modern notation, viz. AD, rather than the Hebrew system in use back then, which started with the Biblical date
of creation (and in which 842 AD would have been 4602 Anno
Mundi). I have tried to retain a flavor of the times by translating some terms and using others in transliteration, where, by my
judgment, readability will not be needlessly hampered. Most special terms are listed and explained in the below. I have used the
modern terms such as "Iconoclast" throughout rather than the
needlessly verbose "followers of the Isaurian heresy." I also refer to
specific geographical features in modern terms, such as the Sea of
Marmara (rather than the Propontis), the Black River (Mavropota-
mus), and Anatolia (to refer to the region that makes up modern
day mainland Turkey and which would probably have simply been
called "Asia" back then), but retain, somewhat inconsistently, a
phonetic spelling for some people's names where, I believe, it adds
richness.

In almost all cases I have retained modern English spelling
where place names are involved (Bosporus instead of Vosporos,
Macedonian rather than Makedonian, and Constantinople rather
than Constantinopolis). However I have chosen to use "Augusta"
as well as Empress depending on the context (not every consort
of an Emperor was a designated ruler) but have decided to stick
to Emperor rather than use the Greek term *Vassilleos* (to avoid
confusion with a major character's name).

This brings up an unfortunate aspect of writing about this period — infants were frequently baptized with names from a limited
pool of possibilities, invariably associated with historical acts of
benevolence or great import, mostly Christian in origin or construction. The abundance of names prefixed with "Theo" (Greek
for "God") is one example, and I hope you will not be confused
between Theodora, Theophilos, Theoktistos, etc. To avoid inun-
dating you further with numerous references to similarly-dubbed
yet very different minor characters I have renamed some of them.

The above is particularly true of the very common name Constantine. To avoid confusion with the original Constantine the Great I have tried to use alternatives wherever possible. For example, I refer to Vassilis' first born as Constantinos. Also, the scholar Cyril was born with the name Constantine. He only adopted the name Cyril late in life, when he took holy orders, but I have used the latter throughout. I trust that scholars will forgive me this gloss.

On the subject of names, I should point out that the use of nicknames was both common and a common source of ridicule. It is important to understand that ridicule was, in itself, a form of humor at court, and probably a release from the tedium of hours of ritual and procession. The epithet "Dickbreath" is my invention, but Constantine "the Shitter" is my translation of Constantine V's court moniker *Copronymus* (literally, the dung-named). Many nicknames were in even worse taste, at least from a modern point of view, and I have omitted mention of these from this text.

A final note, which will be expanded further online, centers on historicity. Virtually all the characters existed, though any information on their motives, and frequently on their origins, is extremely sparse. If my interpolation of the events they experienced and the decisions they made — based on available fact — jars with what the recorded histories say, it is partly in those instances where the main sources disagree. Much of the history of the characters portrayed is colored by a hagiographical approach to relating events. The effect is to remove the less appealing bits and focus on the 'holier' aspects of the life being related. I refer here mainly to the events of Vassilis' arrival in Constantinople, which are shrouded in mystery, as is his birth.

I posit that Vassilis' arrival happens as a result of meeting Methodios and Cyril in Pliska. I should say quite clearly that there is no evidence to suggest that the brothers were sent to Pliska this early, nor that they would have come across Vassilis. However it is obvious from the texts that the Bulgar were quite familiar with Christianity long before the baptism of Boris-Michael. I do not believe that the alleged conversion of the Khan's sister in Constantinople would have sufficed to inform the Bulgar court, and suggest that an *in situ* influence was required — hence my decision to send Methodios and Cyril there before their famous mission to the Moravians, as allegories of what was probably a gradual infiltration or presence of Greek-speaking monks in Bulgaria. As for Vassilis, the official genealogies disagree quite fundamentally on the path he took to reach Constantinople. I would argue that he would have had to know someone like Methodios in the court in order to be brought to the attention of the Emperor's inner circle. Evidently, he was 'talent-spotted' in the wrestling match I describe, which I find far less satisfying an explanation than the one I have adopted.

What is the likelihood that Ingerina would have written down a story of the kind? Small, but not zero, I would argue. The keeping of journals among women is not known to have been common practice in the Eastern Roman Empire, but there are some examples – the most famous being a history of the life of the Emperor Alexios Komnenos, written early in the twelfth century, by his daughter, Anna Komnena. Once again, I hope scholars will understand that my goal has been to create the kind of narrative which modern readers might find accessible while being as true to the customs of the period as possible, given all the uncertainties which we are left with, nearly twelve hundred years after the events related here transpired.

Characters and special terms

Abbasid – One of several terms (among others such as Ishmaelites or Hagarenes) that the Romans might have used to denote in a generic way the predominantly Muslim nations that occupied huge stretches of the Mediterranean, from Andalusia and across North Africa to southeastern Anatolia, including major islands like Corsica, Sicily, and Crete. In fact, the Abbasid were just one of several dynasties which the Romans would have encountered – another would have been the Umayyads, dominant in southern Spain.

Admiral – A military commander with the title of *Droungarios tou Ploimou*, or Admiral of the Imperial Fleet, the latter usually stationed in the Golden Horn.

Akritai – Literally "border tenants". Successive Roman Emperors since the sixth century had begun a policy of devolving more responsibility to regional administrations, through the creation of semi-autonomous military provinces known as Themes (see below), and in order to deal with the increasingly fractious nature of border politics. Thus Akritai is a non-specific term used by an increasingly myopic Imperial administration to refer to inhabitants of the settled regions at the edge of the Empire who maintained the border through their presence and encountered, on a fairly regular basis, numerous barbarian tribes in the north, as well as Muslim nations and their supposedly heretical Christian allies to the east.

(Omar) al-Aqta, the Emir of Melitene – Ruler of part of south eastern Anatolia, the capital of which was Melitene. He is a formidable source of instability to eastern Roman territories in Anatolia.

Antigonus – Vardas' young son, precociously appointed general in his teens before his father's unfortunate demise.

Augusta — A title for an Empress who reigned as the female equivalent of an Emperor. It is important to note that not every consort of an Emperor was crowned an Augusta. This honorific allowed the bearer to rule by decree, hold court, and wear Imperial clothing, in short behave as an Emperor in every respect. As an aside, Irene was the only Augusta to go one step further and seal her decrees and letters with the male honorific for Emperor — Vassileos.

Augusteon — The central forum in the Great Palace complex and the site of formal announcements to the court, and Imperial weddings.

Ayia Sofia, Ayia Eirene — Literally "Holy Wisdom" and "Holy Peace," these names refer to two churches at the center of worship for many centuries. The original Ayia Sofia was erected in the fourth century as a rectangular basilica, possibly by Constantine the Great, and rebuilt after fires in the fifth and sixth century, in the latter case by Justinian who gave it its enormous vaulted dome. It is still a wonder to behold: the dome conveys the illusion from within of suspension without visible support. The Ayia Eirene is older by some thirty years and was built by Constantine the Great. Both still stand today.

The Balcony — The *Kathisma* (literally "The Seat") was the partially covered Imperial viewing balcony at the side of the Hippodrome, connected directly to the Daphne Palace complex by special passageways, seating the Emperor and his family along with selected courtiers so that they could enter the box unseen and enjoy the chariot races in private. It was also used for Imperial announcements.

Bishop's Meadow — The Battle of Bishop's Meadow, also known as the Battle of Lalakaon, was fought in 863 AD in central Anatolia near a tributary of the Halys River. This was a victory for New Rome and marked the end of a long period of often unsuccessful campaigning against the Abbasid.

The Blues and the Greens — The only two surviving sporting, military, and political factions out of an historical four (the Reds and the Whites had ceased to function two centuries before), with their origins in the now powerless talking shop that had become the Senate, these hereditary "associations" extended into all levels of society. Their main role lay in influencing popular opinion, providing a focus for allegiance in sporting events, and reinforcing links with tradition through their participation in ceremonial functions. Their leaders were senior courtiers who sat at the Emperor's table.

Boris(-Michael) — Nephew of Presian, the first Bulgar Khan in our story, and Khan himself from 852 AD onward. Boris takes the name of Michael for his baptism.

Caesar — An honorary title for the second most senior statesman, second in rank only to the Emperor.

Caliph of Baghdad, al-Mutawakkil — The Abbasid supreme ruler of one of several Muslim empires active across Africa and the Middle East at the time, he was open to diplomatic relations with Constantinople, culminating in the exchange of prisoners on two occasions, thanks partly to the work of Photios and Cyril.

Caliph of Córdoba — An Umayyad supreme ruler, whose ancestors had broken away from the Abbasid Caliphate and established themselves in southern Spain. The Umayyad Caliphs also extended their presence throughout the islands of the Mediterranean.

Cataphract — An elite cavalryman in the primary assault troops of the land forces, clad in chain mail or plated armor (as was his mount) and armed with sword, mace, or lance.

Charles the Frank — Charlemagne.

Chief Imperial Secretary — The duties of a *Protoasekretis* might have covered a wide remit. Given Photios' experience and learning, it probably included the provision of general advice to the Imperial family as well as the role of Comptroller of the Treasury on occasion.

Christoferos — The third Logothete (Secretary of State) in this story and a distant cousin of Ingerina's.

Companion — A translation of the Greek term *Parakoimomenos*, literally "He who sleeps alongside," this was the honorary title of Lord Chamberlain, given to a leading courtier who was entrusted with the care of the Emperor's person. This was typically one of the most sought after roles for a eunuch.

Comptroller — *Sakellarios* in Greek, this was the chief official in charge of the Treasury.

Constantinos — Vassilis' first son, by his first wife, Maria. He is not to be confused with references to Constantine the Great — the first Roman Emperor who founded Constantinople, or the Emperor Constantine VI — the blinded son of the earlier Augusta, Regent Irene, or passing mention to the official Constantine Myares.

Damianos — Michael's boyhood companion, later Companion of the Bedchamber.

(Lady) Danielli — A rich merchant widow from the city of Patras in the Peloponnese, in southern Greece, her trading empire covered the known world.

Daphne — Name given to a central area within the Palace complex housing the main Imperial Quarters. Its focus was a large courtyard with lawn, fountains, trees, and hedges.

Demestikos — Full title: *Demestikos ton Scholon*, literally "Domestic of the Schools". This position began, in the fifth century, as a title for the Head of the Palace Guard and evolved, by the ninth century, to the role of Commander in Chief of the armed forces.

(Father) Diomedes — Pastor of the Church of the Mother of God Valinou along the southern shores of the Golden Horn.

Eparch — Municipal Governor of the City, akin to Lord Mayor in modern terms.

Epi tou Kanikleiou — Literally "Keeper of the Inkstand," a title for the most senior civil servant, in the first instance held by Theoktistos along with the title of Logothete, and then by Dekapolitessos, Michael's father-in-law.

Eudokia — Symvatios' second wife and one of the many Eudokias at court, hence the confusion and rumors caused by Vardas' dallying with the ladies.

(Eudokia) Dekapolitessa — Michael's neglected wife, daughter of Dekapolitessos, a court official.

First Lady — The title of Zoste Patrikia, or "Noble lady of the girdle," was the most important and perhaps the only specific female rank beneath Augusta — other women bore the titles of their husbands. As well as making the bearer first within the Gynaeconitis, this title conferred with it a very high rank at Court, ranking even above the title of Magistros.

Gemma — Member of Theodora's retinue both before and after the Regent is banished, and an associate of Ingerina.

General — In Greek *Strategos*, or *Strategoi* (pl.), these military commanders reported to the Logothete and had full responsibility for a Theme. On campaign, generals ceded both strategic and tactical control to the Emperor and his immediate advisors if the latter chose to be involved actively in the engagement.

Golden Horn — The remarkable natural harbor of Constantinople, essentially a deep, curved bay, opening out onto the Bosporus. It stretches far enough inland to function both as a port and naval base, but is narrow enough to seal by laying a set of gigantic chains across its mouth, should the need arise. Though the opposite shore did not form part of the City, it had been settled since ancient times by locals, and by the ninth century it had started to become a place for foreigners to occupy, especially merchants from the west.

Grozdan — A Bulgarian envoy.

Gryllos — Literally, "Pig". He was Michael's court jester.

Gynaeconitis, and the role of women — "The court of the women" was a generic term both for the areas that high-born women congregated in during the day and for the gatherings themselves. These provided an environment which was practical and comfortable, especially in great houses such as the Daphne Palace, for carrying out the many duties which were not only expected of women, but which they also felt they were best at. Though the poor often did not have the luxury of having access to such quarters, women of all classes were expected to be the main source of knowledge regarding children, health, food, plants, music, dance, and the weaving and making of clothes, even at court. By spending most of their waking hours together women could carry out these activities collectively and efficiently, often learning on the job, so to speak. This was not a place of confinement, though men would have felt quite out of place, and thus seldom were present except for good reason, such as when the Augusta wished to conduct some item of business away from the more male-dominated Throne Room.

Hall of the Nineteen, and dining — A vast banqueting hall connected to the Palace complex , it comprised nineteen windowed apses, nine to a side and one at the far end, in which tables were set with Roman couches around them. The couches were arranged in a "C" shape, with their armrests closest to the table in the center, so that one could recline with the right arm and take food and drink with the left. The most senior person at the table sat on the extreme right of the "C", followed by the second most senior on the extreme left, in descending order of rank from left to right. The innovation of cutlery was just being introduced, which did not lend itself particularly well to this old Roman style of eating. Hence it was not long before the practice of eating in the seated position was adopted as more practical — something monastics and the lower classes had been doing for centuries.

Hippodrome — Literally "The horse road," this was a half-mile long, U-shaped, Coliseum-like stadium at the center of Constantinople standing at the center of public life for everyone. It could seat more than fifty thousand, and served as a venue for chariot races as well as a forum for Imperial declarations.

(Ali) ibn-Yahya, the Emir of Tarsus — Ruler of Arab-held Armenia, the capital of which was Tarsus. He was a close ally of Omar al-Aqta.

Iconoclast, Iconodule — Icon destroyer, Icon worshiper. Icons were sacred images of Mary, Christ, the saints, and holy martyrs venerated by all members of the early Church. Iconoclasm was a multi-faceted religious crisis, similar to the Inquisition in its single-mindedness, but targeted at the physical obliteration of religious images. Priests and individuals in the public eye who refused to give up Icon worship, such as Icon painters, also suffered, but perhaps also the common folk as well, we can't be sure.

Ignatios — A senior extremist Iconodule clergyman closely aligned with the Pope, and the third patriarch in this tale. He is appointed by Theodora after Patriarch Methodios dies, then is deposed by Michael and Vardas to allow Photios to be appointed. The rivalry between Ignatios and Photios is one of the catalysts of the great schism between eastern and western Churches.

Inger — Ingerina's father — he was probably an emissary to Constantinople from the Norse lands who adopted the

Hellenized last name of Martinakios. This is why Ingerina is sometimes referred to as Martinaka.

(Augusta and Regent) Irene – The first Empress to reverse Iconoclasm, living approximately half a century before.

John Chaldis – A disaffected young commander in the Palace Guard.

John Daniellis – Lady Danielli's adolescent son, an intimate of Vassilis' in Patras.

John the Grammarian – The first patriarch in this tale and a staunch Iconoclast, and scholar.

Karveas – Leader of the Paulicians, an Iconoclast sect that rejected Theodora's restoration of Icon worship. His people lived in northeastern Anatolia and formed alliances with the leaders of several Muslim emirates (see Ali ibn-Yahya and Omar al-Aqta).

Kleisourai – Literally "guards of the mountain passes", this was the name given to the more militarized Akritai who lived in the mountainous regions of southeastern Anatolia and who came into regular conflict with the Abbasid.

Leo – Ostensibly Vassilis' third son, but very likely Michael's first born by Ingerina. A child who is probably Vassilis' second born, and Ingerina's first-born, dies at birth. Ingerina addresses him throughout the text.

Leo the Mathematician – An Iconoclast scholar who became metropolitan (senior archbishop of a provincial diocese). He travels to Baghdad but returns to help found the University of the Magnaura.

Logothete – Full title: *Logothetis tou Dromou*, literally "Master of the Ways" or "Master of the Courier Service", the highest title in the civil administration, this role encompassed the roles of Secretary of State and Foreign Secretary.

Magistros – A formerly administrative title of high rank, usually associated with membership in the Senate, this role was evolving into more of an honorary title during the late ninth century.

Magnaura – Probably a corruption of the Latin *Magna Aula*, literally "great hall," this was the Senate House within the extended Palace complex, which also provided a venue for the re-founded University of Constantinople.

Maria — A courtier in the Bulgar court, daughter of a Bulgar father (see Tervel) and a Greek mother from Thessaloniki, later Vassilis' first (common-law) wife.

Marianos — Vassilis' oldest brother, some ten years his senior, later a common foot soldier who rises to the rank of cavalry squadron commander, one of the highest ranks in a Theme.

Methodios (the Patriarch) — The second patriarch in this tale, a moderate Iconodule, and Theodora's spiritual adviser (not to be confused with Methodios the monk).

(The) Paulicians — See reference to Karveas above.

(Pope) Nicholas I — Pope of old Rome and partly responsible for initiating the schism with the Eastern Church.

Oryphas — Eparch of Constantinople, later an Admiral of the Fleet and a close associate of Vardas.

Patriarch, or Pope — The five most senior clergymen of the medieval Church bore these titles. The title of Patriarch was used actively by four of them: the Patriarchs of Constantinople, Alexandria, Antioch, and Jerusalem. But by the ninth century, the title of Pope, borrowed from the Patriarch of Alexandria in the sixth century, had become the norm for the Bishop of Old Rome.

Presian — The Khan of the Bulgars until his death in 852 AD, and Boris' uncle.

Spatharios, Protospatharios — *Spatharios* means "Sword Bearer," a member of the Imperial bodyguard and one of a number of titles of intermediate rank for non-eunuch courtiers. The next step up was *Protospatharios*.

Stephen and Alexander — Vassilis' fourth and fifth sons by Ingerina.

Stoudion and the Stoudites — The Stoudion was perhaps the most learned and powerful of the monasteries in Constantinople, whose monks, the Stoudites, had remained staunchly anti-Iconoclastic at all times. They were a political force to be reckoned with, and may almost be thought of as Icon-worshiping "extremists."

Tervel — An elderly Bulgar courtier and Maria's father.

Thekla, Anna, Anastasia, and Pulcheria — The first three are Michael's much despised older sisters, the last a younger sister.

Theme — A Theme (*Thema* in Greek) was a militarized region under the control of a general — or sometimes a count or duke for the older, more established, and hence less militarized Themes — and could vary in size from that of a city to that of the Peloponnese (the whole of southern mainland Greece). New Themes continued to be defined over the years, in response to external conflicts. (See Akritai above.)

Theognostos — An acolyte of Bishop Ignatios.

Theophilitzes — A courtier in semi-permanent residence in Patras, distant cousin to Vardas by marriage and close friend of the Lady Danielli's.

Theotokos — Literally, "Christ-Bearer," this was the epithet most commonly applied to the Virgin Mary in the eastern Church. By the ninth century the veneration of Mary appears to have evolved to cult status in Constantinople. She was considered to be its patron saint, and regularly invoked by everyone at every opportunity.

Throne Room — This was called the *Chrysotriklinos* which can be translated as "Golden Reception Hall". Its main focus was the double-seated throne set on a marble platform raised to eye level at one end. The double seat was meant to emphasize that the Emperor shared this space with Christ, a physical representation of the ancient Roman belief that spiritual and temporal power were united in the supreme ruler.

Thule, Thulians — Terms to describe the Northern lands (most likely modern-day Denmark and Sweden) and those that came from them to Constantinople, which was known to the Norsemen as *Miklagarð*.

Vassilianiscus — A Syrian patrician, newcomer to Constantinople who wins Michael's favor.

Vyzantion — This was an ancient Greek port city taken over in the fourth century by Constantine the Great, and on which he founded Constantinople, which itself means "Constantine's City". Vyzantion is also the origin of the seventeenth century term "Byzantium".

Wasim — An Abbasid youth who encounters Vassilis as a young lad in the forests of Macedonia, and later in the City.